"Marriage? To him? Never!"

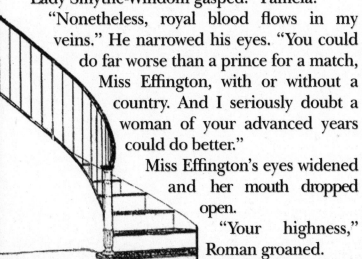

Miss Effington's voice rose. "He's not at all what I want in a husband. Why, he's a prince, and you've just seen how demanding and arrogant they can be. His reputation is dreadful and—"

"I beg your pardon." Alexei brushed aside the fact that he had no desire to wed at all, let alone marry her, and glared. "Dreadful reputation or not, I am indeed still a prince. Arrogance is my birthright. Regardless, most women would cut off an arm to wed a prince."

"I prefer to keep my arms, thank you," Miss Effington snapped. "Besides, you said it yourself, you're a prince without a country. I should think that would diminish your merit as a potential husband somewhat."

Lady Smythe-Windom gasped. "Pamela!"

"Nonetheless, royal blood flows in my veins." He narrowed his eyes. "You could do far worse than a prince for a match, Miss Effington, with or without a country. And I seriously doubt a woman of your advanced years could do better."

Miss Effington's eyes widened and her mouth dropped open.

"Your highness," Roman groaned.

By Victoria Alexander

VICTORIA ALEXANDER

WHEN WE MEET AGAIN

AVON BOOKS
An Imprint of HarperCollins*Publishers*

AVON BOOKS
An Imprint of HarperCollins*Publishers*
10 East 53rd Street
New York, New York 10022-5299

Copyright © 2005 by Cheryl Griffin
ISBN: 0-7394-5434-X

Avon Trademark Reg. U.S. Pat. Off. and in Other Countries, Marca Registrada, Hecho en U.S.A.
HarperCollins® is a registered trademark of HarperCollins Publishers Inc.

Printed in the U.S.A.

This is for my dear friends and fellow rogue authors Patti Berg, Linda Needham, Stephanie Laurens, Susan Andersen, and (rogue at heart) Mariah Stewart. Thank you for holding my hand when I need it held or figuratively smacking me and saying "get over it" when I need that, too. I love you all.

Effington

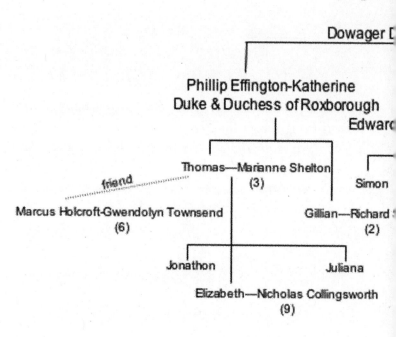

Dowager D

Phillip Effington-Katherine
Duke & Duchess of Roxborough

Edward

Thomas—Marianne Shelton
(3)

Simon

friend

Marcus Holcroft-Gwendolyn Townsend
(6)

Gillian—Richard
(2)

Jonathon

Juliana

Elizabeth—Nicholas Collingsworth
(9)

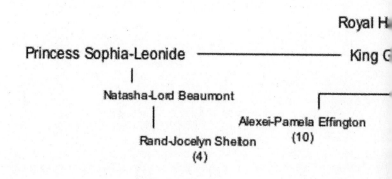

Royal H

Princess Sophia-Leonide ————————— King G

Natasha-Lord Beaumont

Alexei-Pamela Effington
(10)

Rand-Jocelyn Shelton
(4)

& Friends

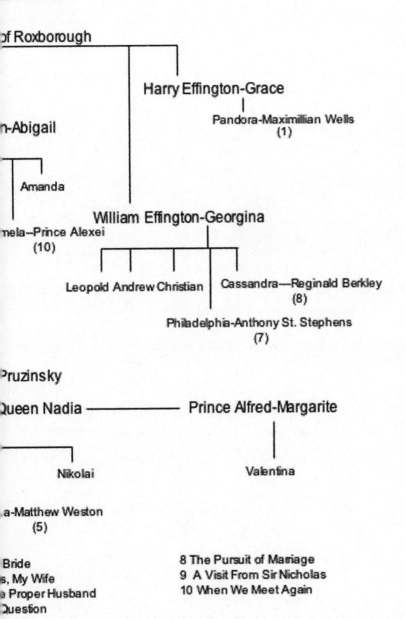

of Roxborough

Harry Effington-Grace
|
Pandora-Maximillian Wells
(1)

n-Abigail

Amanda

mela--Prince Alexei
(10)

William Effington-Georgina
|
Leopold Andrew Christian Cassandra——Reginald Berkley
(8)

Philadelphia-Anthony St. Stephens
(7)

Pruzinsky

Queen Nadia ——————— Prince Alfred-Margarite
|
Nikolai
|
Valentina

a-Matthew Weston
(5)

Bride
s, My Wife
e Proper Husband
Question

8 The Pursuit of Marriage
9 A Visit From Sir Nicholas
10 When We Meet Again

Prologue

Venice, 1818

He was, no doubt, the greatest mistake in her twenty-two years. And the most glorious.

The starlight drifted in through the tall windows in the ornate palace bedchamber to silhouette the profile of his face. It was an exceedingly noble profile—high forehead, strong straight nose, lips just full enough to be at once arrogant and exciting. Even in slumber he had the appearance of royalty, of a man born to rule.

She should leave, and had every intention of doing so before he woke; indeed, she had made him promise to allow her to go before the break of day. Still, at the moment, she could not bring herself to stir from his side.

She started to brush aside the dark hair that had fallen over his forehead but hesitated, her hand hovering over the contours of his face. In spite of the intimacies that had passed between them in this very bed, this simple act seemed rather *too* intimate. Rather too personal. A liberty she had no real right to.

Of course, in truth she had no rights to him at all. Nor did she expect any. She knew full well what to expect when she'd selected him. He'd been chosen for his charm and his reputation with women and the very fact that there was no possibility of a future with him. She had no desire for an emotional entanglement with a man who was not free to return her affection. No, that path led to heartbreak, and she would not tread it again.

She had wanted him for the very reason countless other women had no doubt wanted him: for his handsome face and figure, for the enticing aura of power that surrounded him, and for his royal title. A title that bore responsibilities that precluded any heartfelt morning declarations of affection and commitment. She wished for nothing beyond tonight. Or at least, that had been her plan.

She sighed softly and slipped out of the massive bed, grabbing her cloak from the floor and wrapping it around her naked body like an oversized shawl. She padded to the open doors and gazed out beyond the balcony that overlooked the Grand Canal.

The starlight danced off the waters, and even at this late hour, or rather this early hour, the faint strains of music sounded from somewhere in the distance. Venice and the people who inhabited it did not seem to adhere to the rules that governed other cities. This was a place of magic and passion and all the things that dreams were made of. The kind of place where a young woman with a shattered reputation could begin her life anew as a woman of the world with a man of experience whom she fully intended never to see again. It had been two years, after all, since she'd lost her virtue, squandered it foolishly, really, and it was past time to move on with her life. And why not? She was certainly not the same silly girl she had once been.

She had expected his seduction to be fairly easy. The man had a sizable reputation. Rumor had it that he enjoyed a touch of intrigue, at least when it came to amorous pursuits. Where better to entice him than at a grand masked ball? It was the perfect setting to play to his love of mystery. She had even refused to remove her mask until long after the rest of her clothing had been shed.

What she had not expected was the undercurrent that had run between them from the first. An odd spark, perhaps of recognition of a common spirit, most certainly of mutual attraction and possibly something more. Something intense and indefinable and irresistible.

And really rather wonderful.

From the moment his lips had first brushed her hand there had been the strangest sensation in the pit of her stomach. A physical sense of anticipation, of excitement, of desire she had not truly experienced before. She had allowed it to carry her forward and provide her with a courage she might not have otherwise had.

Certainly, the anonymity provided by the mask helped in that regard. And indeed some of it, much of it perhaps, could be attributed to the nature of Venice itself. The very air of the city had a sensuality and made even a woman with scant experience in the art of love feel like a courtesan. She'd been far more forward and flirtatious than she'd ever been. He'd been intrigued and interested and responded in a manner both exhilarating and gratifying. And she had indeed ended the evening in his bed.

That, too, was not as she had expected. Certainly she knew her previous experience had been cursory and hurried and secretive, but it had been colored, at least on her part, by love, and was therefore exciting—or so she'd thought. She had never anticipated what an experienced lover could provoke in her. How he could bring her senses alive with pleasure. Even now her body still hummed with a tense excitement.

"I do not even know your name." His voice came softly behind her, and she was rather glad he had awakened to join her. He rested his hands on her shoulders, and she leaned back against him.

"Is it necessary then to know my name?"

He paused for a moment, not long in the scheme of things, but long enough to provide a measure of satisfaction, of pleasure really that he might care enough to want to know who she was. At last he laughed softly. "I suppose not. Still, I admit to a certain curiosity as to who has shared my bed."

"Why?" It was her turn to laugh. "I cannot imagine that a man with a reputation as great as yours would be overly concerned with names. It is said you have bedded half the women in Europe."

"Don't be absurd. Half the women indeed. I am not nearly old enough to have bedded even a fraction of that number." She could hear the smile in his voice. "Although I have given it a fair amount of effort."

"No doubt," she said wryly.

"Is that jealousy I hear?"

"Not in the least, Your Highness."

"Pity," he said, more to himself than to her.

In spite of her best intentions her heart sped up, and the oddest sense of something that might well have been hope leapt within her. Utter nonsense of course. She thrust it firmly aside.

"Do you realize you are precisely the right height for me?" He pushed her hair aside and kissed the nape of her neck. "It is extraordinarily easy to kiss you."

"Is it?" She shivered.

"Indeed it is," he murmured against her neck. "You know who I am. It seems entirely unfair that I should not know who you are."

"There is much in life that is unfair. We cannot always have everything we want."

He scoffed. "Rubbish. I always get everything I want."

"Always?"

"Always." Without warning, he spun her around to face him and stared down at her. "I do not permit otherwise."

She sensed he was trying to make out the details of her features in the faint light and was confident he could not do so well enough to identify her. Anonymity was part of the magic of the night. It made no difference at any rate; she would be gone by morning, and there was little chance they would encounter one another ever again.

"I should rather like it, I think, for you to be jealous of the women who came before you."

"Why?" She shook her head. "There are no ties between us. You are a prince and I—"

"Yes?" A hint of eagerness sounded in his voice. "You are?"

She laughed. "I am not a princess."

"Aren't you?"

Her breath caught. How had it happened that what she had intended to have no significance beyond a romantic interlude with a handsome stranger had become rather more important? It was not merely the pleasure he had provided in their hours in his bed, the responses he had coaxed from her, the unexpected joy in their coupling. Something had touched her somewhere in the vicinity of her heart, although such thoughts were the height of absurdity. This was a moment stolen out of time, nothing more than that.

"Although I confess, I do not care if you are in truth a princess or a chambermaid."

She adopted a teasing tone. "And that is which part of your anatomy speaking?"

"My heart," he said without pause.

"Your heart is caught up in the magic of the night, Your Highness." She paused for a moment resisting the impulse to accept his words, embrace them, revel in them. "I understand, as do you, that come the morning, what has passed between us in the darkness will be of no significance. Your Highness—"

"Alexei," he growled, and kissed the curve of her neck.

"Alexei." She shuddered with his name and the feel of his lips on flesh still sensitive from lovemaking. She resisted the urge to melt into his arms. "Alexei, I—"

"What shall I call you?"

"It scarcely matters."

"I must call you something. It is still some time before sunrise, and I do not intend to permit you to go before then."

"We agreed I would leave by dawn."

"But not so much as a moment before."

"I am not entirely certain I can trust—"

"La Serenissima." His hands caressed her back through the silk of her cloak and he nuzzled her ear. "The serene one. That is what I shall call you."

"You're going to name me after Venice then?" She sighed with the pleasure of his touch. "After a city?"

"It is not merely a city."

"And I am scarcely serene."

"Oh, I shall make certain of that." He chuckled, then quieted and turned her around to face out again into the Venetian night, pulling her close against his bare chest and wrapping his arms around her. "I have always loved it here. There is a feel to Venice that touches the yearning in one's soul. It is in the very air we breathe, in the light itself, and unlike anywhere else in the world."

"Such fanciful notions, Your Highness. I would not have suspected it of you."

"I would not have suspected it of myself," he said in a wry manner. "I doubt I have ever said it aloud before but I have long thought this was a place of magic where anything could happen. And no more so than tonight."

She stared out over the wide canal, at the stars overhead and their light reflected in the windows of the ornate palazzi that seemed to grow from the water itself. "A place of dreams."

"Where a prince can be nothing more than a man with

a beautiful woman in his bed. And ask no more from life than that."

"But you are not merely a man."

He blew a long breath. "No, I am not." He paused. "Still, it has been an unexpected and rather extraordinary night."

"Indeed it has."

"I am scheduled to remain in Venice for several weeks. There is nothing to say we cannot share another night as glorious as this one. Or a dozen nights. Or more."

She laughed lightly. "I fear another night with you, Your Highness, and I shall fall madly, irrevocably in love, which can only lead to the breaking of my heart."

"That would be a very great shame. Of course"—his voice was thoughtful—"it could well be my heart that is broken.

"And that would be a greater shame."

"Because I am a prince?"

"Because you will one day be a king," she said softly.

"There are moments when I would rather be a mere man."

"I suspect you could never be a mere man."

He laughed, scooped her up in his arms, and her cloak fell to the floor. She realized he was as naked as she and noted in the back of her mind how odd it was to be in this position and yet not feel at all exposed or embarrassed but rather quite, quite lovely. He started back toward the bed. "You would be very good for me, Serenissima."

"You would be very bad for me, Your Highness."

"Alexei. Tonight, let it be no more than Alexei and—"

"Serenissima?" She laughed.

"Serenissima." Abruptly his mood sobered. "As serene and beautiful and mysterious as the city she is named for."

"Beautiful? I am flattered, as you have not truly seen me."

"And yet I know." He laid her on the bed and stretched out beside her. "My lips have kissed yours and explored the features of your face." He suited his actions to his words. "My hands have caressed the curve of your hip and the length of your legs and the firm, sweet swell of your breasts. I have felt you quicken beneath me at our joining and known the excitement of your release surrounding me."

She slipped her arms around his neck and pressed her body closer to the heat of his. "You are very good at this, Your Highness."

"I suppose I am." He gathered her to him and fell silent for a long moment. She felt his heart beat in his chest against the press of her breasts. His growing arousal nudged between her legs, and her own newfound desire pooled within her. "I could keep you here, you know. At this very minute, there are guards outside the door and others in the room beyond. I could spirit you away without notice, if I so wished, and keep you forever in my bed and by my side."

"Yet you will not do so." Even as she said the words she knew the truth of them. He was a man with unlimited power. A man used to getting exactly what he wanted, yet she hadn't the slightest doubt that, in spite of his threat, he would not do anything to tarnish the memories of this night. He would not do anything she did not wish. "And to what end, Your Highness? I have no desire to be any man's mistress, not even a prince's."

"I cannot offer more."

"I am well aware of the obligations of the heir to a throne."

"Still—"

"Alexei." She brushed her lips against his. "You would grow tired of me before the week is out."

"Never," his lips murmured against hers.

"There is no place for me in your life beyond this one night."

"What is it about this night?" His voice rang hard in the shadows, and he drew away. She sensed him studying her. "You have cast a spell upon me, Serenissima. In truth, I am enchanted. By a woman I have not seen save by the light of the stars. A woman who will share her body but not her name. A woman who initiated seduction yet has had little experience in such matters."

She caught her breath.

"Do not be surprised, Serenissima." He chuckled. "You cannot choose a man of my reputation for this game you play and not expect him to notice you are not what you appear."

"It is not a game, Alexei," she said quietly. "It is my life."

"It could well be my life at risk. You could be an assassin sent to cut my heart out."

"As you can see, I am unarmed."

"Indeed, I made certain of it." A grin sounded in his voice. "Ah, Serenissima, I have no reason to trust you, yet I do." He shook his head. "It is this place, no doubt. In the air. The stars. The music of the water. The magic of the night."

"Alexei." She drew him back to her. "We have this moment and this moment alone. Tonight. Is it not enough?"

"I have never wished for more than this from a woman before," he muttered. "It is most disconcerting."

"Tomorrow you will be Prince Alexei Pruzinsky, the heir to the throne of Avalonia, and the night will have no more significance than a dream."

"And you? Who will you be tomorrow?"

"I will be . . ." She smiled. "I will never be the same again."

"Serenissima." He groaned and met her lips with his, and all rational thought vanished beneath an onslaught of passion and sensation of utter, indescribable delight.

And in the moment before she gave herself completely to the pleasure of his touch she wondered if indeed she could be a woman of the world and share the beds of other men or if whatever had passed between her and this one man on this magic night was far and away too wondrous and unique to know ever again.

He was indeed a glorious mistake.

And she'd never forget him.

One

When I see London again I shall be the picture of propriety. I shall behave in a respectable manner always. And I shall try very hard to hold on to the woman I have become.

Miss Pamela Effington

Four years later . . .

"Well done, Clarissa." Pamela Effington pulled off her mask and grinned at her opponent. "You nearly had me for a moment."

"*Nearly* is an understatement, dear cousin." Clarissa, Lady Overton, drew off her own mask and shook her dark hair free. "Another few seconds, and the point would have been mine."

Pamela laughed. "Fortunately, there was no time left."

"Fortunate indeed." Clarissa slashed the blade of her fencing foil through the air. "Next time, I shall claim victory."

"As you did in our previous match." Pamela shook her head with good-natured humor. "We are well suited, cousin."

"Indeed we are." Clarissa studied the foil thoughtfully. "But is it really necessary, do you think, for a woman to be skilled with a sword? It's not as if we should ever be forced to fight a duel for our honor."

"I'm not certain a woman can ever have too many skills or too much knowledge. Besides, it stirs the blood, or at least mine, and is excellent for the body and the mind. And I, for one, find it both stimulating and quite enjoyable."

Clarissa raised a brow. "You sound precisely like Aunt Millicent."

"I'm not the least bit surprised as I quite agree with her about a great many things." Pamela handed her mask and foil to Monsieur Lucien, the fencing master, with a nod of thanks.

"Of course you would." Clarissa handed her own things to Monsieur Lucien. "Fencing, doing anything women do not typically do, makes you more of an—"

"Don't say it." Pamela's voice was firm. "I am not in the mood for yet another discussion of my character flaws." She started toward the grand entry in the ornate ballroom they had used for their fencing lesson.

The ballroom occupied a good portion of the first floor of an impressive house in the very best part of Vienna that belonged to an Austrian count, an old and dear friend of Lady Smythe-Windom, their Aunt Millicent. Of course, there didn't seem to be anywhere in the world where there wasn't a very old and very dear friend of

Aunt Millicent's. In all the years of their travel together, not one such friend of their aunt's had ever failed to invite them to stay for as long as they wished. It was a grand way to live even if, on occasion, the unsettled nature of their lives had bothered both Pamela and Clarissa. Still, it was what each woman had chosen for her own reasons.

"Nonetheless, I am going to say it." Clarissa trailed after her cousin. "You like fencing and anything else that's unconventional and a shade scandalous because it's precisely what an Effington female would enjoy."

"I am an Effington female." Pamela stifled a long-suffering sigh. Clarissa had brought this subject up over and over again in recent months and over and over again, Pamela had managed to deflect the discussion. She headed down the corridor that led to a series of salons designed for music and games and whatever else the residents of a house like this desired.

"The flaw isn't in being what you are but rather in trying to be something you aren't," Clarissa called after her.

"Indeed," Pamela muttered.

It was easy for Clarissa to make pronouncements. She simply didn't understand and probably never would. Clarissa was Pamela's cousin on her mother's side and hadn't the least idea what it was like to be an Effington. Especially a quiet, reserved, shy Effington.

Oh, certainly, Pamela's cousin Delia had been considered "quiet" until scandal broke around her head. And then Delia's twin sister Cassandra, who everyone thought was headed for the worst kind of scandal, well, wasn't.

And of course, there was Pamela herself, whose behavior no one had ever worried about, who, at the advanced age of twenty, when she certainly should have known better, had fallen deeply and passionately in love with George Fenton, the son of Viscount Penwick. At least she had thought she had, and had, with rapt abandon and no consideration to the consequences, lost her virtue to him. It was, as her brothers had muttered in a dark and forbidding manner once her ruination was known, the quiet ones you had to keep your eye on.

It wasn't simply her nature that had set Pamela apart from the vast numbers of Effington relations. She had never particularly looked like a member of the family, who were all in all an attractive lot, the women universally pretty, some of them quite beautiful, the men typically handsome and dashing.

Pamela's mother, a beauty in her own right, had always staunchly declared her oldest daughter was simply late to bloom and would come into her own one day. And indeed, shortly after her twentieth birthday, Pamela had gazed into a mirror and discovered that her tall, lanky body and nondescript features had somehow become rather nice. Even lovely. Unfortunately, the confidence in oneself that was as much an Effington birthright as the name itself had not accompanied the unexpected transformation. Therefore, was it any wonder that Pamela lost her heart, and her innocence, to the first man who showed her a fair amount of attention? Oh, certainly, she had thought George had been sincere in his declarations of affection and had shared her feelings and was intent upon marriage. She had never dreamed said intentions were not in regards to marriage to *her*.

Clarissa, on the other hand, had been born pretty and

even as a child had always had a quiet confidence about her. She'd never had a doubt as to where she belonged or with whom. While the cousins shared a certain similarity in appearance, although Pamela's coloring was far fairer than Clarissa's, and were a scant few months apart in age, the way in which they saw the world was as different as night and day. Odd then that they had been not merely cousins but the very best of friends for nearly all of their lives. Pamela had on occasion wondered if they were so close because Clarissa was not an Effington and Pamela had never especially felt like an Effington.

Until, of course, Aunt Millicent had taken her under her wing.

"Dearest girls," Aunt Millicent's voice sounded from an open doorway. "Do come join me at once. I have the most interesting news."

Pamela turned to enter the room, but Clarissa caught her arm and met her gaze. "Stop it, cousin, and listen to me. What I have been trying to say for months now, and obviously not at all well, is that you have nothing left to prove. You are not the same girl who fled six years ago from London rather than face scandal. You are confident and assured and not the least bit reticent about voicing your feelings or opinions. Indeed, you've become quite accomplished and really rather remarkable I think. I would even say you are"—Clarissa rolled her gaze toward the ceiling—"every inch an Effington. God help you."

Pamela stared at the other woman for a moment then grinned. "I know."

Clarissa's brows drew together. "You do? But you didn't say a word."

"It isn't something one announces. Besides, it didn't happen overnight. I daresay, I've been changing, growing if you will, since the very first day we left London. Perhaps it makes no sense, it doesn't entirely make sense to me, but I haven't at all been trying to become something I'm not, simply trying to find out who I am." Pamela thought for a moment. "I have found that I like fencing and riding at a full gallop and exotic places and dancing until dawn and flirting with delightful men. And I particularly like speaking my mind without fear as to the consequences. In truth I find I quite like Pamela Effington." She cast her cousin a wry smile. "And I can see that was not true six years ago."

"You were entirely too hard on yourself." Clarissa studied her cousin. "I have always liked you."

"You have always loved me." Pamela gave her a quick hug. "As I have always loved you."

"Are the two of you going to stand in the doorway going on forever about Lord knows what, or are you going to come in here." Aunt Millicent's impatient voice rang from the room. "I have the most wonderful news, and I shall burst if I do not share it at once."

The cousins exchanged grins and stepped into the salon.

Aunt Millicent did indeed look as if she would burst at any moment, her usual air of barely suppressed energy heightened, if possible, by excitement. She was the twin sister of Pamela's mother and had used her widowhood and the vast wealth she had inherited to live precisely as she pleased. Indulging in a great deal of travel, an equally great number of gentlemen admirers, and an extraordinary amount of fun. Aunt Millicent always said she had married once for love and refused to marry again for any other reason. Marriage, she claimed, was simply not worth the effort otherwise.

"News, darlings." Aunt Millicent waved a piece of paper at them. "I have the very best of news. Do you remember my aunt Elizabeth?"

"Great-aunt Elizabeth?" Clarissa nodded. "Of course."

"Of course," Pamela murmured. "Who could possibly forget Great-aunt Elizabeth?"

"Indeed the woman was stodgy and stingy and condemning of virtually everyone who did not live their lives precisely as she thought proper." Aunt Millicent wrinkled her nose. "She long disapproved of me. Well." Aunt Millicent beamed. "She's dead."

A heretofore-unnoticed gentlemen cleared his throat.

Aunt Millicent glanced at him and winced. "I didn't mean to imply that I'm especially glad that she's dead. I would not have wished her dead. However, I certainly did not kill her, and as she is dead, we should bravely carry on and make the best of it." She glanced at her nieces. "This is Mr. Corby, a very nice solicitor whose firm handled Elizabeth's affairs and who has furthermore been so gracious as to come all the way from London to bring us this news as well as this letter explaining everything. It appears Elizabeth was involved in a rather unusual incident involving a carriage and a herd of"—she glanced at the gentleman—"goats was it?"

"Pigs," he said under his breath.

"Pigs, yes, of course." Aunt Millicent sighed and cast her gaze downward. "Quite tragic."

"Shouldn't we say a prayer or a few words?" Pamela said in an aside to Clarissa.

Clarissa nodded. "Something I should think."

"Absolutely. Why, I should have thought of it myself." Aunt Millicent folded her hands together beneath her chin, paper still clasped between them, and gazed upward. "Dear Lord." She paused and cast pointed glances at the rest of the gathering. Pamela and Clarissa obediently folded their hands and looked toward the heavens. Mr. Corby hesitated, then followed suit.

"Dear Lord," Aunt Millicent began again, "please grasp Aunt Elizabeth to your loving bosom although"—she frowned—"as Mr. Corby says she entered your domain more than six months ago, I should think if you have not already taken her to your loving bosom, then perhaps she did not ascend in your direction but rather descend—"

"Aunt Millicent!" Clarissa said, eyes wide with shock although Pamela thought she certainly should have expected such a eulogy from their aunt.

"Yes, of course. Speaking ill of the dead and all that." Aunt Millicent glanced upward. "Sorry. Now then where was I? Ah yes." She cleared her throat and again looked piously toward heaven. "Dear Lord, if indeed Aunt Elizabeth is at your gates, please accept her into your kingdom and forgive her for her sins, although I should think you would wish her to explain her behavior first. She always was a rather unpleasant sort." Aunt Millicent thought for a moment. "If, of course, she has already gained admittance, well then, never mind. I'm certain you have more important matters to attend to." Aunt Millicent nodded.

"Forever and ever. Amen."

"Amen," the others echoed in unison.

"Now." Aunt Millicent's eyes sparkled. "Mr. Corby was also kind enough to bring us a number of boring dry legal documents that nonetheless bear wonderful, wonderful tidings."

Mr. Corwin smiled at the cousins. "A substantial inheritance."

Pamela and Clarissa exchanged glances.

"Quite substantial." Aunt Millicent cast them a radiant smile. "Consisting of Elizabeth's grand house in the very best part of London as well as a sizable fortune."

"How perfect for you," Pamela said with a smile of genuine pleasure.

It was indeed perfect. The house Aunt Millicent had shared with her husband was part of the estate that accompanied his title and had gone to his younger brother upon his death. Aunt Millicent had inherited a respectable fortune but no property. She had always claimed it left her free to explore the world, but on those rare occasions when she spoke of her husband or their life together, it was obvious she wished for a permanent residence, a home to replace the one she had lost.

"Oh no, dearest. It is not my inheritance alone." Aunt Millicent shook her head. "It is to be shared among the three of us. It is ours."

Clarissa gasped. "Ours?"

"I don't quite understand. Why am I included in this?" Pamela drew her brows together. "I barely knew Aunt Elizabeth, and I had the distinct impression she had never approved of my mother's marriage."

"You must remember there was a great deal in this world of which Elizabeth did not approve. In spite of the Effington wealth and prestige and the fact that the head of the family, your uncle, is the Duke of Roxborough, the Effingtons did not quite meet her standards. She always was rather a snob." Aunt Millicent shrugged. "She did not approve of me either, yet I, too, am her beneficiary. It makes no sense, but there you have it."

"If you would permit me, Lady Smythe-Windom." Mr. Corby smiled at Aunt Millicent, and it was obvious that the solicitor was yet another man who had fallen under her spell. Even at the age of five-and-forty, Aunt Millicent was still an attractive woman and had a vibrancy about her that made her quite irresistible to all manner of men, ranging from nobility to servants. "Lady Gorham's affairs were always handled by an older member of the firm, and while I never had direct dealings with her, it is my understanding that she felt Miss Effington was not a typical representative of her family."

Clarissa snorted in unladylike manner. "She has obviously not seen you for a very long time."

"Obviously," Pamela said under her breath.

It was obvious as well that Elizabeth had no knowledge of Pamela's fallen state, which came as something of a surprise. She thought everyone in the world—or, at least, in *their* world—had heard of her disastrous ill judgment and subsequent moment of weakness. Certainly her family had claimed, both in letters and visits through the years, that there had been far greater scandals to capture the ton's attention subsequent to hers. Why, the loss of virtue of one young woman was scarcely worth mention-

ing after the initial burst of gossip. She had certainly believed them in a rational portion of her mind, but even so
she simply hadn't been able to bear the humiliation of her
downfall. At least not then.

An unbidden thought struck her: What would her family
think if they knew George was not her only indiscretion?

"Furthermore, she expressed a great deal of concern as
to Lady Smythe-Windom's continued way of life as well
as its influence on Miss Effington." He glanced at
Clarissa. "And Lady Overton. She felt with this legacy all
three of you would be able to live a proper, respectable
sort of life."

"Respectable is such a vague word," Aunt Millicent
murmured.

"What utter nonsense." Disdain rang in Clarissa's
voice.

Pamela's chin raised. "Our lives are completely respectable."

"I have no doubt of that," Mr. Corwin said firmly. "Indeed, now that I have met Lady Smythe-Windom for myself I think your aunt's fears were nothing more than the
product of an unyielding disposition coupled with advanced age. In addition, you must realize that what is not
at all uncommon on the Continent is seen in an entirely
different light in England. Like your aunt, we English
have a tendency to be a touch"—he bit back a smile—
"stodgy ourselves."

"Not all of you surely?" Aunt Millicent cast him her
brightest smile.

A blush colored his cheeks, and the cousins traded private grins.

"Not all," he said, then shook his head slightly as if to clear it. "Now then"—he pulled a sheaf of papers from a black satchel—"to begin with, your signatures are required on several of these documents. Your funds have been placed in an account in the Bank of England. As for the house, it is my understanding it is ready for immediate occupancy." He stepped to a nearby writing desk and laid out the documents.

"Details regarding the house are oddly vague, as Lady Gorham had not lived in London for a number of years, preferring to spend her time in a manor in the country which, under the terms of a nearly century-old lease, reverted to the owners of a nearby estate upon her death. I am told, however, the London residence has been kept fully staffed and meticulously maintained." He dipped a pen into a conveniently placed inkstand. "Ladies, if you would be so kind."

Mr. Corby continued his endless explanations of the details of precisely what they were signing and the arrangements regarding their newfound wealth and property. Although Pamela nodded and smiled at what she hoped were appropriate moments, she was too stunned to concentrate on what he was saying. His words were as incomprehensible as if he were speaking a foreign language.

Pamela, Clarissa, and Aunt Millicent were now, to be blunt, rich. Obscenely, delightfully wealthy. Pamela's family had always had money, of course, and on her marriage she would have a rather significant dowry, but this was her own. She would never have to depend on her family's support again. She could *choose* to marry, she had always wished to marry, but did have to face the fact that the chances were slim at the advanced age of six-and-twenty. But now she didn't have to wed if she didn't wish to do so. She could support charities, sponsor artists, do nearly anything. She could indeed choose her own future, her own fate.

And they had a home of their very own as well. Clarissa's family home had passed to a distant relative upon her father's death. The house she had shared with her husband had belonged to his parents, who had begrudgingly allowed her to remain in residence for more than a year after his death. It was at that point Aunt Millicent had invited Clarissa to join her on her travels. Both aunt and niece were in nearly the same circumstances after all, both having lost a husband they loved as well as a home, although Aunt Millicent had a great deal of money and Clarissa barely any. Scarcely a week later, Pamela had fallen from grace and desperately wished to leave London as well. The trio had not seen fit to return to England since.

"If there is any assistance I can lend you regarding your return to London"—Mr. Corby paused to sprinkle sand on the signatures—"do feel free to call on me. I am currently in residence at the Hotel—"

"What do you mean by return to London?" Pamela stared at the solicitor.

Mr. Corby frowned. "My apologies, Miss Effington, I thought you understood. To lay claim to your inheritance, all three of you must present yourself in person to a representative of the bank. That will start the process, rather involved and complicated really, but the transfer of amounts like this takes a bit of time. However, within a month, possibly less, your money will be available to you. Further-more, you must take up residence in the house."

"Take up residence?" Clarissa's eyes widened. "You mean return to London to live?"

Aunt Millicent looked shocked by the very idea. "Per-manently?"

"For now at least." He thought for a moment. "There is no particular time period of residency specified in Lady Gorham's will although I should think as little as a year should suffice to meet the terms of the bequest."

"A year," Clarissa said slowly.

"A year," Pamela echoed.

"I have not lived anywhere for a full year in, well, years," Aunt Millicent said under her breath.

Mr. Corby raised a brow. "Does this present a problem?"

"No," Pamela said without thinking. Her gaze locked with Clarissa's. "I am ready to return home. I miss En-gland more than I can say. I miss my parents and my sis-ter and my brothers and everyone else in my family. In truth, I have been thinking of returning home for some time now." Her gaze slid to Aunt Millicent. "These years have done more for me than I can say, and I shall always be grateful to you, but—"

"It's past time to return home," Aunt Millicent said firmly. "We have all been away far too long." She turned to the solicitor and cast him a blinding smile. "Mr. Corby, we are most grateful for your assistance thus far, and you can be certain we will indeed call on you in London should it become necessary."

"Of course." Mr. Corby gathered his things together, started toward the door, then paused. "Lady Smythe-

Windom, I hope this does not seem improperly forward, but I should be delighted if you would do me the honor of joining me for supper this evening."

"I would like nothing better," Aunt Millicent said in that way she had that made every man feel as though she would indeed like nothing better than to be with him and him alone.

A few moments later the gentleman took his leave.

"I have no reason to go home. No one I have missed, no one who has missed me." Clarissa heaved a resigned sigh. "Yet I, too, miss England."

"Good. I could never go without you." Pamela turned to her aunt. "Aunt Millicent?"

"I should be happy to accompany you both back to England. However I must confess, and I'm not entirely sure why I feel this way but"—Aunt Millicent blew an anxious breath—"permanent has an altogether frightening ring to it."

"Nonsense." Pamela studied her aunt in disbelief. "Nothing scares you."

"And surely you don't think we could live in a grand house without you?" Clarissa stared. "Or anywhere without you. Aside from Pamela's family, you are the only family I have left in the world."

"That's very dear of you, but—"

"It's been a long time since you lived in London." Pamela adopted a tempting tone and moved to her aunt's right. "You cannot tell us you haven't missed it."

"Well, I suppose . . ." Aunt Millicent murmured.

"And if we leave Vienna as soon as possible, we shall be back for the start of the season." Clarissa stepped to

Aunt Millicent's left and lowered her voice seductively. "You do remember the season, don't you? The routs, the balls, the soirees."

"The gentlemen," Pamela added.

Aunt Millicent bit her lip, a thoughtful look in her eye. "I have always loved the season."

"I suspect, given what Mr. Corby didn't say as well as what he did, that it's entirely possible that if we don't all join in this legacy, together"—Pamela heaved an overly dramatic sigh—"none of us will get any of it at all."

Clarissa shook her head in a mournful manner. "What a great pity that would be."

"It did sound that way, didn't it?" Aunt Millicent's brows drew together.

"Indeed it did." Clarissa nodded.

"I daresay Great-aunt Elizabeth probably arranged it this way because she knew you would be reluctant to return home." Pamela adopted a casual tone. "Just the thing she'd do, too, reaching out from beyond the grave—"

"To toy with us." Clarissa sighed. "To get the very last word even beyond—"

"That's quite enough." Aunt Millicent glanced from Pamela to Clarissa, then shook her head. "I can accept defeat when I am faced with it. I cannot guarantee permanence, but we shall see. Very well then, my dears." She took her nieces' hands in hers and drew a deep breath. "Let us go home."

Two

"Out with it, man. What are you trying to say?" Alexei Frederick Berthold Ruprect Pruzinsky, crown prince and heir to the throne of the Kingdom of Greater Avalonia, Servant of the Doctrines of St. Stanislaus, Guardian of the Heavens of Avalonia, Protector of the People, glared at the man who had once been his loyal chief of staff, was now an equally loyal friend, and still in charge of his affairs, financial, and to a certain extent, personal as well. "I cannot possibly be—"

"Penniless?" Dimitri Petrov, formerly Captain Petrov, offered helpfully. "Destitute? Impoverished? Without a pot to p—"

"That's quite enough," Count Roman Stefanovich said in the very same tone he had honed to a fine art during his regrettably brief service as chief advisor to the heir to the throne. The count glanced at the notebook in his hand, drew a deep breath, and turned his attention back to his prince. "It is not as dire as all that, Your Highness."

Alexei narrowed his eyes. "Precisely how dire is it, Roman? What is the true state of my finances?"

"As you know, your grandfather saw fit to protect a sizable portion of his personal wealth by placing it in the Bank of England more than half a century ago, during a time of great upheaval in Avalonia," Roman began. "Wisely, as it turns out, even though the crisis had passed, he thought it prudent to allow the funds to remain and accrue interest in the event it was ever needed by the rightful heir to the throne. It is now a substantial, indeed, an impressive fortune."

"Yes, yes, as you said, I know all that." Alexei gestured impatiently. While in many ways Roman was brilliant, he had the most annoying tendency to reiterate the entire history of an issue rather than simply get to the point. "Precisely why I have chosen to make England, a country I have never been overly fond of, my home."

"Although, your sister and your cousin do reside here," Dimitri pointed out. "Besides, England is as far away as one can get from Avalonia and not have to cross the Atlantic."

"There is that," Alexei said darkly.

It still grated on him, this exile from the land of his birth to a country he found no more than bearable, but what choice did he have? He refused to leave Europe altogether and the Americas certainly held no interest for him. Nasty, uncivilized places from what he'd heard. No, as unappealing as he had always considered England, and London as well, it was the only acceptable option. As soon as Roman could locate a suitable estate for purchase somewhere outside of London, it was Alexei's intention to forsake the city altogether. He had always been a sociable sort, indeed he had relished attending grand balls in Vienna, masquerades in Venice, even soirees in London when necessary, but that too had changed in the six months since his father's death.

Alexei now wanted nothing to do with English society or society *anywhere* for that matter. His desire at the present was for solitude, the kind that allowed a man to examine his life and come to grips with his own mistakes as well as accept the forces of fate he could not control. He wanted—no *needed*—a haven for himself and for the handful of retainers, servants and, in the case of Roman and Dimitri, friends as well who had remained loyal to him and accompanied him into exile. He owed them that much and indeed more.

"Unfortunately," Roman continued, "the very reasons your grandfather originally chose the Bank of England, its secure and conservative nature, make it difficult to access the funds at the present time."

"Why?" Alexei asked, even though he already suspected the answer.

"Russia, Your Highness. As Avalonia is now part of the Russian Empire, the bank, as well as the British government, wishes to be certain the Russians have no claim to the money." Roman paused to choose his words. "Apparently the English have no desire to annoy the tsar."

"What about annoying me?" Alexei snapped although once again he knew the answer.

Silence fell in the room. Roman and Dimitri traded wary glances. It was not at all fair of Alexei to take his frustration out on them, and he well knew it.

"My apologies, old friends." Alexei ran a weary hand through his hair. "It is most prudent of the British government to do whatever necessary to avoid strained relations with Russia. I would do the same in their place. I am, after all, a sovereign without a country, and any annoyance on my part is of scarce importance to the English or anyone else."

"Nonetheless, there is a question of loyalty to longtime friends and allies," Dimitri said staunchly.

Alexei laughed, a harsh, deprecating sound. "In the world we inhabit, Dimitri, loyalty between countries has more to do with power than friendship. Avalonia's power has always been tenuous, consisting of nothing more than the strategic nature of its geographic location in the world. I have long known and accepted, as my father did before me and his father before him, that our very existence was contingent on the benevolence of those more powerful countries around us." The muscles in his jaw tightened. "We can thank Napoleon's rampage across Europe for Russia's decision to annex Avalonia to secure its own position before Prussia or Austria chose to do so."

"Damn the French," Dimitri muttered. "And the Russians as well."

"It does no good to condemn half the world, Dimitri," Roman said coolly. "Although I admit to sharing your feelings, they neither change the situation nor help."

"We should have fought to the death," Dimitri blurted, then caught himself. Regret reflected in his eyes, and he bowed toward Alexei. "Forgive me, Your Highness, I did not mean—"

"You most certainly did, and I cannot fault you for it. You have showed remarkable restraint in recent months in not pressing the issue. It is duly noted and appreciated more than you can know." Alexei blew a long breath. "I myself shall regret every moment, with each breath that I take until the end of my days, that we did not fight to retain our independence."

"To what end, Your Highness?" Roman's voice was low and intense. Roman had always been a diplomat, Dimitri a warrior. Roman alone understood full well the decisions Alexei had made. The reasons behind them and the dreadful cost.

Russia had announced its intention to annex Avalonia within days of his father's death, before Alexei could be crowned king. The tsar's representatives had given him a choice no man who was born and raised to rule his country and serve his people should be forced to make. Alexei could still ascend to the throne, but he would be nothing more than a ceremonial leader, a figurehead to be displayed at state functions and formal celebrations. Not even a puppet with the pretense of authority. No more than a symbol of a country that would, for all intents and purposes, no longer exist.

Or he could choose exile. Leave Avalonia forever and forfeit all claims to the throne.

"To what end indeed," Alexei said more to himself than to the others.

His younger brother, Nikolai, had urged full-fledged resistance. Nikolai had demanded they take up arms against Russia and fight to the last Avalonian left standing. Alexei had been forced to send his brother out of the country for his own safety.

Nikolai was young and impetuous. He had not spent his life in training to rule and to put the welfare of his people above all else. Russia had stopped Napoleon's progress when the rest of the world had failed. Avalonia would have been nothing more than a minor and short-lived irritation beneath its feet. The country would have been crushed, the land laid waste, the population decimated. Fighting the Russian Empire would have accomplished nothing more than the final satisfaction of being able to die for one's country. What little country would have been left.

The threat of rebellion was precisely why Alexei had chosen exile. As long as he remained in Avalonia there would be the possibility of revolt. He would have been a constant reminder of what had been lost. Those loyal to his family and to an independent Avalonia would have used him as a symbol around which to rally forces for rebellion. And ultimately, his people would die, and his country would be destroyed.

He had had no choice. To save his country and his people, he had to leave it forever. Pity he could not take his heart with him.

Alexei was more than willing to die for his country. He would have considered it an honor, even a right. But he would not allow his country to die for him.

"The world has moved on, and so, too, shall we." Alexei forced a firm note to his voice. He no longer had a country, a home, but he had two very good men—two very good friends—who had followed him into exile and a handful of servants who had chosen loyalty to their prince over the place of their birth. Their future, indeed their very survival, was now in his hands. "So, how bad are my finances, Roman?" He waved at the room around them, a large library that had become the men's favorite place in the huge, if somewhat shabby, London house Roman had arranged to lease. "Can we retain the roof over our heads at least?"

"That was never in doubt, Your Highness." Indignation colored Roman's voice at the very thought that he had not taken care of this particular matter. "We paid the required rent in advance for the next six months."

Alexei raised a brow. "We had the money for that?"

"I said the situation was not dire." Roman huffed. "Although admittedly said payment did deplete our resources. You have a minimal amount of funds on hand, not what you are used to, of course, but something at any rate. I understand the nobility in this country, when finding themselves in similar circumstances, live to a great extent on credit."

"Credit?" Dimitri brightened.

"No." Alexei shook his head. He had seen far too many nobles in his own country succumb to the lure of credit to their financial ruin. He had never understood the temptation of credit before now. "I would prefer to avoid that route as long as possible."

"Excellent, Your Highness." Roman nodded his approval. "We shall simply have to curtail our expenditures, particularly those of a frivolous nature."

"What?" Alexei adopted a wicked grin. "No expensive baubles for whatever beautiful creature strikes my fancy."

Dimitri's grin matched his prince's. "That scarcely seems frivolous to me. Why, I would call it a necessity of life."

"No doubt you would. Both of you." A reluctant smile curved Roman's lips. "Even I can see the advantages in the presentation of a costly trinket in the attaining of the affections of a lovely woman. However," his expression sobered, "such indulgences must be eliminated for the moment. In point of fact, you—in truth we, all of us— shall have to adhere to a rather strict"—he flipped open his notebook—"budget."

"A budget?" Alexei traded glances with Dimitri. This would be most amusing under other circumstances. As it was, it simply added insult to injury. Certainly, his government had followed a budget, but never in his life had Alexei had to operate under personal financial limits. The world had indeed changed.

"A budget." Roman paged through the notebook, his voice firm.

"You said it was not dire," Dimitri muttered.

"Nor is it," Roman said, without looking up. "You can, Your Highness, continue to live in your accustomed style for the most part although a reasonable element of frugality would be wise. Nothing drastic, mind you, staff does not need to be let go—"

"Thank God," Dimitri said under his breath.

"—however Captain Petrov and I will both have to accept a severe reduction in our wages."

"What?" Dimitri stared.

"Which we will do gladly and in a most gracious manner." Roman leveled a firm look at Dimitri.

The other man smiled weakly. "Gladly."

"You do realize I cannot permit that." Alexei met Roman's gaze. "Given the circumstances, it is a most generous, even charitable offer but—"

"Forgive me, Your Highness, it is neither generous nor charitable." Neither Roman's gaze nor his voice wavered. "When the captain and I chose to throw our lot in with yours we knew full well that life in the future would be uncertain."

"Apparently you knew more than I," Alexei said wryly.

"As I often do, Your Highness." The smile in his eyes belied the tone of his voice. "It is precisely why you depend on me."

Alexei had depended on the count's counsel for the last three years. Roman had long been one of Alexei's few true friends but had only served as chief of staff after the man who had previously held that position had proven to be a traitor in league with Alexei's cousin Valentina's plot to overthrow the king.

"Do keep in mind, Your Highness, this is a temporary state," Roman said, leafing through his notebook. "I am certain your accounts will be available to you fairly soon."

Alexei studied the other man. "How soon?"

"Given the cautious nature of British banking and the intricacies of diplomacy," Roman studied the open page, then looked at Alexei with a confident air, "a few months at the most. No longer than autumn surely."

"But in the meantime we need to be"—Dimitri shuddered—"frugal?"

Roman cast him a quelling glance. At moments like

these, Alexei was hard-pressed to remember that Roman was no more than a scant handful of years older than the other men.

"I see." Alexei thought for a moment. "Then our plan to buy an estate in the country is at a standstill?"

"Not at all, Your Highness," Roman said quickly. "We can certainly continue our search for the right property. Such things take time, as do the negotiations for sale."

"But I cannot actually purchase said property at the moment?"

Roman shook his head. "Regrettably, no."

"So we are trapped for the time being in London."

"Like rats," Dimitri muttered. Dimitri shared his prince's opinion of London and England.

"Hardly, Captain," Roman said coolly. "London is one of the great capitals of Europe, and it is the start of the social season here. Even though His Highness has chosen to keep his presence quiet and therefore will not be receiving invitations to any number of festivities, there remain no end of inexpensive amusements we can avail ourselves of if we so choose."

"Of course there are." A firm tone sounded in Alexei's voice and he feigned enthusiasm. "Museums and galleries of art and libraries and the like." He glanced at Roman, who nodded. "Why in this very room there are enough books to keep us busy for years."

"Books?" Skepticism sounded in Dimitri's voice. He had never been overscholarly.

"An excellent idea, Your Highness." Roman's voice rang with approval. "We could all spend these next few months improving our minds, expanding our intellectual horizons. Such a pursuit would not only be beneficial but a great deal of fun as well."

Dimitri met Alexei's gaze. "Fun?"

Alexei grinned. He was not much more of a scholar than his friend, and the idea of spending the next few months expanding his intellectual horizons held little appeal. At once, it struck him that he really had no idea how he would spend the upcoming months or years, or the rest of his life for that matter.

From the moment he had made his decision to give up his birthright and his country he had lived—or rather existed—in a maelstrom of emotions that would have overwhelmed him if he had so permitted. Instead, he'd ignored them or perhaps controlled them, pushed them to the back of his mind, the back of his heart, and had focused all his efforts and energy on simply putting one foot in front of the other. On functioning as if nothing out of the ordinary had happened. On remembering to breathe. He had made the decisions he had needed to make about his departure, and that of those who chose to accompany him, efficiently and with a minimum of sentiment. He had decided upon England and had further decided to reside quietly in the country. Possibly as a way to avoid a world he no longer had a place in and avoid as well a future he had never considered.

Or perhaps as penance.

His responsibilities, his very life, had changed dramatically. He had no idea what tomorrow might hold, but today it was indeed up to him to make the best of it. For himself and for his friends. He had no choice.

"We have scarcely been in London a fortnight, gentlemen." Alexei clasped his hands behind his back and paced the room. "It seems to me we have several options as to how to occupy our time in the coming weeks or"— he winced in spite of himself—"even months. I can abandon my desire for anonymity. We can indeed make our presence here known publicly and be feted, wined and dined in the manner to which we are accustomed."

"An excellent idea, Your Highness." Dimitri tried and failed to hide the enthusiasm in his voice.

"If that is your preference." Roman's manner was noncommittal. "I have heard the English are exceptionally fond of visiting royalty."

Alexei raised a wry brow. "Even those without a country?"

"From what I understand, especially those without a country. There is an element of romance and, oh, what is the right word"—Roman thought for a moment—"accessibility I should think, perhaps even mystery or—"

"Sympathy? Pity?" Alexei pressed his lips together. "I have no desire to be pitied." He paused and gazed out the window that overlooked the back gardens. "My sister is expecting her second child and cannot travel. I have already sent word to her and my cousin informing them of our presence here but no one else. We shall live quietly and in a reserved manner for the duration of our stay in London. Perhaps, at some point, when we have found a suitable estate and have settled into life here . . ." Then what? Would he wish to partake of society's amusements one day? Or would he prefer to spend the rest of his life in seclusion, dwelling on the past? Even given his current melancholy temperament it was not a pleasant prospect.

He was scarcely five-and-thirty years of age. Far too young for his days to be at an end.

"As you wish, Your Highness." Dimitri heaved a sigh of resignation.

A discreet knock sounded at the door.

Alexei nodded at Roman, who stepped to the door and pulled it open.

"I beg your pardon, Your Highness." Graham, the servant who acted as both butler and majordomo and was indeed the manager of the household, stepped into the room. "You have a caller."

Roman waved him off. "His Highness is not receiving visitors today."

"Precisely what I explained to the lady, my lord, but she was very insistent. And sir"—Graham paused in a manner that might have been termed dramatic if the butler was given to such emotions—"she has baggage."

"Baggage?" Roman frowned.

"A lady?" Dimitri grinned.

"A great deal of baggage," Graham added.

Alexei thought for a moment. As far as he knew, his presence in London was not common knowledge. Still, they had not been overly secretive, simply discreet. They would not be difficult to locate for someone determined or desperate enough to do so. He nodded at the butler. "Show her in."

The butler took his leave, and Roman stepped toward Alexei, concern sounding in his voice. "Your Highness, is that wise?"

Alexei shrugged. "Probably not. However, a lady with all her worldly possessions in tow might well have fled her home precisely as we have."

Dimitri's brows drew together. "An exile from Avalonia perhaps?"

"Perhaps." Alexei nodded. "As such we cannot turn her away without so much as a word."

Roman shook his head. "Still, Your Highness, you cannot—"

"Alexei!" A tall, dark-haired woman swept into the room. "Dear, dear cousin, how are you?"

At once, Dimitri stepped in front of Alexei and instinctively reached for the sword he no longer carried.

"Valentina?" Alexei stared in disbelief. The Princess Valentina Pruzinsky, his cousin and for much of his life his nemesis, was the last person he expected to see here or indeed ever again. He narrowed his gaze. "What in the name of all that is holy are you doing here?"

"I am here because you are here, cousin." She cast him a brilliant smile.

"Allow me to run her through, Your Highness," Dimitri said out of the corner of his mouth. "Slay her where she stands."

"Ah, the ever-loyal Captain Petrov." Valentina fluttered her lashes at the soldier. "It is so good to see you are as charming as ever."

"You do not have a sword, Captain," Roman said coolly, his gaze never leaving Valentina. "However, I believe there may well be a pistol in the house somewhere."

"Do try to control yourselves, gentlemen." Valentina rolled her gaze toward the ceiling. "I realize we might well share a less than pleasant history—"

"Less than pleasant? Less than pleasant!" Dimitri sputtered, his eyes darkening with outrage.

"I should term it deadly myself." Alexei stepped around Dimitri and studied his cousin. "You attempted to seize the throne from my father and fomented revolution among the people."

"And failed rather miserably I might point out. Besides, that is all in the past." Valentina waved off the comment. "It is over and done with. Ancient history as it were. Scarcely worth mentioning now."

Alexei gritted his teeth. "You nearly caused the death of my sister in your efforts to steal the jewels that are Avalonia's heritage."

"I did not try to steal them." Valentina huffed. "I was trying to *recover* them. They were missing, if you recall, and had been for a fair number of years. And, in point of fact, Tatiana was not killed and suffered no more than a momentary inconvenience. Why, some might even call it a rather extraordinary adventure."

"I could strangle her with my bare hands, Your Highness," Dimitri said in a low voice.

Alexei ignored him. "Why are you here?"

"Why?" She glanced down at her hands and began to draw off her gloves in a slow and deliberate manner, an obvious effort to buy time to choose her words. "I have come to apologize and make amends."

Roman stared suspiciously. "Amends?"

Dimitri snorted in disbelief. "Apologize?"

Alexei drew his brows together. "Do you expect me to believe you?"

"No," she said, her gaze still focused on her hands. She pulled off one glove and started on the other. "In truth, I have no idea how to go about this. I'm not sure I have ever apologized for anything before."

At once it struck Alexei that if indeed his proud, imperious cousin meant what she said, this was exceedingly difficult for her.

"However," she drew a deep breath and met his gaze directly, "I am sorry for . . . everything."

Dimitri scoffed.

"Everything?" Alexei said coolly.

"I will not lie to you, especially as there is no reason to do so now. Everything I have ever done was done for the good of my country. For most of my life, I believed my family and, ultimately, I were better fit to rule Avalonia than you and yours. Every action I have taken was toward achieving that end."

"This is an apology?" Dimitri said in an aside to Roman.

"No." Valentina's eyes narrowed at Dimitri. "This is an explanation. I will apologize for my actions but not my beliefs. Indeed, if I had succeeded, we might still have a home today."

"If you had succeeded, there would have been vast bloodshed when Russia finally chose to seize Avalonia." Alexei's voice was cool and unemotional, but his jaw clenched. "Great numbers of our people would have been slaughtered, the country destroyed."

She paused for a long moment, then heaved a resigned sigh. "Possibly."

Alexei raised a brow. "Surely you are not admitting you might well be wrong?"

"Exile, cousin, gives one a great deal of time to think. I

had never especially considered the right or wrong, in a moral sense, of my actions, only what I thought was best for my country." Her eyes glistened. "Avalonia was my soul and the soul of my father. He was too weak to challenge your branch of the family for leadership, but what he lacked he instilled in me.

"However, circumstances, the way life has changed, that is, have led me to regret the actions I have taken in the past. Indeed, I accept now that my methods may well have been . . . well"—she shrugged—"*wrong*, again in a moral sense, and for that I am sorry, but I shall never apologize for the reasons for them."

Alexei stared at her for a long moment. She appeared sincere, but he did not trust her and probably never would. Still, the reason for the discord between her side of the family and his no longer existed. There was nothing left to fight over. At this point, she had nothing to gain with her apologies.

"Why are you here?" he asked once again.

"I thought it was time that you and I mended the rift between us. We are family, after all, and, in truth, we have very little family left. And if we are not bound together by blood, then surely we are bound together by loss. I also thought . . . that is to say I felt . . . or rather I wished . . ." She floundered, obviously at a loss for words.

"Yes?" Alexei prompted.

She grimaced and her gaze met his. "I had nowhere else to go."

"Of course," Roman murmured.

"Ah-hah!" Dimitri smirked. "I suspected as much."

Valentina ignored him. "My funds are seriously depleted. Indeed, I have very little money left at all. My country is gone. I am a widow twice over—"

"And where does the fault lie for that?" Dimitri said darkly.

It had long been rumored that the deaths of both Valentina's first and second husbands were at her hand. Of course, both gentlemen were well past their prime when they had married her, and neither had gone to his final reward in a manner or at an age that could be considered untimely. Still, the gossip had lingered probably because Valentina had not been married to either of them for much more than a year. And they had both had substantial fortunes.

She slanted Dimitri a look that could well prove the demise of any man. Husband or otherwise. He didn't so much as flinch. She turned her attention away from the captain in a manner that could only be described as regal. Alexei had the most unreasonable urge to grin.

"Cousin. Alexei. Your"—she closed her eyes for a moment as if to gather strength—"*Highness*. I am throwing myself on your mercy as it were. As a citizen of Avalonia and a member of your own family I am asking for, well, sanctuary. A haven. Asylum I should think."

"Asylum?" Alexei stared in disbelief then laughed. "I have no asylum to offer. I am not a church offering sanctuary, and I am no longer the sovereign of a country."

"Perhaps asylum was the wrong word." She stepped toward him. "What I need is a home, Alexei. I have not lived my life in a manner that would ensure friends, and you are my only family. Allow me to join your"—she cast a disgusted glance at Dimitri—"household. I am not

without certain skills, you know. I am an excellent hostess and, as you have no wife, when you entertain—"

"I have no intention of entertaining." Alexei's voice
was firm.

Valentina's eyes widened. "Why on earth not?"

"His Highness has no desire to partake of society,"
Roman said staunchly. "He much prefers a more solitary
existence at the moment to reflect and ponder the future."

"You can't possibly be serious." Valentina scoffed. "Regardless of the state of the world, you are still a prince of
Avalonia, the head of the Royal House of Pruzinsky, which
carries certain responsibilities, social at the very least. It is
your duty to present yourself in public if only to show the
world that we may be beaten, but we are not destroyed. Besides, one makes all sorts of valuable contacts that—"

"To what purpose?" Alexei snapped, his gaze boring
into hers.

The very room itself held its breath. Valentina stared at
her cousin, a myriad of emotion flashing across her face.
At last she drew a deep breath. "I do not know. But I will
not hide myself from the world."

"Nor will I, cousin. I have no intention of becoming a
hermit. I am simply not yet ready for the trivialities of society. Therefore, I have no need of a hostess."

"Alexei," Valentina began, but Alexei held up a hand to
stop her.

"However," he continued, "you are family and may
join us."

Concern pulled Roman's brows together. "Perhaps it
would be prudent—"

"You can't mean that, Your Highness." Shocked colored Dimitri's voice. "It would be like inviting a viper into our midst."

Valentina snorted. "A viper? Surely you can do better than that, Captain."

Dimitri ignored her. "She has spent her entire life trying to seize power and destroy you and your family. She has buried two husbands and no doubt put them in their graves herself. She is not to be trusted."

Alexei grinned. "I have no intention of trusting her."

"I certainly wouldn't if I were you," Valentina murmured.

Dimitri frowned. "You do not?"

"Not at all. In fact, I think she needs to be watched closely."

"Oh, I do." Valentina nodded firmly. "I do indeed." She shrugged. "In truth, cousin, I have done nothing to earn your trust. Until you are confident of my motives it is only wise to be cautious. I would be extraordinarily careful in your place."

Roman nodded. "Caution is certainly wise, Your Highness."

"Excellent." Dimitri nodded with satisfaction. "I should hate to think you would be taken in by a few contrite phrases of apology."

"Then allow me to put your concern to rest," Alexei said smoothly. "I think Valentina should be watched every moment she resides with us. Night and day—"

"I could not agree more." Enthusiastic approval sounded in Dimitri's voice.

Alexei bit back a grin. "I furthermore think she should be watched only by someone who has my absolute trust."

"Absolutely." Dimitri nodded.

Roman grinned.

"Someone I would trust with my very life," Alexei continued.

"With your life, Your Highness," Dimitri said firmly. "No one less will do."

"And that, old friend," Alexei paused for emphasis, "would be you."

"Of course, Your Highness, who else—" Abruptly Dimitri realized what he was agreeing to. "Me?"

"Him? The ever-sanctimonious, too perfect, Captain Holier-than-thou?" Valentina huffed. "I would prefer to be tossed in a dungeon and left to share my days with vermin rather than be under his eye. I despise him."

Dimitri folded his arms over his chest and scowled. "And I detest her."

"I am not suggesting a match between the two of you." Alexei wanted to laugh aloud but forced a stern note to his voice. It was really most amusing. Both Dimitri and Valentina looked stricken. It could not be helped, of course. Even if he still had an entire army at his disposal, Dimitri would be his choice for this particular assignment.

"Valentina." Alexei met his cousin's gaze with a hard, level look. "This is a condition of your joining us. It is not negotiable." He turned to Dimitri. "The circumstances we find ourselves in dictate this choice, Captain. There is no other. However, even if I had all the resources of Avalonia still at my disposal, there is no one I trust more than you." Alexei smiled a wry sort of smile. "And no one I trust less than she."

Dimitri's gaze locked with Alexei's for a moment, then

he heaved a resigned sigh and nodded a bow. "As you wish, Your Highness."

Alexei chuckled and leaned closer to his friend. "At the very least, the princess will give you a way to occupy your time other than by expanding your intellectual horizons."

Dimitri smiled in a rather pathetic manner. "That is something at any rate."

"If the two of you are quite finished, I should very much like to be shown to my rooms." Valentina smiled in an overly sweet manner. "I find all this groveling to be rather fatiguing."

Dimitri cast Alexei a pleading glance. "Day and night?"

Alexei grinned.

"You may take pleasure in the knowledge that I am no more pleased about this than you are. I do, however, acknowledge it as the, oh, *penance* I must do to gain my cousin's trust. We shall simply have to make the best of it." Valentina started toward the door. "I assume the servant who showed me in can show me to my quarters. Captain, my bags are in the foyer. Come along."

"I'm not carrying your bags," Dimitri said indignantly, but followed her out the door nonetheless.

Their voices lingered in the hall. Valentina said something Alexei didn't quite catch. Probably for the best.

"Or I shall be forced to throttle you with my bare hands," Dimitri responded.

"Oh, Captain, would you?" Valentina's laugh rang in the hall.

Alexei and Roman traded grins.

Roman shook his head. "That shall certainly provide some needed amusement. Do you think she is sincere?"

"I do not know, but we shall see. She has little to gain, as I have little left to lose." Alexei sank down into the nearest chair. "Roman?"

"Yes, Your Highness?"

"Does our frugality extend to the purchase and consumption of spirits?"

"It would seem to me that is a necessary expenditure," Roman said solemnly. "However, I believe a well-stocked cabinet comes with the house."

"Good." Alexei breathed a weary sigh. "As it seems rather necessary at the moment."

Roman crossed the room to a decanter of brandy and glasses conveniently placed by Graham on a table near the fireplace. It struck Alexei, not for the first time, that not so long ago there would have been half a dozen footmen in any room he inhabited, ready to do such mundane tasks as pour brandy at a moment's notice. While the house was considered fully staffed, it simply was not a royal palace.

Roman poured two glasses and handed Alexei one. "It has been an interesting day thus far, Your Highness."

"Interesting? Hah." Alexei took a long drink of the brandy. "I have no money, and my traitorous cousin has come to live with me. I can scarcely wait to see what tomorrow will hold."

The familiar noise of a throat being cleared sounded from the doorway.

"Or possibly yet today," Alexei muttered.

"It is said many events happen in threes," Roman observed mildly.

"Begging your pardon, Your Highness." Graham cleared

his throat once more, stepped farther into the room, and snapped the door closed behind him.

"More callers, Graham?" Alexei said with a resigned smile.

"Ladies?" Roman chuckled. "With baggage no doubt."

"Indeed, sir. Quite a bit of baggage, as well as a fair number of servants."

Alexei raised a brow. "Avalonian exiles perhaps?"

"I don't believe so, Your Highness." Graham's brow furrowed slightly.

Alexei stared. For the first time since their arrival, and he suspected one of the few times ever, the butler seemed distinctly nonplused.

"These ladies are most definitely English and," the butler paused then straightened his shoulders, "they maintain, well, that is—"

Alexei's jaw clenched with impatience. "Yes?"

"The ladies say this is their house." Unease shaded the butler's face. "And they have come to claim it."

Three

If I ever see His Highness again, I shall pretend not to know him. I shall be cool and collected and serene. And I absolutely shall not let him so much as suspect that he owns my heart.

Miss Pamela Effington

"I daresay, I am at a loss." Aunt Millicent gazed around the foyer as if she had never seen such a grand entry before. "This is all very odd."

Pamela and Clarissa exchanged worried looks. It was exceedingly curious for Aunt Millicent to be at a loss about anything, but from the moment the three women had stepped foot on British soil a subtle change had come over their confident aunt. Aunt Millicent had, well, *softened* was the only word for it. Pamela wondered if *permanent* wasn't the only difficulty her usually self-assured aunt had with returning to London.

A butler had shown them in, then left them standing in a manner that would be considered quite rude—and indeed unforgivable—were it not for the stunned look on his face at their announcement that they were the new owners of the house.

Although the servant was well aware of the demise of his late mistress, even if she had rarely resided in this particular house, he was not merely taken aback, he looked as if he had just been hit. Pamela had the distinct impression uncertainty of any kind was an unfamiliar state for him, and he had no idea how to proceed. He had murmured something confusing about awkward situations and leases and financial obligations, then begged their patience, indicated he would return, and fled the foyer.

"One of us should probably do something," Clarissa murmured although she showed no signs of doing anything whatsoever. Of course, Clarissa had always been rather too reserved, or too polite, to take matters into her own hands. Exactly as her cousin had once been.

Well, those days had passed.

"Indeed one of us should." Pamela nodded firmly and considered exactly what that something should be. She glanced at the door on the far side of the foyer where the butler had vanished. He had obviously gone to speak with someone. "And the place to start might well be with whoever is in that room." She started toward the door.

"Is that wise?" Clarissa trailed behind her. "Perhaps we should wait here."

"Or leave," Aunt Millicent added brightly. "Florence is lovely at this time of year."

Pamela cast her a reassuring smile but did not slow her step. "As is London."

She reached the door, pulled a deep breath, and braced herself for whatever might be in that room.

"I really think we should wait to be announced," Clarissa said under her breath.

"To whom?" Pamela shook her head. "It seems to me there should be no one here at all to whom to be announced. Yet this house does not have an unoccupied air."

"Mr. Corby did say it was kept staffed and well maintained," Aunt Millicent offered.

"Still, there is a distinct difference between maintained and lived in. No, there is something decidedly odd here, and we should waste no further time in getting to the bottom of it." Resolve rang in Pamela's voice. "This is our house, soon to be our home, and the beginning of entirely new chapters in our lives. I have no intention of starting this very first page with indecision and hesitation. It is time, dear ladies, to claim what belongs to us."

A groan sounded from one woman, and a sigh came from the other. Pamela had no idea which came from whom and didn't care. The very act of decision, of seizing the moment with both hands, filled her with the most invigorating sense of strength and power. The oddest thought struck her that this feeling was probably familiar to everyone else in her family. Indeed, this might well be her birthright. She grasped the door handle.

"Wait," Aunt Millicent said.

Pamela glanced at her.

"I have something of a confession to make." Aunt Millicent wrung her hands together.

Pamela frowned. "Now?"

"I would prefer never to now, however . . ." Her aunt

drew a deep breath. "I daresay the two of you are too young to remember this, but after my husband died I became quite close to a certain gentleman—"

"How close?" Pamela asked.

Clarissa raised a brow. "How soon?"

"Nearly two years." Aunt Millicent fixed Clarissa with a firm stare. "A perfectly proper amount of time. I was more aware, or rather more concerned, about such insignificant things as propriety then." She turned to Pamela. "We were, well, betrothed."

Pamela widened her eyes in surprise. "To be married you mean?"

"Yes, well, betrothed does often mean to be married," Aunt Millicent said sharply, then paused and blew a resigned breath. "Although not necessarily in this case."

Pamela and Clarissa traded glances, but neither said a word.

"It was that annoying question of permanence, you see." Aunt Millicent's brows pulled together. "I simply couldn't promise permanence, for the rest of my days, until death and all that. I had promised it once, and it wasn't at all permanent as Charles had the nerve to die altogether too young. I found I couldn't do it again, so I left London."

Clarissa nodded sympathetically. "On your travels."

"Exactly." Aunt Millicent cast her niece a grateful smile.

The faintest memory of whispered gossip nipped at the back of Pamela's mind. "When, exactly, did you leave?"

"Before we were to marry." Aunt Millicent's smile was entirely too innocent.

Pamela narrowed her gaze. "How much before?"

Aunt Millicent glanced away as if she were idly look-ing for something or rather looking at anything but Pamela. Her voice was deceptively casual. "Moments, I should think."

Clarissa gasped. "Moments?"

Aunt Millicent refused to meet her nieces' eyes. "He might well have been awaiting my arrival at, oh, what is the place I'm thinking of?"

Pamela held her breath. "Church?"

"Excellent, my dear." Aunt Millicent smiled weakly. "He was waiting at the church to be wed when I decided I would rather travel than marry. It wasn't at all polite of me, and I did send him a very nice note of explanation; actually, I sent it to my sister, but still and all . . ." Her gaze slipped to the door.

Pamela stared. "Surely you don't think this spurned suitor of yours is here?"

"No, of course not," Aunt Millicent murmured. "Al-though stranger things have certainly happened in this world." She pulled her gaze from the door and met Pamela's. "I simply thought you should know *everything* before we did *anything* that was irrevocable."

"I fear I am somewhat confused." Clarissa's glance darted between her cousin and her aunt. "What does any of that have to do with any of this?"

"Nothing at all really. I just thought I should explain my reticence to return to London. Permanence, whether in regards to residing in a particular city or a specific house or marrying a certain man, should be given a great deal of consideration and is not to be embarked upon lightly. Once we step through that door and claim this house, there can be no turning back." Aunt Millicent sighed. "That's really all I meant."

"Your point is certainly well-taken." A firm note sounded in Pamela's voice, even as she wondered precisely what the point really was. Not that it truly mattered at the moment. "Now if there's nothing else."

"Oh, I'm sure I could think of something," Aunt Millicent said under her breath, then started, as if unaware she had said anything aloud, and favored her niece with a bright smile.

Pamela once again grasped the door handle, opened the door, drew a deep breath, and stepped inside.

The overagitated butler was on the far side of the room addressing two seated gentlemen and paying far too much attention to the queries of the as-yet-unseen gentlemen to note Pamela's presence until she was nearly upon him.

She mustered an authoritative tone she hadn't known she possessed and noticed yet another surge of strength within her. "Mr. Graham, wasn't it?"

At once, the seated gentlemen jumped to their feet. She ignored them and pinned the butler with an unyielding gaze. "Mr. Graham, I demand you explain your behavior at once."

The butler's eyes widened. His mouth opened and closed and opened once more. Something that might have been panic flashed through his eyes, replaced almost at once by resignation. He heaved a slight sigh. "It appears we have something of a problem, Miss Effington."

"And what precisely would that problem be, Mr. Graham?" She met the butler's gaze directly.

"The house is leased for the season, Miss Effington," Graham said reluctantly. "As it was last year and the year before that and nearly every year since Lady Gorham ceased coming to London."

"This is absurd." Pamela's brows pulled together. "My aunt's solicitor said nothing about this."

"I am not entirely sure Lady Gorham's solicitor was aware of the situation," Graham said under his breath.

"I don't understand." Pamela studied the man carefully. She had the distinct impression he was not being entirely honest. "Did Lady Gorham know what you were doing with her house?"

"Absolutely, miss." The butler's voice rang with indignation that she would suggest such a thing. A bit too much indignation perhaps. "Lady Gorham long ago permitted me to rent the residence for the season, as it proved impossible to maintain the house and staff without a steady income."

"Be that as it may." Pamela crossed her arms over her chest. "Lady Gorham is now deceased. Indeed, she has been deceased for more than half a year's time. This house is now the property of Lady Overton, Lady Smythe-Windom, and myself. And we fully intend to occupy it."

"Before you unpack your belongings, please allow me to introduce myself, Miss Effington. I am Count Roman Stefanovich." One of the gentlemen, tall and distinguished in appearance with a vaguely foreign lilt to his voice, stepped forward and bowed. "At the moment, and indeed for the better part of the next six months, this house has been quite properly, and I might add, quite legally, leased by my party."

She stared in annoyance but held her ground. "Regardless, my lord, your lease was agreed to under the mistaken belief as to the ownership of this house. As my aunt was already dead at that point, it seems to me Mr. Graham did not have the authority to reach such an agreement."

"Nonetheless," the count said smoothly, "there are universal principles in law, even in England I believe, based on the concept of past practices." He raised a shoulder in a dismissive shrug. "You could certainly challenge our claim in the courts of your country; however, I would wager that by the time the question was settled it will be past the date of the expiration of the lease and would be a moot point."

"The only point I see is most pertinent." She narrowed her eyes. The man was altogether too clever and most annoying. "This is to be my home, and I fully intend to take up residence here at once. Not six months from now."

"Miss Effington, I am certain we can come to some accommodation that will best suit us all," the second gentleman interjected in a smooth and most diplomatic manner.

Pamela drew a calming breath, prayed for strength, and prepared to do battle with yet another stranger who was probably as clever as his friend. But this was her new home, her new life, and she did not intend to let it slip through her fingers—even for no more than six months—because of some absurd agreement she'd had no say in.

"My dear sir." Pamela turned to address the count's companion and froze. Surely, it couldn't be . . . Her breath caught and her chest tightened. It simply wasn't possible—

Behind her, Aunt Millicent gasped. "Your Highness!"

Your Highness? Alexei?

Prince Alexei Pruzinsky, heir to the throne of the Kingdom of Greater Avalonia, smiled apologetically at her aunt. "Forgive me, my lady, but I fear you have me at a disadvantage. Have we met?"

Have we met? Sheer panic surged through Pamela. He had Aunt Millicent at a disadvantage? Hah!

"I couldn't possibly expect you to remember, Your Highness, you meet a great many people and have a great many responsibilities. I am Lady Smythe-Windom." Aunt Millicent sailed past Pamela, once again her old self, curtseyed, and extended her hand to the prince. "Besides, it was years ago, in Venice if memory serves."

Venice. Pamela groaned to herself. Of all the princes Aunt Millicent had ever met and all the places she had ever met them in, why had she met this particular prince in Venice? Oh certainly, Pamela had met him in Venice, but neither her aunt nor her cousin knew the gentleman Pamela had dallied with in that city was the very same gentleman who was now occupying her house in this city.

"Ah yes, Venice, that explains my lapse of memory." The prince took Aunt Millicent's hand and raised it to his lips.

Did he remember Pamela? Probably not. In truth, she didn't wish him to remember. Hadn't she taken great pains at the time to conceal her identity and ensure he would not recognize her if ever they met again? Indeed, he had never even seen her face other than by the faint light of the stars. And why would he remember her? She was simply a minor indiscretion in a lifetime of indiscretions for him.

"Oh?" Aunt Millicent raised a curious brow.

Of course, Pamela remembered Venice and a night of sheer magic in the bed of a prince as if it were yesterday. A night illuminated by the very essence of starlight and accompanied by the faintest hint of violins in the far distance and water gently caressing the docks.

"Only Venice could erase the memory of meeting a woman as lovely as you." His lips brushed across the back of Aunt Millicent's hand, his gaze never left her aunt's. His was the polished manner of a man well used to flirtation. To seduction.

And Pamela remembered him as well. Everything about him. The dark intensity of his eyes, the tender skill of his touch, the very timbre of his voice when he had murmured endearments in the throes of passion. She had remembered him during the long, lonely hours of the night in the years that had passed since then and joined with him again in the freedom of her dreams. And she had remembered him each and every time she'd so much as considered sharing another man's bed, which really did rather muck things up.

"I daresay I have always found Venice to be rather amusing," Aunt Millicent said with a flirtatious smile of her own.

"Venice is much more than amusing." He released Aunt Millicent's hand and paused for a moment as if recalling the delights of Venice to mind.

The prince had given her an evening so truly wonderful, Pamela had never wished to spoil it with anyone else. It—or rather he—had quite dashed her plans to become a woman of the world.

"Venice is unique on this earth. There is nowhere else

like it. It is a place of dreams." An enigmatic smile lifted his lips. "La Serenissima."

La Serenissima? Pamela sucked in a sharp breath, tried to catch herself, and choked. Then coughed and choked again or perhaps coughed again. Regardless, the odd, strangled sounds emanated from her with a total disregard for her desire to remain as unnoticed as possible at this moment and instead ensured the attention of everyone in the room.

Aunt Millicent stared at her with concern. "Pamela, my dear, are you all right?"

"Quite," Pamela gasped, struggling to catch her breath. Of all the times she had dreamed of meeting the prince—*Alexei*—again this was not at all as she'd imagined. She had rather thought she'd be elegant and collected and not sputtering and gasping like a dying fish.

The butler, obviously far better trained than he had appeared thus far, hurried to her side with a glass of water, and she accepted it gratefully. She sipped the water and glanced discreetly at Alexei. He studied her with an expression that mixed concern and amusement and carried no hint of recognition whatsoever. Excellent. She had no desire for so much as a slight breath of scandal, and his recalling their night together might well be the first step toward a scandal of immense proportions. After all, it was one thing to lose one's innocence in the misguided belief that one was in love and quite another to seduce a prince as the launching of a life of experience.

"Pamela?" Clarissa stepped up beside her and peered into her face. "Are you certain you're all right?"

"I am quite recovered, thank you." Pamela flashed a polite smile at the gathering, and tried and failed to avoid

Alexei's clear brown eyes. They held a touch of ordinary curiosity but nothing beyond that. She brushed aside the tiniest bit of what might well have been disappointment.

"Your Highness, do allow me to present my nieces." Aunt Millicent gestured at the younger women. "Clarissa, Lady Overton—"

Clarissa murmured a polite greeting.

"And Miss Pamela Effington." Aunt Millicent nodded at Pamela. "I fear she's rather outspoken these days."

Alexei chuckled. "I am well aware of that."

"We've never met," Pamela said quickly.

"Indeed we have not. I would most certainly remember such a meeting." Alexei studied her. "I was simply referring to your confrontation with Graham and Count Stefanovich."

"Of course," she murmured, and prayed her cheeks did not appear nearly as hot as they felt.

"It is indeed a pleasure to make your acquaintence, dear ladies. I am Alexei Pruzinsky." He nodded a bow. "And I am at your service."

Count Stefanovich frowned. "Your Highness, your title, your position—"

"Is as moot a point as others that have come up today." Alexei met the other man's gaze. "We are embarking upon a new life, Roman. It is time to leave the trappings of the old one behind."

The trappings of the old? Pamela stared, then realized exactly what he was speaking of. She had read that his country had been annexed by Russia, and he had relinquished all right to the throne. He was indeed embarking upon a new life. One he could never have imagined.

"You will always be a prince, Your Highness," the count said in a low voice. "It is the right of your birth. Who you are."

Alexei considered the count thoughtfully. Her heart twisted for him. He was a man made to rule. How could he leave his heritage behind him? Indeed, how could he go on at all?

"Your Highness, I understand your desire to put the past behind you," Aunt Millicent said quickly. "But I for one would be most uncomfortable referring to you as anything other than Your Highness, and I daresay others would feel a similar discomfort."

Alexei smiled wryly. "Do you really think so, my lady? I am a prince without a country after all."

"To my mind, it scarcely matters." Aunt Millicent nodded firmly. "You have always been a prince, and regardless of the political state of the world, you remain so. I think your behavior and that of others in regard to you should continue to reflect that position."

"I appreciate your sentiment, but the very world itself has changed and so, too, should I." Alexei shrugged. "Regardless, it is not a question to be decided now."

"What are you doing here?" Pamela said without thinking.

Alexei's brow rose. "You are indeed outspoken. Very well, Miss Effington, the answer is quite simple. I am living here."

"We have leased this house," Stefanovich said firmly.

Pamela huffed. "I am well aware of that. I meant what are you doing in England?"

"I have nowhere else to go." Alexei chuckled. "It is a

depressing state to find oneself exiled to a country that has never held a great deal of appeal. I do have relations residing in England though, and they appear fairly content with their lot. I have no intention of living in London for the rest of my days, however; I propose to purchase an estate in the country. That plan has now been delayed so, for the moment, this house is my residence, the residence of my staff and of my cousin. Our home, as it were." He met Pamela's gaze, and a distinct challenge glimmered in his eyes. "And I have no intention of leaving."

She stared at him, ignoring the unsettled feeling churning in the pit of her stomach, and raised her chin. "And I have no intention of allowing you to stay. This is my house now, soon to be my *home*, and I want you and the count and anyone else you may have with you to vacate the premises immediately."

"Pamela!" Aunt Millicent's voice rang with shock. Aunt Millicent had always been overly fond of princes or royalty of any kind. She could count among her friends members of most of the royal houses of Europe. Indeed, she collected royalty as one might collect precious gems.

"That's not at all gracious of you," Clarissa said under her breath, and laid her hand on her cousin's arm. "Surely there is somewhere else we could stay in London until their lease expires?"

"Where would you suggest?" Pamela's words were addressed to Clarissa, but her gaze stayed locked with Alexei's. "Neither you nor Aunt Millicent has property here. It is the start of the season, and I suspect there is not another acceptable residence available in all of London."

"There are hotels," Aunt Millicent offered.

"Ladies do not stay in hotels." Pamela narrowed her eyes and ignored the amusement that now shone in the prince's eyes. The blasted man was enjoying this. "I have a perfectly acceptable house right here, and I have no intention of living anywhere else."

"We could always stay with your family," Clarissa said hopefully. "Your parents or perhaps even the duke and duchess would no doubt be more than happy—"

"No." Pamela's voice was sharp, and she jerked her gaze to her cousin. "That will not do."

Clarissa and Aunt Millicent traded resigned looks. Pamela had no intention of explaining to these gentlemen why she had no desire to return to the homes she had spent the better part of her life in. She loved her family and had no doubt of their love for her. But she had become a competent, independent woman in the years since she'd left London. She had the most unreasonable fear that all she'd gained would be lost, that returning to her previous home would return her to her previous character, and that she would not risk. Especially when there was no need to do so.

"Mr. Graham." Pamela nodded at the butler. "Please see to it that whatever amount the prince has paid for the lease of the house is returned to him and send a footman at once to the Clarendon or the Pulteney to see if there are accommodations available for the prince and his party."

"That might be rather awkward, miss," Graham said in a decidedly reluctant manner.

Her gaze snapped to his. "Which part?"

"Hotels are notoriously full at this time of year and," Graham winced, "as for the money . . ."

She did not like the look on the butler's face one bit. "Yes?"

"It cannot actually be returned," he said slowly. "That is not entirely. Or rather not all of it." He shrugged apologetically. "Expenses, miss."

"Very well." Pamela gritted her teeth. "I shall refund their money out of my own funds."

"That, too, might be awkward, Pamela. Have you forgotten that we have yet to receive the financial portion of our inheritance? Mr. Corby said the funds would not be immediately available." Aunt Millicent glanced at the count. "Unless it is an extremely reasonable amount?"

"It was exorbitant," Stefanovich said dryly.

Aunt Millicent heaved a delicate sigh. "I'm afraid exorbitant is out of the question."

Pamela cast her aunt a beseeching look. "Couldn't you—"

"Oh, I certainly could, but I have a much, much better idea than refunding the prince's money and sending him on his way." A considering light shone in Aunt Millicent's eye. "I suggest we take up residence here as we have planned and—"

"And?" Pamela held her breath.

"And," Aunt Millicent continued, "we allow His Highness, and the rest of his party, too, of course"—she glanced at Alexei—"you did say there was a cousin here as well? A royal cousin I presume?"

Alexei nodded. "A princess."

"A princess? Oh I do like that. A prince and a princess under my roof, I can't wait to tell my sister." A wicked gleam sparked in Aunt Millicent's eye. "As I was saying, we allow them to remain—"

"Never!" Pamela glared.

"Oh my," Clarissa said faintly. "Here?"

"As our guests," Aunt Millicent finished with a flourish.

"Delightful," Stefanovich muttered.

"How very clever of you to think of such a solution, Lady Smythe-Windom." Alexei stepped forward, took Aunt Millicent's hand in both of his, and gazed down at her. Surely he wasn't going to kiss her hand again? That would be entirely too much even for a man of his reputation. "I am in your debt. If there is ever anything I can do for you in the future, please do not hesitate to ask."

"I'm certain I can think of something." Aunt Millicent stared up at him with a smile that hinted of all sorts of things. Naughty, wicked things.

Immediately a number of naughty, wicked things that could be done with Alexei flashed through Pamela's head, and for a moment her knees weakened. She pushed the thoughts aside and struggled for control. "Aunt Millicent." She drew a deep breath. "I don't want this man and his entourage in my house."

"It is really not much of an entourage," Alexei said thoughtfully. "Not at all like the old days. What do you think, Roman?"

"No, Your Highness." The count shook his head regretfully. "Our number is woefully small in comparison to the old days."

"Indeed." Alexei sighed in a dramatic matter. "Why, it is little more than a handful really. Aside from the count and myself, there is Captain Petrov, our respective valets, a few drivers and stable hands, whatever servants my cousin has, and of course, our cook." He leaned toward Aunt Millicent in a confidential manner. "He is most extraordinary, Lady Smythe-Windom. Why, the cook here has completely allowed him to have his way in her kitchen, and I suspect, given his mood since our arrival, has furthermore allowed him to have his way—"

"And do not forget your cousin, Your Highness," Stefanovich cut in.

"I could never forget Valentina." Alexei's voice carried a hint of resignation.

"There now, Pamela." Aunt Millicent cast her niece a satisfied smile. "Why, there are so few of them, and this house is enormous, we shall scarcely know they're here." She glanced at the butler. "Would it overly tax the staff to have a larger party in residence?"

"Not at all, my lady," Graham said with a subtle but definite air of relief.

"Excellent." Aunt Millicent nodded. "If you would be so good as to inform them of all this."

"At once, my lady." Graham nodded a bow and took his leave.

The moment the butler closed the door behind him, Pamela threw her hands up in frustration. "Of course we'll know they're here. Everyone will know they're here. The entire world, no doubt, will know they're here. He's a prince. It's difficult to hide the presence of a prince. And any possibility of respectability or propriety will be out of the question."

"Nonsense," Aunt Millicent said firmly. "I am a widow and the Countess of Smythe-Windom. There is nothing the least bit improper about my having royal guests upon my return, indeed, my triumphant return, to London. Beyond that, Clarissa is a widow and eminently proper as well. And we have long served as your"—Aunt Millicent's gaze locked with her—"chaperones."

Pamela opened her mouth to reply, then thought better of it. Aunt Millicent had been her teacher, mentor, guide, and dear friend but all three women knew she had been a dreadful failure as a chaperone. And none of them would have had it otherwise.

She looked to her cousin for assistance. Clarissa appeared as helpless as Pamela felt. Pamela drew a deep breath. "I still don't think—"

"Effington was it?" Alexei said thoughtfully. "Are you any relation to the Marquess of Helmsley?"

"Thomas is my cousin." She narrowed her eyes. "Why do you ask?"

"Because it changes everything. Helmsley is married to the sister of the Viscountess Beaumont. The viscount is my cousin." Alexei smirked. "You and I are related."

Pamela snorted. "Distantly and by marriage. It scarcely counts."

"It most certainly does." Aunt Millicent grinned. "A prince in my family. I never imagined such a thing, and I quite like it."

"I do not. I don't care what he is, I still don't think it's the least bit proper having him under this roof. Besides"—Pamela aimed an accusing finger at him—"this man has a notorious reputation. He is reputed to have shared a bed with half the women in Europe."

"Oh not nearly half although I do appreciate the compliment." Alexei grinned. "I am not really old enough to have bedded half . . ." He paused as if recalling something, then shook his head. "Regardless, Miss Effington, while I admit to having earned that reputation, I regret to confess I have not entirely lived up to it in recent years." He shrugged. "My life has been far too complicated with matters of state and politics, rebellion and crisis to concentrate on pursuits of a more amorous nature. You need not worry about my presence in your household. I shall make no attempt to seduce you."

Pamela gasped. "I never imagined . . . that is I did not think—"

"Regardless of what wicked thought might have been in your mind, cousin dear"—Alexei strode to the nearest chair, dropped into it in a most unprincely manner, picked up a glass from the table beside the chair, and raised it in a salute—"we are relations, and you cannot throw someone who is a member of your own family into the streets."

"I should like nothing better than to do precisely that. And do you realize you're sitting while I'm standing?" She glared. "How indescribably rude of you."

"Not at all. I am well used to sitting while everyone else stands in my royal presence. What say you, Lady Smythe-Windom?" Alexei nodded at Aunt Millicent. "Is it entirely proper for me to sit?"

Aunt Millicent glanced from Alexei to Pamela, a speculative look in her eyes. Pamela's heart sank. Her aunt had far better insight than anyone ever credited her with. Aunt Millicent turned her attention back to Alexei. "You are a prince, Your Highness, and doing as you wish is entirely proper."

He laughed and got to his feet. "You are indeed gracious, Lady Smythe-Windom, but your niece was right. It was inexcusably rude. Even for a prince." He turned to Pamela and bowed. "My apologies, Miss Effington."

Pamela stared at him for a long moment. Here was a man who had lost everything that was of importance to him. His home. His country. His very purpose in life. He, too, was attempting to start anew. She would have sent him away from what might well be his only sanctuary at the moment because she feared he would reveal her secret and cause yet another scandal. It was not the least bit gracious or noble or even nice.

Not at all the thing an Effington would do.

"No, it is I who should offer my apologies, and beg your forgiveness. I am the one who has been rude. Regardless of the circumstances we find ourselves in, this is my home, and I should have been as gracious as my aunt." She bowed her head and dropped a deep curtsey. "Forgive me, Your Highness."

"Of course," he murmured.

She glanced up and met his gaze. Curiosity and appreciation shone in his eyes. Precisely as it had four years ago. Her breath caught.

"Now that that question is resolved, we should make our plans." Aunt Millicent tapped her forefinger thoughtfully against her bottom lip. "I must send out cards announcing my—*our*—return to London. Then, of course, the invitations will pour in. Perhaps we can have a small soiree ourselves. Or better yet, a ball. This house cries for a grand ball, and I doubt it has seen one for many years." Aunt Millicent practically glowed with anticipation. "Just think how exciting the season will be with a prince in tow. Why, we can have an event in his honor. Something unique. A reception perhaps or a masked ball—"

"No," Pamela blurted.

"No," Alexei said at precisely the same time.

A frown creased Aunt Millicent's forehead. "Why ever not?"

"My dear Lady Smythe-Windom, I fear I have not made my position clear." Alexei's voice was firm. "That I am here during your social season is nothing more than mere chance. I have no desire to attend balls and soirees, indeed, I have no intention of partaking of society in any manner whatsoever. I quite agree with Miss Effington. I do not wish to make my presence in London, even in this house, known. Therefore, I am sorry to spoil your plans, but I refuse to be towed anywhere."

"Oh dear, Your Highness, I'm afraid I have not made *my* position clear." Aunt Millicent smiled sweetly, and Pamela braced herself. She had seen that smile before. "There is a condition to your residency."

Alexei grimaced. "You wish to tow me."

"Nothing so dire I assure you, Your Highness." Aunt Millicent cast him a pleasant smile. "I simply wish you to court my niece."

Four

If ever I find her again I shall confess that she, unlike any other woman, has stayed in my dreams and even, I suspect, in my heart. Still, as I have nothing to offer her it is best that I never see her again. I do not even know her name.

His Royal Highness,
Prince Alexei Pruzinsky

Miss Effington gasped. "Court me? *Me*?"

Alexei stared at the Lady Smythe-Windom. "You mean with an eye toward marriage?"

"Marriage? To him? Never!" Miss Effington's voice rose. "He's not at all what I want in a husband. Why, he's a prince, and you've just seen how very demanding and arrogant they can be. His reputation is dreadful and—"

"I beg your pardon." Alexei brushed aside the fact that he had no desire to wed at all, let alone marry her, and glared. "Dreadful reputation or not, I am indeed still a prince. Arrogance is my birthright. Regardless, most women would cut off an arm to wed a prince."

"I prefer to keep my arms, thank you," Miss Effington snapped, her resolution to be grateful apparently forgotten. "Besides, you said it yourself, you're a prince without a country, *Mr.* Pruzinsky. I should think that would diminish your merit as a potential husband somewhat."

Lady Smythe-Windom gasped. "Pamela!"

"Nonetheless, royal blood flows in my veins. The blood of generations of kings of Avalonia and the nobility of Europe. The same blood that shall flow in the veins of my children." He narrowed his eyes. "You could do far worse than a prince for a match, Miss Effington, with or without a country, and I seriously doubt a woman of your advanced years could do better."

Miss Effington's eyes widened, and her mouth dropped open.

"Your Highness." Roman groaned.

Alexei ignored him and stepped closer to Miss Effington in what he fully intended to be a most threatening manner. He stared down at her and noted in the back of his mind that she was really quite lovely when she was stunned into silence and wondered as well why he had not noticed before. Her unusually dark eyes contrasted nicely with her fair hair. Her skin was smooth and touched delicately with peach, and she was the perfect height for him. Just tall enough to allow him to easily kiss the nape of her neck if he so desired. He did rather enjoy kissing the nape of a lovely neck. Not that he would kiss this neck of course. Indeed, he had barely met this woman, but already he had had more than enough of her.

"Miss Effington," he said in a low growl meant for her ears alone. She glared up at him and stood her ground. An admirable, if annoying, quality. Her gaze locked with his, and for one extraordinary moment he was not entirely sure if he wished to chastise her or kiss her. And for one moment it seemed entirely possible she would kiss him back. Ridiculous idea, of course. He brushed the thought away and began again. "Miss Effington."

"Mr. Pruz—" She sighed. "Your Highness?"

There was something unique about the woman though. Maddening and most exasperating but unique nonetheless. Rather a pity he had promised not to seduce her.

"Your Highness?" she repeated, arching a delicate brow.

"Women, Miss Effington, have always had a remarkable propensity to throw themselves at my feet. I would be foolish indeed if I did not understand that a great deal of my attraction lay in my title and wealth and the power I wielded."

"And without that power?" Her voice was low, as if her anger had mellowed, faded to something much more . . . enticing. Upon reconsideration, it wasn't an actual promise.

"I do not yet know, Miss Effington." In truth, his remark about not seducing her was nothing more than an offhand comment. Scarcely carrying the weight of a true vow. "But I am confident that my charms are not contingent on my title."

"Confident or arrogant?" An odd intensity shone in her eyes, and he knew without question she was as intrigued by him as he was by her.

"It scarcely matters." What would she do, indeed what would the entire room do, if he pulled her into his arms this very moment? Would Lady Smythe-Windom allow even a prince that liberty? Probably not. Pity. "Your eyes are lovely, Miss Effington."

"Come now, Your Highness. If that is a display of your charms, surely you can do better." Her voice had a slightly breathless quality.

"Indeed, I could, Miss Effington." He leaned closer until there was scarcely more than a whisper between them. "Shall I tell you about your lips then? Full and ripe and begging to be kissed?" His gaze slipped to her lips and back to her eyes. "Or shall I speak of the perfection of your skin? Or the—"

"Your Highness," Lady Smythe-Windom's exasperated tone rang in the room. "No one save Pamela can hear whatever it is you're saying because you are standing entirely too close to her, and it is most improper. However, I shall let it pass because she has not yet slapped your face, and you have not yet wrapped your hands around her throat. I am assuming this lack of violence is an indication that for now at least you have resolved your differences."

Alexei glanced into Pamela's dark eyes and was more than satisfied to note a flicker of what might have been indecision. How very interesting. Possibly even exciting. He straightened and stepped back.

"For now." Alexei met the other woman's gaze. "However, I have no intention of marrying Miss Effington or anyone else at the moment."

"Nor do I," Miss Effington said quickly although not

with the same vehemence as she had a moment ago. "Not at the moment, that is."

"If the two of you will allow me to explain my idea, you'll find I am not proposing marriage. That would be absurd. Even I can see you have nothing in common save an instant dislike of one another, although I daresay successful marriages have been built on substantially less," Lady Smythe-Windom said coolly. "What I am proposing is nothing more than courtship."

"Courtship without marriage," Alexei said slowly.

"You've always been rather good at that, Your Highness," Roman said under his breath.

"Well, I for one do not see the point of it." Clarissa shrugged. "Marriage is the culmination of courtship. Courtship without marriage is like marriage without—"

"And as no one here is interested in marriage, at least not now and not to each other, this should work out rather nicely." Lady Smythe-Windom cast Alexei a brilliant smile, and he suspected he would come to fear that smile. "It's really very simple, Your Highness. Six years ago, Pamela was involved in—oh what is the word?"

"Dear Lord." Pamela sank into the closest chair and covered her eyes with her hand. "Take me now."

"An indiscretion," Clarissa offered.

"And scandal. The silliest of scandals really as the world sees such things but scandal in England nonetheless." Lady Smythe-Windom lowered her voice in a confidential manner. "Involving a truly despicable young man who should have been drawn and quartered for his crimes."

"Miss Effington? The oh so very concerned with propriety Miss Effington? I must say I am shocked." Alexei bit back a grin. "Apparently I am not the only one with a dreadful past."

Miss Effington muttered something he did not hear, and he thought it for the best.

"Needless to say she was ruined." Lady Smythe-Windom sighed regrettably.

"Was she indeed?" Alexei wondered just how serious this ruination was. From what he had seen of the English through the years, it could well have been something the rest of the world would scarcely note as significant at all. Or it might have been an incident even he might consider truly scandalous.

Miss Effington moaned, buried her face in her hands, and seemed, if possible, to sink even lower into the chair. Alexei was fairly certain if a large fissure opened up in the floor at this very moment, Miss Effington would quite happily throw herself into it.

Lady Smythe-Windom nodded. "Indeed she was although in London there is a minor scandal every third day and something really tasty every week or two. By the next season it might well have been forgotten altogether. Therefore, there was no need for it, mind you, but Pamela took it upon herself to leave the country and join me in my travels. She has not returned to London since."

This was extraordinarily interesting. The Miss Effington he had met today did not at all strike him as the type of woman to flee her home because of a bit of scandal. Today's Miss Effington did not appear to be frightened by anything. Apparently she was not entirely as she appeared.

"Now that Pamela has returned, she would prefer if society forgets about her past. The very best way to do that is on the arm of a prince." Lady Smythe-Windom beamed.

Miss Effington jerked her head up, confusion on her face. "What?"

"If I understand her correctly, what your aunt is trying to say, Miss Effington," Alexei paused to choose the right words, "is that no one will care or probably even remember an indiscretion of—how long ago?"

Miss Effington rolled her gaze toward the ceiling. "Six years."

"Six years? That is a long time in exile." He had scarcely been away from his homeland for six months, yet it already seemed a lifetime. "At any rate, the past will not matter in the least if in the present you are seen in the company of a prince who is quite obviously captivated by you, in a most respectable way of course. Any memory of your long-ago indiscretion will be swept away by the brilliance of the match you have now made."

Miss Effington straightened, her eyes wide. "That's very good. Very good indeed."

"It is, isn't it?" Lady Smythe-Windom grinned in a most immodest manner.

"Beyond that, when our charade is at an end, and you have sent me away for whatever reason your aunt devises—"

"Infidelity would work, Your Highness," Roman suggested. "It is an excellent reason for a lady to sever a relationship. And when the gentleman in question has a reputation as impressive as yours, infidelity is practically to be expected."

"Brilliant observation," Alexei said dryly. "I shall keep it in mind. As I was saying, in the wake of our ill-fated liaison, I suspect you shall have no problem finding a suitable match if you so wish. Men always see a woman who is already taken, particularly one who was desired by royalty, as more attractive than one who is available." Alexei glanced at Lady Smythe-Windom. "Am I correct thus far?"

"Indeed you are, Your Highness." Lady Smythe-Windom nodded with enthusiasm. "And it shall be even better if, as you suggested, the two of you are betrothed."

Alexei started. "As I suggested? I do not recall suggesting anything of the sort."

"It did indeed sound that way, Your Highness," Roman said under his breath. "The brilliance of the match comment I believe."

Pamela stared at Alexei. "And you are willing to do this?"

"Absolutely not." Alexei huffed. "I have already said I do not wish to make my presence in London known. That precludes attendance at any society function whatsoever and completely eliminates the public exhibition of a betrothal."

"That's that then although, in truth, it scarcely matters." Miss Effington rose to her feet, resolve in the very line of her body. "I am more than capable of resuming my life and venturing into society without a prince. Indeed, I had fully expected to do so."

"Your Highness, this is a condition of your residing in our home." Lady Smythe-Windom fixed him with an uncompromising gaze. "If you refuse, regardless of Count

Stefanovich's assertion that legal action will take a considerable amount of time, I will initiate such action. That, and the fact that I will not hesitate to tell the biggest gossips in London that you are here, will effectively end your desire for anonymity and privacy.

"I do hope you realize that, aside from anything else you are seeking to avoid, an eligible prince residing in London, regardless of whether he has a country or not, will become the target for every lady with a marriageable daughter in England. I daresay the matters of state, politics, rebellion, and crisis you mentioned a moment ago pale in comparison to the battles that will be waged for your hand." She favored him with a pleasant smile. "However, it is entirely your choice."

"I see you are not as gracious as you first appeared." Alexei stared.

Lady Smythe-Windom folded her hands in front of her and stared back, her gaze and her smile unwavering. If one didn't know better, one would have believed her to be innocuous and quite harmless. Obviously erroneous assumptions. Even so . . .

"I will not be forced into this absurd farce against my will."

"Your Highness." Roman stepped quickly to his side and murmured low in his ear. "Do not forget we do not have the funds to rent another house and, even if she refunds our money, there is nothing available save perhaps a hotel, and that would provide no privacy whatsoever."

"There is that," Alexei murmured.

"It is entirely possible as well that the bank might look with favor upon a man who will soon become part of one of England's most notable families and release your funds with greater speed. Indeed, I shall make it a point to query our man at the bank on the question later today."

"No real choice then?" Alexei said out of the corner of his mouth.

Roman shook his head. "None that I can see, Your Highness."

"I thought not. Very well." Alexei straightened and drew a deep breath. "However." He summoned his most charming smile, the one guaranteed to melt the heart of even the most resistant virgin, and aimed it at Lady Smythe-Windom. "As your guest I should be delighted to lend my assistance in whatever manner you desire."

"Are you certain?" Miss Effington moved toward him, and her gaze searched his cautiously. "Even given the circumstances, it is rather a lot to ask."

"There are far worse things in this world than pretending to be in love with a beautiful woman and attending endless parties and, I suspect, having rather a good time of it." He smiled down at her and shrugged. "I suppose, Miss Effington, I cannot hide forever although I had hoped to do just that for at least a short while. Besides, my schedule is surprisingly free at the moment, and I find myself with a great deal of time on my hands."

"I am most appreciative, Your Highness." For the first time since he had met her a smile curved her lovely lips. And did something decidedly odd to the pit of his stomach.

"Mark my words, it shall all work out beautifully. Your Highness. Count." Lady Smythe-Windom gave the gentlemen a satisfied nod, then started toward the door. "We shall further discuss our plans over dinner this evening.

In the meantime, my nieces and I will spend the remainder of the day settling in and reacquainting ourselves with the house."

"You should inform your family of your return," Lady Overton said to her cousin.

"My family." Miss Effington winced. "I had completely forgotten about my family. They shall certainly wish to meet"—she cast Alexei a weak smile—"my fiancé."

"He'll make a grand impression, which, after all, is precisely why we're pressing him into service," Lady Smythe-Windom tossed back over her shoulder. "It's been years since I've been here, you know. I see Elizabeth did nothing to keep the place up. We shall certainly . . ."

The younger ladies trailed after their aunt.

Alexei stared at the closed door and absently accepted a glass of brandy from Roman. "What just happened here?"

"What happened, Your Highness, is that we are apparently at the mercy of those who are erroneously called the weaker sex. Lady Smythe-Windom, Miss Effington, and, I suspect, even the quieter Lady Overton are a force to be reckoned with."

Alexei snorted. "And do not forget Valentina. Even if her reformation is genuine, she will still be a force as well."

"Your Highness, I could never forget Valentina."

Alexei took a long sip of the liquor and let the warmth of the alcohol flow through him. "Why is it that Englishwomen place such importance on the sheer number of women a man has been with? The last time I was with an Englishwoman she said precisely the same thing about my having bedded half the women in Europe."

Roman chuckled. "It is a charge not entirely without merit, Your Highness." He paused for a moment. "It was the owner of the earbob, was it not? The last English-woman to make such a charge? The lady from Venice?"

Alexei nodded.

"And that was?"

Alexei blew a long breath. "Four years ago."

"Yes, of course," Roman said quietly.

It was not at all odd that Roman was not acutely aware that the interlude in question had occurred precisely four years ago this March past. He had not held his position then. It was before the days of Valentina's effort to seize power and her corruption of Alexei's former chief advisor. Before the day his sister had left Avalonia to marry an English lord, and Dimitri was still in command of her safety. Before Alexei's world had changed irrevocably.

Alexei had told both friends the story on more than one occasion, usually late in the night after copious amounts of liquor and tales of lovely ladies from the other men. Tales of another time.

In those days Alexei had indeed lived a life that could well be considered excessive, at least to the English, although he had never particularly considered it such himself; nor had he ever been chastised for it. Oh, he had never shirked his responsibilities or his obligations. He had simply lived as princes not yet ascended to a throne tended to live: lavishly, with an eye toward the next entertainment and the next enthusiastic, accommodating lady.

He still was not sure why that particular night and that particular lady had stayed in his mind. Lingered like a melody he could not get out of his head always playing faintly in the distance. She had lost an earbob in his bed. A pretty thing, made of Venetian glass. Not at all valuable but charming and unique. He had kept it in his waistcoat pocket ever since. An odd sort of talisman that as a child he would have thought of as magic. It was not, of course, but he held on to it nonetheless. Just as he had his memories.

In truth, it had bothered him somewhat, this grip she held on him. Certainly she was lovely from what he could tell although he had not seen her face save by the light of the stars. But he had had any number of beautiful women, and he had certainly had lovelier. Nor was she particularly skilled at lovemaking but rather quite, quite sweet and most enthusiastic and well, *loving*, even though that was not precisely the right word. How could it be for a single night of passion between strangers?

He had given that night a great deal of thought through the tumultuous years that had followed in those rare, odd hours when nothing else demanded his attention. The moments after he had dropped into his bed alone at night, exhausted, or the moments before he rose in the morning. Appropriate enough, he supposed, as he had been with her again and again in his dreams. He had tried to tell himself it was neither the lady nor the evening but rather the unique combination of factors: Venice and the mystery of not knowing who she was and perhaps, yes, even magic.

For good or ill she had touched something in him. His soul perhaps. One would have thought he was too cynical, at least when it came to women, to be touched. He had wondered if it was because she, of all the women he had experienced, seemed to want nothing from him. Marriage had been out of the question. He had been destined then to make a marriage of political advantage. Nor did she want the prestige of becoming his mistress or even the panache of being seen in his company.

And if it was his child she had sought, to what end? She had never again contacted him, so he had assumed there was no child of their union. He suspected he was very much like the men in his family who had never produced large numbers of offspring. His parents had had only three children. Even so, Alexei had always been particularly careful in that respect and did not, to his knowledge, have unknown children scattered across Europe. At any rate, he no longer had a crown and a country to pass to a child, little to offer at all save his name.

He was a prince without a country haunted by the memory of an unknown woman about to embark upon a fraudulent engagement with a lady who was obviously not at all as she appeared. It would be most amusing if it were all happening to someone else. As it was, it was his life. His new life. His new, absurd, ridiculous farce of a life.

But it did have the oh-so-delectable and completely unique Miss Effington as a rather large part of it, at least for the moment. Life might be rather amusing after all.

"Did you notice her perfume, Roman?"

Roman frowned in confusion. "Whose perfume?"

"Miss Effington's." Alexei pulled his brows together and tried to recall where he had smelled that scent before. "It is most intoxicating and vaguely familiar."

"I had not noticed, Your Highness." Roman paused for a moment. "But then I was not nearly as close to the lady as you were."

Alexei ignored the suggestion of impropriety in Roman's comment and swirled the brandy in his glass. "She is rather lovely though, isn't she?"

Roman chuckled. "Which one?"

"All of them really, but I was referring to Miss Effington."

"She is attractive enough."

Alexei glanced at Roman and raised a brow.

"I simply thought the quiet one more classically lovely." Roman shrugged. "Personal preference, no doubt. I have always been rather fond of dark-haired beauties with green eyes."

Alexei grinned. "Her eyes were green?"

"Indeed, they were. A charming emerald color. Most exquisite. But even they are not her most appealing feature."

"Oh?"

"He best feature was that she was remarkably quiet and well-mannered." Roman sipped his drink. "Unlike her cousin."

Alexei laughed. "I daresay Miss Effington is unique among women. She has a great deal of spirit and knows precisely what she wants."

"She is outspoken and stubborn and most annoying."

"Which only serves to make her more of a challenge. She makes a man's blood race."

"A clever man would indeed race, fast and as far away as possible," Roman said under his breath.

"But where would be the fun in that?" Alexei shook his

head. "No, Roman, if we are trapped in this farce, I see no other choice but to enjoy it. I suspect Miss Effington is not at all as she pretends to be. She is rather an enigma."

"A mystery then, Your Highness?"

"I have always rather enjoyed puzzles." Or at least he had once.

For the past three years he had done nothing but fight against plots and schemes, most engineered by Valentina, to keep his family on the throne and keep his country united. He had been successful, and by the time of his father's death, Avalonia was indeed peaceful, its people content, and his family's rule assured. Not that it mattered now, of course. Avalonia was a part of Russia, and he could do nothing save accept it.

Why not turn his attention to a puzzle he could unravel? As he had told her, he had a great deal of time on his hands.

"And I daresay I shall enjoy this one. Besides, a ruined Miss Effington is an entirely different matter than a proper Miss Effington." Alexei took a sip of his brandy and grinned. "And a great deal more interesting."

Five

 If ever I see the overly sanctimonious and oh-so-righteous Captain Petrov again, I shall do all in my power not to shoot him on the spot. It shall not be easy.

Her Royal Highness,
Princess Valentina Pruzinsky

The man had ruined her life as surely and thoroughly as George had. If she wasn't on her guard every moment, he would probably do it again—or rather *she* would do it, but it would be entirely *his* fault.

Pamela paced across the large bedchamber in the suite of rooms she had chosen as much for its location in the farthest corner of the house as for anything else.

Prince Alexei Pruzinsky of the Kingdom of Greater Avalonia was the very last person she'd ever thought she'd see again and, for the most part, the very last person she ever wished to see again. Oh, certainly she had always known there was the possibility of coming face-to-face with him on a ballroom floor in Paris or at a garden party in Greece or in a hunting lodge in the Alps, but she was prepared for that. Indeed, she had a dozen or more charming, witty phrases rehearsed for their introduction because, of course, he wouldn't recognize her. Even so, she had at least twice that many prepared in case he did. What she was not at all ready for was his presence in her very own house.

If there was a saving grace at all, it was that the house was more than sufficient in size for the prince's party as well as the new owners and could likely accommodate a small army as well. Indeed, it rivaled her uncle's home— Effington House—in size. Pity it did not do so in grandeur. The house was not quite shabby, but it was sorely in need of renovation. Yearly rental might well have kept the building standing upright and the roof in adequate repair, but had obviously paid for little else.

Well, it was her house now, at least a third of it, and improvements would certainly be made. Not that that was of any concern at the moment.

No, right now she had to decide what she would do about His Highness. Although *do* was not entirely accurate. There was nothing she could *do* about him.

Pamela paused by the window, rested her hands on the sill and gazed unseeing at the back gardens, relatively small but at least from this vantage point, apparently better kept than the house itself.

There were, as she saw it, several specific problems. First of all, if Alexei recognized her and acknowledged their past, she would be the subject of scandal all over again. However, after considering the matter rationally, she conceded that particular concern might not be at all valid. Alexei might well have been a rake in the past, might well still be for all she knew, but the man she'd met this afternoon also struck her as a man of honor.

Even if he should remember their brief interlude, and realize she was the lady behind the mask, she suspected he would not allow that knowledge to become public. She could be wrong about his character, but apparently she would have ample opportunity to find out, as they would be spending a great deal of time in one another's company.

And that was the second problem. The more she was with Alexei, the greater the chances of a slip of the tongue on her part. How on earth could she fully guard against that? After all, she had dreamed of the blasted man. Relived every moment spent together. If she wasn't careful, she might well call him "Alexei" instead of "Your Highness." At the very least, he would think her forward and presumptuous. The last thing she wanted was his recognition or recollection of her. She was not ashamed of their night together, even if she was a tiny bit embarrassed by her patently seductive actions. It was simply that it was in the past, and she preferred it stay firmly in the past. Long ago and best forgotten.

Even worse than all else, she suspected she had fallen more than a little in love with him on that single night so many years ago. Oh, certainly the mere idea was the height of absurdity. No one fell in love after one night. One needed to get to know another person, become well acquainted with character and temperament, before one could truly declare oneself in love. Granted, she had thought she had known George rather well and had been horribly mistaken as to both his character and her own feelings. The love she had fervently declared for him hadn't lasted quite as long as the sheer humiliation of his betrayal.

Whatever it was she felt for Alexei had lingered for four long years. It might well not be love at all but a sort of unrepentant lust wrought by a man overly skilled in the art of lovemaking. Regardless of its definition, it obviously still held her in its vile grip. She'd been hard-pressed not to fling herself into his arms this very afternoon when he had been blatantly flirtatious and standing entirely too close. There was something about the resonance of his voice and the intensity in his eyes and the memory of his touch that even now weakened her knees and her resolve.

Still . . . an odd thought struck her, and she straightened. Wasn't it entirely possible that it was the memory of the man, the dream, that enthralled her? It had been four years, after all, and it was to be expected that time and distance had changed what was no more than an enjoyable evening into something far more spectacular that it had in fact been. If there was love involved at all, it might well be for a man who did not really exist. Perhaps she needed to determine her true feelings for this all-too-real prince before she did anything whatsoever. Perhaps the way to do that was to get to know this prince—this man—better. She had shared his bed, but in truth she did not know him at all.

She glanced at the aged French clock on the ladies' desk by the window. There were still a few hours remaining until dinner. If she hurried, she could dress and be downstairs well before Aunt Millicent and Clarissa. If she were lucky, Alexei would be downstairs already. If she were smart, she'd make certain of it.

She sat down at the desk and penned a quick note. She would have a footman deliver it to Alexei at once. Oddly enough, the simple act of doing something rather than waiting for something to happen eased her anxiety. Certainly she didn't expect this meeting to resolve her questions about her own feelings. Nor did she expect anything whatsoever on Alexei's part. However, it was a first step. Better yet, it was on her terms. Why, her response to him today could well be attributed to nothing more than shock at seeing him again. This evening she would be prepared. She would be charming and clever and perhaps even use some of those phrases she had practiced just for such an occasion.

Pamela would be every inch the perfect hostess and better, every inch the perfect fraudulent fiancée for a deposed prince. Besides, she had charmed him once with a mask on and her clothes off. Surely it would not be much more difficult sans mask and fully dressed.

Still, an annoying voice in the back of her head that refused to understand she was trying to start a new, respectable life, whispered in a most wicked manner that it might well be easier—but it would certainly not be as much fun.

"Your Highness." Miss Effington sailed into the parlor with a lighthearted air and a charming smile. One never would have imagined that a scant few hours ago she had been a termagant ready to throw him bodily into the streets.

"Miss Effington." Alexei met her halfway across the room, noted wryly the symbolism, and took her hands in his. "You are looking exceptionally lovely this evening."

She arched a brow. "Very polished, Your Highness. Yet another example of your charm?"

His gaze met hers, and he raised her hands to his lips. "Only if it is successful." He brushed his lips lightly across the back of one hand, then the next. "Regardless, its success does not diminish its truth." All the while he kept his gaze fixed firmly on hers. "You are indeed a vision."

"And you are indeed well practiced in the art of charm. Nonetheless, I will concede your point." The corners of her lips quirked upward in the satisfied smile of a woman who knows she looks her best.

"Excellent. I detest false modesty." He lowered her hands but did not release them and continued to stare into her eyes.

Admittedly, it was a technique of seduction that was most effective. This meshing of his gaze with hers created an impression of intimacy even in a crowded room and he had perfected it. Not that it was a particular hardship gazing into eyes like hers. They were luminous and very dark, with a hint of sensuality, suppressed probably in spite of her ruin, but still almost . . . erotic. And shaded with intelligence.

Alexei had never been overly fond of intelligent woman. Politically, they were dangerous. Valentina was a prime example of just how dangerous they could be. Personally, clever women were never satisfied and had always wanted more than he'd been willing to give. Political favors, preferential treatment at court, a permanent position in his bed, commitment of some sort. Of course, his life was different now. He had nothing of that nature left to give, or rather, left to lose. Regardless, he had meant it when he had told Miss Effington that his charms were not contingent on his title. It was obviously time to prove it.

And what better way to prove it than with an intelligent woman? This particular intelligent woman.

"What else do you detest, Your Highness?"

"Mutton," he said without thinking.

She laughed. "Mutton?"

"Even as a boy I never liked mutton." He shuddered. "I have always considered it rather repulsive." He paused to think. "And Avalonian brandy."

"Avalonian brandy? I've never tasted it."

"Consider yourself blessed."

"You don't like it then? And I gather it's from your country?"

"From what *was* my county," he corrected. "No, Avalonian brandy may well be the only thing I do not miss. Dreadful, bitter stuff that we are—*were*—forced to drink for state celebrations in some sort of gastronomical barbarism dictated by tradition. It is made by a monastic order, and I suspect the making of it is penance for their sins and the drinking of it penance for ours."

"Do you require penance for your sins then, Your Highness? If so, I should be most willing to hear your confession."

"Would you grant absolution as well?"

She shrugged. "I suspect it depends on the sins."

"And what of your sins, Miss Effington?"

"I daresay, Your Highness, my sins would pale in comparison." She firmly pulled her hands from his. "You would no doubt find them very, very dull."

"I cannot imagine that." He chuckled. "However, as neither of us is inclined at the moment toward confession and therefore penance, and as there is thankfully no Avalonian brandy available at any rate, I thought perhaps a glass of champagne before dinner would be appropriate. To toast our betrothal." He glanced past her. "Graham?"

Graham stood by a sideboard along the wall behind Miss Effington and at once uncorked a bottle and poured two glasses. Alexei was certain Miss Effington had had no idea the servant was in the room, yet she did not show so much as a twinge of surprise. How very interesting. The thought flickered through his mind that she would have made an excellent queen.

Graham brought her a glass. She eyed it with a touch of skepticism. "I do hope the wine cellar is better maintained than the rest of the house."

"The wine cellar is exceptional, miss." Graham's tone carried a hint of indignation that she would suspect otherwise. "We have found through the years that a superb selection of wine and other spirits is essential toward attracting a respectable tenant for the season. As is the outer appearance of the house and gardens. Therefore, maintenance in those areas has always been of paramount importance."

"And the interiors simply let go?" Her manner was casual, as if her question was of no significance whatsoever, and accepted the glass.

"Not at all, miss," Graham said coolly. "Necessary repairs are made continuously. However, it's been rather a long time since Lady Gorham paid any particular attention to this house at all. Indeed, *we* thought she had forgotten our existence altogether. In recent years, the income from the yearly rental is all that has sustained us. You should know as well that after wages were paid, the remaining proceeds went into maintenance." He lifted his chin and stared down a rather long nose. "No one has profited in any way, Miss Effington. The books for the house are entirely in order."

"Do accept my apology, Graham, if I have offended you." Miss Effington shook her head. "That was certainly not my intention."

"Of course not," Alexei said smoothly, and took the remaining glass from the butler. "It is to be expected that one would have a certain number of questions when the reality of a situation is not entirely as one expected."

"That's it exactly." She nodded. "I simply had no idea that the house was so . . . so . . ."

"Warm and welcoming," Alexei said firmly. "With a delightful sense of having been loved and well cared for." He nodded at the servant. "That will be all for the moment, Graham."

"Of course, Your Highness." Graham paused. "And might I extend my congratulations upon the occasion of your betrothal."

"Thank you, Graham." Alexei smiled pleasantly.

The butler nodded curtly and took his leave. That was that then. Once a servant, any servant, was in possession of information such as this, it was certain to become common knowledge. Although it scarcely mattered he supposed. Alexei had agreed to Lady Smythe-Windom's scheme after all. He simply had not expected it to begin immediately.

Still, there were far worse fates than the pretense of affection toward a lovely woman.

"Expectations aside, how does it feel to be home at last, Miss Effington?"

"I have missed London more than I ever anticipated and missed my family, too, of course." She sipped her wine thoughtfully. "However, this house is scarcely my home. Yet. In fact, I don't think I've stepped foot in the place before now."

"Not at all?" he said curiously. "I was given to understand you had inherited it from a relative?"

"Oh, I did, along with my aunt and my cousin." Miss Effington idly stepped away, wandering around the large parlor with a critical eye. "It was willed to us by my great-aunt, who did not approve of the way Aunt Millicent has lived her life."

"Yet she left you this house?"

"And her fortune as well. All in hopes that it would encourage better behavior on the part of my aunt, thus saving my cousin and myself from a life she viewed as inappropriate. Inappropriate being in the eye of the beholder. To my own mind, Lady Smythe-Windom's life has always been exceptionally appropriate."

"Again in the eye of the beholder."

"Exactly." Miss Effington smiled in a wry manner. "Aunt Millicent did indeed live what anyone would view as an eminently proper life until she became a widow, at which point she discovered an aversion to permanence and a penchant for doing precisely as she pleased. Of course, she had the funds to do so then. She abandoned London for the adventure of travel and has only returned a time or two since. Most recently six years ago. That was when my cousin and I decided to join her."

"Ah yes," He sipped his champagne casually. "After the scandal."

She cast him a sharp glance. "Indeed."

"I think, as your fiancé, I should know something about that particular incident." He signed in feigned regret. "In the interest of avoiding misunderstandings between us in the future if for no other reason."

"Your Highness, there shall be no misunderstandings because there is no future. No real future, that is. Beyond that"—she squared her shoulders and met his gaze—"I should very much prefer that we agree that in regards to our private lives you shall not discuss my past, and I shall not discuss yours."

"I rather like discussing my past, in regards to my private life, that is."

She frowned. "You do?"

"Indeed I do. Of course, it is different for a man I suppose. A reputation for bedding—what was it? Ah yes, half the women in Europe. Such a reputation is rather a badge of honor, you know, among men."

She snorted. "It's nothing of the sort. I think it's in extremely bad taste to sample indiscriminately the charms of one woman after another."

"But then you are not a man." He allowed his gaze to slide over her. "To my everlasting gratitude."

She ignored his comment and studied him curiously. "You are proud of your reputation then?"

"*Proud* is not entirely the right word; however, I do take umbrage at your use of the word *indiscriminately*. I was always most selective."

"My apologies."

"Accepted." He brushed aside the less-than-sincere note in her voice. "I do not make excuses for my past, Miss Effington, as I have nothing to be ashamed of. If I have lived my life with a certain recklessness, a particular abandon, enthusiasm as it were, it was because I knew there would soon come a time when it would no longer be mine to do with as I chose. The life of any monarch belongs to his people. As mine would belong to my people when I ascended the throne. Until that point, however, I intended to have a very good time." He smiled wickedly. "And I did."

"I have no doubt of that."

"Nor should you. However you should also keep in mind that when one is in line to inherit a throne and rule a country, one's every move, every act, every comment, becomes a topic of discussion and fodder for gossip. I will concede to you, and you alone, Miss Effington, and it pains me to do so, that my reputation is exaggerated—"

She scoffed.

"Although not greatly." He grinned then continued. "However, there are certain expectations—"

"To bed half the women in Europe?"

"No. That is simply a pleasant benefit. There is the expectation that because you are destined to rule, in every way, you shall be larger than life allows. You cannot behave like other men, nor are you bound by the limits of other men, because you are not like other men. Your intelligence, your ability to command loyalty, your courage, even your appetites are expected to be greater than ordinary men."

"Disregarding the question of appetites, there have been any number of kings, even here in England, who have scarcely met such standards."

"Regardless of royal blood, men are still flesh and bone and subject to the failings that are inherent in all of mankind. But the kings who are successful in their rule, whose countries are prosperous and whose people are happy, are those who do indeed try to live up to those higher expectations." He drew his brows together and considered his words. "It is not always possible, indeed, it is a continuous challenge, but it is the responsibility of power and privilege."

She studied him for a long moment. Her voice was cool, but there was a spark of amusement in her eyes. "All that to explain your behavior with women?"

He grimaced. "More than you wanted to know perhaps?"

"Not at all. In truth I found it fascinating. One never stops to think of the difficulties of a man born to your station, only of the more enviable trappings." She paused. "Do you miss it?"

"There is a great deal I miss although, once again, Miss Effington, this is a concession only to you, I have not played the role of carefree prince for a rather long time."

He paused to pull his thoughts together. He was not entirely sure why he chose to tell her all this, although it was scarcely a secret. Still, he was not accustomed to confiding in anyone, with the occasional exception of Roman or Dimitri. He blew a long breath. "Three years ago, my cousin, Valentina, attempted to seize power. My father was ill at the time, and it was my responsibility to thwart her efforts. I was successful, and while my father did regain his health somewhat, since that time I have been far too busy with matters of state to resume my previous wicked ways. Admittedly, I rather miss them." He glanced at her. "Did I mention I had a great deal of fun?"

She smiled. "In passing."

"Inevitably, there is a moment in one's life when one is forced to accept the responsibility of one's position. Make no mistake, I was fully prepared to do so. I was nothing if not well trained. After my father's illness, I essentially ruled by his side although we took great pains not to let it appear as such. Weakness, Miss Effington"— he met her gaze firmly—"is not acceptable."

"Not up to the standards."

"Exactly. By the time of his death, I was king in all but title and crown. It is a dreadful thing to lose a monarch. Quite another to lose a father." He shrugged as if it didn't matter. "He was a good ruler. A good man."

Alexei swirled the wine in his glass and watched it for a silent moment. He had not truly realized until now that he had had no time to mourn his father. Certainly there had been a state funeral, official mourning for a king. But Russia had moved far too quickly to allow any time for a son to mourn a father. Alexei's every waking moment had been spent trying to come up with a way to save his country.

"Was he a good father?" she asked softly.

"As good as a man who considers himself the father of an entire country can be to one child in particular, I think. When I was a boy, he used to let me watch from a hidden spot in the Grand Hall in the palace when he held court. Later, he and I would discuss his decisions. I see now it was a way to teach me what I needed to know not merely to rule but to rule with an eye toward both justice and the benefit of the people as a whole. They are not always one and the same you know." He smiled with the memories of his father's lessons. "He was a man who loved his country and his people, but I never for a moment doubted he loved his son as well."

"You miss him." It was more a statement than a question.

"Yes I do. I miss my father, I miss my king, and I miss my country. And I regret more than I can say that I shall never see either of them again. Yet, that is that way of life, Miss Effington. Greetings and partings." He tossed back the rest of his champagne and strode across the parlor to where Graham had placed the bottle. He refilled his glass and noted a slight unsteadiness in his hand and a rather significant thirst. Odd and most annoying. Particularly given what he had just said about weakness. Still, he couldn't recall ever speaking of such intimate matters with anyone before and had no idea why he was doing so now. Almost as if she were really the woman he would spend the rest of his days with.

He drew a calming breath and turned back to her with a pleasant smile. "Now then, Miss Effington, I believe it is your turn."

Her eyes widened. "My turn for what?"

"Confessions of an intimate nature." He raised a glass to her. "In spite of our aversion to confession, it appears I have done precisely that. It is now your turn."

She shook her head and smiled. "I think not."

"Come now, Miss Effington. Surely you can tell me something about yourself? It needn't be scandalous, I shall take any scrap of information you deign to deliver. About your family at the very least. As your fiancé, it will be expected that I know something beyond your name and the color of your eyes. It does seem to me if we are to—"

"My father"—a note of resignation sounded in her voice—"is the brother of the Duke of Roxborough, and, as you already know, Thomas, the Marquess of Helmsley, is my cousin."

"Hence our own distant familial connection."

"*Very* distant," she said firmly. "To continue, Lady Smythe-Windom is my mother's sister. Clarissa, Lady Overton, is my only cousin on my mother's side of the family, the daughter of my mother's older sister. My father, however, is an Effington, which means I have three sets of aunts and uncles and a total of eight first cousins, a number of whom are married, thus providing a host of endless relations. I have two brothers and a sister. There are any number of more distant relatives by marriage—"

He raised his hand. "Including myself."

"In addition, my grandfather had three brothers who left England to make their fortunes in America years ago, and today there is a rather large branch of the family there as well. No doubt producing Effingtons right and left, although I have lost notice of them. My mother would know more. I could ask her if you're curious."

"I am curious about everything pertaining to you, Miss Effington, and while I do find what you have revealed thus far to be fascinating, I admit I was hoping for something a bit more personal than an explanation of your genealogy."

"I have no intention—"

"I am not asking for your innermost secrets." He gazed toward the ceiling. She was not merely intelligent but stubborn. No matter, so was he. "I only wish to know you better. Not simply who your family is, who you are in name."

"My name *is* who I am, Your Highness." She considered him for a moment as if assessing whether or not he was worthy of her confidence. "I am an Effington, and Effingtons are known to be honorable and outspoken and stubborn."

"No!" He gasped in feigned surprise. "I never would have suspected such a thing."

"I can certainly understand your shock." She laughed, then sobered. "In truth, Your Highness, as odd as it sounds, it took leaving London and my family to become more like them. I know it makes no sense, but I had always felt rather, well, intimidated by my family. It was always as if I were trying to jam my foot into a shoe that simply did not fit." She cast him a wry glance. "It's not entirely easy living up to expectations, you know."

"I may have heard that somewhere before."

"And recently, too, no doubt." She laughed again, and the sound echoed through his veins. Most delightful. "Now then." Her tone was abruptly brisk and not the least bit delightful. "I requested you meet me here before the others join us for dinner because there are a number of matters we should discuss."

"I believe we were in the process of discussing a number of matters."

"These matters are about the endeavor we are about to embark upon."

"Endeavor?" He laughed.

"Well, what would you call it?"

"Farce. Charade. Mockery. Sham. Trav—"

"I prefer endeavor." She huffed. "At any rate, my aunt and I agree it would be best if no one knew I was as much an owner of the house as she."

He pulled his brows together. "Why?"

"Primarily because it would appear much better if you were a guest in the home of the widowed Lady Smythe-Windom rather than—"

"In the home of a never-married woman. Of course." He shook his head. "You English have an absurd sense of propriety, but I shall do as you request."

"I do appreciate it. Also, I think it would be wise if no one, save those of us who already know the truth, know that our endeavor—"

"Our pretense. Our deception. Our—"

"Yes, yes all of those." She waved his words away impatiently. "Our lie, if you prefer, as it is indeed a lie. And do keep in mind it was not my idea. Nor did I think it an especially good idea in the beginning."

"And now?"

"Now, Your Highness, I think . . ." She tossed back the rest of her wine, set the glass down, and smiled in a bemused way as if she couldn't believe her own words. "I think, why not? I should much rather reappear in society as the fiancée of a prince than as the pathetic subject of whispers."

"Do you not think people have forgotten your . . ."

"Indiscretion? Mistake?" She crossed her arms over her chest and glared. "It was an indiscretion and a dreadful, dreadful mistake. There. Are you quite happy now?"

"Not at all. It was obvious that it was an indiscretion of some sort. After all, the word *ruined* was tossed about. The question is"—he studied her curiously—"precisely what kind of indiscretion."

"Your Highness, I—"

"I mean, was it a compromising position that could be easily explained away—"

"Your High—"

"Or was it something rather more explicit? Caught in the act as it were."

"Your Highness!" Her eyes widened with indignation. "I daresay—"

"No, no, Miss Effington." He held up a hand to quiet her. "I will not ask you to elaborate. I understand your hesitation to delve into the sordid nature of your past."

"Sordid nature!" She glared.

"It was not sordid then?"

"No." She huffed. "It was a case of incredibly poor decisions made for what seemed to be excellent reasons at the time by a woman who was not thinking as rationally as she should have been."

"The gentleman in question must have been exceptionally charming then?" He grinned. "Not unlike myself."

"Exceptionally charming indeed. You are as arrogant

as I first thought." Abruptly, she turned her back to him. "What is the color of my eyes, Your Highness?"

"Brown," he said without hesitation. "Although brown does not do them justice. They are . . . the color of sable. Deep and rich and luxurious with a promise of warmth and—"

"And that will suffice."

"Did I pass your test?"

She turned back to him. "It was scarcely much of a test. You were looking at my eyes just a moment ago."

"Yes, but you were not confident that my mention of them was nothing more than idle flattery. Part of my well-practiced charms no doubt." He stepped closer and gazed down into her eyes. "This farce will be rather more difficult, Miss Effington, if you neither trust me nor like me."

"Oh dear, Your Highness, I'm afraid you don't understand at all." She heaved a regretful sigh. "I do like you. And therein lies the problem."

He frowned. "I see no problem."

"The entire purpose of our fraudulent engagement is to allow me to reenter society in a respectable manner. Should I throw myself into your arms or worse yet into your bed, it would ruin everything."

He narrowed his eyes. "Are you saying there is a possibility of that?"

"Of ruining everything?"

"No, of throwing yourself into my arms or, better yet, into my bed?"

She smiled a noncommittal smile.

Alexei stared. This Miss Effington was an interesting mix of invitation and innocence. A moment ago, Alexei would have wagered her sordid past consisted of no more than one momentary indiscretion. She just did not seem the type of woman to engage in random intimacies. Now he was not entirely sure.

He smiled back. "Miss Effington, you are rather a mystery."

"Am I, Your Highness?"

"I have always enjoyed mysteries. The solving of riddles. The unraveling of puzzles. That sort of thing."

Her gaze locked with his. "Do not for a moment imagine that I shall allow unraveling of any kind."

"Ah but, Miss Effington, is that not the purpose of engagements?" His gaze slid to her lips and back to her eyes. He was near enough to kiss her. "To get to know one another better?" It would scarcely take any effort at all to lean closer, to touch his lips to hers. "To learn the secrets of the person you have chosen to spend the rest of your life with?" What would she do if he did?

"My secrets are scarcely worth learning." Her voice was slightly lower and distinctly seductive. Did she want him to kiss her?

"Oh, I doubt that, Miss Effington. Regardless, I suspect it would be a great challenge to uncover your secrets." His lips were a bare whisper from hers, and the scent she wore wafted around him. Inviting and quite irresistible. "I enjoy a challenge nearly as much as I relish a mystery."

"Nonetheless, Your Highness." Her words were scarcely more than an enticing whisper. "There shall be no unraveling nor uncovering."

She did indeed want him to kiss her. He could see it in

her eyes, and he was never wrong about the invitation in a lady's eyes. But whether she would allow it or not was another question. "Oh, but there will. Before this farce of ours is ended, Miss Effington, there shall be unraveling and uncovering and any number of other delights."

"Even a prince cannot overcome every challenge."

"Just as with my charms, my ability to meet a challenge does not depend on my title. You should know as well"—he slipped his arms around her and noted again what a perfect height she was for him—"that I always get what I want."

She braced her hands on his chest but neither pushed him away nor pulled out of his arms. Oh, she would most certainly allow his kiss. "Always?"

"Always. I do not permit otherwise." He lowered his lips to meet hers and had the most remarkable feeling that this might be more important than a mere kiss. And felt as well as if he were about to tumble over a cliff into a crevasse of unknown depth and oddly welcomed the adventure of the fall.

"Alexei! Cousin!" A horribly familiar voice rang from the doorway. "What wonderful news!"

Six

 If ever I see the traitorous Princess Valentina again, I shall resist the urge to strangle her with my bare hands. Which is more than she deserves.

Captain Dimitri Petrov

"I cannot tell you how thrilled I am to hear this." A striking, dark-haired woman, a few years older than Pamela, swept into the room as if she owned it. "Even if I did have to hear it from a servant."

Alexei gritted his teeth, cast Pamela an apologetic look, and released her. Pamela resisted the immediate urge—no, the need—to leap away from him as if he had suddenly burst into flames. Instead, she forced herself to step easily out of his arms, in the manner of a woman who had just been caught in an admittedly improper, but nonetheless understandable, embrace with the man she intended to marry. In truth this woman, whoever she was, had saved Pamela. Not from Alexei but from herself.

"What news would that be?" Alexei said with a resigned air.

"I tried to stop her, Your Highness." An irate gentleman with a murderous gleam in his eye stalked after the woman. "But she is impossible."

"And you are an ass, Petrov," the lady tossed back over her shoulder. "But even you cannot dampen my excitement at this news." She moved to Pamela, grabbed her hands, and kissed the air by one cheek, then the next. "My dear, let me be the first officially to welcome you."

Alexei groaned.

"Welcome me to what?" Pamela said slowly.

"The family of course. The House of Pruzinsky. The ruling house of the Kingdom of Greater Avalonia." The lady wrinkled her nose. "Or rather what *was* the ruling house. I should probably stop calling it such."

"Forgive me, but"—Pamela chose her words carefully—"who are you?"

"Allow me to introduce my cousin." Alexei's voice was edged with a long-suffering air. "Princess Valentina Pruzinsky."

"You shall call me Valentina, as I know we shall be very close." The princess favored her with a brilliant smile. "And I shall call you?"

"Pamela." Pamela stared at the other woman. "Valentina? You're the one who—"

"Yes, yes, I am the one. I shall always be known as *the one*. It is my cross to bear." The princess's eyes narrowed with suspicion. "Did he call me wicked?"

"Not that that would be especially inaccurate," the gentleman—Petrov—muttered.

Alexei blew a long breath. "I did not call you wicked. You claim to have changed, and—"

"As indeed I have," Valentina said brightly.

"And until such time as you prove otherwise—" Alexei leveled his cousin a look that was worthy of a prince or a king. The oddest thrill tripped up Pamela's spine. "I am willing to give you the benefit of the doubt." He turned toward Pamela. "And this is perhaps my oldest friend in the world. Captain Dimitri Petrov, formerly the captain of my guards."

"You must be the enchanting Miss Effington." The captain stepped to her, took her hand, and raised it to his lips. "While I must admit to a moment of shock"—he shot a questioning glance at Alexei—"I can certainly see why His Highness was swept off his feet by your loveliness."

"Do not be an idiot, Petrov." Valentina rolled her gaze toward the ceiling. "They have obviously met before. Why, I strongly suspect she is the real reason why he decided to take up residence in this dreadful house in this wretched country." She glanced at Pamela and gestured aimlessly. "I do mean that in the best possible way, of course."

"Of course," Pamela murmured. "There is often more than one way to think of dreadful and wretched."

Valentina nodded approvingly. "I have always thought so."

Pamela tried not to stare at the other woman and failed miserably. The princess was nothing short of mesmerizing. Oh, not in appearance, although she was undeniably beautiful, but there was an air about her of command or strength or resolve. It struck Pamela that this lady would be a formidable, even deadly, enemy. If she had indeed changed—could she be as good an ally? Or even friend? Alexei would need friends in the future.

Petrov snorted in disdain. "As the words *treacherous* and *murderous* have more than one meaning."

Valentina turned to him with what, by any definition, was a truly murderous look. "Captain, I realize, given my past misdeeds, earning your trust will be only less difficult than transporting myself to the moon. I realize as well that you do not like me, you have never liked me, but as I have never liked you either, that is of scant importance. However"—her eyes narrowed—"if you do not refrain from using words like *murderous* I shall forget the repentance of my sins and my determination to reform and do all in my power to rip the heart from your chest." She cast Pamela a pleasant smile. "In the best meaning of the phrase, of course."

"Of course," Pamela said weakly.

"You should be in a cold, dark dungeon where you can do no harm." Petrov glared down at the princess.

"You should be stuffed and pickled and fed to small creatures with exceptionally sharp teeth," Valentina snapped.

"Stop it at once. You should both be restrained in some manner, and at this particular moment I would be inclined toward chains for both of you. You are like quibbling children." Once more Alexei's voice took on the commanding tone of a king. It was really quite exciting. His wry gaze caught hers. "Welcome to my family, Miss—" a private smile lifted his lips—"Pamela."

Perhaps it was the faint foreign inflection of his words

or perhaps it was that he had never said it before or perhaps it was simply that he had murmured it over and over again in her dreams, but there was something about the way he said her name that made it sound intimate and personal and special. *Pamela.*

Serenissima.

"Your Highness." She drew a deep breath and returned his smile. "Alexei."

"I told you, Petrov." A smirk sounded in Valentina's voice. "Two people who have just met do not look at one another as these two do."

"Perhaps," Petrov muttered.

"And extremely clever of you, too, cousin, to keep your feelings hidden for so many years." Valentina gave Alexei an approving glance.

Pamela caught her breath.

Alexei shook his head in confusion. "What are you talking about?"

"Come now, Alexei, I may have given up any number of my previous pursuits, but I have not given up thinking as well." She cast him a condescending look. "You and I both know that until now you were not free to marry where you might wish but were expected to wed for the purpose of political alliances. That you did not do so before now is obviously the hand of fate."

"Fate?" Alexei said cautiously.

"Fate, destiny, whatever you wish to call it. Cousin, you may be able to fool any number of people, but you cannot fool me. In spite of Petrov's feigned shock at the news of your betrothal"—she cast Petrov a disgusted glance—"and not the least bit convincing I might add."

Petrov shrugged.

Valentina turned her attention back to Alexei. "I know very well you were last in England three years ago, and I know there are distant connections by marriage between her family and ours. It is not at all far-fetched to assume that the two of you met at that time but there was nothing you could do about your affection for one another. Now that there is, you have rushed back here, to her very house, to proclaim your intentions."

Alexei nodded. "That does make perfect sense."

"And to my mind, cousin, you could not have made a better match."

"He couldn't?" Pamela stared at Valentina. "Why not?"

"Why, my dear, you are an Effington." The princess looked shocked that Pamela would even ask such a question. "It is not as if you were true royalty, but your family is headed by a duke, which in this country is most respectable. Personally, my experience with the Effingtons has not been especially pleasant." She leaned toward Pamela in a confidential matter. "A nasty little incident a few years ago at a reception. Little more than a misunderstanding really, although I doubt their memories of me are overly fond."

"Fond?" Dimitri scoffed. "I cannot imagine why they wouldn't be. Oh certainly, there was the potentially fatal incident with the balloon and a question of theft, as well as a few nasty threats, and we must not forget the shooting."

Valentina ignored him. "I will confess that, at the time, I was not especially impressed by Effingtons. I thought them all rather sanctimonious and, well, annoying. Still, I am more than willing to give them a second chance, and I am certain they will not hold my past behavior against Alexei. I am confident they are far too good for that. Besides, one cannot choose one's relatives after all." She gestured dismissively. "At any rate, cousin, they have a great deal of power, politically and socially, and an even greater fortune. You are exceedingly clever to return to claim her as your bride. Why, I would wager her dowry alone will put us—or rather you—back on firm financial ground."

"Oh?" Pamela raised a brow at the revelation. Alexei without a fortune might well be as devastating for him as Alexei without a country.

Alexei's eyes narrowed. "Dimitri?"

"She is a wicked, wicked woman, Your Highness," the captain muttered, then shook his head in bewilderment. "I have no idea how it happened, it just slipped out. One moment I was talking about nothing in particular, and the next I was telling her of the state of your finances. I suspect"—he lowered his voice—"she is a witch."

"Or you are an idiot," Valentina said pleasantly, then turned back to Alexei. "It is not the least bit shameful, cousin. Europe is filthy with deposed royalty: kings and princesses and counts and endless other titles all running about with no idea where their next penny will come from. Or"—Valentina's gaze slid pointedly to the champagne bottle on the table—"their next glass of champagne."

Alexei nodded at Dimitri, who clasped his hands behind his back and adopted an innocent air. "I am afraid I see no extra glasses, Your Highness."

"There are no extra glasses at the moment, Valentina,

118

so you shall have to wait," Alexei said firmly. "And I do know where my next glass of champagne, as well as my next penny, will come from."

"How delightful for you." Valentina sniffed and crossed her arms over her chest.

He ignored his cousin and turned his attention back to Pamela. "Miss—Pamela—I should explain."

Abruptly it struck her that if she were really his fiancée and had just heard of the state of his finances she would be more than a little concerned. And probably rather upset.

"Yes," she said slowly. "I believe you should."

"A temporary financial crisis, nothing more." Alexei shrugged. "It should be resolved within a few months."

"Were you going to tell me about this?" She raised her chin and met his gaze directly. "Or were you going to keep this from me until after we were wed?"

His brow furrowed, his words were cautious. "I did not think informing you was necessary."

"If one were a suspicious sort, one might think your return to London had more to do with my prospects than your heart." She forced a note of indignation to her voice. This pretense was really rather enjoyable, especially given the total confusion on Alexei's face. "Indeed, one might think your urgent desire to wed was prompted by financial need rather than affection."

"Pamela, I can assure you I—" Abruptly his expression cleared and a gleam of amusement sparked in his eye. "My urgency is prompted only by my desire to have you as my wife, by my side, for the rest of my days."

Before she could so much as open her mouth to respond, he moved to her and swept her into his arms. "I was a fool when last we met not to have abandoned my duties and responsibilities for love. But we have been given a second chance, and I shall not lose you again." He grinned, and it was all she could do to keep from laughing aloud.

"Then it's not my dowry or my inheritance that you want?" She fluttered her lashes at him and felt him suppress a laugh.

"I want you and only you." His voice rose with the passion of his words. "I do not care if you haven't so much as a penny to your name—"

"Although it would be a great pity," Valentina said behind him.

"It does not matter to me if you are a member of a prestigious family or nothing more than a chambermaid." His voice rang dramatically in the room.

Pamela glanced over his shoulder. Valentina stared with rapt attention, Petrov with a bit of confusion, but it was obvious both cousin and friend accepted their ruse.

Her gaze slid back to his, and she grinned. He nodded slightly in silent acknowledgment.

"I loved you then and I love you now and I shall not lose you again." Perhaps his voice rang a shade too dramatically. Still, it was most effective.

Besides, there was not a doubt in Pamela's mind that Alexei was enjoying this act of theirs. And why not? The man probably hadn't had a truly frivolous moment in years. The least she could do was continue their performance.

"Do you?" A hopeful note sounded in her voice, matching his in drama and overacting. It was great fun.

"It's been so long, and I scarcely dared to think, to imagine, to dream . . ."

"And I have spent every moment since our last moment together"—he gathered her closer and gazed into her eyes—"thinking, imagining, dreaming of no one save you."

Pamela stared up at him. He was very good at this. Of course, he would be. He had no doubt practiced fine phrases exactly like these with endless numbers of women.

"Still"—a realistic quiver sounded in her voice, and she clutched at the lapels of his coat—"you are now, as you have always been, a prince. And I am merely—"

"You are the stars that show my way in the night, the sun that warms my flesh in the day." His gaze bored into hers. His brown eyes were endless and mysterious and enticing. One could well imagine true affection there. It was rather easy to forget it was nothing but an act on his part. And on hers as well. "The light that feeds my soul."

Except that she had indeed thought about him, imagined being in his life, dreamed of being in his arms.

He lowered his lips to hers.

"Your Highness. Alexei." Her voice was barely more than a whisper. "I think perhaps, at this point, we should—"

"Do be quiet, Miss Effington." His gaze slipped to her lips and back to her eyes. "I know precisely what we should do at this point."

His lips met hers, and for a long moment she didn't breathe. Couldn't breathe. She closed her eyes and at once was swept back through the years and the miles to a night of sheer magic. Desire, sweet and aching and nearly forgotten, washed through her, and it was all she could do to remain standing and not melt into a pool of wanton need at his feet.

He raised his head and stared down at her, a perplexed expression on his face. "Miss Effington—Pamela—"

"Yes?" she said a shade too eagerly.

"For a moment I thought. That is to say . . ."

"Yes?" She stared up at him.

"Have we . . . Have you and I . . ." His puzzled gaze locked with hers. "Have we met?"

"Have we . . ." *Once. On a starlit night filled with magic and mystery and memories to last forever.* She drew a deep breath and forced a light note to her voice. "How very unflattering to think that you would have forgotten such a meeting."

"I would not have forgotten," he said simply. "Never." He studied her for a moment, then shook his head and stepped away.

It was wise, of course, his putting some distance between them, that is. She was extraordinarily tempted to do precisely as she had threatened earlier and throw herself into his arms. Just as tempting was the urge to remind him of their night together. Still, that wouldn't do at all if indeed her desire was for a proper, respectable life. Bringing to mind a long-ago liaison that was strictly for purposes of beginning an entirely different kind of life altogether was not especially sensible. No, it was best that he not recall their past.

Unless, the idea flashed through her mind, her desire for him was greater than her desire to reclaim her position in society.

"Good evening, Your Highness." Aunt Millicent breezed into the parlor with her usual air of an accomplished actress making her first entrance. Clarissa, accompanied by Count Stefanovich, trailed in her wake, their appearance together surely no more than coincidence. Pity.

Aunt Millicent headed toward Alexei, then caught sight of Valentina and pulled up short. "You must be His Highness's cousin, the princess."

"Indeed I must." Valentina smiled smugly.

The two women considered one another much as one warrior might appraise another. Valentina looked to be about Alexei's age and therefore a decade or so younger than Aunt Millicent. Regardless, both were sophisticated, well traveled and clever, and to all appearances, evenly matched.

"I have heard a great deal about you," Aunt Millicent said in a pleasant manner.

"Oh?" Valentina's eyes narrowed. "From my cousin, no doubt?"

"Not at all. His Highness has scarcely mentioned you. However, in certain circles on the Continent your name has come up on occasion." Aunt Millicent's voice was cool. "You have rather an . . . interesting reputation."

"Really?" The princess's expression brightened. "How interesting?"

"Extremely." Aunt Millicent studied her curiously. "I have heard words like *wicked* and *dangerous* and *treacherous* used in reference to you."

"Ah yes, the good days . . ." Valentina sighed then shrugged. "Alas, I have reformed. I have given up my previous ill-advised methods of achieving what I want."

Petrov snorted again, and again Valentina ignored him.

"Have you?" Aunt Millicent nodded thoughtfully. "It's been my experience few people, even those with the best of intentions, ever truly change."

"Well, few people lose their country, their fortune, and two husbands," Valentina said sharply. "Few people are forced to face the fact that all they have left in the entire world is a handful of relations, most of whom despise them. It is quite a revelation."

"I can see where it would be." Aunt Millicent stared with obvious fascination. "It must be extremely difficult to reform. To give up one's wicked ways."

"You have no idea." Valentina heaved a heartfelt sigh.

"Particularly when one has enjoyed one's wicked ways," Aunt Millicent said.

"I did have rather a lot of fun," Valentina murmured.

"Has she really changed?" Aunt Millicent glanced at Alexei.

Alexei shrugged. "We shall see."

"We shall all, no doubt, be smothered in our beds," Petrov muttered.

Valentina cast him a look of disgust.

Aunt Millicent looked at him with a definite spark of interest in her eye. "I can think of any number of things I'd prefer to have happen in our beds."

Clarissa choked. The count stepped forward to make the necessary introductions. A moment later, Aunt Millicent was engaged in animated conversation with the princess, who appeared to quite enjoy the discussion, and Petrov, who seemed to do little more than scowl. Which might well work in his favor as Aunt Millicent had always had something of a fondness for brooding men of a military nature. Alexei said something under his breath to Stefanovich, who then traded glances with Clarissa. Alexei murmured an apology to Pamela, and he and the count stepped aside for a private word. No doubt to relate what had transpired with the princess and Petrov.

Graham appeared from nowhere with a tray of champagne-filled glasses, and the room took on the air of a celebration. Odd in and of itself since most of those here knew the betrothal of Pamela and the prince was a sham. Still, it didn't seem to matter.

Clarissa stepped to Pamela's side and accepted a glass of champagne. Her gaze roamed curiously over the gathering. "It appears everyone in the household now knows about your engagement."

Pamela took a glass for herself and waited until the butler had moved out of earshot. "I always find it amazing how quickly news of this nature travels within a house. It's been no more than half an hour since the butler overheard us."

Clarissa scoffed. "Within a house? I daresay all of London will know of your *excellent match* before you and His Highness so much as step foot upon a ballroom floor."

Pamela winced. "It's all happening rather quickly, isn't it?"

"Indeed it is."

Pamela's gaze slipped to Alexei. He and Stefanovich were obviously discussing something of importance, at least judging by the expressions on their faces. "Just this morning I was barely aware of his existence."

"And this evening you are about to embark on a grand farce designed to fool all of London."

Alexei caught Pamela's eye, and he smiled and raised his glass in a slight salute. Her stomach fluttered, and she returned his smile.

"It is a farce, isn't it, Pamela?" Clarissa sipped her champagne thoughtfully. "You aren't planning—"

"Certainly it's a farce," Pamela said quickly. "I don't even know the man. And he is a prince after all. Regardless of his current circumstances, I daresay he is still considered most eligible for the hand of some princess or other. Therefore, there can never be anything of a permanent nature between us. He is simply doing me a great kindness."

"Because he has no choice."

"Nonetheless, it is quite gracious of him." Pamela glanced at her cousin. "Why on earth would you suggest I might think there could possibly be more between us?"

"Oh, I don't know. No reason really." Clarissa shrugged. "There's something in the way you look at him . . ."

"Nonsense." Pamela brushed away the comment. "I look at him the very same way I look at any man who is as dashing and handsome as he is."

"The count is every bit as dashing and handsome, yet I haven't noticed you looking at him in the same manner."

"The count is not posing as my fiancé," Pamela said firmly. "It's to be expected that I should look at Alexei—"

Clarissa raised a brow. "Alexei?"

"As well as it is expected that I should call him by his given name."

"Yes, of course," Clarissa said, her voice overly casual. "Aunt Millicent says she met him in Venice during our stay there a few years ago."

"She did say that, didn't she?" Pamela's tone matched her cousin's as if this was indeed an insignificant observation.

"I don't remember meeting him," Clarissa continued. "Did you?"

"Not that I recall," Pamela murmured. "One meets so many people in so many places. It is one of the true benefits of travel to my mind."

"Indeed. The meeting of any number of people. So difficult to bring one particular meeting to mind." Clarissa paused. "However, I do vaguely recall a gentleman that you met that I did not, at a masked ball I believe, who occupied your attention for the better part of a night."

"Yes?" Pamela met her cousin's gaze directly and held her breath. She had no intention of lying to Clarissa, but she had no desire to reveal Alexei's name now. It simply muddied up everything.

"A night that was rather more important to you than you had planned."

Pamela raised her chin a notch. "Yes?"

Clarissa studied her for a long moment, then shrugged and sipped her champagne. "Just something I happened to remember. I daresay it's of no significance now."

"None whatsoever." Pamela pushed aside a twinge of guilt. It really wasn't a lie. Or at least not a complete lie. She hadn't so much as a single doubt that their night together wasn't the least bit significant to Alexei. Therefore, it wasn't the least bit significant to her. Now.

Clarissa's gaze drifted to Alexei and the count. "Still, even if you didn't meet him in Venice, there is something in the way you now look at—"

"As there is something in the way you look at Count Stefanovich," Pamela said curtly.

A most unusual smile curved the corners of Clarissa's lips. "Is there?"

Pamela stared. "You've scarcely met him."

A speculative smile accompanied by a distinct gleam in Clarissa's eye. "Indeed, we've exchanged no more than a dozen words."

"I cannot believe that you . . . why you've never—"

"Then perhaps it's time I did." Clarissa glanced at her. "It's your influence you know."

Pamela gasped. "Mine?"

"All that 'becoming an Effington' nonsense, I think. As well as being back in London. I did dread it; there are far too many memories here for comfort, and not all of them good." She smiled wryly. "Yet, even though we have been back in the city for no more than a day, it feels rather, I don't know, right to be here. As if this is where I belong and have always belonged. And that feeling carries with it a rather remarkable sense of assurance and confidence."

"I don't know what to say." Pamela stared for a long moment. On one hand, she did rather hate being, even in part, the impetus for her cousin's deciding to do whatever it was she was obviously deciding to do with the handsome count. On the other, well, certainly it was past time Clarissa actually did something. Anything. In the years since her husband's death it had been as though she were waiting for something as yet unidentified and unknown.

"Save perhaps"—she grinned—"to wish you the very best of luck."

Clarissa laughed lightly. "I am most appreciative, but I daresay I'm not the one who needs luck." Sympathy shone in her eyes. "Have you given any thought as to what you will tell your family?"

"My family?" Pamela widened her eyes. "Dear Lord, I haven't considered my family at all."

"Well, you probably should." Clarissa sipped her wine. "You can't possibly tell them the truth if you want to fool the rest of the world."

"I should hate to deceive them, but they've never been especially good at keeping secrets, especially secrets of this magnitude. I love them of course, but . . ."

Pamela shook her head. She quite liked her family, indeed, she couldn't think of an Effington she *dis*liked. But her mother in particular could not be counted on to keep a secret as delicious as this one. Her younger sister was probably no different. Her father and brothers would doubtless think it would do no harm to tell a cousin or an uncle and everyone in the family would know everything within days.

"No." Pamela squared her shoulders. "It's best if they never know the truth. Besides, what possible harm could it do? My parents, indeed, my aunts and uncles and everyone else will be quite pleased I have returned on the arm of a prince. Beyond that, the whole thing will be over and done with soon enough."

"Of course," Clarissa said without so much as a hint of conviction in her voice.

Pamela frowned. "Whatever are you thinking?"

"Nothing of any significance really." Clarissa's gaze returned to the count. "Only that no matter how careful you might be, life has a rather interesting way of changing your plans and changing as well what you think you want."

"I know what I want," Pamela said firmly. "I want to be who I was always meant to be, in the position I was meant to be in."

"Dear cousin, I should be careful what I wish for if I were you."

"What do you mean?"

"Only that you always wanted to be like the rest of your family in temperament. And while I think you are unique, in these years away from them you have indeed in many ways become an Effington."

"We've established that." Pamela narrowed her eyes. "What is your point?"

"It's been my observation that, while the end result is always interesting, few ventures involving members of your illustrious family ever turn out as expected." Clarissa smiled. "And this has all the markings of one of them."

"Miss Effington and I have met before." Alexei directed his words to Roman but kept his gaze fixed firmly on Miss Effington—Pamela.

Roman frowned. "Are you certain?"

"I am indeed. I was not until I kissed her—"

"You kissed her?"

"Part of the act." Alexei waved away the question. "Nothing more than that." Although there was a great deal more than that even if he could not quite ascertain what at the moment.

It was a simple kiss. Nothing really uncommon about it in terms of length or passion, yet somehow it was extraordinary. Indeed it was rather shocking and most compelling. He was certain those lips had met his before, but surely he would have remembered. Why, her eyes alone would linger in one's memory for at least a lifetime. It made absolutely no sense that she could possibly have slipped his mind. Even if he did not always remember everyone who made his acquaintance, he did pride himself on remembering those he had kissed. And if he had kissed her before, why had she pretended they had never met?

It was definitely a mystery. Intriguing and most delightful. And solving it would be great fun, especially since it would mean, indeed, it would require him to kiss her again. Over and over and over again. Why, with any luck at all, it would be a most difficult mystery to solve.

"Did her aunt not say you had met in Venice?"

Alexei nodded. "Unfortunately, I do not remember the meeting. No doubt it was at one gala or another, a crush of guests, an endless blur of faces and names."

"You forgot the aunt; is it not possible that you forgot the niece as well?"

"No," Alexei said firmly. "I would not forget her."

"Your Highness." Roman paused thoughtfully. "You commented on her charging you with having bedded half the women in Europe. Is that not the exact phrase another Englishwoman, another Englishwoman in Venice, once used with you? Is it possible—"

"Do not be absurd. Miss Effington is not at all the type of woman to engage in an evening predicated on nothing but desire and mystery. I scarcely know her, but I am already confident of that."

Although there was her unexpected comment about throwing herself in his arms or his bed . . . Regardless, the very idea of Miss Effington being the one woman who had joined him in his bed and remained in his soul was utter nonsense.

Still . . . absently he touched the glass earbob in his waistcoat pocket. "I want you to determine where she and I might have met."

"As you wish." Roman's voice was casual. "Lady Overton might well have some insight into that."

"Indeed she might." Alexei chuckled. Roman had obviously taken a liking to the quiet lady. And why not? It was past time he found a wife and a life of his own. "One more thing, Roman."

"Yes, Your Highness?"

"I need you to make a few discreet inquiries as well."

"Regarding?"

"The scandal that led Miss Effington to flee London six years ago. I should very much like to know the details of the incident that ruined her reputation as well as the name of the man involved."

Roman frowned. "Your Highness, are you sure—"

"Oh, I am indeed. After all, Roman, I am her betrothed. I would hate to appear an idiot should some reference be made to it. Besides, our Miss Effington is full of secrets." Alexei watched Pamela laugh in response to something her cousin said, and he smiled slowly. "And before this escapade of ours is over, I shall know each and every one of them."

Seven

When I see my sister again I shall not let her know that the life I chose has been anything but wonderful. I shall never let her know that I may not be completely happy with the decisions I have made and the path I have walked. And I shall never let her know that just possibly she was right.

Millicent, Lady Smythe-Windom

Dinner was a delightful occasion. Or as delightful an occasion as dinner could possibly be when some of those present were marking a betrothal that didn't exist, while others were pretending said betrothal was not merely legitimate but a triumph.

Petrov spent most of his meal glaring suspiciously at Valentina, who variously ignored and baited him. Aunt Millicent seemed to find them both fascinating and alternated her attention between the princess and the captain, leaving Pamela, Alexei, Clarissa, and the count to engage one another in conversation. Which would have been enjoyable had not Clarissa turned most of her efforts toward unabashed flirtation with Stefanovich, who did not hesitate to flirt back. And then there was Alexei. He was the consummate guest, dividing his attention evenly among the ladies, but he had the most annoying way of watching her when he thought she wasn't looking. But, of course, she was.

Dinner had all the reality of a dream in which one is terribly confused, has no idea where precisely to go but is desperate to get there, and doesn't realize until far too late that she is absolutely naked. By the meal's end, Pamela had had quite enough and begged off any further involvement with the rest of the company, claiming weariness from travel and an aching head, only part of which was untrue, and fled to her rooms.

Sleep, however, was as elusive as clarity. She'd tossed and turned through the long hours of the night in a bed that had seemed remarkably inviting at first but was in truth little more than a torturous device composed of twisted sheets and tangled blankets. Even nature itself was taunting her with the pale, growing light of dawn. Pamela heaved a frustrated sigh, tossed off the covers, and slid to her feet.

It was obvious that whatever feelings she still had for Alexei had not dimmed with the passage of time. Whether those feelings were merely of a lustful nature or something more significant she had no idea. All she knew was that she wanted to be in his arms and, God help her, in his bed. It was no way to begin a new life of respectability.

She paced the room, vaguely noting the threadbare feel

of the carpet against her toes. He had certainly been charming enough tonight. No, more than charming.

Four years ago, Alexei had the charm of a man confident in his ability to have whatever he wished, women and anything else. That confidence did not appear to have lessened, at least not regarding women, but seemed to have tempered.

In addition, he was rather *more* than he had seemed to her upon their last meeting, although admittedly they had not a great deal of conversation regarding such serious matters as the responsibility of rule or the expectations of princes. Still, there was a decidedly different air about him now. Richer, deeper as if he had indeed been forged by fire and emerged whole and strong. And if there was a shadow of sadness across his eyes, a suggestion of regret in his voice, it was subtle and private and nothing he would ever reveal or admit or acknowledge. At least to anyone other than himself. It all made him rather remarkable and quite admirable.

She had thought he would make a good king when first they'd met. Now she suspected he would have been great.

Four years ago he had been a prince she could share a delightful evening with. Today, he was a man she could possibly love.

If she didn't already, of course.

Just a few hours ago she had thought that one needed to get to know a man before one could fall in love. Since then Alexei had revealed a great deal about himself both in what he had said and what he hadn't said. Even aside from the way his touch made her weak, the man was most intriguing. Indeed, in this one conversation she knew more about him, about who he was rather than what he was, than any man she'd ever met. Including George.

Alexei Pruzinsky, once the heir to the throne of the Kingdom of Greater Avalonia, was a good man. She could certainly do far worse.

The thought pulled her up short.

Where on earth had that come from? Their engagement was an act—a deceit concocted by her aunt to help reestablish Pamela in society. The very idea that it could be more was absurd. After all, Alexei was a prince. Why, she'd just told Clarissa that regardless of his political status, he was still eligible for a royal match.

But to what end? With his country now little more than a region of Russia, his value as a political match was minimal. A marriage to him offered nothing in terms of alliances. Certainly his bloodline alone assured that he could marry a minor princess from an equally minor country. But if that was what he wished for his life, it made no sense for him to be in England wanting nothing but privacy and solitude. Besides, Alexei was not the type of man who would be happy as the consort to a princess. What kind of woman, what kind of life would make him happy?

And what would make her happy?

Certainly Pamela wanted to resume her life, a proper and respectable life, the life she would have had if she hadn't been such a fool. If not for her mistake with George, she would have made a suitable match, become a wife and mother, and taken her expected place in society. She would have done precisely what was expected of her.

Instead, she had fled England to travel the world. She

had walked in the footsteps of the Caesars in Rome, traced the paths of the great philosophers in Athens, climbed the pyramids. She had studied the world's greatest art in Paris and been moved to tears by the music of Beethoven in Vienna. She had met great men, composers and artists and writers, those with power granted by birthright or fortune or talent. Upon reflection, it hadn't been an exile at all but a grand adventure.

And it had made her the woman she was today.

Good Lord. She sank down onto the bed. How could she have thought, even for a moment, that she could pick up where she had left off? Or that she would want to? Certainly, she wished to be wed and have a family of her own, but throwing herself back into the marriage mart might not be the best way to accomplish that. After all, she was no longer eighteen or even twenty. And she hadn't been particularly successful at attracting suitors when she was younger.

She scrambled off the bed and crossed the room to stand before a cheval mirror. Her reflection was distorted by aged glass and the pink light of the new day. Immodest as it was to admit, she was rather nice-looking now, even lovely, where she hadn't especially been before. Still, appearances aside, men did seem to prefer younger women for wives. Perhaps because they were rather malleable and yet to be formed. Pamela shuddered. She feared she was rather distinctly formed at this point.

Yet she did want to be accepted back in society. With luck, this ruse with Alexei would accomplish that. And she did want a husband. She studied the image in the mirror with a critical eye. She was clever and she was pretty and she came from an excellent family. Even if she were older than the other eligible ladies this season, she was certainly not yet on the shelf. She simply needed to find the right man. A man who could appreciate who she was. A man who wouldn't concern himself in the least with a long-ago scandal. Such a man might well be rare, but with Alexei's help she would at least attract his notice. What did he say about a woman already taken being much more desirable than one who is readily available?

As for Alexei, it was absurd to think even for a moment that there could be anything between them aside from that annoying question of lust. She would simply have to ignore the way her mouth went dry when he gazed into her eyes, or how her heart leapt when he brushed a kiss across her hand, or the manner in which her legs seemed barely able to support her when he took her in his arms.

Alexei was indeed someone she could love given the right circumstances. But the circumstances weren't anywhere near right, and she couldn't imagine they ever would be.

No, this was definitely the best course for her life. She nodded at the reflection in the mirror. She wouldn't regain her position in society as much as she would carve out a new place with Alexei's help. Oh, they could certainly be friends. At least as long as he, or anyone else, never knew that for one single night they'd been significantly more than friends. She wasn't entirely sure what, if anything, he'd do if he discovered their shared past, and she preferred not to find out.

She climbed back into bed, curled around her pillow, and closed her eyes. Determination washed through her.

She would put Alexei out of her mind as anything other than a means to an end. Her decision brought a surprising sense of relief and a deep weariness. Perhaps now she could rest.

In the last moments before sleep finally claimed her she wondered if she could keep him out of her dreams as well.

Alexei nodded a pleasant good day to the footman who opened the door one beat ahead of him. The house might not be in the best of repair, but the servants were impeccably trained and the facilities for his horses were in excellent condition. Indeed, Alexei's mount might well be better housed than the rest of his party.

He had long been in the habit of an early-morning ride, and even here in London retained the practice, finding Hyde Park limiting but still suitable for his purposes. He quite looked forward to the day when he could ride, without restriction, in the countryside. At the moment, however, the park would have to do. At least his new life offered the benefit of a solitary ride rather than one accompanied by a retinue of retainers. Solitude in which to consider any number of questions including how on earth he got himself into an absurd feigned engagement and, more importantly, the women who shared this farce.

The more he thought about it the more he was convinced he and Pamela had indeed met. Why then would she pretend they had not? And why did *he* not remember *her*? It made no sense at all unless one subscribed to Roman's theory that she was the lady he shared a single night with in Venice.

Serenissima.

It was not possible. He had never seen her face, but he did not doubt if he ever met her again he would know her at once, without hesitation, without question. His soul would recognize hers. Plato and the ancient Greeks believed that man and woman were originally one being, split by the gods and condemned to spend their lives searching for their other halves. Alexei had dismissed the idea as foolish romantic nonsense until one memorable night and one unforgettable woman.

No, whatever Miss Effington was hiding, that was not her secret.

He started toward the dining room. In the scant few days since his arrival the staff had become quite adept at anticipating his needs, and breakfast would be waiting on the sideboard. He was becoming rather fond of the servants here, particularly Graham. After all, the man had managed to run the house, lease it year after year, keep the exterior and the grounds pristine even if the interior was lacking, and do it all without attracting undue attention from either the owner or her solicitors. When Alexei at last purchased an estate in the country he would probably need additional staff, and he doubted he could find better than Graham and the others. If, of course, he could induce them to leave the new owners. That might not be nearly as difficult as getting them to leave the house itself, which he suspected commanded a great deal of loyalty. After all, it was their home.

The sound of female voices drifted from the parlor and caught his attention. He drew his brows together in annoyance. So much for solitude. He rather expected Roman or Dimitri or both to join him shortly at the breakfast table, if they were not already there, but Lady Smythe-Windom did not strike him as the type of woman who would be about at this hour. Still, that was definitely her voice. He was not at all sure he was ready to hear just what new and diabolical schemes she had hatched during the night. She probably had him and her niece saying false wedding vows before a fraudulent minister to further this absurd scheme of hers. Why, before he knew it, there would be children frolicking about his feet. Still, children did require a legitimate wedding night and any number of intimate nights thereafter.

He grinned. What a delightful thought. The least he could do for the lady who had put such a pleasant idea in his head and brightened his mood considerably so early in the morning was bid her a good day. He turned and stepped into the parlor.

Lady Smythe-Windom was dressed for an outing and accompanied by an exquisite young woman attired in a similar fashion. The two were perched on a sofa and engaged in lively conversation with Valentina, who was dressed for riding. Alexei stifled a laugh. Perhaps greeting the day in a timely fashion with a legitimate pursuit was part of her effort to change her ways. Of course, they had all retired rather early last night. There was simply little else to do.

Dimitri and Roman stood flanking the fireplace, the captain with arms crossed over his chest watching Valentina every second, and Roman, who observed the ladies with a definite air of amusement.

"Good day, ladies." Alexei strode into the room. "You are looking lovely this morning, Lady Smythe-Windom."

"Your Highness." Roman stepped forward. "Allow me to—"

"Am I, Your Highness?" Lady Smythe-Windom gazed up at him with an assessing eye and an amused smile. She extended her hand. "How lovely?"

He bowed over her hand, lifted it to his lips, and met her gaze. "Exceptionally."

"Really?" Lady Smythe-Windom's eyes widened innocently.

Valentina smirked. "Do you think she is lovelier this morning than she was, oh, say, last night?"

Alexei laughed and straightened. "Most definitely lovelier."

Lady Smythe-Windom's smile was decidedly smug. "And younger too perhaps?"

"The very breath of youth," he said firmly.

"They say there is always a good twin and not so good twin." An irate feminine voice rang from the doorway. Alexei turned to find Lady Smythe-Windom, or rather someone who looked exactly like Lady Smythe-Windom, or exactly like the lady seated in front of him, save for her dress, lounging in the doorway. "I was the good twin."

"Not for long." The first Lady Smythe-Windom rose to her feet. "I daresay you've rectified that in recent years."

"You can be assured I have given it my very best efforts." The newly arrived Lady Smythe-Windom moved toward her twin. "Still, I would never coerce a prince into saying I looked younger and lovelier than my sister."

The sister glanced at Alexei. "Do forgive me, Your Highness, if I coerced you in any way. Or if I deceived you. I am Abigail Effington. Lady Edward. Pamela's mother."

"Yes, of course." He should have known the moment he realized there were two of them. She couldn't possibly be anyone else.

"Abigail." Lady Smythe-Windom met her sister in the center of the room.

Lady Edward eyed her twin. "Millicent."

The resemblance between the women was nothing short of remarkable. Alexei wondered if it went beyond appearance, although if appearance was any indication, the sisters did not seem especially pleased to see one another. A distinct tension hovered in the air between them.

"I wondered if you were ever going to return home," Lady Edward said.

Lady Smythe-Windom shrugged. "As did I."

Lady Edward narrowed her eyes. "Are you still as reckless, single-minded, and prone to doing precisely as you please as you once were?"

"Most certainly." Lady Smythe-Windom studied her sister. "And have you remained as stubborn, arrogant, and convinced that you and you alone are right as you used to be?"

Lady Edward nodded. "Absolutely."

"Good. I was afraid that you had changed."

"Never." Lady Edward laughed and threw her arms around her sister.

The two women embraced amidst laughter and banter and the odd tear, each apparently trying to get years of conversation into a few bare moments. Alexei breathed a sigh of relief. What an odd relationship these Englishwomen had. A moment ago he was certain they would come to blows and had been prepared to throw himself bodily between them although he had not relished the idea. Fortunately, it was now obvious that they held one another in great affection.

Roman moved to Alexei's side. "I did try to warn you, Your Highness."

Lady Smythe-Windom disentangled herself from her sister's embrace. "I should have warned you as well."

"I daresay I could have used a bit of warning." Alexei smiled wryly. "It is rather frightening to discover there is more than one of you."

"I can see where it would be, but I meant that I should have warned you that Abigail would try to get you to say something terribly complimentary to her at my expense." Lady Smythe-Windom cast her sister a long-suffering look.

Lady Edward laughed. "You would have done precisely the same thing if you had thought of it first."

"Yes," Lady Smythe-Windom said smugly. "But I would have done it much better."

"Hardly." Lady Edward laughed and took her sister's hands. "I understand you have taken exceptionally good care of Pamela."

"Of course I have." Indignation furrowed Lady Smythe-Windom's brow. "I would never let anything happen to Pamela or Clarissa either for that matter."

"Of course not. I'm not talking about keeping her safe. I'm talking about . . ." Lady Edward nodded in a significant manner toward Alexei. "Him."

Alexei started. "Me?"

Lady Edward cast her sister a radiant smile. "You've done a splendid job."

"Have I?" Lady Smythe-Windom said cautiously.

"Prepare yourself, Your Highness," Roman said under his breath.

"Indeed you have. Although, I do wish you had written me, at least of the possibilities." Lady Edward shook her head. "We could be much farther along by now."

"I have written you faithfully once a month for most of my life." Lady Smythe-Windom stared in confusion. "Farther along with what?"

"I have been telling her all about Pamela and Alexei," Valentina said with a fond smile at Lady Edward. "We have been discussing arrangements for the wedding."

"The wedding?" Lady Smythe-Windom slanted Alexei a quick look.

"You have?" Alexei stared at his cousin.

"Most certainly." Valentina nodded. "Oh I know this will not be as lavish as a state wedding, but it is the joining of the House of Pruzinsky and the House of Effington—"

"I'm not sure that I'd call it a house exactly," Lady Edward murmured.

"Family then. Regardless"—Valentina shrugged— "there should be some sort of celebration, and I for one intend to do all I can to assure that it goes well." She leaned toward Alexei and met his gaze. "The very least I can do, cousin, is to help you start your new life in a splendid manner since I am, to a certain extent, responsible for your old life being a wee bit complicated now and again. You may thank me later."

"Thank you?" Alexei's voice rose.

"Think nothing of it." Valentina smiled smugly.

"A bit complicated?" Dimitri scoffed. "Now and again?"

Valentina ignored him. Lady Edward and Lady Smythe-Windom exchanged glances.

"I told the ladies it was perhaps a little early for wedding arrangements," Roman said smoothly.

"Nonsense," Lady Edward said firmly. "From what the princess has been telling me, His Highness and Pamela have waited far too long already."

"Yes, but," Lady Smythe-Windom chose her words carefully, "they just saw one another again yesterday and immediately realized . . . that is, well . . . this has all happened so quickly—"

The young woman seated on the sofa heaved a heartfelt sigh. "I think it's terribly romantic."

"As do I." Valentina grinned at her cousin. "Terribly."

The most absurd sense of panic twisted Alexei's stomach. Apparently it was not enough that he had lost his country. Now these women wanted to take away his freedom as well. It was one thing to pose as Pamela's fiancé but something entirely different actually to marry her as part of the act regardless of the considerable appeal of a wedding night and endless nights with her in his bed. The specter of frolicking children once again appeared about his feet.

No. The children vanished. He had spent his life knowing he would have little say in the selection of a bride. That had changed along with everything else, and he bloody hell would not be forced into a marriage simply because an absurd scheme went awry.

"Lady Edward." Alexei fixed the woman with a firm look. "Before this goes any further, I feel I must inform you—"

"He must inform you . . . or rather . . ." Lady Smythe-Windom cut in, "your husband. Yes of course, that's it. Pamela's father. Edward that is." Her expression brightened. "His Highness feels simply dreadful that he did not have the opportunity to do all this properly and ask for Pamela's hand. He should certainly do that before there are any actual wedding arrangements made." She turned toward him. "Isn't that right, Your Highness?"

Alexei narrowed his gaze.

Roman leaned closer, his voice for Alexei alone. "Do keep in mind the bank, Your Highness."

Alexei blew a long breath. "Indeed, Lady Smythe-Windom, I feel"—he gritted his teeth—"dreadful."

"I thought as much." Relief flickered across her face, and she offered him a grateful smile. "And do call me Aunt Millicent."

"Not precisely the name I had in mind," he said under his breath.

"Edward would quite like that." Lady Edward nodded approvingly. "And I appreciate the gesture as well although I'm not entirely certain it's necessary given Pamela's age and well . . ." She waved dismissively. "It scarcely matters now I suppose." Lady Edward favored Alexei with a glowing smile. "Now that she has made such an excellent match and for love. I could not more delighted."

Alexei sighed. "Lady Edward—"

"We are all delighted, my lady," Roman said smoothly. "For the happiness of Miss Effington and His Highness."

"And we shall all be able to mark the occasion in a grand manner. Our timing is nothing short of perfect. Lady Edward's family is hosting a ball a scant two days from now." Excitement sounded in Valentina's voice. "It will be the perfect place for an official announcement."

"What will be the perfect place to announce what?" Pamela stood in the doorway, staring in obvious confusion. She looked rather charmingly disheveled as if she had just been awakened and dressed hurriedly. Alexei had the most absurd desire to sweep her into his arm and carry her back to her bed.

"Whatever are you . . ." She stepped into the room and her eyes widened. "Mother? Amanda?" Pamela flew across the room and into the arms of her mother and the younger lady, no doubt her sister.

The next few minutes were a repeat of the earlier greeting between the older ladies but louder and longer, and amazingly enough, with even greater enthusiasm. Especially as Lady Smythe-Windom—or rather Aunt Millicent—threw herself into the fray. Even Valentina seemed pulled toward the knot of excited women, who appeared to be something of a force of nature not unlike a whirlpool sucking in everything in its path.

"Dearest, you look wonderful." Lady Edward held her eldest daughter at arm's length and considered her thoughtfully. "Travel obviously agrees with you."

"I've had a grand time, Mother," Pamela said. "But I am very glad to be home."

"But you're not home really. I mean you're here." Lady Edward glanced around the room and shuddered. "In this place, Great-aunt Elizabeth's house—God rest her soul—rather than in our home. It's simply not right."

Apparently, Lady Edward was not aware that Pamela was a partial owner of the house.

"Right or not, this is where I shall stay." Pamela shook her head. "I cannot go back to where I lived any more than I can go back to who I was."

"She is most welcome here," Aunt Millicent said quickly. "I don't know what I would do without Pamela and Clarissa. Indeed, I think of them as more than mere nieces. They are as close to me as if they were my own daughters." She heaved a deep sigh. "I was never blessed with children of my own, you know."

Lady Edward snorted. "You were never especially fond of children."

"I find I quite like them once they've ended all that childhood nonsense," Aunt Millicent said in a lofty manner. "When they've entered into adulthood they're very much like . . . people."

Pamela laughed. "Thank you, Aunt Millicent." She drew a deep breath and turned to Lady Edward. "Mother, it is precisely because I am an adult that I would prefer not to occupy the very same quarters I occupied as a child. I know most unmarried women of my age do so. However, I have never wished to be one of them."

She looked her mother directly in the eye. "I fear I have become too . . . independent to return to the life I lived as a child, in the place where I resided as a child. It sounds silly, I suppose, and I do hope you understand but, well, there you have it."

Lady Edward studied her daughter for a long moment. "Your letters were more accurate than I'd thought, Millicent, although I'd suspected as much from the manner in which Pamela's own notes changed through the years."

Lady Edward cast a critical eye over her daughter. "She has changed a great deal."

Aunt Millicent grinned. "She has become one of them."

"It was inevitable, I suppose, it is in her blood. But I cannot say it is not for the best." Lady Edward cupped her daughter's chin in her hand and smiled into her eyes. "You always were entirely too reserved and quiet for a member of this family. I rather feared that at some point you might simply burst from the strain of restraint."

"She did burst, Mother, in a way that is," Amanda said in a matter-of-fact manner. "With Penwick? Don't you remember?"

Penwick? Alexei glanced at Roman, who nodded slightly.

Lady Edward shot Alexei a quick, assessing look. "We all remember, dear, but it's in the past and best forgotten. There is no need to bring it up now."

"Tell me about the ball, Mother," Pamela said. "Unless you've failed to mention it in your letters, you haven't hosted a ball in years."

"Actually, it's to be held at your aunt and uncle's. At Effington House," Lady Edward murmured.

"At Effington House? The last time *I* can recall a ball you hosted at Effington House it was for . . ." She narrowed her eyes. "Mother?"

"It's Amanda's coming-out ball." A note of reluctance sounded in Lady Edward's voice. "However, I see no reason why we cannot make an announcement there."

"Absolutely not." Pamela looked horrified at the very suggestion. Excellent. Alexei was rather horrified by the prospect himself. She turned to her sister and took her hands. "Amanda, it's your ball. You should be the center of attention, and absolutely nothing should distract from you."

"Pamela, dear, nothing will," Amanda said with the confidence of a woman who is secure in her own beauty. Somewhat unusual in one so young although her appearance certainly justified it.

Amanda was substantially shorter than her older sister, but there was a distinct resemblance. Amanda's fair hair was a shade darker than Pamela's, her brown eyes a bit lighter. She was delicate where Pamela was stately, and she had an almost ethereal, angelic air about her. She would have most of the eligible men in London seeking her favors in no time, if they were not already.

"You've been away for six endless years. We've only seen you once, when we met you in Paris the first year you were gone. I have missed you dreadfully. Of course, I am terribly excited about the ball—it's my official entry into society after all—but it is for me, and I should be able to have whatever I wish in regards to it. And I should like nothing better than to share it with my only sister. Besides, an announcement will be made at some point somewhere. Why not at my party?" Amanda grinned in a most wicked manner, and all sense of saintliness vanished. "The announcement of my sister's impending marriage to a real prince and his presence—" She looked at Alexei in a most suspicious manner. "You will be present, won't you?"

Alexei smiled wryly. "As it is my betrothal, I would not dare miss it." In truth, he was beginning to wonder where all this would end, and he did rather hate to leave an opera before the final aria had been sung.

"It will make my ball the talk of the season." Amanda leaned toward her sister confidentially. "Lucy Berkley's ball is next week, and she's been saying hers will be the event of the year. I hardly think so now."

Pamela glanced at her mother. "Lucy Berkley?"

Lady Edward sighed. "Her oldest and dearest friend in the world."

Amanda chortled in a most unangelic manner. "I can scarcely wait to see exactly what shade of green she turns when she hears this."

Pamela chose her words carefully. "Still, we only just arrived in London yesterday, and as His Highness and I haven't seen each other for years, well, it all seems to be happening rather quickly."

"Precisely what I said," Aunt Millicent muttered.

"But why wait when one is in love?" Valentina said.

"Why wait indeed?" Lady Edward winced. "For marriage, that is."

"I . . . I . . ." Pamela cast him a pleading look. He smiled encouragingly. "I would prefer to wait before a formal announcement is made. After all, it has been some time since His Highness and I parted. I simply think it would be wise for the two of us to reacquaint ourselves with one another before we go rushing into public announcements. Don't you agree?"

He stared at her for a long moment. It would be nothing more than a postponement but to what end? He had given his word after all. Alexei had always been something of a believer in the idea that if one was about to be immersed in freezing water, it was best to plunge right in. The initial shock was intense, but ultimately it was far easier to accept. Besides, it was all becoming quite amusing.

"I do agree, my dear." He bit back a grin. "With your sister."

"You do?" Amanda's eyes widened.

Pamela's brow furrowed. "You do?"

"Thank God," Aunt Millicent said under her breath.

"How wonderful." Lady Edward sighed with relief.

"My dear, Miss Effington." He stepped closer to Amanda, took her hand, and raised it to his lips. "I can think of no greater reason to announce my intentions publicly toward your sister than that of making your Miss Berkley as green as she could possibly be."

"We are going to get along extremely well, Your Highness." Amanda grinned, and the most enchanting dimple appeared at the corner of her mouth. At once Alexei felt a wave of sympathy for whatever young man she eventually set her sights on. He would not have a chance.

Pamela stared at him. "I really think it would be wiser to wait until we have spent some time together—"

"Nonsense." He met her gaze firmly and tried not to laugh at her obvious annoyance. He was rather enjoying this. "Getting to better know one another is the precise reason for an engagement, particularly as we are not marrying for purposes of politics or alliances. We are following our hearts, Pamela, wherever they may lead us. They have led us to this moment, and we cannot ignore them."

She stared at him. "We can't?"

"No, we cannot." His gaze meshed with hers, and he stepped closer to her. "It is our hearts that tell us that no matter how ill-advised this might seem when viewed rationally and logically, it is nonetheless right and true." He took her hands in his. "It is our hearts that called out for one another through the miles and years that separated us." He kissed one hand, then the next, his gaze still locked with hers. "And it is our hearts that have at last drawn us together again."

Pamela's mouth dropped open. "Oh my."

"That *was* terribly romantic," Valentina murmured.

"I can't tell you how pleased I am," Lady Edward said in a low aside to her sister."

"We are all pleased." Aunt Millicent's voice carried a distinct note of speculation.

Alexei ignored them and continued to stare into Pamela's dark eyes. "I warn you, Pamela, I intend to use every moment until the ball working to ease your fears. We shall spend a great deal of time together."

She stared up at him. "I shall look forward to it."

"Properly chaperoned of course," Lady Edward said with a firm voice.

Alexei released her hands, noting a distinct reluctance to do so and a definite loss when the warmth of her fingers left his.

"Now there are a number of details we should discuss . . ." Lady Edward began, the other ladies joining her to express an opinion or make a comment save for Pamela, who appeared momentarily befuddled. Excellent. He liked having her befuddled.

Alexei stepped out of the way, nodding and smiling when necessary although, in truth, he was superfluous to the discussion and paid it no heed whatsoever. They could be planning to release white doves over his head for all he cared.

No, he was intent upon watching Pamela. It was most annoying to acknowledge she knew something he was not privy to. No doubt that was precisely why he had declared they would spend a great deal of time together before the ball. Oh certainly, he fully intended to take advantage of that time to kiss her again and quite thoroughly, both in the interest of refreshing his memory and, more, because he very much wanted to.

"Now that we have everything well in hand"—a brisk note sounded in Valentina's voice and she headed for the door—"I am off to follow my cousin's example and ride in the park." She directed her words over her shoulder but didn't turn around. "Are you coming, Petrov?"

Dimitri's jaw clenched, and he shot Alexei a desperate look. Alexei shrugged and shook his head in apology. The captain cast his gaze toward the heavens as if now seeking divine help.

"Captain," Valentina called.

Dimitri closed his eyes for a moment, muttered something to himself, and followed after the princess.

"We should be going as well. There are endless details that must be attended to before the ball." Lady Edward turned to her older daughter and embraced her. "I have missed you more than I can say. Promise me you will never stay away so long again."

Pamela nodded, her eyes bright. "I do promise, Mother. I have missed you as well."

"We shall have a grand time at the ball, Pamela." Amanda gave her sister a quick hug then turned to Alexei

and extended her hand. "Thank you again, Your Highness, for agreeing to make my ball the very best of the
season."

He obligingly brushed his lips across her hand and
tried not to laugh. "I shall do what I can, Miss Effington."

"I say, you don't happen to have a brother do you?"
Amanda said thoughtfully. "Young and quite handsome,
perhaps?"

He laughed. "I do indeed have a brother, Miss Effington. And yes he is a good deal younger than I and considerably more handsome. At least in the opinion of ladies."

"Really?" Amanda adopted an innocent manner. "Do
you think he might be persuaded to come to the ball as
well?"

"In the interest of besting Miss Berkley, I am certain
he could be induced to make an appearance—"

Amanda opened her mouth, but Alexei held up a hand
to stop her.

"—if I knew where he was, and I am afraid at the moment I do not."

"What a pity." Amanda's brow furrowed with thought.
"Perhaps you can make an attempt to find—"

"That's quite enough, Amanda." Lady Edward ushered
the girl toward the door. "You have an engagement announcement, and a prince and a princess attending your
ball. I daresay that's more than sufficient to dampen the
spirits of your dearest friend."

"It is, isn't it?" Amanda flashed him a smug grin, and
he grinned back. She would indeed be a handful for any
man with the courage to attempt it.

After a flurry of farewells and promises to meet tomorrow, the two ladies departed, leaving Pamela, Alexei, Roman, and Aunt Millicent.

Aunt Millicent turned to the others with a pleasant smile. "That went well."

"Well?" Pamela's voice rose. "Well? I would scarcely call it well. Announcements at balls? Wedding arrangements? Don't you think this is all going too far?"

Aunt Millicent widened her eyes. "What do you mean, dear?"

"What do I mean?" Pamela sputtered. "I mean, I have just lied to my mother."

Aunt Millicent scoffed. "Come now, Pamela, you fully intended to lie to her before she so much as stepped foot in the door."

"Yes, but intending to lie to her and actually doing it are two entirely different things," she snapped, then turned her attention to Alexei. "As for you—"

"I thought I did an exceptionally good job." Alexei tried and failed to hide the satisfaction in his voice. "What do you think, Roman?"

Roman nodded. "A thrill ran though my blood, Your Highness."

"Exceptionally good?" Pamela stared. "Exceptionally good?"

"Does she do that a lot?" Alexei asked in an aside to the older woman. "Repeat what you have just said, I mean."

"I've never noticed it before now." Aunt Millicent studied her niece. "She is rather upset though."

"Upset, of course I'm upset." Pamela rubbed her hand across her forehead and paced the room. "This has gone far beyond what I expected. Granted, I should have expected it, all of it, and I admit a great deal of this is my fault. It seemed like such a simple little plan when it was proposed yesterday, but it has grown out of all proportion. I didn't think of the ramifications. I didn't think—" She pulled up short, her eyes wide. "We must call it off. At once."

Aunt Millicent snorted. "We shall do nothing of the sort."

"Why not? We could say . . . oh, I don't know." She turned a pleading glance to Alexei. "What could we say?"

"We could claim"—Alexei glanced at Roman—"insanity? That would do, would it not?"

"Absolutely, Your Highness," Roman said solemnly. "European royalty has used insanity as an excuse for ill-advised behavior since time began."

"Then it could work," Pamela said eagerly. "Besides, a legitimate argument for insanity could be made by anyone looking at this scheme."

"Don't be absurd." Aunt Millicent crossed her arms over her chest. "Even insanity will not save us. First of all, far too many people know of this alleged engagement, and I daresay Lucy Berkley will know within the hour and will doubtless tell her mother. Who will hasten to tell her good friends and so on and so forth. Not all of them will believe insanity."

"Are you sure?" Pamela said weakly.

"Positive." Aunt Millicent nodded. "Besides, even if they did, once started, insanity is a nasty rumor to dispel."

"Indeed it is." Alexei shook his head in a mournful manner. "There are any number of royal houses whose members are as sane as you and I, but even so, they cannot dispel the belief that they are mad, and their every action is viewed accordingly."

"Of course there was that particular princess from some kingdom, whose name escapes me now, who was continually batting at flies that did not exist." Roman said. "Do you remember?"

"Indeed, I do." Alexei thought for a moment. "She ate them too as I recall. Most distressing. Although in that instance I believe she was at least a little deranged."

"Very well then." Pamela blew a long breath. "Insanity will not work, but surely—"

"No," Aunt Millicent said firmly. "There is no way to extricate us from this situation at this point without causing a huge amount of embarrassment and scandal as well. Far too many people know. Any hope you have of being accepted in society will be dashed. I will admit I did not expect it to escalate quite in the manner it did, and perhaps the entire plan was not properly thought out—"

"It was not thought out at all." Pamela's voice was grim.

"But we are in it now, and we were in it the moment the butler heard the news. We shall just have to carry it off as best we can. Besides"—Aunt Millicent drew a deep breath—"if my sister ever learns the truth, she will never let me forget it. She will hold this over me for the rest of my days."

"As well she should!" Pamela glared. "You don't ever intend to tell her then?"

"I haven't decided." Aunt Millicent considered the question. "However, if it works, she'll be quite pleased."

"Good Lord." Pamela closed her eyes and clenched her fists, obviously searching for calm. Or she might have been praying. At last she drew a deep breath and opened her eyes. "Very well then. We shall play our parts, and this farce may not be our downfall after all. Now, if you will excuse me, I feel the need to lie down for a while with a cold cloth across my head."

Alexei raised a brow. "Headache?"

"Brought on by a severe lack of sleep. I had a great deal on my mind. Not nearly as much as I have now, however." She nodded and headed toward the door.

"Miss Effington," he said without thinking.

She turned back. "Yes?"

He smiled his most engaging smile. "I cannot think of anyone I would rather be trapped with in a farce."

The corners of her lips quirked slightly in a reluctant smile. "I see even this morning's encounter has not dimmed that infamous charm of yours."

"That is one of the very best things about charm. It rises to the occasion."

"I daresay it will have numerous opportunities to rise in the coming days." She sighed and again started to take her leave.

"Oh, and Miss Effington, I meant it when I said I wished to spend every moment together."

She paused for a long moment, heaved another sigh, of surrender perhaps, then glanced back at him over her shoulder, a genuine smile on her face. "Good."

Before he could respond she had disappeared through the doorway.

"I, too, have a number of things to attend to." Aunt

Millicent studied him thoughtfully. "And I, too, meant what I said."

"Oh?" Alexei said absently, still staring at the doorway. Whatever had she meant by *good*?

"About chaperones, Your Highness," Aunt Millicent said.

Alexei laughed. "You do not trust me then?"

"You look at her in a way that does not encourage trust, Your Highness. Worse, she looks at you in precisely the same way." Her eyes narrowed. "I'm not sure I trust either of you."

Alexei shrugged. "It is simply part and parcel of the act, *Aunt Millicent*."

"See that it is, Your Highness." She considered him for another moment, then nodded, bid them good morning, and swept from the room.

Alexei stared after her thoughtfully

"That was very good, Your Highness," Roman said.

"What?"

"The soliloquy about hearts reaching for one another through the years."

"Yes, it was, wasn't it." Odd, for a moment when he had gazed into her eyes, he had meant everything he had said. "Have you had the opportunity to query Lady Overton about Pamela's past or their travels for an idea as to where she and I might have met?"

"Not yet, Your Highness." Roman chuckled. "But I will."

"And you caught the name the younger Miss Effington mentioned?"

"Penwick?" Roman nodded. "I shall look into it at once."

"Excellent."

"Your Highness," Roman said slowly. "It does strike me that if you are not extremely careful, you could end up married."

It was an intriguing thought and not entirely distasteful. Still, it was the height of irony that when he was heir to a kingdom and had the world to offer the lady who would be his wife, he had had no choice in the selection of a bride. Now that he could marry whomever he pleased, he had nothing to offer save his name, and that was of little consequence these days.

No, he had no intention of marrying anyone. As for Pamela, there was something brewing between the two of them. He felt it as surely as he felt the beat of his own heart and knew as well that she felt it, too. He had no idea where it would lead, but she was no innocent virgin. She was a strong-willed, independent woman responsible for her own decisions. And an insurmountable challenge for any man.

Except, perhaps, for him.

Eight

When I see my sister again I shall not let her suspect even for a moment that while my life has been everything I have ever wished and I am truly happy, still, I cannot help but envy on occasion, the path she chose of wonderfully exciting new places and interesting new men. And I will never, ever let her know that there is the tiniest possibility that I could ever think she was right.

Abigail, Lady Edward Effington

"Good day, Your Highness." Pamela's horse cantered up beside Alexei's, and she slowed him to a walk. "A lovely morning for a ride, don't you think?"

"Indeed I do, Miss Effington." Alexei smiled a warm welcome as if he were genuinely glad to see her. "And made all the lovelier by your presence."

Pamela raised an approving brow. "Very good, Your Highness."

He grinned. "I thought so." He glanced behind her. "Have you managed to escape without a chaperone, or is your aunt lurking somewhere in the bushes?"

"Don't be absurd. This is far too early in the day for Aunt Millicent. She considers anything before noon to be obscene. My mother's visit yesterday is the only thing that would have roused her from her bed."

"Then I am safe for the moment?"

"For the moment." Pamela laughed. "She has been rather vigilant of late."

"Vigilant?" Alexei snorted. "I have been surrounded by armed men whose sole duty it was to protect me from assassins who were not as vigilant as your aunt. I must confess I have never before spent a full day and an entire evening without once being able to manage so much as a moment alone with whatever woman I intended to spend a moment alone with. She watched us, or rather me, like a hawk eyeing a rabbit."

"Perhaps she thought you were the hawk and I was the rabbit?"

"Do you think I am the hawk?"

"You do have that reputation, you know."

"Ah yes." He sighed in a regretful manner she didn't believe for a moment. After all, he had already confessed to having thoroughly enjoyed his past. "My reputation. Surely we can put that behind us?"

"Have you?"

He grinned in a most wicked manner, and a delightful chill raced down her spine.

"I do have chaperones," she said abruptly, then winced

164

to herself. Good Lord, she sounded like a frightened, well, *rabbit* for lack of a better word. A virginal rabbit at that.

This was ridiculous. She was well used to flirtatious banter, and she'd had years of practice with men every bit as polished in the art as Alexei. Prince or not, he was merely another man. She would do well to remember that and treat him as such. Still, there was scarcely another man alive who could make her heart skip a beat simply by walking into the room.

Pamela shrugged in an offhand manner as if the question of chaperones, present or not, wasn't of the slightest significance. "Lady Overton is directly behind us."

Concern furrowed his forehead. "Alone?"

"No, Count Stefanovich is accompanying her."

"I see." He chuckled.

"What exactly do you see?"

"Only that Lady Overton and Roman are the perfect chaperones. Mature, discreet and,"—he glanced behind them—"and still nowhere in sight."

"Precisely why I asked them to accompany me."

"Oh?"

"I have never before spent a full day and an entire evening without once spending even a moment alone with whatever gentleman I had intended to spend a moment alone with." She grinned.

He considered her thoughtfully. "The rabbit usually prefers not to spend any time at all with the hawk."

"Yes, but we have yet to decide which of us is the rabbit." She leaned toward him and lowered her voice. "And which is the hawk."

"Excellent, Miss Effington." He laughed. "Well said."

"Indeed it was." She tilted her head and studied him. "You called me Pamela yesterday. Are we back to Miss Effington then?"

"I only called you Pamela when we were around the others because it seemed appropriate to the illusion. However"—he met her gaze directly—"I would be honored to call you by your given name if you wish."

"I do."

"Very well then." He smiled. "Pamela."

Perhaps he should call her Miss Effington. The way he said Pamela, as if he were savoring the sound of it on his tongue, did decidedly odd things to the pit of her stomach.

"And I would much prefer you to call me Alexei rather than Your Highness. In truth, it seems rather hollow now, vestiges of the past and all that. I do not mind it so much with Roman or Dimitri or your aunt but with you"—he glanced at her—"it seems so . . . impersonal. I have never been in an engagement before, fraudulent or otherwise, and I suspect impersonal is to be avoided."

"But you've been called Your Highness all your life. I can't imagine your mother did not refer to your father in the same manner."

"He was a king, she was a queen. They were bound by traditions and expectations that no longer exist for me. My life is substantially different from that of my parents." The faintest hint of regret showed in his smile, so slight as to be overlooked altogether if one weren't acutely aware of the changes in his life.

They rode side by side in silent companionship. She

had decided to join him this morning because they hadn't had a chance to talk alone since the evening of her arrival. She thought it wise, if they were to appear publicly in just two days, to become at ease in one another's presence. She found it as annoying as he did never to be able to speak privately, thanks to her aunt. There was much she wished to know about him—what his thoughts were and what he now wanted for his life. Surely a fiancée would know such things.

"Why have you never married?" she asked without thinking. It was the first thing that popped into her head and the one question she'd wondered about for years.

"I have a brother," he said simply.

"A brother? I don't understand."

"My brother, Nikolai, was next in line for the throne should anything happen to me. Therefore, there was no particular urgency to wed and produce an heir. I should have married years ago, I suppose"—he slanted her a quick grin—"but I was having entirely too much fun."

"I recall some mention of that."

"And then my father fell ill, there were political problems—"

"Caused by the princess?"

"*Encouraged* by her more than caused. Even she never had the power to do more than stir the pot although she did manage to stir it to a frenzy." Alexei shrugged. "Avalonians have always been easily roused to a good fight. We are a very passionate people."

"Indeed." At once she recalled quite vividly exactly how passionate the one Avalonian she knew could be when roused. She pushed the thought aside.

"Perhaps I was avoiding the inevitable, but I was too busy to give the search for a bride my attention. In truth, I had always thought I had more than enough time to find a lady who would not only serve as wife but as queen. One does think that, does one not?"

She drew her brows together. "That there is enough time to find a wife?"

"That there is enough time for everything one has planned. That life will continue as it always has." He paused, obviously gathering his thoughts. "I knew the world was changing, Pamela, thanks in great part to Napoleon's rampage as well as any number of other factors. Among them the progress of mankind itself I suppose. Countries that had existed independently from time immemorial were vanishing into one empire or another. Claimed or conquered by greater powers. I knew Avalonia's position was precarious. It always had been. But what one knows in a logical, rational sort of way has little to do with the emotion of it all. One's acceptance of the reality of the state of the world on an intellectual level has nothing whatsoever to do with what is felt in one's heart.

"And that, while an explanation of sorts, is certainly not an answer." He chuckled. "In truth, I suppose, I never found a bride who would be both politically advantageous and personally palatable."

"I can see where politically advantageous as well as personally palatable would be difficult."

He shook his head. "You have no idea."

They approached the Serpentine, and he glanced at her. "Would you care to walk by the lake for a bit?"

"That would be lovely." She smiled. "Alexei."

The moment she said his name aloud she wished she hadn't. There was an enormous difference between using his given name when there were others present and calling him Alexei when they were alone. It was indeed personal and extremely intimate. Worse still, she had always thought of him as Alexei in her memories and her dreams. With every minute in his company, it was more and more difficult to keep her memories and dreams separate from the here and now.

He dismounted, then moved to help her down. His hands fastened around her waist, and she slid off her horse and into his arms. He made no effort to pull away. She made no effort to move. For a long moment they stared at one another.

"You are an excellent rider, Pamela." The look in his eye, of admiration and invitation, quite took her breath away. "I do not know how women can abide sidesaddles."

"I've ridden astride on occasion in the country, and I quite prefer it." His hands were still lightly on her waist, hers rested on his shoulders, and she wondered that she continued to breathe.

"Do you?" His voice was low, intense, and resonated in her blood.

"I met an Italian countess once who had a pillow in the shape of a leg that she would affix to her saddle so that it appeared she was riding properly when, in truth, she was riding"—she swallowed hard—"astride."

"Was she?" His gaze drifted to her lips then back to her eyes. "Astride you say?"

"Oh my, yes." Her heart pounded in her ears. "I have

often thought it quite a clever ruse and well worth the effort for the . . . the . . . *ease* of riding"—she struggled for breath—"astride."

"And the pleasure?" The word was a caress, a promise.

"Most definitely." Absently she wet her lips. "The pleasure."

"Miss Effington." He drew her closer. "Pamela."

"Yes?" Her voice was barely more than a whisper.

"Do be quiet," he said, and his mouth met hers in a kiss at once firm and tender.

For an endless moment his lips caressed hers in a gentle exploration. Teasing, tempting, inviting. Heat pooled in the pit of her stomach. She wrapped her arms around his neck, and he pulled her tighter against him. She could feel the heat of his body through the layers of clothing separating them, the solidity of the muscles of his chest, the hard lines of his thighs. Desire, hot and aching, washed through her. He deepened his kiss and crushed his lips to hers as if he felt it, too. As if the need that gripped her flowed between them, binding them together. His mouth plundered hers, demanding and hungry, and she responded in kind with a greed of her own. Lord help her she wanted him now as she had wanted him every day and night for the past four years. Wanted his lips on hers, his hands on her naked flesh, his legs entwined with hers—

Alexei wrenched his lips from hers, held her out at arm's length, and stared. "Where in the name of all that is holy have we met?"

"What?" She gasped for breath. "What are you talking about?"

"Where have we met before, Pamela?" His voice was sharp with frustration. "It is a simple enough question."

"Simple? No doubt but . . ." She shook her head to clear it, more than a bit frustrated herself. "Why are you asking it now? At this particular moment? I know I was not the least bit concerned with . . . with questions! At least not of that nature!"

His brows drew together, and he glared at her. "Because for some absurd reason you are pretending that we have never met when I am certain that we have."

She stared in disbelief, shrugged off his hands, and moved away from him. Another moment in his arms, and she would have been willing, even eager to tell him anything he wanted. She would have thrown caution to the winds and confessed everything. Now, however, she wasn't at all sure she wished to reveal so much as her own name. He was just so . . . so . . . commanding and *royal*.

She chose her words carefully. "Why are you so certain that we have met?"

"I never forget a woman I have kissed. And a woman I have kissed never forgets me." His manner was lofty in a matter-of-fact sort of way, as if there was no possibility that his kiss would not be memorable.

"Come now, Your Highness." Pamela snorted in disdain. "Given the vast numbers of women you have kissed, I cannot believe you remember each and every one. Nor can I believe they remember you."

"I do, and they do."

"Nonsense. One kisses so many men, and so few are worth remembering."

"Perhaps that is why one becomes embroiled in scandal, ruined, and is forced to flee one's country!"

She sucked in a hard breath.

At once regret showed in his eyes. "Pamela, I—"

"At least I still have a country to flee from," she said without thinking, turned on her heel, and stalked off.

How could he have said something like that to her? Worse, how could she have said that to him? A dreadful sense of shame rushed through her. How could she have said that to anyone let alone to him? She knew what losing his country had done to him. It was not at all the type of hurtful thing she would ever have said to anyone, but the blasted man did things to her. Made her say and feel things she no idea she was capable of. Certainly his own snide comment warranted her reaction, but still that was no—

"You are not getting away that easily," he called after her. A moment later he grabbed her elbow and whirled her around to face him. "That was a vile, wicked thing to say, Pamela."

"I know." She drew a deep breath. "And I regret it more than I can say. You did not—"

"I deserved it. My comment to you was contemptible and mean in spirit. I do not know what it is about you, Pamela. I find myself saying things I should not say and thinking things I have no right to think."

"Oh?" She jerked her chin up. "What kinds of things?"

He yanked her hard into his arms. "I think about the feel of the silken heat of your naked skin against mine."

"Stop it." She pushed against him, but he would not let her go.

"Never." He bent his head and murmured against the

side of her neck. "I think of the manner in which your eyes will darken in the throes of passion."

"Stop," she said again, rather weakly and without the least bit of conviction, and tried to hang on to her anger. And failed.

"I think about the sounds you will make when I give you pleasure you have never imagined."

"Alexei . . ." She shuddered as much with his words as his touch.

"I think about the way your scent will linger on my pillow after you have gone."

"Dear Lord." She could barely gasp out the words. "You have had a great deal of practice at this."

In the tiny, rational part of her mind that still cared about respectability, she noted that while it was extremely early—indeed the park was nearly deserted—this was still a public place, and a display such as Alexei nuzzling her neck in a manner that left her weak was simply not permissible. If she could gather enough strength of will, and if her legs did not collapse, she would tell him so. Any moment now.

"I have thought about you, dearest Pamela, every day, every hour, every minute since we first met." His voice was intoxicating, tempting and irresistible. "Do you recall? The first moment we met? The first time we kissed?"

"Yes, of course." She struggled to breathe, to think. "The first . . . when we . . ." Realization struck like a dash of cold water, and she pushed out of his arms. "You are a beast! A royal, impossible beast! Does it matter if we have met before? Or kissed before?"

"Yes. I am never wrong about things like this. Besides"—he narrowed his gaze—"I dislike secrets, and you, my dear, have secrets."

"Any secrets I might or might not have are none of your concern. You are not, in truth, my fiancé."

"I dislike dishonesty as well."

"Do you?" She tilted her head and considered him. "Yet here you are about to embark on a public deception. Apparently you have no trouble with hypocrisy."

"This is entirely different. I had no choice."

"Then dishonesty is acceptable if one can justify it?"

He gritted his teeth. "Pamela—"

"I have not been dishonest with you, and I deeply resent your implication that I have. I have not told you a single falsehood, nor have I misled you in any way. What I have done is keep my secrets, as you call them, my own." She wagged an accusing finger at him. "I told you on the very first night I preferred to keep my life, my past, private. I know that is difficult for you to understand as you revel in yours and insist on boasting about it."

"I do not boast. I have never—"

"And furthermore"—she thrust out her hand to quiet him—"as much as you claim to dislike dishonesty, I dislike"—she fairly spit the word—"arrogance."

"Arrogance?" He practically sputtered the word. "Arrogance?"

"Yes, arrogance!"

"You cannot possibly be accusing me of arrogance." He stared in complete disbelief. "I have no need of arrogance. Arrogance is for men who need to prove their worth to the world. I am simply confident in the knowl-

edge of who I am and have no need to prove anything."
He crossed his arms over his chest. "I am a prince."

"You don't think you're arrogant? Hah!" She planted
her hands on her hips and mimicked him in her most sarcastic imitation of an overly dramatic European accent.
"I nevair forgeet a woman I ave keessed, and a woman I
ave keessed nevair forgeets me. Do forgive me, Your
Highness, but having now kissed you, I think it was eminently forgettable."

He glared at her. "I do not sound like that."

She shrugged dismissively.

"I speak nine languages fluently, and I scarcely have an
accent in any one of them, let alone one that sounds like a
bad actor in a worse play."

"The accent was not the point."

"Nonetheless, I am highly insulted." Indignation rang
in his voice.

"That was precisely the idea," she snapped, turned, and
started back toward the horses. "If you would be so good
as to help me up, I should like to return home now.
Alone."

"As you wish." He stalked past her to reach the horses
a step or two before her. "I know I would like nothing better than for you to return home. Alone."

He hoisted her onto the sidesaddle in a manner that
could barely be called civil and not at all lingering and
turned away pointedly. Not that she cared, of course.

"I shall leave you in the capable hands of Lady Overton. I see that she and Count Stefanovich are but a short
distance away." His manner was crisp and cool, and she
would have liked nothing so much as to smack him on the

top of his head, very hard. It would have been extremely childish and just as extremely satisfying.

"Excellent." She wheeled her horse around and urged him to a canter.

She spotted Clarissa and the count up ahead and at once slowed to a walk. She could well use a few minutes to consider what had just happened.

Never in a hundred lifetimes would she have imagined he would recognize her from a kiss. She should have paid more attention to that moment the other night when he had asked if they'd met. It had simply slipped her mind. After all, he hadn't been as insistent about it then as he had been now.

Was there really any harm in telling him at this point? Certainly in the beginning she'd feared he'd say something and shatter any possibility of a proper, respectable future. Now she knew he would never say a word. She was confident of his discretion and his honorable nature. In truth, there really wasn't any reason at all why she shouldn't tell him.

Unless, of course, he didn't remember the night they'd shared. It was entirely possible one night spent with one particular woman was insignificant in the story of his life. There had probably been countless such nights with an infinite number of women. Why would she expect that he would remember the one spent with her? And if, or rather, *when* he didn't remember?

It would be quite the most devastating thing she'd ever experienced. Certainly it was foolish on her part to place so much importance on a single night, but it was the most wonderful night of her life. To learn it meant nothing whatsoever to him—well, George's betrayal would pale in comparison.

No, she'd much prefer never to have him know they once spent an enchanted evening together rather than take that risk.

"Clarissa, Count Stefanovich." Pamela nodded in greeting. "Clarissa, I should like to return home now. That is if you would not mind accompanying me."

"Of course," Clarissa said with a smile.

"And I believe I shall join His Highness." The count's gaze met Clarissa's. "It has been a most enjoyable morning, Lady Overton."

"Indeed it has, my lord." An enigmatic half smile curved Clarissa's lips. The very same smile she wore every time Stefanovich was around.

The count touched his hat, turned his horse, and headed off.

Pamela raised a brow. "A lovely morning?"

Clarissa watched him ride off, that content smile lingering on her face. "Following a rather exceptional evening."

"Oh?"

Clarissa pulled her gaze away from the count's retreating figure. "I like him, Pamela. Quite a lot. I never thought I'd ever like a man again as much as I do this one."

"He is probably as vile as his prince," Pamela said grimly.

"He is not the least bit vile, and I doubt that his prince is either." Clarissa glanced at her cousin. "What has His Highness done?"

"He is convinced that I have grave secrets, and he insists

on knowing what they are. He is both arrogant and demanding, royal if you will, none of which I find especially attractive."

"Grave secrets?" Clarissa laughed. "I hardly think so."

"He does. He insists we have met somewhere before and is most annoyed that I will not confirm his conviction." She headed her horse toward the far distant park gate.

Clarissa's horse walked beside Pamela's and for a few minutes they rode in silence.

"So," Clarissa said at last. "Have you?"

For a long moment Pamela said nothing at all. At last she heaved a sigh of surrender. "Perhaps."

Clarissa nodded in a knowing manner. "The prince is the gentleman from Venice, isn't he? The one who never saw your face? The one you've been dreaming about ever since?"

Pamela nodded. "You don't sound at all surprised."

"I'm not. In spite of your denials, I suspected it all along." Clarissa chuckled. "Between your reaction when you first saw him, Aunt Millicent's recalling that she had met him when we were in Venice, and the way you look at him, well, it was obvious."

"Do you think Aunt Millicent knows?"

"She might. That could be precisely why she is so determined to keep the two of you apart. Or she could think now that we are back in London, she should at last become a responsible chaperone."

"As opposed to a chaperone who encouraged both of us to experience life however we wished?"

"She never was a traditional sort of chaperone,"

Clarissa said wryly. "However, I should think it's more than likely that she's noticed not merely the way you look at him but the way he looks at you as well."

"He looks at all women that way." Pamela waved away the comment. "He is that sort of man."

"Perhaps, but there is something in his eyes when his gaze settles on you. Something I cannot quite define . . ." Clarissa shrugged. "Of course, I know nothing about men." She paused. "Are you going to tell him that he's right then? That you have indeed met? In truth, much more than merely met."

"No." Pamela shook her head. "I never expected that he would recognize me. Indeed, I took great care to make certain of that. But if he doesn't remember that particular night at all, and I would be surprised if he did, well, I don't want to know. It would be most humiliating and, frankly, rather devastating." She blew a long breath. "Besides, I have no idea how to approach the subject. I can't simply walk up to him with an 'I say, Your Highness, it's the most amusing thing but we did indeed meet several years ago, in your bed if I recall.' "

"That would be rather awkward."

"Awkward? Hah! No." Pamela set her jaw firmly. "It's best that I say nothing at all."

"I see." Clarissa studied her. "And what if he does remember?"

"I don't know." Pamela thought for a moment. "I've never seriously considered that."

"What if he has spent the last four years thinking about you? Dreaming about the unknown woman who shared his bed in Venice? What if, beyond a number of other things, that is the real reason, a reason of the heart as it were, why he has never married? What if he has been looking for you?"

Pamela scoffed. "That's absurd." Even so, it was an idea worth pondering. "Is it possible, do you think?"

Clarissa glanced over her shoulder in the direction the count had taken and smiled. "Anything is possible, cousin dear."

"Do you realize this changes everything?" Pamela reined her horse to a halt. Excitement sounded in her voice. "If indeed he has thought about me the way I have thought about him, why there is no reason we can't be together."

"You said he would still be a match for a princess."

"Nonsense." She shrugged. "I was being kind. What princess would have him without a country? Politically, he's practically worthless."

"Pamela!"

"Oh, come now, Clarissa, you know it's true. But I'd have him. Indeed, I want him. I've always wanted him. And we'd be perfect together. A prince and an Effington."

"An exiled prince," Clarissa said cautiously.

"And I'm a ruined Effington. We were made for each other!" Pamela grinned with sheer delight. "And we are already engaged. It's scarcely any distance at all from betrothed to wed."

"It's not a real engagement. Besides, you don't know—"

"You're right I don't." Pamela drew her brows together and thought for a moment. "But you can find out for me."

"Me?" Clarissa's eyes widened. "How?"

"The count will know. I would wager he and the captain know all of Alexei's secrets." Pamela chuckled. "No doubt His Highness has all sorts of secrets. Probably why he wants to know mine."

Clarissa narrowed her eyes. "How, precisely, do you propose I get this information from the count?"

"The same way women have always gotten information from men," Pamela said blithely. "After all, you are sharing his bed and—"

Clarissa gasped. "I most certainly am not!"

"You said you had an exceptional evening."

"I did." Clarissa sputtered with indignation. "We talked. We strolled in the garden. We gazed at the stars. We kissed. Once!"

"Oh." Pamela considered the other woman. "But you will be sharing his bed?"

"I have no intention—"

Pamela raised a skeptical brow.

"Very well, I have every intention." Clarissa huffed. "But I am certainly not going to slide into a man's bed just to get information about another man for you."

"Of course not." Pamela forced a shocked expression to her face. "That would be wrong."

"Yes, it would."

"However," Pamela said in a casual manner, "if you find yourself in his bed and the subject happens to come up—"

"Pamela!"

"Goodness, cousin, it's not as if I am asking you to seduce him." Pamela leaned forward eagerly. "At that point, the seduction part of it will have already been accomplished. I'm simply asking that afterward, or before if you prefer, not during, as that would be most awkward and would definitely arouse suspicion among other things, that you ask a few casual questions about—"

"Very well, I'll do it," Clarissa snapped.

"Really?"

"Yes." Clarissa sighed. "I will find out what you need to know although I might not do so in Roman's bed. When I join him in his bed it will be for reasons that have nothing to do with you or the prince. And you and His Highness will be the farthest thing from my mind."

"Of course. And you certainly do not need to question him while in his bed. It just seemed that as you are obviously, well, probably, rather soon I suspect—"

"Yes, yes, probably." Clarissa blew a long breath. "I have no idea why I've agreed to do this."

"I do." Pamela grinned. "Because I am your dearest friend in the world, and you would do anything for me. Because if I were indeed to marry Alexei, the count would be free to follow his own heart. Because as you are obviously going to end up in the count's bed anyway, it might as well serve a dual purpose."

Clarissa met her cousin's gaze firmly. "You do realize there is still every possibility that he does not remember that night. Only a few moments ago you said you didn't want to know. Have you changed your mind?"

"Yes. No." Pamela drew a deep breath. "Yes. It seems a risk I must take." She paused to find the right words. "I have always wondered, or perhaps hoped, that our night together meant as much to him as it did to me but I knew that was more than likely a forlorn hope. Being with him now, the way I feel about him—"

"You care for him then?"

"It seems rather absurd, I know, and in truth it could just be unrepentant lust, but I'm very much afraid I would like to spend the rest of my days finding out." She winced. "So much for my intentions of a respectable life."

"But you do want marriage?"

"I do, but only with him, which does rather defeat the entire purpose of Aunt Millicent's feigned engagement plan." Pamela fell silent for a long moment, then sighed. "I never told you, but I could have become his mistress four years ago. I did not want that then, nor shall I accept it now. If that one night was as special to him as it was to me, then there might well be a chance for a future. If not"—she squared her shoulders—"then I shall never tell him what we once shared. I shall put the past behind me and rely on what we seem to have between us now."

"Well, I shall do all I can to find out what Roman might know. It's not really that much to ask." Clarissa cast her a reluctant smile. "And I do intend to enjoy every minute."

Pamela laughed. "As I intend to enjoy being the fiancée of a prince. Real or otherwise."

Clarissa studied her cousin. "Is he really what you want?"

"I hadn't realized it until now, but he is not merely what I want." Determination sounded in Pamela's voice. "One way or another"—she grinned—"he is what I will have."

"Have you learned anything yet?" Alexei asked the moment Roman pulled his horse up beside him.

"And a good day to you, Your Highness," Roman said with a wry smile. "How was your chat with Miss Effington?"

"Perhaps the most irritating conversation I've ever had." Alexei shook his head. "I am never certain if I wish to take her in my arms and kiss her senseless or wrap my hands around her neck." He glanced at his friend. "Do you think I have an accent that sounds like something from a poorly acted play?"

"Not at all, Your Highness," Roman said indignantly.

"Or that I am arrogant?"

Roman hesitated, then chose his words with care. "Arrogance is a question of degree I should think."

"Then I am?"

"I believe I would use the word *proud.*"

Alexei snorted. "Semantics."

Roman bit back a grin.

"Miss Effington thinks I'm arrogant."

"Nonetheless, she likes you. A great deal I should think."

"I suspected as much." Alexei grinned.

Roman laughed. "It's fairly apparent in the way she looks at you when she thinks you are not looking. Which is rather difficult to do as you seem to be watching her every minute."

Alexei winced. "Am I that obvious?"

"Perhaps not to everyone, Your Highness, but I have been in your service for some time and your friend for much longer."

"Does Lady Overton think she likes me?"

"Forgive me for saying so, Your Highness," Roman

said, choosing his words with care, "but Lady Overton and I have found any number of subjects to discuss other than you and Miss Effington."

"Yes of course. And somewhat arrogant of me to think you would spend your time in the company of a beautiful woman in a discussion of my concerns. My apologies, Roman."

"Accepted." Roman grinned. "Nonetheless, in the course of a discussion of interest to Lady Overton and me, I was able to learn about the scandal in Miss Effington's past."

"Excellent." Alexei held his breath. He really had no idea what to expect. He was fast learning that expectations when it came to Pamela were rather pointless. She was a continuing source of surprise. "Go on."

"According to Lady Overton, Miss Effington was extremely shy and not overly attractive as a child. She did not—what is the word she used? Ah yes, *bloom* as it were until she was nearly twenty. It was almost inevitable, therefore, that she would fall in love with the first man who paid her any notice." Roman shrugged. "Unfortunately for Miss Effington that was a scoundrel named George Fenton, now Lord Penwick. Apparently, she believed his intentions were honorable when they were not. Unbeknownst to Miss Effington, his marriage to the heiress of a substantial fortune had been arranged in his childhood."

"I see," Alexei said grimly. It was not an uncommon story although he would have thought Pamela was more intelligent than to be fooled by such a man. Still, she had been young and naïve, and women often do stupid things in the name of love.

"Her family might have kept Miss Effington's indiscretion from becoming public knowledge had Penwick not bragged about his conquest. Gossip being what it is, Lady Overton said everyone knew of it in no time, and Miss Effington's reputation was ruined."

"Why was Penwick not made to marry her?"

"Her family certainly could have forced such a marriage, but when she discovered he was promised to someone else, Miss Effington realized he did not share her affection and further realized she had been something of a fool. She refused to consider marriage and wanted nothing whatsoever to do with him."

"That is the Miss Effington I have come to know." Alexei nodded with satisfaction. While it was perhaps not the wisest course for a ruined young lady of good family, it showed a fair amount of courage.

"She then joined her cousin and her aunt, and they have traveled the world ever since, only returning to London when they inherited the house." Roman paused. "Her cousin says she has changed a great deal from the reserved, quiet creature she once was."

"Quiet and reserved?"

"Difficult to imagine I know, Your Highness, yet Lady Overton swears it is true."

"Miss Effington said something about that. What was it?" He thought for a moment. "Something about having worn a shoe, no, having *been* a shoe that did not fit."

Roman's brow furrowed. "That makes no sense."

"In truth, Roman, it does. Not everyone is fortunate enough always to understand his own nature. To never doubt his own worth or abilities and to have the confidence such understanding provides. Or if you will"—he smiled—"the arrogance."

"Then arrogance is not necessarily a bad thing, Your Highness."

"You are a loyal sort, Roman."

Roman laughed. "Indeed, I am. There I was alone with a woman who may well be all I have ever wanted—"

Alexei pulled his horse to a stop and stared. "What?"

Roman grimaced. "Not precisely what I had planned, but—"

"But this is not the sort of thing one does plan." Alexei slapped his old friend across the back. "It is the sort of thing that smacks you across the face when you least expect it."

Roman nodded reluctantly. "The sort of thing that twists your stomach until you wonder that you can eat at all."

"That turns you into a blithering idiot."

"Precisely at the very time you need all your wits about you."

"That makes you question your sanity for even thinking for a moment that a woman as annoying as she is could be the one woman who has captured your heart."

Roman chuckled. "Your Highness, I daresay Lady Over—"

Alexei continued without pause. "The sort of thing that brings to mind absurd questions of forever and until death and all those things that cannot possibly work because you are who you are."

"Your Highness, I cannot imagine—"

"And makes you realize when you had the world to offer you could give nothing but your heart, and now all you have is your heart and nothing else." His words seemed to come of their own accord. "So it is beyond ridiculous to so much as consider the idea of falling in love, let alone marriage, even if at the point that you realize it you realize as well that it might be too late."

"Your Highness—"

"That you may have already lost your heart, but it scarcely matters because you cannot burden her with what you have become, with the pathetic remains of your life because, in truth, regardless of how you feel, there can be no future for the two of you. And you care for her too much to allow her to share a fate you detest and condemn her to watch you wallow in regret for the rest of her days."

Roman's mouth dropped open, and he stared.

At once, Alexei was struck by what he had said. Just how much he had revealed. Not just to Roman but to himself. He had not realized how he felt about himself and his future. And he had not noticed he had been falling in love. Why would he? He had only felt even remotely like this once, and he never saw her face. Now he knew full well the face of the lady who had captured his heart. He could see it with his eyes closed. The curve of her cheek. The arch of her brow. The sable darkness of her eyes.

Not that it mattered.

He shrugged his comments off. "You do understand I am speaking in a strictly theoretical sense."

"Theoretical? Exactly what I was thinking, Your Highness." A casual note sounded in Roman's voice. "In a nontheoretical sense, would you care to know what else I have discovered about Miss Effington?"

"As you went to the trouble . . ." Alexei's tone matched his friend's as if anything regarding Pamela was of no particular concern.

"Only that it is entirely possible Miss Effington was indeed your mysterious liaison in Venice. The dates of your respective stays in that city four years ago overlap considerably."

"I see." Was it at all possible? Just two days ago he had been certain it wasn't. Now . . .

"Are you going to confront Miss Effington then?"

"She denies we have ever met. No, upon reflection . . ." Alexei searched his memory. "In truth, the blasted woman does not deny it at all, she simply evades the question. Or twists it to her own advantage. One minute I'm demanding to know where we have met, the next I am an arrogant ass." He chuckled. "Oh, she is a devious creature."

"As are you," Roman said smoothly. "What do you intend to do?"

"I intend to find out the truth, and I will use whatever means at my disposal. I may not know her face, and I may well have enjoyed any number of other women in my life, but I have never forgotten so much as one detail of that night. If she is the one, I will know." His blood quickened at the thought.

"Seduction?"

"Reunion. An entirely different thing from seduction."

"And if this woman who has already apparently captured your heart is the woman who has long haunted your dreams, what then Your Highness?"

What then indeed?

"I do not know. I never imagined I would find her again even if I have always believed there was an element of destiny in that particular night. If they are one and the same . . . I shall face that revelation when, or if, I come to it." He narrowed his gaze. "Miss Effington insists on playing a game with me, Roman. She has laid down a challenge with her refusal to answer my questions, and if she has nothing to hide it makes no sense. However, I have no particular aversion to games, and I always win. And that, old friend, is not arrogance but a simple statement of fact."

"It is a dangerous game, is it not, Your Highness?" Roman's voice was casual, as if his words did not matter. "Your heart may already be at stake, and to my knowledge you have never risked your heart before."

"There is risk in any game where there is only one victor."

Perhaps there could be no future with Pamela or Serenissima. Perhaps there could only be today.

"My life seems to be filled these days with things I have never done before. With a fate that is uncertain. This is no different. But I have always enjoyed games, puzzles, and the like. And regardless of the outcome"—he smiled in a wry manner—"I intend to enjoy this one."

Nine

 When I see Millicent again I absolutely will not allow her to see that she once broke my heart. I shall be remote and aloof. Furthermore, I shall resist the urge to put her over my knee and spank her thoroughly. After her years abroad she might well like it.

Sir Winchester Roberts

"Miss Effington—Pamela—I am so pleased you agreed to see me." Alexei crossed the library floor to greet Pamela with an eager step. Her heart fluttered at the look in his eye. "I feared after our ride this morning you would avoid me. You were gone most of the day."

"I was with my family. It was most enjoyable. As for avoiding you—nonsense." Pamela favored him with her brightest smile. One would never have imagined a scant few hours ago she had been ready to throttle him. Of course, he had been ready to throttle her as well. "Be-

191

sides, I could scarcely ignore a note as charming as yours, Your Highness." She held out her hand.

"Alexei."

"It held the proper tone of apology then?" He raised her hand to his lips.

"Indeed it did."

"An appropriate amount of remorse?" His gaze locked on hers.

"Appropriate, yes."

"As well as regret." He turned her hand over and kissed the inside of her wrist. "Repentance."

She arched a brow. "It was not that long a note."

"Do you forgive me then?"

"Yes, of course." As much as she would have left her hand in his forever, she pulled it away. "What, specifically, am I to forgive you for?"

He gasped in feigned disbelief. "Why, for my boorish, arrogant attitude, of course. Your secrets are your secrets, your past is your past. And if we have indeed met in the past, and you do not wish to acknowledge it, I can only imagine you have your reasons."

"You can?" She studied him curiously. Alexei did not strike her as the kind of man to give up easily.

"What I cannot imagine is what they are although any number of possibilities come to mind."

"Do they?"

"I have a surprisingly fertile imagination on occasion, Pamela, and I have been allowing it free rein to speculate on the question of why a woman I have met, indeed, a woman I know I have kissed—"

"Because you never forget a woman that you kiss?"

"Exactly."

"Dare I ask what answers you have arrived at?"

"I was hoping you would." He clasped his hands behind his back and paced the room in perfect imitation of a Latin tutor she'd had as a girl. "First, I thought perhaps you had had a horrible accident and lost your memory entirely."

She shook her head. "I don't recall ever losing my memory."

"Ah, but then you would not remember if you had, would you?"

"Excellent point."

"Then I considered the possibility that the kiss in question was an embarrassment for one of us, or both of us, and you have therefore hidden it away with other unpleasant memories of your past."

She stifled a smile. "Not a good kiss then?"

"Rather far-fetched I know, but a possibility nonetheless. Next, I wondered if perhaps my kiss had, well, spoiled you for anyone else, ever, and you had thought it best to put it out of your mind altogether." He glanced at her. "In the interest of avoiding disappointment in the future of course."

"I see." She bit her lip to keep from laughing. "If your kiss—"

"On further thought, I believe it would more appropriate to call it *our* kiss."

"Very well. Either *our* kiss was so dreadful I would not wish to remember it or so wonderful I would force myself to forget it because"—she shook her head in confusion—"how was that again?"

"Because you would compare every other man to me and"—he flashed her a wicked grin—"they would not fare well."

She laughed.

"You must admit that last part sounds quite conceivable."

"Rather an arrogant answer though, don't you think?"

"Yes, well, apparently arrogance is my cross to bear in addition to my charm. What do you think of my theories?"

"Very good." She grinned. "Quite plausible."

"Do any sound, oh, accurate?"

She thought for a moment. "I should term them interesting rather than accurate."

"I am glad you think so." He bit back a smile, then waved at a tray bearing a teapot, cups, and a biscuit plate placed on one side of the table near the fireplace. The ever-present decanter of brandy and glasses remained on the other side of the table, thanks to the always efficient Graham. "Would you care for refreshment? I thought you might like tea or even brandy if you prefer. This late in the day, I enjoy a good brandy although it may well still be too early for you."

"Tea would be fine. I suspect I shall need all my wits about me."

Alexei grinned in a most knowing way that did the oddest things to the pit of her stomach.

This would never do. In another minute she would throw herself into his arms. She drew a steadying breath and glanced around. "Is Graham hiding in the shadows, or shall I pour it myself?"

Alexei chuckled. "Neither Graham nor your aunt is anywhere to be found at the moment. I have made certain of it."

"Have you?" She moved to the tray, poured a cup then perched on the edge of a sofa. "Why?

"Because I wish to speak with you alone."

She narrowed her gaze. "Why?"

He laughed. "Come now, Pamela, you need not look at me that way. I have apologized. I have even groveled a bit—"

"Hardly."

"Admittedly I do not grovel well." He shrugged. "I have had very little practice."

"I should be happy to help you do something about that." She smiled sweetly.

"I am certain you would. Another time perhaps." His tone was brisk. "As to your question, I simply do not think we know each other well enough to be able to carry off this charade of ours. We appear in public for the first time tomorrow, and there are any number of things I do not know about you."

She sipped her tea and studied him over the rim of her cup. "What would you like to know?"

"Well, I think a man who intends to marry a woman would know, oh, say, what color she prefers."

"Blue."

"The blue of the sea during a storm or the blue of the sky at midday?"

"A storm I should think," she said without pause. "I rather like storms."

"Excellent choice." An intriguing gleam sparked in his clear, brown eyes. "Flowers?

"Roses."

"Of course. Red?"

"Yellow."

"How every interesting." He sipped his brandy thoughtfully. "Composer?"

"I like any number of composers. Haydn, Bach." She thought for a moment. "Schubert."

"Books?"

"Far too many to mention." She set down her cup, rose to her feet, and moved to the nearest bookshelf. Her gaze skimmed the spines of books that looked as if they had not been disturbed for years, but she was far more aware of Alexei pouring himself a brandy than of any of the titles before her. "I have always rather liked stories of adventure. *Emmeline* was a favorite when I was a girl, as well as *The Mysteries of Udolpho* and *Cecilia*."

"You prefer stories of adventure primarily about women then?"

"Yes, I do. But I also liked *Robinson Crusoe*." She glanced at him. "And *Tom Jones*."

"How very interesting," he murmured.

She laughed and returned her attention to the shelves and a set of Shakespeare's plays. "I like Shakespeare, of course, but only the comedies. I find the histories and tragedies far too dark in spirit. Although I have always been fond of *Antony and Cleopatra*, in spite of the ending."

He moved to stand behind her and studied the shelves. If she turned abruptly, there was a very good chance she would be in his arms. And then there was an excellent possibility he would take the opportunity afforded to him to kiss—

"What about *Romeo and Juliet*?" He reached out and traced a title with the tip of his finger. "I thought women, particularly women with a penchant toward romance, liked *Romeo and Juliet*."

"And you think I have a penchant for romance?"

"I do not know." She felt him lean closer. His words sounded beside her ear. "I rather hope so."

"Do you?" She held her breath. "Why?"

"Because I have a fondness for romance myself." His words were low and seductive, his breath warm against her ear.

She swallowed hard. "I have never been particularly fond of *Romeo and Juliet*."

"No?" His lips brushed the side of her neck. "You do not care for Romeo's declarations of love?"

"His declarations are meaningless given the end of the play." She shook her head and tried to ignore the altogether wonderful sensations he was expertly producing. "I fear I find it entirely too sad."

"I can certainly understand that." He nuzzled the crook of her neck, and delight shuddered through her. "They do die at the end after all."

"The entire story is heartbreaking. Star-crossed lovers doomed never to be together. Yet they could love no one else. They were destined for each other, one made for the other as if halves of the same whole."

He stilled. "Do you believe in that sort of thing?"

Was he always going to do this? Just when she was about to melt into a puddle at his feet, he changed the subject. It was becoming most annoying. "What sort of thing?"

"Destiny. That two people might be fated for one another? Halves of the same whole?"

"Yes," she said slowly. She hadn't when she'd first met him, but then all she had intended was a single night. She'd had no idea that night would stay in her dreams, in her heart, forever. Indeed, only today had she come to the realization that they were perfect for one another. That he was most likely the only man in the world for her.

He straightened. "Which play of Shakespeare's do you like best then?"

She sighed. "*All's Well that Ends Well* I suppose."

"And your favorite sweet?"

"I don't know." She wanted nothing more than to bang her head in frustration on the bookshelves. "Strawberry tarts."

"Do you prefer dogs or cats?"

"Dogs." This was absurd.

"Your favorite place?"

"Ven—" She caught herself and whirled to face him. "Vienna."

He braced a hand on the bookshelves on either side of her and grinned. "Ven-Vienna? Charming place. I believe I visited there once. The food wasn't very good though if I recall."

"I meant to say Vienna," she said in a lofty manner.

"You meant to say Venice."

He had her effectively trapped between his arms. Not necessarily a bad position to be in if one weren't trying to evade questions and one's own growing desire. "Very well then, I confess."

He chuckled. "I thought you might."

"I did indeed start to say Venice, but then I changed

my mind." She smiled. "I decided that in truth I preferred Vienna."

"Come now, Pamela." He looked annoyingly smug as if he could read her very thoughts.

Surely he couldn't have connected her to the woman he had met in Venice? It was entirely far-fetched even to consider that Pamela and Serenissima would be one and the same. Unless, of course, he did indeed remember their night together, and had somehow managed to match her presence there with his. He did claim a fertile imagination after all.

Still, did he care? Was it at all significant to him, or was this simply one of those puzzles he enjoyed unraveling?

"You cannot possibly prefer Vienna, or indeed anywhere else in the world, to Venice."

"And yet I do." She met his gaze coolly.

"Do you?" His gaze searched hers. "Why?"

She shrugged. "It's one of the great capitals of the world. It is the center of art and music—"

"And coffeehouses."

"And coffeehouses." She laughed.

"And yet"—he leaned close and brushed his lips lightly across hers—"it is lacking in the very element that makes Venice so very special."

"Oh?" Dear Lord he was good. He fogged her mind and muddled her senses. Was it really necessary to ignore her own desire?

"Magic," he said softly.

"I daresay Vienna has magic." After all, it wasn't as if they hadn't been together before.

"Do you realize, Pamela, you are precisely the right height for me?" His gaze bored into hers.

She raised her chin slightly. "I hadn't noticed."

"It is extraordinarily easy to kiss you. As if you were made just for me."

"Perhaps you were made for me?"

He chuckled. "Perhaps."

She drew a deep breath. Either she was going to drag him bodily to his bed, or it was time to put some distance between them.

"Is there anything else you would like to know about me?" she said in a casual manner that belied the hammering of her heart.

"I should like to know everything about you." He kissed the altogether too-sensitive spot below her ears. "Where to touch to make you tremble as you are doing now."

"I'm not trembling," she said in a voice that wasn't the least bit steady.

His lips whispered against the base of her throat. "Where to kiss you to feel your skin flush beneath my lips."

She tried to ignore all the images his words brought to mind. "This really isn't—"

"Or whether you will call out my name in—"

"That's quite enough," she said in the firmest manner she could muster. "You are being entirely inappropriate. Quite scandalous and impertinent, and I should slap your face very hard for that."

He grinned. "Would you?"

"No. You would like it entirely too much." She gathered the fragments of her resolve, ducked under his arm, and stepped out of reach. "Need I remind you, Alexei, the

entire purpose of our engagement is to restore my position in society with the eventual goal of finding a suitable
husband."

He snorted. "You would not be happy with a suitable
sort of husband."

She stared. "Why on earth not?"

He shrugged: "I simply cannot see you with someone
suitable. You would be bored within a week."

"Don't be absurd." She moved to pick up her teacup,
carried it to the brandy decanter, poured a healthy dollop
into her cup, and took a long swallow. Aunt Millicent
had always said, and Pamela had always agreed, a touch
of brandy in tea, or perhaps it was a touch of tea in
brandy, helped to steady one's nerves. Her nerves could
certainly use steadying at the moment. "I shall probably
be quite content."

He raised a brow. "Content?"

"Happy. I meant to say happy. Even blissful."

"Rubbish." He picked up his glass and swirled his
brandy. "I have met any number of Englishmen, and
aside from my cousin and yours as well perhaps, I have
never met one who is not dull, rather sanctimonious, and
surprisingly arrogant."

"You're arrogant."

"Yes, but my arrogance is justified."

She rolled her gaze toward the ceiling.

"You have spent years traveling, visiting any number of
foreign lands, meeting any number of interesting people.
I would wager it has changed you rather dramatically."

"I've already admitted to that."

"I do not mean the manner in which you have become

more like the rest of your family. That was obviously always a part of your nature that you had yet to develop and came with age and experience and probably the absence of the influence of the Effingtons."

"Probably," she said wryly, and took another sip of the brandy-laden tea. It was really quite tasty.

"What I mean is that you are different in the way in which you see the world. Certainly, through your years of travel you have spent a great deal of time with the elite of society, the wealthy, royalty, and the like, but you have, as well, experienced cultures and customs of countries you never would have known had you not left England."

"Travel is always something of an education. It's part of the enjoyment of it."

"And I suspect it has made you far less likely to accept the suitable sort of husband you would have accepted six years ago."

She drew her brows together in annoyance. "Even then I certainly wouldn't have accepted anyone, just for the sake of marrying."

"No, I daresay you would not."

"Not that I think you're at all correct about Englishmen, mind you, but what kind of man do you think I should marry?"

"Someone with an adventurous nature. And courage, of course. I suspect marriage to you would require a fair amount of courage."

"Thank you."

"I am not entirely certain that was a compliment." He chuckled. "You require someone with a fair amount of in-

telligence as well. You have an exceptionally sharp mind."
He raised his glass to her. "*That* was a compliment."

"Again, my thanks."

"Beyond that, you need someone who can appreciate
the uniqueness of your character. Who will not try to
mold you into the perfect, docile creature Englishmen appear to prefer. Who will see you as a challenge that stirs
his blood."

"A challenge to stir the blood?" She laughed. "That is a
compliment."

"Indeed it is." His gaze met hers, and her breath
caught.

"Dare I hope to find such a paragon?" *Although in
truth I have found him already.* "Indeed, he seems too
perfect to be a mortal man."

"Ah, but he is not perfect, Pamela." He sipped his
brandy and studied her thoughtfully. "You would not do
well with perfect, nor would perfect do well with you.
You need a man who would challenge you as much as you
challenge him. A man to do battle with."

"And what of love?"

He chuckled. "Love is an interesting question."

"Have you ever been in love?" She held her breath.

"I do not know." He shrugged. "Perhaps. Perhaps not."

"Surely you would know if you—"

"I see your rules are for you alone."

She shook her head. "What do you mean?"

"Simply that you wish no discussion of your past, yet
mine is apparently a topic of vast interest."

"You like discussing your past."

"Much of it I do." He shook his head. "But not this."

"Why not?"

"It is entirely too personal."

"More personal than your romantic conquests?"

"Apparently."

She studied him for a moment. "Was your heart broken then? At some time in the past?"

He sighed. "You certainly have no understanding of the word *no*, do you?"

"I simply think there are some things a fiancée would know about her betrothed," she said lightly.

"I do so enjoy having my words turned around to suit you. Very well then, Pamela, no." His tone was firm. "My heart has never been broken. It was . . . twisted once, even bent perhaps, although I did not realize it until much later."

"Oh?" Her own heart sped up.

"It was a moment, nothing more than that. Stolen really from the realities of life." He shrugged. "It was never intended to be more than a moment and yet . . ."

"And yet?"

"And yet it was." He paused, and she wondered if he was thinking about their moment or if it was something altogether different. At last he drew a deep breath. "And you?"

"And I what?"

"Have you ever been in love?"

"Excellent change of topic, Alexei." She laughed softly.

His gaze met hers, sharp and intense as if he could see right through her. "And only fair that you answer."

"Yes, I suppose it is." She sipped her tea. "I thought I was in love once, but I was mistaken."

"Only once then?"

"I was mistaken only once, yes."

He stared for a moment then laughed. "And I daresay I shall get no more from you than that."

She grinned. "Am I still a challenge then? Still a mystery to be unraveled?"

"Always I suspect." His tone was mild, but the look in his eye remained.

"But not today." She drained the last of her drink, placed her cup on the table, and rose to her feet. "Clarissa and I have errands, and I must be off."

"Pity. I had rather hoped to spend the rest of the afternoon together to . . . talk."

"Just to talk?"

"You are annoying." He heaved a resigned sigh, set his glass down, and, before she could say a word, moved to her and took her in his arms. "Most annoying."

His kiss was hard, decisive almost, as if he were claiming her as his own. And, dear Lord, she wanted him to claim her, mark her, own her. As she would own him in return. She wrapped her arms around his neck and reveled in the power of the need that tied them together. No, more than mere need. Recognition. Of the half that made her whole. Did he feel it as well? Or did he feel nothing but lust? And did she care? Here and now she was in his arms, and here and now, little else mattered.

She pulled back and stared up at him, her voice annoyingly breathless. "Are you planning on seducing me?"

His voice was nearly as unsteady as hers. "What? Here? Now? In a library?"

She nodded. "Here and now?"

"A library is rather cursory, is it not?" He blew a long breath. "And rather insulting as well, I should think."

"Insulting?"

"Why, it shows a definite lack of planning." He grinned slowly, in that wicked way he had that shivered through her blood. "No, I had not really thought about seduction in a library, but it has a certain appeal I suppose. Particularly"—he brushed his lips across hers—"right now."

She couldn't help a slight sigh. "Then you weren't planning to seduce me?"

He chuckled. "I do rather like the note of disappointment in your voice."

"I am not disappointed," she said indignantly, and tried to push out of his arms, but he held her fast.

"Oh, do not mistake my words, Pamela. I fully intend to seduce you." His gaze searched hers. "Or perhaps I shall allow you to seduce me."

She gasped. "Why, I would never . . ."

"Never?" His brow rose.

"Well, perhaps once." She wrapped her arms around his neck and pulled his lips back to hers. She kissed him until she felt her knees might well buckle beneath her, then reluctantly drew away. "Or twice."

"Only twice?"

She stepped away. "You are very good at this. Your reputation is well-founded."

"Surely you did not doubt it?"

"Not for a moment." She caught his gaze, an unyielding note in her voice. "I should warn you, Alexei, I am entirely serious about my desire for marriage. I will not allow emotions or desire or lust to sweep aside good judgment."

"I expect no less of you." He paused, as if choosing his words. "I should warn you as well, Pamela, I have no intention of marrying. Ever."

A heavy weight settled in the pit of her stomach. She ignored it and kept the tone of her voice matter-of-fact. "As long as we understand one another." She nodded. "Then I shall see you at dinner?"

"I would not miss it." His voice was as cool as his eyes, and she had no idea what he was thinking.

"Until this evening then." She forced a pleasant smile and headed toward the door.

Her own thoughts were muddled and horribly confused. She wanted him now and wanted as well to be with him for the rest of his days. And if she could not do so as his wife, would she be willing to settle for less?

She had no idea. She only knew she could not live without him.

"Pamela."

"Yes?" she said without turning around.

"You do realize my intentions have not changed? I want you in my bed, and I will have you."

She hesitated for an endless moment, her fingers on the door handle. At last she drew a long, shuddering breath and cast him a brilliant smile over her shoulder.

"I shall look forward to it."

The door snapped closed behind her, and he stared at it unseeing.

What in God's name was he thinking? Or was he thinking at all?

He was right. He knew it now as surely as he knew his own name. He should have realized it from their first kiss, but he never would have imagined the irate Miss Effington would be the inestimable Serenissima. His Serenissima. The woman of his dreams.

He snatched up his glass, strode to the brandy decanter, and refilled the glass, ignoring the way the liquor sloshed over the side. He tossed it back with an unsteady hand and immediately filled the glass again.

And he never would have known at all if not for this absurd farce of an engagement. Indeed, if not for being thrown in one another's company, he never would have suspected the truth. Never would have found her again.

But to what end?

Alexei pulled the earbob, her earbob, from his waistcoat pocket and stared at it. The Venetian glass caught the late-afternoon sunlight and twinkled in his hand as if it had a life of its own. As if it was magic.

He never imagined he'd find her again. He had toyed through the years with the idea of searching for her, but he had no idea where to start. Shortly after his sojourn in Venice his life had become far and away too embroiled in matters of state and politics and the survival of his country to pay any attention to matters of the heart. Besides, he had nothing save an earbob and the memory of a face seen only by starlight, and even that grew vague with the passage of time and far too many dreams, until he was not certain what was memory and what was illusion.

But he remembered the feel of her skin beneath his hands. And the way her body meshed perfectly with his. And her kiss.

It struck him now that even before he had realized the truth, possibly from the very moment Pamela had ordered him out of the house, there was something about her that had called to something in him. Something indefinable but no less compelling. And struck him as well that whatever he felt for her, and he feared it was indeed love, had blossomed well before he so much as suspected Pamela and Serenissima could be one and the same.

Still, it made perfect sense. Regardless of name or circumstance, she was half of his soul. He knew it four years ago, and he knew it now. She was his fate, his destiny. His love.

To what end indeed?

He had meant everything that he had said to Roman this morning. He could not allow the woman that he loved to share his fate. It was bad enough that he had allowed Roman and Dimitri to share it. He had no country, no future and, for the moment at least, no money. His fate was as uncertain as the winds. He had nothing to offer her except his heart, and that was simply not enough.

No. The best thing he could do for Pamela was proceed with their farce exactly as it had first been planned. He would play the perfect royal fiancé and ensure her acceptance into London society. He would make certain every man who saw her saw her through his eyes until she found a man she could marry. Then he would allow her to break it off with him and make sure the rest of the world saw her actions as wise and justified.

And there would be no more talk, or thought, of seduction.

She would never understand any of it, of course. He

Ten

When I see him again I shall apologize profusely and beg his forgiveness. Or, better yet, I could simply flee the country. Yes, I like that.

Millicent, Lady Smythe-Windom

"Your Highness?"

Effington House, the London home of the Duke of Roxborough, was certainly not a palace, but it was most impressive nonetheless, as were the festivities. The grand ballroom was overflowing with guests, the din of the crowd drowning the efforts of the musicians. Still, Alexei scarcely noticed. His gaze skimmed the gathering, searching for one guest in particular.

Pamela and Lady Overton had spent the day with her family in preparation for the evening, and he had not laid eyes on her since dinner last night. She had been remarkably quiet at dinner, but then, so had he.

"Your Highness?"

Even Lady Smythe-Windom had abandoned him,

claiming a need to be present before the start of the ball. He and Roman had arrived a scant half an hour ago. If there was a saving grace to tonight, it was that he needn't worry about anything Valentina might say or do. Given her past encounters with the Effington family, they had agreed that the princess, and therefore Dimitri as well, would not attend the ball. It was an indication of Valentina's desire for reformation that, while she was not at all happy, she grudgingly agreed her absence was for the best.

Alexei rather envied her at the moment. Here in Pamela's uncle's house he was remarkably ill at ease. In truth he could not remember ever having been so ill at ease before. It was not the deception of their false engagement that bothered him. After all, he had had no choice in the matter, and ultimately all this was in Pamela's best interest. No, it was his own turbulent emotions that set his nerves on edge. How could he possibly spend an entire evening, a week, a month as an attentive fiancé, then keep his distance from her? It was the height of irony to realize the pretense of a man in love had become reality. And acting as if he did not care about her was now the deceit.

"Your Highness!"

"Yes," he snapped, then drew a deep breath. "My apologies, Roman. You were saying?"

"I was wondering if something was amiss. You have not been your usual self since our arrival. No." Roman studied him thoughtfully. "You have been pensive and re-mote since yesterday."

Alexei smiled in a grim manner. "My engagement is about to be publicly announced. My *feigned* engagement.

Surely under such circumstances any preoccupation on my part is understandable."

"Understandable but . . ." Roman shook his head. He stopped a passing waiter long enough for them both to exchange empty champagne glasses for fresh ones. "That is not what is on your mind."

"Perhaps I simply dislike being on display." Alexei did indeed feel as if all eyes in the room had been on him from the moment he was announced. As if he were the topic of any number of whispered conversations, the target of pity.

"You have always been on display, as it were, Your Highness." Roman paused. "However, I am well aware that this is your first public appearance since . . ."

"You can say it aloud. My first public appearance since Avalonia ceased to exist. Since the loss of my father and my country and my home." *Since my failure to preserve my nation's independence and my father's legacy.*

Roman sipped his champagne in a casual manner. "My king and my country and my home as well."

Alexei stared at his friend. "Of course. My apologies. It is easy to forget the loss is not mine alone." He took a bracing swallow of his champagne. Silly, frivolous stuff, but he was rather fond of it. "Do not think I am feeling sorry for myself or wallowing in self-pity."

"I would never think such a thing," Roman said mildly. "I think this has less to do with the loss of a country than the loss of a woman. And in that respect, perhaps a bit of sympathy for yourself, even a moment of wallowing, is to be permitted."

"Do not be absurd. I have not lost Miss Effington. She was never mine to lose."

"Lady Overton and I noted a great deal of tension between the two of you last night."

"Of course there was tension," Alexei said, his tone a shade sharper than he wished. "We are about to embark upon an enormous deception." He glanced around the crowded room. "Where is the blasted woman anyway? How long can it take to repair a dress?"

They had been greeted upon their arrival by Pamela's parents, Lord and Lady Edward, the younger Miss Effington, and Lady Smythe-Windom. Lord Edward had been cordial but not overly friendly, as if he were assessing Alexei's suitability as a husband, in direct contrast to Amanda, who appeared quite overcome with glee at Alexei's appearance. Lady Edward had told them Pamela and Lady Overton had retired to repair some sort of problem with Pamela's dress, and they would return shortly. Immediately thereafter Alexei and Roman had been besieged by one introduction after another. One curious conversation following the next with any number of people whose names he could not possibly remember. That, too, was an indication of his state of mind. He had always had an uncanny ability to recall names.

"Your Highness." Roman nudged him and nodded toward a doorway at the far end of the room. "I believe the repair has been completed."

Alexei glanced in the direction Roman indicated. His breath caught.

Pamela was a vision wrought from magic and fire and every dream he'd ever had. She stood chatting with Lady

Overton and another woman, but he saw no one save her. Even the crowd seemed to fade away like ships enveloped by fog.

Pamela wore a gown of a shimmering copper color, and even from this distance he could see it enhanced the fair tones of her skin and the golden hue of her hair and the sable of her eyes. She looked every inch a goddess. Every inch a queen. A dream—his dream—at last come to life.

Serenissima.

Her gaze caught his, and a radiant smile lit her face. His heart twisted, and he steeled himself against the desire to rush to her side, take her in his arms, and carry her off. And never let her go. This was going to be considerably more difficult than he had imagined.

"She is remarkable." A note of awe sounded in Roman's voice.

"Indeed she is," Alexei said softly.

Roman paused. "With your permission, Your Highness, I intend to marry her."

"You intend to . . ." Alexei stared then chuckled. "You are speaking of Lady Overton."

"Clarissa." Roman said her name as if it were a prayer or a promise, and Alexei couldn't help a brief stab of envy.

He brushed it aside. "You do not need my permission, old friend, but if you wish for my approval, you have it. As well as my wishes for every happiness."

"I always thought I was happy or at least content with my life. I certainly never thought a woman was necessary to make my life complete. Of course, I had never met this particular woman." Roman sipped his wine, but his gaze lingered on Lady Overton. "I had no idea." He glanced at Alexei. "We should join them."

"And so the farce begins," Alexei said under his breath. He could do this, of course. He had played far more treacherous games on the fields of politics, where the stakes were considerably higher. Only his heart was at risk now. Unfortunately, so was hers.

"Your Highness?" A footman appeared at his side bearing a silver salver holding a folded note.

Alexei accepted the note, read the brief lines, then glanced at Roman. "It seems the father of my intended would like to have a word with me."

"That could be a bit awkward," Roman murmured.

"I cannot imagine why," Alexei said wryly.

A few moments later Alexei entered the Effington House library. A most impressive room with book-lined shelves reaching toward the heavens. As much an expression of significant fortune as of scholarly pursuit.

"The collection was amassed primarily in the last century. Volumes have been added on occasion as warranted." Lord Edward glanced around the room. "But this room looks essentially as it did when I was a boy."

"And did you read a great many of these as a boy?"

"I confess I did not read many I was not forced to read. My brother Harry was much more inclined toward academic pursuits than any of the rest of us." Lord Edward chuckled. "I fear I have never been overly scholarly."

Alexei smiled. "Then we have that in common."

"That and my daughter." Lord Edward nodded in a brisk manner and moved to sit behind a desk as impressive as the rest of the room. He gestured at the chair in front of the desk. "Do sit down, Your Highness."

"I believe I would prefer to stand, Lord Edward," Alexei said slowly.

"This is not an inquisition, you may let down your guard." Lord Edward glanced up at him. "Indeed, I would offer you a brandy, but this will not take long. It is nothing more than a business matter I should like to dispose of so that we may enjoy the remainder of the evening."

"A business matter?" Alexei sank into the chair.

Good Lord, he wasn't referring to Pamela's dowry as a business matter, was he? Certainly marriage negotiations between heads of state regarding the union of their respective offspring were considered matters of business as well as affaires of politics, but this was decidedly different. To all appearances this was a love match. Or at least it was supposed to be.

Lord Edward shuffled through several papers laid out on the desk in front of him. "It has come to my attention that you currently have a significant fortune on deposit in the Bank of England."

"Go on." Alexei narrowed his gaze. He could have denied it of course, but it seemed rather pointless.

"I understand you have been unable to draw on the account, indeed you have been denied any access to it at all. Political absurdity of course but there you have it." He looked at Alexei. "Am I correct?"

"About political absurdity or my inability to claim my own fortune?"

"Both."

"Yes."

Lord Edward nodded. "The matter has been taken care of. Your funds will be at your disposal within the next few days. Probably as soon as tomorrow or possibly as long as a week but no longer." Lord Edward cast him a satisfied smile, then got to his feet. "Now, then, I suggest we return to the party."

"That is it?" Alexei stood slowly. Surely there was more to this meeting with Pamela's father than this? "That is all you wish to discuss?"

Lord Edward's brow rose. "Is there something else we should talk about?"

"I thought you would want to talk about Pamela. About my intentions and my prospects and that sort of thing."

"Your Highness, I know your prospects down to the last penny. At least financially. I know as well your political status and your personal reputation." His expression was reserved, cool, and considering, and once again Alexei had the distinct impression the man was measuring his worth. "You played the rake exceedingly well up until a few years ago, when political affairs in your country demanded your full attention. You have scarcely left Avalonia since. From all accounts, you are considered both intelligent and honorable.

"While I do not specifically know your plans for the remainder of your life, aside from my daughter, that is, a man with a fortune as large as yours has the luxury of time to decide on the path for his future. As for your intentions, given that I am to make an announcement later in the evening—oh, and I did think we could do that right before we go into supper if that meets with your approval?"

Alexei stared.

"Yes, I thought it would. As I was saying, as I am announcing your engagement, I am assuming your intention is marriage."

"Then we have nothing else to discuss?" Alexei said slowly. "Nothing else you wish to talk about or to ask me?"

"I believe I already know a great deal." Lord Edward studied him for a moment, then heaved a resigned sigh, settled back into his chair, and waved for Alexei to sit. "I was afraid of this."

Alexei sat down and chose his words carefully. "Afraid of what?"

"That you would wish to have a long, earnest discussion about whatever men in your position wish to have long, earnest discussions about. It has been a very long time since I had such a discussion with the father of the woman I intended to marry, and I remember little of it save the unrelentingly earnest nature of the talk." He opened a drawer, pulled out a bottle of brandy, set it on the desk, then retrieved two glasses. "This will take longer than I expected."

He filled the glasses and pushed one across the desk toward Alexei. "To begin with I suppose you probably wish to know how I knew of your financial difficulties and the other details of your life."

"Not at all." Alexei shrugged. "Your brother is the Duke of Roxborough and has a great deal of power. Furthermore, I assume you have any number of business interests and therefore know people who would be willing to provide such information. I would quite frankly consider it ill-advised on your part if you had not made certain inquiries regarding the man your daughter intends to marry."

Lord Edward chuckled. "Well said, Your Highness." A frown furrowed his forehead. "Should I continue to address you as Your Highness? It will seem decidedly odd to do so after you are officially a member of the family. What should I call you?"

"Whatever you would call any man who would marry your daughter," Alexei said smoothly.

"Damn lucky, Your Highness. I would call him damn lucky." Lord Edward took a sip of his brandy, settled back in his chair, and studied Alexei. "Do not for a moment think that I am not exceptionally fond of my oldest daughter."

"As well you should be, Lord Edward."

"She was a bright child and lovely as well. At least in my opinion, but I am only the father and apparently know nothing of such matters." He paused as if choosing his words. "I do not wish to see her make another mistake with her life. However, she is also a grown woman soon to be the recipient of a substantial inheritance that will make her, at least, financially independent. That, coupled with her age, means she can do precisely what she wishes with her life, and I daresay she will. To be honest, at this point, she has no practical need for a father or, for that matter, for a husband."

Alexei took a swallow of his brandy, noted the excellent quality, and waited.

"Independence is not what I would wish for her. I have always wanted her to marry and have a family of her own. Needless to say, I was delighted to learn she had indeed found a suitable match."

Alexei smiled in a noncommittal manner but held his

tongue. He was willing to go along with the deception, but he did not care to lie outright to this man.

"Even in the short time I spent with her today," Lord Edward continued, "I could see she has changed substantially in the years she has been away. She is a woman who knows her own mind now, God help you.

"I always thought she would, you know, come to know her own nature, that is. A pity it did not occur sooner." Lord Edward's gaze narrowed. "You are aware of her past, are you not?"

Alexei nodded.

"Good. I don't think a marriage should be based on deception." The older man paused for a moment. "At least not an inordinate amount of deception. A touch of deception between a man and wife, however, is acceptable. Adds a hint of mystery and all that." He grinned, tossed back the rest of his brandy, and got to his feet. "If there is nothing else?"

"I do not think . . . yes." Alexei stood and met the other man's gaze. "It is about the incident that caused Pamela to leave London."

"Perhaps," Lord Edward chose his words with care, "any questions you have should be addressed to Pamela."

"No, Lord Edward," Alexei shook his head. "This is for you."

"Very well."

"It is my understanding that Pamela did not marry the gentleman in question because she did not wish to. Given the circumstances, why was she not made to marry?"

"Regardless of scandal, I would never force any of my children to marry against their will. Marriage is far too permanent a state to enter into reluctantly." Lord Edward paused for a moment. "You must understand, while she is most intelligent, Pamela was not wise in the ways of men. She was never especially flirtatious as opposed to her sister. Amanda has been able to wrap men around her fingers since the moment she could walk.

"Indeed, I would hazard to say Pamela has read more books in this library and the libraries of all the members of the family than most of the rest of us. In spite of her feelings for this man, she was wise enough to realize a bad marriage is worse than none at all." He chuckled. "It was the first time I suspected her quiet and reserved demeanor was not her true nature."

"I see." Alexei nodded. "I must ask as well why you or your sons did not defend her honor."

Lord Edward raised a brow. "A duel you mean?"

"Yes."

"My dear sir, dueling is illegal in this country."

Alexei shrugged. "Nonetheless—"

"Pamela forbid us to do so. She said, and she was right, that a duel would only end in more scandal and possibly tragedy. She had by then already decided on her own course of action."

"Travels with her aunt?"

Lord Edward nodded. "She said if any of us initiated a duel with Penwick, she would learn of it, and she would never return home."

"Because she cared for him?" Alexei held his breath. It was long ago, and Pamela herself claimed she had been mistaken about her feelings for Penwick. Still, what a woman might say aloud was not always the same as what she might feel.

"I prefer to think it was because she cared for us."

"Regardless—"

"Regardless." A definite gleam of satisfaction showed in Lord Edward's eye. "The moment Pamela was safely out of England, Penwick suffered a nasty beating at the hand of an unknown assailant. And at his own home no less. It was weeks before the bruises faded enough for him to appear in public."

"Your sons?"

"Did not duel with the gentleman, as per their sister's wishes. Indeed, they gave him a sporting chance to defend himself. Even going so far as to let him select which of them would thrash him." Lord Edward chuckled. "To my knowledge, Pamela is still unaware of the incident."

"I see."

"And while I don't think it has any significance, you should probably be aware," Lord Edward's gaze met Alexei's, "that Penwick's wife died a few years ago and he has not yet remarried."

"And?"

"And nothing at all. Simply something I thought you should know. You should know as well that I would rather have you wed my daughter than have her marry Penwick. Of course, it is Pamela's choice, not mine."

"Of course." And who would Pamela's choice be? Did she know Penwick was free to marry now where he was not free six years ago? And more importantly, did she care?

"You should know something else as well. I should not like to see my daughter embroiled in another scandal. Regardless of the veneer of sophistication she has acquired, I suspect she remains more fragile than she appears. Penwick broke her heart. I will not allow it to be broken again."

Alexei raised a brow. "Perhaps I am mistaken, Lord Edward, that sounds suspiciously like a threat."

"Not at all, Your Highness." Pamela's father smiled pleasantly, but his gaze was hard and unyielding. "It's a promise."

"Where on earth do you think he disappeared to?" Pamela skimmed the crowd. She well knew from past experience once you lost sight of someone in the overly packed Effington House ballroom, only luck and prayer could bring them back into view in a reasonable amount of time. "He was there just a moment ago, then I turned to speak to Lady Frederick, and now he seems to have vanished."

"Leaving poor Count Stefanovich to his own devices." Clarissa's gaze fixed on the count. "Fortunately, he is making his way through the crowd."

Pamela glanced at her cousin and grinned. "My, that is fortunate."

"Indeed it is. For me." Clarissa laughed. "As for you, now that we have a moment to ourselves do you wish to tell me what has been on your mind all day?"

Pamela shrugged. "What could possibly be on my mind?"

"Besides His Highness?" Clarissa grinned. "I have no idea."

"I don't know what to do about him." She blew a long breath. "He wants me, cousin, as much as I want him."

"Well then—"

"But he claims to have no interest in marriage. And does so in a tone that brooks no argument and allows no discussion."

"That is a problem."

Pamela forced a casual note to her voice. "Have you, by any chance, discovered whether or not—"

"No," Clarissa said firmly. "I have not forgotten my promise but the opportune occasion to"—she grimaced—"*interrogate* the count has not yet arrived."

"Pity," Pamela murmured. "If I recall interrogation can be quite—"

"Pamela!"

"My apologies." Pamela grinned. "But teasing you is entirely too much fun to resist. And I do appreciate that you have agreed to help me. I just have one more, tiny favor to ask."

Clarissa narrowed her eyes in suspicion.

"In the course of your interrogation, perhaps you could find out why Alexei is so adamant about not marrying."

"I could do that, I suppose."

"Thank you." Pamela breathed a sigh of relief. "My very future depends on it."

"Your future?" Clarissa studied her for a moment. "I don't like the sound of that."

"I have a decision to make."

"I don't like the sound of that either. What decision?"

"It's really quite simple. Alexei is the only man on earth that I wish to spend my life with, and I will be with him." Pamela drew a deep breath. "Even if I cannot have him as my husband."

"I feared as much." Clarissa moved closer to her cousin, her gaze searching Pamela's. "Are you quite serious about this?"

Pamela shrugged. "I'm afraid I am."

"It sounds as if you have already made your decision," Clarissa said slowly.

"Perhaps." Pamela's stomach twisted. Long ago she had intended Alexei to be the first man in her new life as a woman of experience. Instead, he had turned out to be the only man. His declaration yesterday that he would never marry had made her think long and hard about what she was willing to give up to have him.

"I thought you did not wish to be his—"

"Mistress? I don't. And I won't, not really. As I have my own fortune now, I will never have to be dependent upon him for my keep. My existence will not be contingent on his whim."

"Pamela, I—"

"Clarissa, I would rather be with him in whatever manner necessary than live the rest of my life without him."

"I see." Clarissa thought for a moment. "Do you intend to tell him then?"

"Tell him I am willing to join him in his bed for the rest of my days without benefit of marriage?" She snorted. "I may well be in love, but I have not completely lost my mind. No. What I am willing to do and what I will do are two entirely different things."

"I'm afraid I don't understand."

"Neither do I, dear cousin. I haven't the vaguest idea what will ultimately happen between us. Perhaps we are destined only for one night together. Well"—she flashed the other woman a wicked grin—"one more night to-gether." She sobered, and her resolve hardened. "I want to have his children, Clarissa. I want to grow old with him. I want to spend the last moments of my life looking into his brown eyes. I shall give up whatever I must for that."

"What if he does not care for you?" Clarissa said slowly.

"At last, the heart of the matter." Pamela smiled in a grim manner. "I think he might care for me. There is something quite wonderful in his eyes but . . ." She shook her head. "In truth I don't know how he feels. He is an expert at flirtation. His touch, his kiss, his words . . ." She heaved a heartfelt sigh. "He is very good."

"Apparently," Clarissa said wryly.

"I am willing to sacrifice everything I have long thought I wanted for him, but I cannot make him love me. And as much as I want to be with him, I will not give up both marriage and love."

"Pamela." Clarissa laid a hand on her cousin's arm. "It's not too late to stop this charade. Your father has not yet made his announcement. And in truth not that many people know of this engagement of yours as of yet, and—"

"Don't be absurd." Pamela scoffed. "Even if I sound a bit melancholy at the moment, I have certainly not given up. It could well be that by this time tomorrow, His Highness will have fallen head over heels for me and will realize he cannot live without me. As his wife preferably. No, I shall act out this comedy of ours until the final curtain falls.

"Besides, if I am to spend my life living in Great-aunt Elizabeth's house with Aunt Millicent or, worse, alone, I should at least like to have memories of my royal engagement to look back on."

"Nonsense. I will be with you always," Clarissa said staunchly.

"You, my dear loyal cousin"—Pamela linked her arm through Clarissa's—"will no doubt be wed before the month is out."

"Roman has not spoken of marriage."

"He will, I am certain of it. If only to save you from living out the remainder of your days with a bitter old crone."

Clarissa laughed. "I cannot imagine you being a bitter old crone."

"Oh I intend to be extremely bitter as well as quite annoying, demanding, and irascible. And absolutely eccentric." Pamela laughed. "Do believe me when I say you are far better off with your Count Stefanovich than you would ever be with me."

"Talking about me again, Lady Overton?" Count Stefanovich stepped to Clarissa's side, took her hand, and lifted it to his lips. "Did I fare well in the discussion?"

"I have not yet decided, my lord." Clarissa's gaze met his, and they could have been quite alone rather than in a crush of ball guests for all the notice they took of anyone else.

Pamela's heart caught at the look that passed between them. She was at once distinctly envious and most pleased for this cousin who was her dearest friend. Clarissa well deserved to find happiness again.

"Good evening, Miss Effington." The count reluctantly dropped Clarissa's hand to take Pamela's. "Delightful gathering thus far."

"My mother will be very pleased you think so," Pamela said lightly. "Is His Highness enjoying himself as well?"

"I rather doubt it at the moment, Miss Effington." The count chuckled. "When last I saw him he was on his way to a meeting with your father."

"My father?" Pamela's voice rose. "Why would he wish to speak to my father?"

"First of all, Miss Effington, it was not His Highness who wished to speak with your father, but your father who asked to speak with him." Stefanovich looked distinctly amused. "And secondly, it is my understanding that fathers of ladies about to be wed often wish to speak with the gentleman involved regarding any number of issues."

Pamela groaned. "Dear Lord, take me now."

The count laughed. "I cannot imagine it is as bad as all that." He leaned closer to her, his words for her alone. "Take heart, Miss Effington. The play has just begun, and who knows how it may end."

"Is the ending in doubt?" Pamela's gaze met Stefanovich's.

"I daresay the ending is always in doubt when the play is being written as it is performed," he said.

"Then is it a comedy or a tragedy we play, my lord?"

"It is a farce, Miss Effington." Stefanovich smiled. "Nuances of the plot will determine its end, but by its nature, it is most amusing and enjoyable."

"For the audience perhaps," Pamela said wryly.

The count chuckled. "I suspect the enjoyment of the actors is directly proportional to their skill."

"And skill is yet to be determined?" She laughed. "I must confess I have never embarked upon a stage of such magnitude. Indeed, any deceptions I may have undertaken in the past pale in comparison to this."

"I imagine the difficulty increases without props, costumes"—he paused—"masks, that sort of thing."

"A mask would be most welcome at the moment." The light tone of her voice belied the clenching of her stomach. Surely it was no more than a coincidence that the count had mentioned masks. "As would my fellow actor."

"Isn't that His Highness now?" Clarissa nodded toward the main door.

Pamela followed her cousin's gaze. Alexei stood gazing over the crowd in a distinctly regal manner. Tall and handsome in his evening clothes, he looked every inch the prince he was. Her gaze met his across the ballroom floor, and he smiled. Even from here, he made her heart catch. Alexei nodded a greeting and started in her direction.

"I wonder how he fared," the count murmured.

"It's past time to find out." Pamela started toward him.

"Perhaps you should wait until he . . ." Clarissa's words trailed behind her.

Pamela should indeed wait for him to approach her, it was the proper thing to do after all, but at the moment she didn't especially care. Nor did she especially care what had passed between Alexei and her father. At this particular moment, she simply wanted to be with him. Foolish, of course, but then what about the two of them had not been rather foolish?

She made her way around the ballroom, ignoring the dancers on the floor and stopping what seemed like every inch or two to speak with people she had not seen in years. All of whom seemed genuinely pleased to see her. Not one of whom seemed the least bit censuring. Certainly, she had not been in London society since her ruin, but London society had apparently proceeded quite nicely without her. She wondered if indeed people had forgotten about her mistake, or perhaps there had been so many varied and assorted scandals since hers, it was simply no longer of great interest.

It was odd being here again. She had changed, but much around her remained exactly as it had always been. The ballroom was awash with swags of brightly colored silk draped over every doorway and every window. Ribbons fluttered from sconces and columns. Huge flower-filled urns occupied various niches, flanked entries, and marked even those private alcoves that had long provided meeting places for lovers or those who would be lovers. The house was decorated in very much the same manner as it had been for her coming out and for that of each of her female cousins. The coming out of a female Effington was a grand affair that traditionally called for the use of the Effington House grand ballroom. This was, after all, the family's ancestral home in London. Aunt Katherine, the Duchess of Roxborough, took it as her responsibility, indeed her right, to have those milestone occasions in her house although, in truth, she simply delighted in the excuse to have a ball. Uncle Phillip, the duke, bore it bravely, if with considerably less enthusiasm than his wife, as his duty as the oldest brother and the bearer of the family title.

It was a most familiar setting, yet never had it seemed so special, almost magical. Pamela met Alexei at what was very nearly the halfway point of the room. If this was indeed a farce, there was no better place to begin than the center of the stage.

Pamela favored him with her brightest smile. "Good evening, Your Highness."

"Miss Effington." Alexei took her hand and raised it to his lips, his gaze never leaving hers. "You are looking exceptionally lovely this evening."

She laughed. "And you are as charming as ever. Still, your words will quite turn my head."

"Nonetheless, you are a vision. A dream come to life." His gaze bored into hers. "A memory."

"A memory?" She held her breath.

"Of a moment caught in time."

She forced a carefree note. "Only a moment?"

"A moment at once unexpected and lingering forever." His voice was intimate and low and shivered through her. "Of light and magic and . . . passion."

"You do realize people are staring at us?" Not that she cared. Or indeed noticed that there was anyone at all save the two of them.

"In my experience, the English have always had a tendency to stare." A look of hunger showed in his eyes, and it was all she could do not to fling herself into his arms.

"Perhaps they are staring because you have held my hand entirely too long." *Or perhaps they, too, can feel what it is between us. That pulls us inexorably together. Can you not feel it, Alexei?*

"Or perhaps it has not been long enough." He released

her hand with a reluctant smile, and her heart ached with the loss of his touch.

She drew a steadying breath. "I understand you were speaking to my father."

"It was most enlightening." He chuckled.

"Oh?" Her brow rose. "I am not at all certain I wish you to be enlightened by my father."

"And why not?"

"You might learn all my secrets. Unravel my mysteries, and where will I be then?"

"Where do you wish to be?" His tone was light, belying the intensity in his dark eyes.

With you. Always. "You are a dreadful flirt, Alexei."

"Not at all, Pamela." He grinned that wicked, well-practiced smile of his. "I am excellent at flirtation. Do not forget my reputation."

She laughed. "I thought you wished to put that behind you?"

"Did I say that?" He drew his brows together. "It does not sound at all like me."

"I know." She heaved an exaggerated sigh. "You are annoyingly proud of your reputation. But you did indeed say that."

"Ah well"—he shrugged—"apparently I have forgotten."

"I have not."

"Interesting, do you not think"—his voice was matter-of-fact, but his gaze locked with hers—"that I would forget something so recent and yet other occurrences from rather long ago are as fresh as yesterday?"

"Are they?" Her heart thudded in her chest.

"They are." He stared at her as if trying to see into her

very soul. Time seemed to stretch and stop altogether. She was conscious of nothing beyond his dark eyes, the heat of his body close to hers, the feel of her blood throbbing in her veins. And a yearning that threatened to overwhelm her. It was a mere second or an entire lifetime, but at last he shook his head slightly, like a man awakening from a deep sleep, and smiled. "It occurs to me that we have never danced together. We should have made it a point to do so before now. Part of the charade and all that."

"Of course." Her voice was oddly breathless.

"It is rather unusual for a man never to have danced with the woman he intends to marry after all." He sighed in an overly dramatic way. "Yet another thing that has slipped my mind in recent days. It appears, Pamela, you have the remarkable ability to befuddle my mind."

She tilted her head and cast him a flirtatious smile of her own. "Just your mind?"

"No," he said in a manner that indicated this particular discussion was closed. "They are playing a waltz, and there is little in the world that I like quite as much as dancing the waltz with a lovely lady in my arms." He held out his hand. "Would you do me the great honor of this dance?"

"I should like nothing better." She placed her hand on his and allowed him to lead her onto the dance floor. A moment later she was in his arms.

He held her in the correct manner, with precisely the proper amount of space between them, but it scarcely mattered. They fit together as if they were cast from the same mold. Moved together as if they were one. Halves of the same whole. But then she knew they would.

The glittering lights, the festive gowns, the crowded ballroom, the colors and the music all swept her back to another ball and another time. Venice. A night of improbable magic. And even with the mask she'd worn, then as now, his gaze never faltered from hers. He led her perfectly through the steps of the dance, and they moved together with an ease that could only have come through practice. Or fate.

Far too soon the music faded, and they stopped. He escorted her off the floor.

"Your father wishes to announce our engagement before we go into supper."

She drew a deep breath. "Alexei, regardless of my aunt's threats I cannot hold you to your agreement. If you do not wish—"

"My dear Pamela, I have nothing to lose in this endeavor and very little else to occupy my time at the moment." His gaze searched hers. "However this comedy of ours ends, the risk is truly yours and yours alone. This is your world and has little to do with me. If the truth of our engagement is made known, you are the one who will suffer the scandal. Even now we have dug too deep a hole to climb out of with any measure of grace. As your aunt pointed out, the moment your mother and sister believed we were betrothed, any number of others knew as well."

"They have never been known to keep anything as interesting as this to themselves."

"I shall not abandon you to face another scandal alone. I gave my word, and I shall not go back on it now. I am entirely at your disposal."

"Are you?" She smiled slowly. "I should warn you, Alexei, I will take full advantage of your generosity."

"Will you indeed?" His dark eyes twinkled with amusement. "I shall look forward to it."

She studied him for a long moment. "If you are certain—"

"I can think of nothing else I would rather do than pretend to be in love with a beautiful woman. And better yet, have a beautiful woman pretend to be in love with me.

"Besides, I have yet to leave a well-acted play before the final curtain." He grinned. "I would so hate not to see how it all ends."

Eleven

 If I ever see George again, I can only pray I see him before he sees me to enable me to avoid him altogether. It is a dreadful thing to come face-to-face with the stupidity of one's youth. Or in this case, George.

Miss Pamela Effington

"*P*amela dear, I must speak with you at once." Aunt Millicent hooked her arm through her niece's and propelled her toward one of the open doors that led onto the terrace.

"Aunt Millicent, I am waiting for His Highness." Pamela craned her neck to look back over her shoulder. "It is nearly time for supper and—"

"Goodness, Pamela, there are far greater matters to be concerned with at the moment than food." Aunt Millicent steered her through the doors, barely slowing until they had reached the stone balustrade at the far end of the broad terrace to a discreet, secluded spot as far from the

237

doors as one could get. But even here, flower-filled urns scented the night air, and candelabras cast a warm glow.

"There now." Aunt Millicent glanced from side to side as if to make certain they were alone. "This will do."

"This will do for what?"

"I need your assistance. I am in something of a quandary." Aunt Millicent wrung her hands together. "Do you realize virtually everyone who is anyone is here? As well as a great number of those who are no one in particular?"

"It is quite the crush," Pamela said slowly. "Amanda is beside herself with excitement."

"Yes, yes, of course she is. An enormous success and all that." Aunt Millicent waved away the comment. "But you don't understand—everyone is here. *Everyone!*"

"We've just established that." Pamela drew her brows together in confusion. "And you're right, I don't understand."

"Obviously, I am not making myself clear." Aunt Millicent turned and paced a few feet in one direction, through the flickering circle of light cast by the candelabra, then turned on her heel and paced back. "When I say everyone is here I don't really mean *everyone*. Although it certainly could be everyone given the vast horde in the ballroom. Goodness, we are packed in there like pigs to slaughter. Indeed, I thought it was really rather warm and quite stuffy, didn't you?"

Pamela stared. "Aunt Millicent, you're babbling."

Aunt Millicent pulled up short and gasped. "Have you ever heard me babble before?"

Pamela bit back a grin. "Not that I can recall."

"God help me then." She resumed her pacing. "I used

to babble, you know, when I was younger. I babbled all the time. Indeed, my sister often threatened to smack me if I did not stop."

"I can certainly understand that," Pamela murmured.

"I knew I should never have returned to London. I knew this would happen if I returned for any length of time at all. First babbling, then, well, in truth the babbling did not come first, but rather—"

"Aunt Millicent, what are you talking about?"

She stopped in the light of the flickering candles, drew herself up, and proclaimed in an overly dramatic manner. "*He* is here."

"He? Who?"

"Winchester Roberts."

Pamela shook her head. "Who?"

"Sir Winchester actually."

"I'm sorry but I don't—"

"The man I didn't marry!"

"The man you didn't . . ." At once Pamela realized what Aunt Millicent was trying to say. "The one you left waiting at the church?"

"The very one." Aunt Millicent twisted her hands together. "I don't know that he has seen me, but I saw him. I've managed to avoid him thus far, but it is just a matter of time. He probably knows I am here. Pamela"—she clutched her niece's arm—"you must help me escape."

"Escape what? The ball?"

"No, not the ball." Aunt Millicent shook her head. "London. I must leave London at once. Italy is nice at this time of year. Or Switzerland. Or perhaps China? I've never been to China and it's very, very far away. I could—"

"Don't be absurd." Pamela pried Aunt Millicent's rather painful grip from her arm. "It's been what? Twelve years now? Why, the poor man probably doesn't even remember you."

"Of course he remembers me." Indignation sounded in her aunt's voice. "He was in love with me. Even if I hadn't publicly humiliated him, he would certainly remember me for that reason alone. Not remember me indeed."

Pamela tried not to laugh. Aunt Millicent was deadly serious about this. "Perhaps it's time you faced him then? Even apologized?"

"Apologized? Oh, no, I couldn't. I should of course, but . . ."

Aunt Millicent resumed her pacing. "You see, he was such a very nice man, and I was extremely fond of him—"

Pamela raised a brow. "Fond?"

"Possibly more than fond. I might have loved him as well but he simply . . . well he didn't . . . and I wasn't . . ." She paused and met her niece's gaze. "He deserved better, Pamela."

"Better than being left waiting at a church?"

"Well, that, of course, but better than I." Aunt Millicent blew a long breath. "You see, Charles had been dead a mere two years. Not a very long time really to become accustomed to being without the first true love of your life."

"No, two years is not long at all," Pamela said softly.

"I fully thought I was ready to go on with my life, but I wasn't. And marriage is such a very permanent thing after all. Even though I did have feelings for Winchester, it simply didn't seem fair to saddle him with a wife for the rest of his days, and I was unsure of whether or not I wished to be a wife again. At least the kind of wife he should have. Did I say he was a very nice man?"

"You mentioned it."

"Yes, well, he was. Possibly, he still is. Which is precisely why I cannot face him." Genuine despair sounded in Aunt Millicent's voice. "If I stay in London, it's inevitable that eventually our paths will cross. And I have no idea what to say to him."

Pamela considered her aunt for a long moment. The only other time she had seen her this flustered was a few days ago, right before they'd discovered Alexei had taken up residence in their house. Then, as now, it was because of this one particular gentleman. Certainly Aunt Millicent had been involved with any number of gentlemen through the years, but none, to Pamela's knowledge, had ever produced this effect on her. How very interesting.

Pamela chose her words carefully. "Surely, through the years, you have thought of what you might say?"

"On occasion, perhaps. In those odd moments when one's mind is not otherwise occupied. When one is soaking in a tub or awaiting sleep at night, one's thoughts might drift to what might have been and what, under the proper circumstances, might be said." Aunt Millicent sighed. "I have thought that I might say I'd been a fool. That leaving him was an enormous mistake, possibly the biggest of my life and that I deeply regret my actions. Offer my apologies, of course, ask for his forgiveness, that sort of thing."

"You could also say that you missed me," a deep, masculine voice said from the shadows.

Aunt Millicent sucked in a sharp breath and stared at a

point over Pamela's shoulder. Her eyes widened, and even in the faint light Pamela could see her aunt's face pale. Pamela turned to meet the owner of the voice, obviously Sir Winchester.

A tall gentleman, perhaps a year or two older than Aunt Millicent, stepped into the light. He was distinguished in appearance, indeed, quite handsome really, with dark hair touched at the temples with silver. Very dashing.

Aunt Millicent stared in total disbelief and obvious shock.

Pamela stepped toward him and extended her hand. "Sir Winchester, I presume?"

"And you must be Miss Effington." He smiled and kissed her hand. It was an extraordinarily nice smile.

"Must I?" Pamela returned his smile. She liked him immediately. "Couldn't I be someone else?"

"You could, I suppose." He nodded thoughtfully. "However, when I saw your aunt dragging you out here and asked a gentleman who you were, he was quite positive as to your name."

Pamela laughed. "You have me then."

"Would you two stop being so cordial to one another," Aunt Millicent snapped. "It's most annoying."

He scoffed. "And I would certainly not wish to annoy you in any way."

Aunt Millicent crossed her arms over her chest. "What are you doing here?"

"I was invited."

"No, I don't mean here in general terms." She huffed. "I mean specifically here on the terrace. Where you were *not* invited."

"We have a great deal to discuss," he said firmly. "I have waited twelve long years for this discussion, Millicent, and I shall not be put off another minute."

"I should probably take my leave now." Pamela edged toward the ballroom door.

"You most certainly will not." Aunt Millicent grabbed Pamela's hand and yanked the younger woman firmly back to her side. "I need witnesses. Possibly even protection. He could . . . he could shoot me. Or worse."

Pamela stared. Her aunt's behavior made her earlier babbling appear positively normal. "What would be worse than shooting you?"

Sir Winchester chuckled. "Do you really think I would shoot you?"

"I would in your place." Aunt Millicent's eyes narrowed. "Why are you being so nice to me?"

"You said he was a nice man," Pamela said under her breath.

"I hadn't planned to be nice at all. You humiliated me in public, and for a long time I plotted all kinds of various and assorted acts of revenge."

"I can well imagine," Aunt Millicent said, in a grudging manner. "And I cannot blame you."

"No, you can't. And I don't believe you can begin to imagine what you put me through. I even considered following you after your abandonment—"

"*Abandonment* is such a harsh word," Aunt Millicent murmured.

"Harsh but true. And then I decided"—he shrugged—"you simply weren't worth the trouble."

"What? Not worth the trouble? How could you, Winchester?" Aunt Millicent glared. "I most certainly am worth the trouble, and you well know it!"

"Aunt Millicent!" Pamela said sharply.

"Well I am." Aunt Millicent glared at Sir Winchester. "I thought I broke your heart?"

"You did," he said simply.

"Then why didn't you come after me?" There was the oddest note in Aunt Millicent's voice. "To break my heart or the very least my neck?"

"Why would I chase after a woman who did not want me?"

"You simply should have, that's all." Aunt Millicent was definitely flustered.

"Would it have made a difference?" he said quietly.

"I don't know," she snapped. "It might have."

"I see." Sir Winchester paused for a moment. "That's something I didn't consider."

"And it changes things considerably, doesn't it?" Aunt Millicent's manner was lofty, as if his actions excused hers.

"Not in the least." The man shook his head, perhaps in an effort to clear it from Aunt Millicent's unique way of looking at the situation. "Blast it all, Millicent, you left me! You broke my heart!"

"We've established that." She waved aside his comment, releasing her grip on her niece. Pamela promptly stepped out of her reach. "You needn't repeat it."

"It bears repeating," he said sharply.

Any minute now, Pamela could make her own escape. This was far too personal a conversation for an observer. She took a casual step toward the ballroom door.

"Yes, well, I am sorry about that." Aunt Millicent huffed. "There, now, I've said it. You have my heartfelt apologies."

"That's it?" His voice rose. "That's all you intend to say? You left me waiting to marry you at a church accompanied by a fair number of family and friends, and you have nothing more to say?"

Aunt Millicent shrugged. "It was inexcusable of me."

"Inexcusable? Hah! You didn't even leave me a note, a letter, nothing!" Sir Winchester's voice rang with anger. "It took hours before I realized you were not coming at all. I had to find out that you had left the country from your sister because you had left a note for her!"

"She's my sister."

"And I was the man you were to marry!"

Because Aunt Millicent might well need someone else present as a deterrent if for no other reason, Pamela sighed to herself and slipped back to her previous position.

"I'm *extremely* sorry," Aunt Millicent said, in a tone that had even Pamela questioning her sincerity.

"Oh that is better." Sir Winchester glared. "*Extremely* certainly makes up for everything! There's nothing like the addition of *extremely* to rectify all of life's ills!"

Still, Aunt Millicent could probably take care of herself. Pamela cast a longing glance at the doors, which were entirely too far away.

Aunt Millicent glared. "I do not recall your being this sarcastic, Winchester."

"I do not recall your being this selfish, Millicent."

Pamela winced.

Aunt Millicent gasped. "Selfish! I most certainly am not selfish."

He snorted in disbelief.

"Well possibly I am just the tiniest bit selfish but . . . but . . ." She smirked. "I don't remember you being quite so sanctimonious."

Pamela groaned.

"Sanctimonious? Sanctimonious?" Sir Winchester sputtered.

"Sanctimonious," Aunt Millicent said smugly.

Sir Winchester gritted his teeth and clenched his fists by his side. Probably not at all a good sign.

"Well, I don't remember you being this"—he paused and his eyes narrowed—"lovely."

"There! That's precisely what I am talking about. That's definitely sarcasm and it simply does not suit you. You are not at all . . ." She stopped and drew her brows together. "Did you say lovely?"

"Yes," he snapped.

"Why?"

He threw his hands up in frustration. "Because you are."

"But I am substantially older," she said slowly.

"And hopefully wiser as well!"

"Hopefully." She studied him for a long moment. "Have you forgiven me then?"

"No," he said sharply, then ran his hand through his hair. "Blast it all, Millicent, I have not forgiven you. I may never forgive you, but the moment I saw you tonight I realized I am the worst kind of fool. Twelve long years, and my feelings for you haven't changed."

"Really?" Aunt Millicent's expression brightened.

He glared.

She paused for a long moment, then drew a deep breath. "Then I confess, I have indeed missed you."

He stared at her.

"We should talk, I think."

"Yes." He drew a deep breath. "We should."

"Not here of course. This terrace is entirely too public. One cannot find a moment alone." Aunt Millicent glanced pointedly at Pamela. "You may leave if you wish."

"Only if you're certain you're no longer in danger of being shot," Pamela said in an overly sweet manner. "By Sir Winchester, that is."

"You may rest assured, Miss Effington, I would never shoot your aunt." Sir Winchester chuckled. "Tempting as it may be."

"Nonsense, no one is going to shoot me. What a ridiculous idea. Winchester." Aunt Millicent stepped to Sir Winchester and gazed up at him. "Would you escort me home?"

He stared down at her. "Now?"

"We do have a great deal to discuss." Aunt Millicent trailed a finger along the edge of his lapel. "It is past time, I think."

He caught her hand and stared down at her. "Indeed it is."

For an endless moment they gazed at one another in a manner that was most intimate and extremely personal.

Pamela looked away and cleared her throat. "I believe I should return to the ballroom."

"Yes, you should," Aunt Millicent said, although Pamela was confident her aunt wasn't paying the slightest attention to her niece. "Do enjoy yourself, dear."

"As will you, no doubt," Pamela said under her breath,

and without pause started across the terrace, leaving the couple alone in the shadows.

This was certainly an unexpected turn of events. Who would have imagined the man Aunt Millicent had abandoned still had feelings for her after a dozen years? And who would have imagined Aunt Millicent would have felt the same? It was obvious from the way she behaved in Sir Winchester's presence that her feelings for him went well beyond any embarrassment at being confronted by the man she had left on her wedding day.

It was something of a revelation. Sir Winchester did not strike Pamela as the kind of man Aunt Millicent usually dallied with. He seemed a solid sort. The type of man one could depend on on a permanent basis. Perhaps that was why Aunt Millicent had left him? Pamela smiled to herself. No, Sir Winchester was not a mere dalliance; he might well be forever.

Without warning a figure stepped from the shadows some feet directly in front of her, and she pulled up short, very nearly colliding with him.

Pamela stifled a stab of impatience. She did need to return to the ballroom and had no desire for polite conversation on the terrace.

She forced a pleasant smile. "Do forgive me, I was paying no attention to where I was . . ."

He stepped into the light.

Her breath caught.

"Good evening, Pamela."

"Have you seen her?" Alexei scanned the crowd impatiently. "It is nearly time for supper, and she is nowhere to be found." He glanced at Lady Overton. "Is this a habit of hers? Is she always this evasive? One would think she was hiding from me."

"Or you were hiding from her." Lady Overton smiled politely.

"Indeed, it is decidedly odd the way the two of you cannot keep sight of each other," Roman observed.

"How can we keep sight of each other when we are constantly being besieged by one person or another wishing to have a private word? Everyone in London must be here." Alexei cast a disgusted look around the room. "I barely managed a single dance with Miss Effington before I was accosted by a gentleman and his overbearing wife who claimed a previous acquaintance, and Pamela was pulled away by some relative she had not seen in years. How many of these blasted Effingtons are there? Tens of thousands no doubt."

"Not quite that many." Lady Overton bit back a smile. "Although admittedly they are a rather large family."

"It occurs to me, Your Highness, that I have not noticed you to be unoccupied in Miss Effington's absence," Roman said.

"Unfortunately no." Alexei blew a long breath. "There are any number of people here I met on my last visit, and a few others I have met elsewhere in the world. All of whom seem eager to renew their acquaintence."

"Wasn't that Lord Westerfield you were speaking to?" Roman nodded at the crowd. "Over there? I believe I met him last year when he traveled to Avalonia."

Alexei nodded. "Westerfield has long been one of the guiding forces behind the Society for the Preservation of

Anglo-Avalonian Brotherhood. Social more than political in nature really, its members all have ties of one sort or another, ancestral for the most part, to Avalonia."

"What did he want?" Roman's gaze met Alexei's.

Alexei shrugged. "Nothing of any significance."

"Oh?" Roman studied him. "The expressions on your faces seemed rather intense for nothing of significance."

"It was a pointless conversation, Roman," Alexei said firmly. "And best forgotten altogether."

Even so, it was difficult to ignore completely Westerfield's suggestion that it might be possible to reclaim Avalonia as a sovereign state if Britain led Austria and Prussia in demanding Russia relinquish control over the country. It was a possibility Alexei had desperately pursued once but with no success. Russia had moved too quickly, and the time and distance between Avalonia and England, or any country that might come to Avalonia's aid, too vast for effective diplomatic pressure. Besides, much of the European world was in awe of Russia's might as well as its ruthless nature. Now, it was too late, the opportunity for diplomatic solutions long passed.

"I believe I saw Pamela step out to the terrace with Aunt Millicent," Lady Overton offered.

"What did I just say?" Alexei huffed. "We cannot keep sight of one another if we are constantly being spirited off for meaningless discussions. She is supposed to be my fiancée, yet I cannot keep her by my side for two minutes. It does not bode well for the marriage, I tell you that."

Lady Overton and Roman exchanged glances.

"And precisely what do the two of you think is so damnably amusing?" Alexei glared.

"Not a thing, Your Highness." Lady Overton's eyes widened innocently.

"Nothing at all." Roman tried and failed to hide a grin. "Except perhaps the fact that you are remarkably on edge."

"You would be on edge, too, if you were about to allow an honorable gentleman, who has just done you a great service, to announce your intentions to marry his daughter, even though you have no real intention of doing any such thing, and the daughter cannot be found." Alexei glared at the open doors on the opposite side of the ballroom that he assumed led to the terrace. "Dare I wonder if she is planning to return, or will she take up residence on the terrace?"

"Perhaps," Roman said slowly, "Miss Effington is having second thoughts about the advisability of your ruse."

Alexei snorted. "Only an idiot would not be having second thoughts. I have had second thoughts from the moment the idea was proposed."

Still, in spite of his earlier reassurances to her, it was entirely possible Pamela had indeed decided not to go through with their charade. The oddest sense of disappointment stabbed him. Certainly he had not been enthusiastic about the idea originally, nor was he especially enthusiastic now, and the wisdom of it all was definitely in question, but he had to admit he was rather looking forward to playing attentive fiancé to Pamela. There was no future to be had with her, of course, but was there really any harm in savoring whatever time he could with the woman he had kept in his dreams, in his heart, for so long? If he was fated to spend his life without her, was this time together too much to ask?

"I imagine a gentleman always has a second thought or two when he is announcing his intentions to wed," Lady Overton said in a casual manner.

"I do not see why," Roman said staunchly. "Once he has realized that the lady in question is precisely what he has always wanted, indeed, what he has always longed for even if he did not realize it, he is a fool to so much as hesitate."

"But what of doubts?" she asked. "Surely he has doubts? Marriage is a remarkably permanent state."

"Doubts are for those who do not know their own minds." Roman's voice was firm.

Lady Overton studied him thoughtfully. "And do you know your own mind, my lord?"

"Indeed I do." Roman nodded.

"And yet you seem to hesitate. How very interesting." She smiled pleasantly then directed her gaze to Alexei. "And what of you, Your Highness?"

"I have no doubts as I am not about to marry. Do not forget this betrothal is nothing but a farce."

"What if it wasn't?"

"But it is."

"Oh do humor me for a moment, Your Highness. If indeed you were about to marry Pamela, would you have doubts?"

"No, Lady Overton, I would not," he said without a moment's pause, and realized he meant every word. "I should consider myself extremely lucky, as I consider her quite exceptional. However, it is a moot point."

"Why?"

"Because Miss Effington has no intention of marrying me nor do I have any intention of marrying her, or anyone. Ever."

"Why not?"

Alexei stared at her. "Earlier this evening Lord Edward said our talk was not on the order of an inquisition. Is that because he had allocated that duty to you?"

"Come now, Your Highness, Pamela's father would never relinquish such an important task. If he felt an inquisition was necessary he would certainly have taken it upon himself to carry it out." Lady Overton laughed. "Any inquisition I may conduct is entirely my own idea."

"To what end, Lady Overton?"

"Pamela is not only my cousin, she is my dearest friend. I am concerned about everything that concerns her. However"—she shrugged—"this is simple curiosity, Your Highness. Nothing more than that."

"Nothing?"

"Not a thing." Her green eyes were wide and completely innocent, and Alexei did not believe her for a moment. There was obviously far more to the quiet, reserved Lady Overton than met the eye. But he suspected Roman already knew that.

"Would you like me to find Pamela for you?" Lady Overton asked. "I shouldn't mind a few minutes on the terrace myself. It's exceptionally warm in here, but then it always is."

"I would be happy to accompany you." Roman offered her his arm.

"No, I shall go myself." Alexei sighed. "It will provide a momentary respite if nothing else."

"I suggest we all go," Lady Overton said brightly. "We shall certainly avoid any hint of impropriety if we are all together."

Roman raised a brow. "Impropriety?"

"The Effington terrace is well-known as a place for private conversation." Lady Overton cast Roman a distinctly seductive look. "It has any number of secluded locations well suited to meetings of a clandestine nature."

A speculative gleam appeared in Roman's eye. "Then we should waste no time in proceeding to the terrace."

Alexei smiled in spite of himself. It was most annoying to be with two people who were as obviously smitten with each other as these two were when Alexei was trying to keep his own emotions in check. He wasn't sure he had ever envied another man before, but he envied Roman now. Roman and Lady Overton had the rest of their lives ahead of them.

He and Pamela only had however long this sham of an engagement lasted.

Of course, there was no reason why they shouldn't enjoy it. Indeed, once he found Pamela, if Lady Smythe-Windom could be avoided, and Roman and Lady Overton encouraged to drift away to their own assignation, a few intimate moments with Pamela on a shadowed terrace under the stars might well be the perfect way to begin doing just that.

Twelve

When I see Pamela again I shall waste no time in declaring myself. I shall marry her at once. She will no doubt be very pleased.

George Fenton, Viscount Penwick

$\mathcal{P}$amela sucked in a hard breath. "George!"

"I heard you were back in London." George gazed at her as if he were a starving man, and she were a roast of veal. It was most disconcerting. "It has been a very long time."

George Fenton, now Viscount Penwick, looked precisely as he had the last time the two of them had stood on this very terrace engaged in a private meeting. Then as now he was an attractive man, a few inches taller than she, with hair nearly as fair and regular features. He didn't appear to have changed at all, at least in appearance.

"Hasn't it though?" she said weakly, and wondered how best to escape gracefully.

She should have been prepared for this encounter; indeed, she should have known George might be here to-

255

night. Or at least realized that she would at some point come face-to-face with him whenever she at last returned to London. She simply hadn't given him more than a passing thought. And even if she had, she never would have envisioned their first meeting to be alone on the Effington House terrace. Dear Lord, she would have avoided the terrace like it was infested with plague if she had so much as suspected this was a possibility.

"Now if you will excuse me." She tried to circle around him, but he moved to block her way.

"A moment, Pamela, please." His voice held a pleading note that might have been quite effective if he had been anyone else. "We have a great deal to talk about."

"We have nothing to talk about." She nodded firmly and started around him again, but once more he stepped in front of her.

"We have not seen each other for six long years."

"And it has not been nearly long enough."

"You have not forgiven me then?" Disbelief sounded in his voice.

"Forgiven you?" She paused for a moment as if giving the question some thought, resisted the urge to scream at him, and forced a pleasant smile to her face. "No."

"You never gave me the opportunity to explain, you know," he said in a reproving manner that quite set her teeth on edge.

"Didn't I?" She gasped in feigned dismay. "How could I have been so thoughtless? Yes, I remember now." She crossed her arms over her chest. "All of London somehow became aware that you and I, well, that you had seduced me—"

"You were scarcely reluctant if I recall." George gave a satisfied chuckle.

"No, George, I wasn't reluctant because I foolishly believed we were in love with one another and planning to spend the rest of our days together."

"I did love you," he said staunchly. "Quite profoundly."

"If you loved me so profoundly, how is it that you allowed everyone to learn of my . . . my indiscretion?"

"It was not deliberate, I assure you. Certainly you can understand. One mentions something to a friend one trusts who then mentions it to someone else and so on and so forth, and before you know what has happened—"

"Before you know what has happened, one's reputation is shattered." She glared. "Did you consider at all what would happen to me the moment you told that trusted friend?"

"That may have slipped my mind."

"And that wasn't all that slipped your mind, was it?" She gritted her teeth. "When I first became aware that our involvement had become public, I thought we could simply marry at once, and any scandal would eventually fade. Imagine my surprise to discover that you were all but betrothed to a lady I had no idea existed!"

"Constance always preferred the country," he said quickly. "She was rather shy that way."

"I was rather shy!"

"But you were exciting, Pamela." He stepped toward her eagerly, and she moved back. "I had never met a woman as exciting as you."

"*I* was exciting?" She couldn't believe he was saying such a thing. Six years ago she would never have used the word *exciting* to describe her or any part of her life. If any word described her then it was, well, *dull*.

"Indeed you were." He nodded vigorously. "You were beautiful and had no idea you were beautiful. It was most exciting. Beyond that, you were passionate and eager and charmingly innocent at the same time. And your family connections were impeccable."

"My family connections?" she said slowly.

"Absolutely. Come now, Pamela, regardless of emotion, I would never allow myself to become involved with any woman whose family connections were not impeccable. One never knows where such involvement might lead."

Had he always been so shallow? She narrowed her gaze. "As my family connections were so impeccable, and I was so exciting and you loved me so profoundly, why did you not beg off your engagement and marry me?"

"Oh, I couldn't possibly have done that." He scoffed as if the suggestion was too ridiculous to consider. "I had given my word after all. Besides, Constance stood to inherit a great deal of money. Far greater, frankly, than your dowry or your expectations. Which she did inherit by the way."

And mercenary. "So you sacrificed love for money?"

"Not at all. I was quite fond of Constance. And you needn't make it sound like that. Like it was"—indignation washed across his face—"wrong."

Pamela stared. This was the creature she had thrown away her future for? How could she ever have thought she was in love with this ludicrous excuse for a man? What an idiot she'd been. And what remarkably poor taste she'd had.

"I am so happy you got what you wanted, George."

"But I didn't, not entirely." A note of reproach sounded in his voice. "If you had just given me the opportunity to talk to you before you vanished from London, I would have explained everything."

"Do forgive me." Sarcasm rolled off her words. "I had all the explanation I needed."

He stared. "I do not remember your being quite so curt."

"I have changed a great deal, George." She waved away the comment. "Curt is the least of it."

"I have changed as well." He paused as if to allow the significance of his words to sink in. "I am widowed now."

"My condolences."

"Which means I am free to wed." An expectant note sounded in his voice.

Good Lord. She groaned to herself. "I wish you every happiness."

"You have never wed," he said pointedly.

"*Yet.*" Her tone was firm. "I have not *yet* wed." She'd really had quite enough of this. "Now if you would be so good as to step out of my way—"

"No, Pamela." George shook his head. "I have no intention of stepping out of your way. Not now. I have waited far too long to be with you again. There are things between us that must be acknowledged."

She stared for a long moment. It was exceedingly satisfying to note that, aside from a bit of lingering anger and an unrelenting desire to rip his throat out, she really felt nothing at all for him. Perhaps irritation at the moment but nothing anywhere near the vicinity of her heart. Certainly George was very much the same although why she hadn't seen his true nature six years ago could only be attributed to the fact that she had been very much a fool. To her credit, she had realized rather quickly after she'd left England that what she had felt for George was not merely a mistake but indeed had no more substance than air.

An enormous sense of freedom accompanied the realization that she'd been right.

"And I have wasted far too much time. Good evening, my lord." She started off, but George grabbed her arm and yanked her into his arms.

"Pamela, don't you understand? I love you, and I have always loved you. I was a fool six years ago, and I shall not be a fool now." He lowered his lips to hers.

"I swear to you, George, if you attempt to kiss me, I shall use my knee to inflict great bodily harm on an area which you would probably prefer to preserve."

He stilled. "You would never do such a thing."

"Oh, but I would, and, furthermore, I would enjoy it. Very much." She smiled in an overly sweet manner. "Do you wish to have children, George?"

He considered her for a moment, then sighed and released her. "You have changed."

"Indeed I have." She smoothed her dress, then glared at him. "Whatever were you thinking?"

"I wasn't thinking." He huffed. "I was swept away by passion."

"Passion?"

"Yes," he snapped. "You are the only woman I have ever felt anything approaching passion for."

"Really?"

"Yes." He nodded, then hesitated. "I probably should not confess such a thing, but as we have been lovers—"

She winced. "I daresay two rather hurried encounters scarcely makes us lovers."

"Nonetheless, we were. Indeed, you were very nearly my first."

"Very nearly?" She had the oddest urge to giggle.

"A maid or two before you perhaps." He shrugged. "They scarcely count. You were my first lady of quality."

"That explains it then," she murmured.

"There was no need for you to leave London. We could have . . ."

"We could have . . . what?" She was almost afraid to hear his answer.

"We could have been together."

"In spite of your marriage?"

"My marriage had nothing to do with us. You could have been my"—he paused dramatically—"mistress."

She stared at him for a moment and struggled against the laughter that threatened to overcome her. "Mistress?"

"It would have been quite wonderful." He sighed with anticipated rapture. "I would have taken excellent care of you."

"Would you?" She could barely choke out the words.

"As I can take care of you now. I have a great deal of money, you know, thanks to Constance and my father's demise. Pamela"—he stepped toward her and grabbed her hand—"it's not too late to recapture what we once had. Marry me now."

"Thank you, but I think not." She tugged at her hand, but he would not release it. "And I should tell you my betrothal to someone else is to be announced tonight."

"I heard mention of that. Some foreign prince as I understand." He sniffed. "One without so much as a country to his name I hear."

She hated to lower herself to George's standards, but there were obviously only certain things he would understand. "Yes well"—she jerked her hand from his—"he does have a substantial fortune."

"Oh, I see." Understanding showed in his eyes. He thought for a moment. "Still, we should not let a simple matter like your marriage stand between us. There are ways to be together."

"George." She clasped her hands together and adopted a hard tone. "If you are proposing the idea of an arrangement of an intimate nature between the two of us, I shall have to decline. I have no intentions of having a"—she closed her eyes for a moment and prayed for strength—"*lover* outside of my marriage."

"Don't be absurd, Pamela. The man's a prince. Royalty sees these things entirely differently than we do." He leaned toward her in a confidential manner. "I'd wager he'll have a mistress before you've been wed a week if he doesn't already."

Her jaw clenched. "Nonetheless—"

"We were meant to be together, Pamela, don't you understand? We are fated to be with one another. Why else are we here together, now, alone? It's destiny I tell you."

"Hardly. Half of London is here, and at some point nearly everyone wanders on to the terrace."

"Yes, but we are here alone."

"I was not alone when I—" She sighed with annoyance. "Were you watching me? Did you follow me?"

"Only driven by the hand of fate," he said quickly.

"As much as I hate to defy fate, George, we are not destined to be together. My fate lies with His Highness"—she paused for emphasis—"as does my heart."

He considered her for a long moment, his look assessing, as if he were a general preparing to redeploy his troops. She did not like that look. "Does His Highness know about your past?"

"You mean does he know about you?"

"Yes."

It was all she could do to keep from cracking her hand hard across his face. As satisfying as that might be, it would probably not be the wisest course of action. George seemed harmless, even comical, but there was something about him she did not trust. She chose her words carefully. "He knows there was a scandal in my past and generally what it was about, but he does not know the specific details."

"Excellent."

"Why?"

"Well, he will not be suspicious of me, of course."

"I fear I'm a bit confused."

"Pamela, dearest, if he does not know who I am, he will never suspect that your lover—"

"You are not my lover!" She resisted the urge to stamp her foot. "Nor will you be. Ever!"

"Fate," George said smugly. "You cannot deny it. It has brought you back to me."

"It brought me back to London!"

"And to me."

"You are incidental."

"I am the only true love of your life."

She stared. "You're completely mad."

"Indeed I am. Mad with love."

"George." She drew a deep breath. "I am going to say this once more, then I am going to return to the ball."

"Capital idea." He chuckled. "It would not do for anyone to catch us out here."

She rolled her gaze toward the heavens. "Listen closely, George. I have no interest in resuming the acquaintence we once had. Whatever it is we shared is over, done with, and in the past."

"Not for me," he said staunchly.

She ignored him. "George, I don't know how to say this kindly, and indeed you have destroyed any tendency toward kindness I may have felt for you. Therefore, I shall just say it quite plainly and in words you can comprehend.

"I would prefer never to see you again. However, as that is unlikely, I will warn you right now. If you pursue me in any manner or do anything that even remotely annoys me, if we run into one another on the street and I find your presence so much as a tiny bit irritating, I shall have my brothers thrash you to within an inch of your life. Or better yet, I shall simply shoot you myself." She smiled in a most cordial manner. "Do you understand?"

"You would never shoot me, although your brothers are a nasty lot." He narrowed his eyes. "Did you know they accosted me and inflicted a brutal beating after you left London? I was bruised for weeks."

"Consider yourself fortunate," she snapped. "I forbade them to duel with you, which means I would not allow them to kill you."

He smiled knowingly. "Because you loved me."

"Because I loved them!"

"And you love me still, as I love you." He stepped closer. "Don't you feel it between us, Pamela? There is an excitement in the air when we are together. A tension you cannot deny."

"Of course there is a tension in the air. You refuse to listen to anything I am saying. You are a lunatic, and you are driving me mad! For the last time." She shook her finger at him. "What occurred between the two of us six years ago was a dreadful mistake in judgment brought on by emotion, and it is best forgotten. I have gone on with my life as should you. I am going to marry Prince Alexei. He and he alone is the man fate has destined me for. I do not care about the state of his country, nor do I care that he has a great fortune. He has my heart, George. And that is the end of it."

George stared at her for a long moment, then shrugged. "I don't believe you."

If she screamed out of sheer frustration, it would probably just attract no end of scandalous attention. Still, it might be worth it.

"Perhaps," a familiar wry voice sounded from the shadows, "you will believe me."

"Your Highness," Pamela said with obvious relief.

Alexei stepped forward casually, as if he had not the slightest intention of planting a fist in this lout's face.

"Your Highness," the lout said, and bowed low in a most obsequious way. Obviously, he was a man impressed by royalty and probably social position and wealth as well.

"Allow me to introduce myself." The lout straightened. "I am Viscount Penwick, and I am at your service, Your Highness."

"Are you indeed?" Alexei said in an indolent manner and studied Penwick for a long moment.

So this was the man who had taken advantage of Pamela's innocence and boasted about it. The fool who had not been clever enough to understand what he was losing when he had allowed her to slip through his grasp. Although Penwick certainly did not look like a man who could sweep an intelligent woman, no matter how inexperienced with men, off her feet and into his bed. He was really rather nondescript, altogether too fair in coloring, and his chin was somewhat weak although Alexei could see where his blond charm might possibly appeal to an impressionable young woman who did not know better.

A distinct sense of gratitude gripped Alexei. After all, if Penwick had not been such an idiot, Pamela might well be his wife right now. It was a dreadful thought. Penwick would have sucked the life from her, and she never would have become the spirited creature she was today. She would never have left England's shores. Instead, she would have lived a life of desperate boredom and probably never even realized it.

And Alexei never would have met either Serenissima or Pamela.

"Why?" Alexei said coolly.

Penwick looked decidedly confused. "Why what, Your Highness?"

"Why are you at my service?" Alexei narrowed his eyes. "Did I not just hear you tell the lady I intend to marry that you did not believe her claim that she does not care for you?"

"Oh, you misunderstand, Your Highness." Penwick

laughed, a distinctly awkward sound. "Miss Effington and I are very old friends, and I was simply trying to renew our acquaintance."

Behind Alexei, Lady Overton snorted in a most unladylike manner.

Alexei raised a brow. "Were you?"

"Indeed I was, Your Highness." Penwick nodded vigorously.

"Obviously the night air has distorted my hearing. I had the impression that you were trying to do far more than renew an acquaintance. Indeed, I thought I might have heard a declaration of affection from you as well as Miss Effington's rejection of said declaration."

"Why, Your Highness." Penwick gasped in dismay. "I would never presume to press my affections."

"I was mistaken then?" Alexei glanced at Pamela. "Miss Effington, was I in error, or has Lord Penwick been both forward and offensive?"

"I say, Your Highness." Penwick stepped forward. "That's not at all—"

Alexei held out a hand to quiet him. "Well, Miss Effington, what say you? Shall I allow him to retreat to the ballroom with apologies all around for the misunderstanding, or shall I slay him where he stands?"

Penwick gasped. "Your Highness!"

"Oh would you, Your Highness?" Pamela said brightly. "You would do that for me?"

"Indeed I would, Miss Effington." His gaze met hers, and his words abruptly carried far more meaning than he had intended. "I would do anything for you."

"Be that as it may, Your Highness." Roman stepped up

behind him. "I might point out that at the moment you are unarmed."

"Am I?" Alexei adopted a note of surprise. "No sword? No pistol?"

"Regretfully no, Your Highness," Roman said with a sigh. "Your cravat is the most dangerous item on your person at the moment."

"It is certainly starched enough to be lethal. Nonetheless it will not do." Alexei shrugged. "I fear, Miss Effington, should you decide to allow me to free this miserable excuse for a man from his earthly bonds, I shall have to make arrangements to do so later."

"A duel, Your Highness?" Precisely the right touch of eagerness sounded in Roman's voice.

Alexei nodded solemnly. "A duel."

"I must protest, Your Highness," Penwick said quickly. "While I would certainly honor any such challenge I should tell you dueling is not legal in this country."

"As I intend to be the victor, that is scarcely your concern. You will not be around to suffer the consequences, and I am more than prepared to do so." Alexei smiled pleasantly. "Now then, Penwick, swords or pistols?"

Penwick's eyes widened. "Your Highness, I—"

"Before you choose, my lord," Roman said in a confidential manner to Penwick, "you should know that His Highness is considered one of the best marksmen in all of Europe."

"Am I?" Delight sounded in Alexei's voice. "I had no idea."

"Swords," Penwick said quickly. "I will warn you, I am rather good with a sword."

"Excellent." Alexei grinned. "There is nothing I like better than a challenge."

"A challenge?" Pamela said to Roman.

Roman nodded. "He enjoys a challenge a great deal. Not at all easy to come by for him, you know. He is excellent with a pistol, but he is the best swordsman in all of Avalonia and I would hazard to guess one of the very best in the world."

Pamela glanced at Alexei. "Is that true?"

Alexei shrugged modestly. "I would admit it, but it would be arrogant to do so."

Pamela bit back a smile.

"Your Highness," Penwick said in an earnest manner. "It has been my experience that Miss Effington does not approve of duels." He turned to Pamela. "Miss Effington?"

"Well, they are frightfully messy things. All that blood. Less with a pistol, though, than a sword, I should think." Pamela looked at Alexei. "Don't you agree, Your Highness?"

"Most certainly. There is scarcely any blood at all with a pistol. But a sword, especially when the severing of a limb is involved"—he shuddered dramatically—"frightfully messy indeed."

Panic shone in Penwick's eyes. "Regardless of the methods, Miss Effington, surely you of all people cannot sanction this sort of activity?"

"It is an interesting question. When I was younger I thought a duel to be a dreadful thing even aside from the illegal nature of the activity. Now, however, it doesn't seem so very bad at all." She shrugged. "I told you I'd changed, my lord."

"Is this what you wish then?" Penwick's voice rose.

Pamela appeared to mull over the question although Alexei suspected she was just giving Penwick time to consider his fate. At last she cast Alexei a resigned look. "I suppose not."

Penwick breathed a sigh of relief. "I do apologize, Miss Effington, if I offended you in any way."

"We shall consider it an unpleasant misunderstanding then and put it all behind us." Alexei cast Penwick his most beneficent smile.

"Yes, of course, Your Highness." Penwick bowed and backed away as if in fear Alexei would change his mind and skewer him on the spot.

"I assume such a misunderstanding shall not happen again? I fear I shall not be quite so," Alexei thought for a moment, "*understanding* as it were if there is a next time."

"Of course not, Your Highness. Do have a pleasant evening, Your Highness. Miss Effington." Penwick nodded once again, turned, and fled.

"Pity really," Roman said, watching Penwick's hasty retreat. "I would have liked to have seen you cut him into tiny pieces."

"Scarcely worth the effort," Alexei said idly. He didn't like the man at all and suspected even if Penwick did not share a past indiscretion with Pamela, Alexei would not like him. He glanced at Pamela. "Imagine him thinking you would be interested in renewing whatever acquaintence you once shared."

"Yes," Pamela said weakly, "imagine that."

"I have seen men like him before." Alexei stared after

Penwick with narrowed eyes. "He is a coward and a weakling. A man who seizes whatever opportunity is presented usually at the cost of those even weaker than himself."

"Yes, well . . . perhaps," Pamela murmured.

Without warning anger, irrational and intense, swept through him, and he stared at her. "I should like to have a private word with you, Miss Effington."

"Lady Overton, perhaps we should return to the ballroom," Roman said smoothly.

Lady Overton's gaze shifted from Pamela to Alexei and back. "I don't know—"

"It's quite all right, Clarissa. I daresay we shall be but a few moments behind you." Pamela's words were for her cousin, but her gaze stayed on Alexei. "The terrace is private, Your Highness."

He snorted. "Hardly. I would not hazard to guess who might next make an appearance here." He nodded past the balustrade. "Where do those stairs lead?"

"To the gardens," Pamela said. "They are quite extensive."

"Excellent." He grabbed her hand and fairly dragged her across the terrace.

"Whatever is he planning?" Lady Overton's concerned voice trailed after them. "I am not at all certain . . ."

"Your Highness," Pamela hissed. "Alexei! Where on earth do you think you are going?"

"You and I are going to have a talk, Pamela." He reached the steps and slowed; he certainly didn't want her tumbling down the stairs. He toyed with the idea of simply picking her up and carrying her into the gardens, but that would be most scandalous, and given that the whole purpose of their current scheme was to help people forget her last scandal and find her a respectable husband in the process, that would not be especially wise.

"Alexei!"

Still, it would be much faster and infinitely more efficient. He stopped abruptly, scooped her into his arms, and continued down the steps.

"What do you think you're doing?" She struggled against him. "Put me down!"

"Quiet!"

She huffed but held her tongue. Good. He wasn't sure why he was so angry, but he was, and his anger was directed at the woman in his arms.

The garden paths were lit with tiny lanterns that would have been most charming under other circumstances. As it was, they shed entirely too much light.

He turned down a substantially dimmer path that branched off from the main walkway and continued until he was certain they were out of sight of the terrace and out of hearing as well. It was a decidedly private spot, lit only by the stars above, complete with a stone bench well suited for his purposes although admittedly he was not entirely certain what his purposes were.

"This will do." He set her on her feet and stepped back.

She fisted her hands on her hips. "This will do for what?"

"I will not allow you to make a fool out of me, Pamela!"

"A fool out of you?" Confusion rang in her voice. "What are you talking about?"

"I am supposed to be your fiancé. I will not permit you

to have secret rendezvous on the terrace or anywhere else for that matter."

"It was not a rendezvous, and it was scarcely secret. Furthermore, it was not my choice. He confronted me."

He ignored her. "For as long as this farce of ours continues I will not allow assignations with any man, but particularly not with that one."

She paused. "With that one?"

"Penwick," he snapped. "I know full well who he is."

"You do?" she said slowly.

"Of course I do. I cannot believe you had the incredibly poor taste to be taken in by that sorry excuse for a man."

"How do you know—"

"Come now, Pamela, I made it my business to know."

"Why?"

"It seemed wise to know precisely what I was dealing with in terms of this charade."

"Congratulations, Your Highness. It seems you have achieved your goal and uncovered my secrets." Sarcasm colored her words.

Indeed I have, Serenissima. "It was scarcely much of a secret. All of London apparently knew."

Her voice was cool. "I was very young."

He snorted. "You were twenty."

"Very well," she snapped. "I was a fool!"

"On that we can agree!"

"Although apparently not as foolish as I am now!"

"We can agree on that as well! It was the height of stupidity to go anywhere near him. Unless, of course, you still care for him?" He was not entirely sure where that question came from or why it made him hold his breath.

"I don't . . ." She paused for a long moment, then drew a deep breath. "I don't see what concern it is of yours."

"It is my concern as long as we are bound together in this masquerade."

"But a masquerade is all that it is, Alexei," she said quietly.

She had not answered his question. And why not? It was most annoying. Aside from avoiding the issue of where they had met before and her refusal to discuss her past, she had always been relatively candid with him. At least he thought she had. Certainly he had not heard the entire conversation between Pamela and Penwick. They had arrived only in time to hear her declare Penwick was driving her mad. But surely he had overheard enough to know she had no interest in the man.

Still, Alexei had not heard her tell Penwick that she did not love him. Was that because he had been privy only to a small portion of the conversation? Or because she had never said it?

And why did it make him so blasted angry?

"Surely Penwick is not the kind of man you wish to marry?"

"What's wrong with him?"

"For one thing he is a pompous, pretentious idiot."

"That's more than one thing."

"I am certain the list goes on," he snapped.

"You're being rather unfair, aren't you?" she said mildly. "After all, you scarcely met him."

He clenched his jaw. "Nonetheless, I am an excellent judge of character."

"Are you?"

"Indeed I am. Penwick is precisely the type of man I have said would not suit you at all."

"Not adventurous enough then for me?"

"No." His tone was sharp. "Do you know what would have happened to you had you not been fortunate enough to escape him?"

"Oh, that was fortunate," she said wryly. "The ruin of my reputation and all."

"I am not talking about that." He waved away her comment. "You would have lived a life of utter propriety punctuated only by complete boredom and never realized how dreadful it was."

"I doubt it would have been dreadful." She thought for a moment. "Not overly exciting perhaps, but not dreadful. He does claim to care for me after all. There is something to be said for that. For love."

"Love?" He scoffed. "In spite of what poets claim, love cannot conquer all."

She was quiet for a long moment. "I do not believe that."

"Believe it, Pamela. Love, be it for a woman or a country or a people, no matter how profound, cannot change what is." A note of bitterness sounded in his voice. "Love can lead you to do what is right for whatever it is that holds a place in your heart. But the cost is great, and payment is taken from your very soul."

"Is it?" She seemed to hold her breath.

He did not answer. He did not know what to say short of declaring she held that place in his heart. And that he would not do. For her.

At last she drew a deep breath. "I do not want to marry without love, Alexei."

"As you wish," he said, as if it did not matter. "I told you once you needed a man who will challenge you as you will challenge him. Perhaps, with such a man, you can find love."

"I understand," she said slowly, "you have always enjoyed a challenge.

The starlight illuminated her face, and at once he was swept back to another time when he had seen her only by starlight. His heart ached at the thought of what he could never have. If he loved her, and indeed that was no longer in doubt, all he had left to give her was a life free from the demons that haunted him.

"I have no desire for marriage."

"No, of course not." She sighed in resignation. "Are we finished here then? Have you said everything you wish to say?"

No. "For the moment."

"You're not going to accuse me of having met you before? Danced with you?" She paused. "Kissed you?"

"No." He shrugged. "It seems pointless. I admit now, I must have been mistaken. If indeed we have met before, it was long ago and best forgotten as obviously I have done."

"I see." She sighed softly. "We should really return to the ballroom now. No doubt we have already been missed." She started off.

"Pamela," he said without thinking.

She halted. "Yes."

"Know that, if we had met before, I would never have forgotten you. The feel of your hand in mine. The scent of your hair on the night breeze." He resisted the urge to pull her into his arms. Only madness lay that way. "The way we would have danced as if we were made for one another."

"Never?"

"Not for the rest of my days."

"And would those memories be enough? For the rest of your days?"

Enough to sustain me through the empty years ahead? No. "One can only hope."

"One should always be careful what one wishes for, Alexei," she said softly, and a moment later she had vanished into the night.

He blew a long breath and started after her. She was the one woman in all of creation meant for him. Indeed, he had fallen in love with her not once but twice. And for her own sake, he would not tie her to him. Life with him would be every bit as dreadful as life with that idiot Penwick. Even love could not overcome the awful regrets that he lived with day and night.

Still, he couldn't help but think she was not the fool.

He was.

Thirteen

 If I ever meet a woman who makes me realize life is incomplete without her, I shall take the steps necessary to keep her by my side for the rest of my days. Although I cannot in truth conceive of such a thing as my life is extraordinarily full.

Roman, Count Stefanovich

Alexei was the perfect prince and very nearly the perfect fiancé.

Even now, dancing yet another waltz with him, which he executed flawlessly, he was, well, perfect.

He had been above reproach from the moment he and Pamela had reentered the ballroom. When Pamela's father had announced their engagement, when they had gone into supper, and when the two of them had danced together, he was charming, cordial, attentive, and . . . perfect. He hadn't uttered a word that wasn't polite or was overly personal, cast a glance that wasn't proper, or done anything whatsoever that anyone, no matter how stuffy, could look askance at. And furthermore, he was right.

She detested perfect.

Pamela wasn't sure what had triggered his outburst in the garden, but she was certain he had feelings of affection for her. Strong feelings if *she* were even half the judge of character *he* claimed to be. Indeed, there was a fleeting moment in the garden when she thought he'd declare himself. It was a very good sign. Whatever barriers Alexei refused to cross regarding love and for whatever reason, marriage, Pamela absolutely would not allow them to deter her. He was the man she was destined to spend the rest of her days with, and she intended to do just that. In spite of him if necessary.

He was quite obviously jealous of George. Apparently, Alexei had not heard enough of her conversation with George to realize she wanted nothing whatsoever to do with him, but surely he had heard her tell George that Alexei held her heart? She tried to remember every word that had passed between them, but she'd been so blasted annoyed it was decidedly hard to recall. Perhaps, if one heard only a snippet and was prone to jealousy, even if one refused to admit his feelings aloud, it might well seem as though she had some feelings for George.

She grinned at the thought. How very . . . perfect.

The music drew to a close, and Alexei escorted her off the floor.

"Whatever do you find so amusing?" Alexei asked coolly.

"Everything." She laughed. "I find the evening to be altogether delightful. I hadn't expected to enjoy myself as much as I am." She fluttered her lashes at him. "And are you enjoying it as well, Your Highness?"

"Quite." His tone was clipped, and she bit back a grin.

Alexei had indeed been perfect since their return from the garden, but he had also been cool and aloof. As if he were holding all sorts of emotions in check. She took that as a good sign as well.

"I daresay the ball is a rousing success. Your sister should be quite pleased."

"She is beside herself with satisfaction." Pamela glanced around and caught sight of Amanda. Her sister was speaking to an extremely attractive young man and obviously flirting with him. And he was obviously flirting right back. "I wonder who that is? Amanda seems quite taken with him."

Alexei's gaze followed hers, and she felt his body stiffen beside her.

"Your Highness." Roman stepped up beside Alexei. "Do you see—"

"Indeed I do, Roman." Alexei nodded slowly. He directed his words to Pamela, but his gaze remained fixed on the gentleman with her sister. The young man glanced in their direction, said something to Amanda, and started toward them. "If you will excuse me, Pamela, I really should—"

"Alexei." She laid her hand on his arm. "Who is he?"

"Simply someone I never expected to see here." A slight smile curved the corners of Alexei's lips, and he watched the stranger approach.

The gentleman was tall, dark-haired, and even more handsome than he had appeared from a distance. It was no wonder Amanda had turned her considerable charms on him. There was something oddly familiar about him as well although if Pamela had met him before, she surely would have remembered. This was not a man one easily forgot.

"Good evening." The stranger grinned and nodded a greeting. "Your Highness."

Who was he?

Alexei's eyes narrowed, but his smile widened. "What are you doing here?"

"I thought it was past time I came to London, especially when I learned you were here. Your sister sends her regards, although I am instructed to tell you she is not at all happy that she had to learn of your impending nuptials through a most indirect, although surprisingly efficient, method involving her mother-in-law, I believe." He leaned toward Pamela in a confidential manner. "A most annoying woman I can tell you."

His grin was infectious, and she returned his smile. Whoever he was, she rather liked him.

"I wrote to Tatiana when I first arrived in London, but I have not yet written her of this." Alexei grimaced. "Is she very angry?"

"Furious," the stranger said with a chuckle. "She would have come to London herself, but she is the size of a cottage. I have never seen a woman quite so enormous. If she does not give birth soon, she will surely explode, and I must confess, I am glad I shall not be around for that."

Clarissa stared as if he were a completely foreign creature. Roman grinned, and Pamela tried not to laugh.

Even Alexei looked amused. "I thought you were in Paris?"

"Ah, yes, Paris. Delightful city, but after a while one gets rather bored with all that pleasure. So I thought I would come to England. It has been far too long since I've seen either Tatiana or you." He turned to Pamela, took her hand and raised it to his lips. "You must be the incomparable Miss Effington."

"Must I?" She raised a brow. "Incomparable?"

"Without a doubt. Only a woman of the utmost charm and character would ever entice His Highness into marriage." His lips brushed across her hand, his gaze fastened firmly on hers. His dark eyes held a spark of amusement or admiration or both and were surprisingly familiar. Pamela would have sworn she had looked into those eyes before. "Unless, of course, I had seen her first."

"Miss Effington allow me to introduce"—Alexei's smile was wry—"His Royal Highness, Prince Nikolai Pruzinsky."

Prince Nikolai grinned in a most wicked manner. "I am the brother you have no doubt heard spoken of in nothing but glowing phrases."

"Oh nothing but glowing." Pamela laughed. This prince obviously took after his brother when it came to arrogance, although he had such a roguish, lighthearted air about him he was almost as irresistible as his brother had been six years ago.

Nikolai turned to Alexei, and the brothers embraced. It was obvious they cared a great deal for each other. She wondered if they'd seen each other at all since Alexei's exile. They drew apart and studied one another in the manner of men who have not been together for some time. Assessing and thoughtful, and Pamela suspected each saw far more than the other might wish.

"It is good to see you, little brother." Genuine affection sounded in Alexei's voice.

Nikolai lowered his voice and leaned closer to his brother. "How are you faring, Alexei? Tatiana worries about you, as do I."

"There is no need for worry. I am becoming accustomed to life as it is now. It is"—Alexei shrugged, his smile resigned—"bearable."

Nikolai's gaze shifted to Pamela and back to his brother. "I can see that." He caught sight of Count Stefanovich, and his smile widened. "Roman!"

"Your Highness." Roman beamed, and the two men clasped hands. "It is good to see you looking so well."

"It appears London agrees with you." Nikolai's gaze slid to Clarissa. "Dare I guess the reason why?"

Roman introduced Clarissa, and Nikolai kissed her hand. The man was remarkably polished, nearly as much so as his brother. He lingered over Clarissa's hand a shade longer than was necessary. It was most effective. Perhaps he was even more practiced than Alexei. Amanda would have to be very careful of this one. Or possibly he would have to be very careful of her.

"And is Dimitri here as well?" Nikolai glanced around the ballroom. "I cannot see him missing a gathering where there are so many lovely women and only Englishmen to appreciate them."

"He is here in London with us, but he is otherwise occupied tonight," Roman said.

Nikolai chuckled. "Of course he would be."

Alexei and Roman exchanged glances

"It is not exactly what you might think," Alexei said. "Our lives have become altogether stranger than you can imagine. The reason for Dimitri's absence tonight is one of the more bizarre aspects of life."

"You shall have to tell me everything then. Indeed, we have a great deal to talk about." Nikolai's tone was light, but an intense gleam shone in his eye.

The oddest feeling of apprehension washed through Pamela.

Alexei studied his brother, his gaze abruptly serious, his tone matching the younger man's. "Later tonight then?"

"Not tonight, brother." Nikolai shook his head. "Indeed, I had not planned on staying this long. I have made other arrangements for tonight."

"Arrangements?"

Nikolai flashed a wicked grin.

Alexei chuckled.

"But before I go, a word?" Nikolai's gaze met his brother's.

Alexei nodded. "Yes, of course."

"The terrace can be extremely private," Pamela said brightly.

Alexei shot her an annoyed glance.

"Excellent." Nikolai nodded. "Indeed, I have always found terraces to be quite convenient for a quiet word or whatever else one requires privacy for."

"The gardens are better," Alexei said under his breath.

"Roman," Nikolai said, "would you be so good as to join us?"

"Certainly, Your Highness. If you will excuse us." Roman smiled at Clarissa, nodded at Pamela, and started off with Nikolai and Alexei.

"Alexei." Pamela said without thinking, and reached to touch his arm.

"Yes?" He paused and raised a brow.

"Do be careful."

He smiled, the first genuine smile she'd seen from him since they'd come in from the garden. "I am only going to the terrace, Pamela, although I daresay terraces can be fraught with danger."

"It's silly I know, but"—her gaze met his—"it's nothing more than the strangest feeling that . . . well I don't know." She dropped her hand. "I said it was silly."

He hesitated, then took her hand and raised it to his lips. "Nonetheless, concern is always appreciated."

Alexei nodded, then followed the others. Pamela watched them make their way through the crowd toward the terrace. An awful nagging feeling of impending doom settled in the pit of her stomach.

"He is a dangerous man, Clarissa." Pamela lowered her voice and stepped closer to her cousin. They were, after all, in the midst of a rather significant crowd, and she would prefer not to be overheard.

"Prince Nikolai?" Clarissa shook her head. "Dangerously charming I would say. The man looks at you as if you were a sweet he cannot wait to savor." She paused. "It's most compelling."

"That's not what I mean although I daresay you're right." Pamela drew her brows together. "There is something about him. I don't know what exactly; I just have the oddest feeling that his presence here does not bode well."

"Pamela." Clarissa drew a deep breath. "Has His Highness, Prince Alexei that is, told you anything about those final days in Avalonia? After his father's death, when Russia was annexing the country?"

"Not really." Pamela shook her head. "He's spoken a bit about his father's death but no more than that. He's never talked about giving up his country. I suspect it is too difficult for him."

"Roman told me His Highness was given the choice of remaining as Avalonia's king in a strictly symbolic position—"

"He would have hated that."

"Or exile. Roman says he chose to leave because he feared revolution would always be a possibility if he remained. And his people and his country would pay the price."

"They could never have triumphed against Russia."

"No." Clarissa shook her head. "It was the only decision possible, indeed, the only way to save Avalonia and its people, but Roman says . . ."

"Yes?" Pamela held her breath.

"Even now it weighs heavily on His Highness. He is torn with regret that he did not choose to fight against the Russians."

"He had no choice." Pamela stared. "It would have been a slaughter. Russia defeated Napoleon. Avalonia would have been no more than a minor annoyance."

The horror of what could have happened took her breath away. Alexei, Stefanovich, Petrov, and countless

Avalonians, including, no doubt, children and women, would have been killed. The country itself would have been destroyed. Russia was renowned for its intolerance of rebellion of any kind. The realization of the dreadful decision Alexei had made tore at her heart.

"Love can lead you to do what is right for whatever it is that holds a place in your heart. But the cost is great, and payment is taken from your very soul."

"He has never talked about it, but then why would he?" Pamela shook her head. "After all, our engagement is nothing but an act. He does not truly intend to spend his life with me."

"Perhaps," Clarissa said slowly, "the regret he carries is why he does not wish to marry."

"And perhaps he needs me more than he knows." She raised a brow. "Is that speculation on your part or have you discov—"

"No," Clarissa said firmly then smiled. "Not yet." She sobered. "Pamela, you should know as well that Nikolai did not agree with his brother's decision."

"He is young and probably quite reckless and—"

"Alexei was forced to send him away for fear he would rally an army and lead it against Russia."

"Alexei was right." An icy hand of dread griped Pamela's heart. "It would have been futile. Nothing short of madness."

Or suicide. The word lodged in her mind.

"Indeed it would have," Clarissa said. "But it is over and done with now. Nikolai may well still disagree with Alexei's actions, but what can be done now? There is probably nothing to be concerned about at all. Besides, it is entirely to be expected that Nikolai would come to join his brother with no more intention than the reuniting of his family."

"You're right, of course." Pamela forced a smile. "The only danger Nikolai presents is to those ladies foolish enough to succumb to the invitation in his eyes."

"Or the broad stretch of his shoulders," Clarissa said, with an amused smile.

Pamela laughed. "The polished charm of his words."

Clarissa joined her, then smoothly turned the topic of the discussion to the blatant flirtation, or perhaps seduction, taking place across the room between a rather notorious, and long-wed, countess and an equally long-married, and not at all to be trusted, lord. It was but one of any number of interesting scenes being played out around the room and no doubt on the terrace as well.

"Pamela, my dear, I heard you were here."

Pamela turned to find another relative she had not yet greeted. A moment later she was engaged in a conversation about something altogether meaningless that she nonetheless pretended had her full attention. Even so, she kept a close eye on the doors to the terrace.

Pamela could well see she was jumping to absurd conclusions based on nothing more than an odd sense of impending doom. In truth, she had nothing of substance to base even that feeling on. It was the height of absurdity to think Nikolai's appearance was anything but innocent.

Still, Pamela couldn't escape the feeling that something was very, very wrong.

* * *

"Dare I ask what you are thinking?" Roman said.

Alexei leaned his forearms on the stone balustrade, clasped his hands together, and stared out into the night. "It was good to see my brother again. It has been far too long."

Nikolai had taken his leave a scant few moments ago. Their talk had been brief. A prelude, nothing more.

"He looks well." Roman paused. "However, that was not what I meant."

"I know." Alexei shook his head slowly. "I am not sure what to think."

"Surely Your Highness, you can't—"

"I do not know," he said sharply, then blew a long breath. "I am sorry, old friend, I should not take my frustration out on you."

"No apologies are needed, Your Highness." Roman paused for a moment. His words were measured. "We have been down this road before."

"I told Nikolai I would hear him out, and I intend to do so. After that." After that . . . what? "I have no idea what he intends to say."

"No, of course not, Your Highness."

"You could say that as though you truly believed it, Roman."

"I could," Roman said slowly. "Although it would be a lie."

"We shall see tomorrow."

Roman did not answer, but his silence said a great deal.

"Now, what are you thinking, Roman?"

"I do not believe you would like it, Your Highness."

Alexei chuckled without humor. "I do not expect to."

"Very well." Roman paused as if choosing his words carefully. Not that it mattered. Alexei knew full well what his advisor, his friend would no doubt say. "I think, Your Highness, it is most unfair."

"Unfair?" Alexei glanced at the other man in surprise. "What do you mean unfair?"

Roman drew a deep breath. "It does not seem fair that a man should have to choose to have his heart torn out twice in the same lifetime."

Alexei was silent for a long moment.

"Your Highness?"

"Someone once said to me," Alexei said slowly, "that much in life is unfair. That we cannot always have what we want. I disregarded it at the time. It had no meaning for me then, as I had always had everything I had ever wanted. I had never imagined life would be any other way, not really." He shrugged. "But it is and is it unfair? Perhaps. Still, such is the way of the world we live in."

"Rather a pity I think."

"It is simply life. It forces you to make the choices you must make whether you wish to or not." Alexei searched for the right words. "One makes the decisions one does in life for the good of all concerned. For their lives or their happiness or their survival but always to their benefit whether they appreciate it or not. Indeed, they may well hate you for it. Still, it is your responsibility, and it carries a great weight."

Roman nodded. "The responsibility of rule."

"Not at all, old friend." Alexei blew a long breath. "The responsibility of love."

* * *

It was going to be a very long night. No, it had already been a very long night.

Pamela lay in her bed and stared unseeing at the ceiling somewhere in the dark shadows above.

The remainder of the ball had been most disquieting. When Alexei had returned from his talk with his brother he, and Roman as well, had been preoccupied and reticent to say much of anything of substance. Alexei was polite, of course, and eminently proper, but she had the distinct impression that his thoughts were far away in a beloved country and a time not so very long ago.

Alexei's behavior was not her only concern. She had caught sight of George too often for comfort. At times the man was but a few steps away. And each and every time she had seen him he had been staring at her with a speculative look in his eye. It was disconcerting and might well be a bit frightening if George had been something other than the fool he was. Still, he was to be avoided.

She turned on her side and cradled her head in her arms. Even the ride home was silent, fraught with unstated concerns and unease. Tension hung so thick in the carriage Pamela wondered if a word said aloud would cause visible ripples in the air like a stone in water. Alexei had retired immediately upon their return, and Pamela had gone to her own rooms a few moments later, leaving Clarissa and Stefanovich to bid one another good night in private.

What had happened on the terrace with Nikolai? What had he said to his brother? It was important, she was certain of it. Regardless of his silence, she could see something preyed on Alexei's mind. Even perhaps on his heart. And it terrified her.

Clarissa might know. Pamela sat up. Roman had already confided in her. Indeed, he had told her far more than Alexei had ever revealed to Pamela. Of course, Stefanovich had probably revealed his feelings to Clarissa as well, or at least did not hide them as thoroughly as Alexei seemed to. Pamela refused to so much as consider the possibility that Alexei might not have feelings for her. She saw it in his eyes and knew it as well somewhere in the very depths of her soul.

She flung off the covers, slid out of bed, and grabbed her wrapper. She had it no more than halfway on when she reached the door and stepped into the hall. While it was unlikely that anyone would be about at this late, or rather, this early, an hour, it was best to be cautious.

Pamela slipped quietly down the dark hall to Clarissa's room, knocked softly, and waited. Her cousin had never been a sound sleeper. A few moments later she tried again with a somewhat firmer knock. She would give Clarissa another moment or two.

"Who is it," a hushed voice sounded from the other side of the door.

"It's me," Pamela said as quietly as possible. Who was it indeed? "Pamela."

Clarissa paused. "What do you want?"

"I must speak with you. Open the door."

"Why?"

"It's important."

Again there was a pause. "Very well."

The door opened just enough for Clarissa to slip into

the corridor. She held her wrapper together with one hand and pulled the door closed behind her with the other. "What is it?"

"Did the count tell you what Nikolai wanted tonight?"

"No." Clarissa sighed. "Is that all?"

"Well, there is more, of course, but that seems to be the most important question at the moment. Did I wake you?"

"No. Or rather yes," Clarissa said quickly.

"I am sorry, but I simply cannot sleep. There are far too many questions and concerns swimming in my head. May I come in for a bit?"

"No," Clarissa said firmly

Pamela frowned. "Why not?"

"Because you can't. Because it's . . . it's very late. Yes, that's it. It's very late, and I'm very tired."

"Don't be silly. We have chatted together in the middle of the night like this any number of occasions. This is absolutely no different."

"Regardless, I—"

At once realization dawned. Pamela sucked in a sharp breath. "Good Lord, you're not alone, are you?"

Clarissa heaved a sigh of surrender. "No, I am not alone."

Pamela stared and wished she could better make out Clarissa's expression. She knew her cousin and the count were on this path, and as much as she thought Clarissa had been far too long without a man in her bed, it was still somewhat shocking to realize her perfectly proper cousin had at last given in to temptation. Shocking and quite delightful.

Pamela grinned. "I should probably go then."

"Yes, you probably should."

"Say, while you have him in this . . . position—"

"Pamela!"

"It's the perfect opportunity to ask about Venice and Alexei's attitude about marriage."

Clarissa huffed. "I hardly think so."

"Still—"

"Still, I shall do what I can, but not at this particular moment. Now"—Clarissa opened the door just wide enough to allow her to slip back into her room—"I am returning to my bed, and I suggest you do the same." She started to close the door.

"Clarissa?"

Clarissa sighed. "What is it now?"

"Was it wonderful?"

"Yes!" Clarissa hissed. "Now go away." The door snapped closed behind her.

A slow grin spread across Pamela's face. Clarissa well deserved to find happiness, and Pamela had no doubt her happiness lay with the count. She would not be at all surprised if they announced their intention to wed in the morning, or at least very soon.

Of course, everyone's happiness might well depend on Nikolai. Pamela's smile faded. Her own speculation was probably absurd. She really knew nothing at all about Alexei's brother save what little Count Stefanovich had told Clarissa. It could well be, with the passage of time, he, too, had accepted the loss of Avalonia. Alexei's serious demeanor after their meeting might have nothing to do with anything remotely dangerous but something distinctly personal. Perhaps a problem with their sister or another relative?

Still, Pamela had never had a feeling of apprehension quite like this before, and she could not ignore it. And there was one person who might be able to give her some answer as to Nikolai's intentions.

She drew a deep breath and started down the hall toward the far end of the house. She reached what she thought was the right door and noticed a faint light coming from under the doorway. Good. At least she wouldn't be disturbing anyone else. She knocked quietly, waited a few moments, then knocked again.

The door opened abruptly. Valentina stood in the doorway, clad in only a sheet wrapped around her. Even in the faint light from the candle or lamp or whatever it was she had burning in her room she looked distinctly annoyed and really rather menacing.

"What do you want?" the princess snapped.

Pamela took a step back. "Could I speak to you for a moment?"

"Could you what? Now?" Valentina's eyes narrowed. "Why?"

"Because you're the only one who might have the information I need."

"Really?" Valentina leaned against the doorway and studied her curiously. "In the middle of the night?"

Pamela shrugged. "I couldn't sleep."

Valentina smiled in a wicked manner. "I do not seem to be getting a great deal of sleep myself."

"There must be something in the air tonight. I . . ."

Valentina chuckled.

Pamela winced. "You are not alone are you?"

"No."

Pamela stared. "It's not . . . surely it isn't . . . it can't possibly be . . . is it Captain Petrov?"

Valentina cast a glance over her shoulder. "Why, indeed it is."

"I thought you hated him"

"Oh, I do."

"And I thought he disliked you as well."

"He detests me."

"Then I don't understand."

"My dear Pamela, that is what makes it all so very exciting. Passion is passion. I despise him, and he cannot abide me. The passion of our distaste for one another is precisely what makes relations between us absolutely glorious." She sighed in a distinctly satisfied manner. "I may have to keep him."

"I see," Pamela said slowly.

Valentina laughed. "You do not."

"Perhaps not." She smiled reluctantly.

"Did you want something then? Or are middle-of-the-night visits some sort of obscure English custom?" Valentina stifled a yawn. "If so, I do not find it the least bit charming."

"Prince Nikolai is here."

"Here? In the house?"

"No, he was at the ball." Pamela paused. "He spoke with Alexei and the count. I believe they have another meeting tomorrow."

"I see," Valentina said slowly. There was a murmured question from somewhere behind her. "Do be quiet, Petrov."

The response was low and muttered, and Pamela was grateful she could not make it out.

Valentina laughed. "That does sound like fun."

Pamela ignored the outrageous ideas that popped into her head about Petrov's unheard comment and what the princess's laugh implied.

"About Nikolai?" Pamela prompted.

"Ah, yes." Valentina thought for a moment. "No doubt he simply wanted to see his brother." She shrugged and started to close the door.

"Your Highness," Pamela said quickly. "Alexei and the count were both pensive and preoccupied after they talked to Nikolai, and, quite frankly, their manner has me concerned."

"Pamela, you may well be seeing trouble where none exists. I daresay—"

"Your Highness, please."

"In truth I do not know what to say. I would suspect Nikolai has not accepted the changes in our world as Alexei has or, for that matter, as I now have. I can well understand his feelings." She paused for a moment, then blew a resigned breath. "I have come to one inescapable conclusion in recent months, and if you breathe a word of this, I shall quite cheerfully slit your throat. Or have it slit, it scarcely matters."

"You needn't threaten me. I don't find you the least bit frightening, you know."

"Not even a little?"

"No," Pamela said firmly, although in truth the princess was more than a little intimidating.

"I have changed more than I thought," Valentina murmured.

"I shall keep your confidence. You have my word."

"Really? Very well then." Valentina paused. "Alexei was right."

"About?"

"His decision not to oppose the Russians." The princess sighed. "I did not realize it at the time, of course, but then in some ways I have always let my passions overrule my head."

Pamela snorted.

Valentina ignored her. "In truth, Alexei had no choice, and fortunately for Avalonia, the wisdom to accept it. Again, if you dare to mention—"

"I won't say a word. What about Nikolai?"

"Nikolai is young, and we are all rather stupid when we are young."

"We certainly can be," Pamela said under her breath.

"I have no idea what Nikolai's intentions are. We shall have to wait until tomorrow. Or rather later today to be accurate. Now then, if there is nothing else?"

"No." Pamela shook her head. "Nothing."

Valentina studied her for a moment. "I am sorry that I was not of more help. You must realize my cousins and I have always been, well, natural enemies as it were. Therefore, I do not know them as well as other people might know members of their family. They do not trust me yet, and there is every chance they never will. It is my burden to bear, and even I can admit I well deserve it. As much as it pains me to confess it, I now truly believe Alexei chose the wisest course for our people and that he will continue to do what is in their best interest. I believe as well, God help me"—she heaved a heartfelt sigh—"he would have made a wise and good, possibly even great, king."

Pamela stared.

"I know, it is all very shocking," Valentina said wryly. "I can scarcely accept it myself."

Pamela nodded slowly. "Good evening, Your Highness, and thank you."

"Yes, yes." Valentina grimaced, stepped back, and closed the door.

Pamela stared at the closed door. She certainly hadn't expected any of that. Oh, not Petrov in Valentina's bed, although that was something Pamela would never have imagined, but Valentina's comments about Alexei. The princess really had changed if she thought her cousin would have made a great king.

Pamela started back toward her room although she doubted even now she'd be able to sleep. She toyed with knocking on Aunt Millicent's door, but she rather feared what she would find there as well. Besides, Aunt Millicent might well try to calm Pamela's fears, but she knew nothing of the situation and could not provide any insight.

There was nothing to be done for it then. She would have to wait until tomorrow. Or later today. Or . . . her step slowed.

She could go directly to Alexei. She would never be able to sleep until she had an answer. Admittedly presenting herself at Alexei's door at this late hour, dressed in nothing but her nightclothes, carried a definite risk.

Was it a risk she was willing to take? She had no particular intention of ending the night in his bed, but she had no particular aversion to it either. Her heart thudded in her chest. She turned on her heel and started toward the far end of the passage. His rooms were at the very end of the corridor, as far away from hers as one could get.

She had had two rather cursory, and unsatisfactory, intimate encounters with George. And one night of bliss and magic with Alexei. If things did not end well between them, or if Nikolai's presence did indeed lead to disaster, it was entirely possible she would have no other chance to be with him again. She knew now respectability was not as important to her as he was. And knew as well if she did not marry him, she would not marry at all.

Once she had chosen him as the man to start her on the path to a life of experience. Now he was the man who held her heart.

And, whether he wished it or not, always would.

Fourteen

If ever I meet a man who can make me feel as my husband did, as if I am the only woman in the world, I shall abandon all sense of propriety and follow my heart wherever it may lead. Right or wrong.

Clarissa, Lady Overton

"What is it?" Alexei yanked the door open and stared. "What are you doing here?"

Pamela stood in the doorway illuminated by the light behind him. She was scandalously clad in some sort of flimsy robe, her hair rumpled, her eyes dark and shadowed.

"I couldn't sleep, and I saw the light under your door."

"Yes, well." He ran his hand through his hair, acutely aware that all he wore was a dressing gown and silk trousers. "That seems to be my trouble as well."

"May I come in?"

"I do not think that would be wise."

"Perhaps not." She shrugged. "However, unless you intend to leave me in the corridor, where I warn you I shall pound on your door, no doubt rousing anyone who may yet be asleep, and as—"

"Come in," he snapped and stepped aside to let her pass. She slipped into the room, the scent that was hers and hers alone drifting in her wake. He shut the door behind her and wondered how grave a mistake it was to allow her in his room and anywhere near his bed. The very same bed where he had dreamed about her, indeed where he had envisioned her, ever since they had first met. Or rather, met again.

She wandered around the room, lit but dimly by the single lamp. "I see your rooms are not substantially better cared for than mine."

"They are sufficient for my needs."

"Still, it's not the luxury that you are used to." She ran her hand along the fringed edge of the window drapes.

"One accustoms oneself to what one must. Besides, it is all of good quality, if a bit worn, and the maids are thorough. In truth, I have scarcely noticed." He narrowed his eyes. "Surely you are not here to check on the suitability of my accommodations?"

"It would seem rather absurd at this hour." She glanced around the room, her gaze settling for just a moment on the bed. Very large, with carved posts and an upper frame for bed hangings long since vanished, it was the kind of bed that fairly invited the partaking of pleasure. A blush swept up her face, and she quickly looked away. "Still, it is my house, at least in part; therefore, you are my guest."

He snorted. "And paying for the privilege."

"Is it so bad then? Staying here with us."

"It is indeed a"—he smiled—"privilege."

She returned his smile.

"What do you want, Pamela?" he said softly.

"First?" Her gaze met his, her dark eyes simmered. His stomached lurched.

He drew a deep breath and nodded. "First."

"I want to know why your brother is here."

He shook his head. "I do apologize, Pamela, but that is really none of your concern."

"Isn't it?" She settled into a chair near the fireplace and studied him. "It seems to me it is indeed my concern as long as we are in this masquerade."

"Well said. Although I have never especially enjoyed having my words thrown back in my face."

"It wasn't really throwing. It was more in the manner of, oh, gently tossing." She grinned. "But with unerring accuracy."

"Very well, then, I dislike having my words tossed at me, gently or otherwise, with unerring accuracy."

"And I dislike avoidance of a simple question," she said coolly.

"A simple question? I would have thought you of all people would have well understood the avoidance of a simple question. A question like oh, let me think. What was it again?" He paused thoughtfully. "Ah yes. Questions such as where have we met before? Or even where have we kissed?"

"I thought you had decided you were mistaken?"

"That is one of the problems with admitting one's mistakes." He shook his head forlornly. "When you do so once, you may well open the doors to doing so again."

"What?" She shook her head in confusion.

"In admitting I was wrong about having met you before I allowed the possibility that the admission of my mistake was a mistake in and of itself."

"That is most confusing, and you well know it." She frowned in annoyance. "You are simply trying to change the subject."

"I am not trying to do anything." He crossed his arms and leaned against the carved post of the bed. "I have already done it."

She narrowed her eyes. "Why is your brother here?"

"He is my brother. We have not seen one another for some time. Indeed, it has been far too long." He paused. "You did not see your brothers for many years. No doubt you missed them."

"Well, yes—"

"I made the acquaintance of both of them tonight. They were pleasant enough although they did seem to view me with a certain lack of trust and a definite touch of suspicion."

She waved away his comment. "They are brothers. They do not trust any men who express interest in my sister or myself."

"And yet they also greeted me with a distinct air of relief and possibly even gratitude," he said thoughtfully. "I wonder why that was?"

She stared at him for a moment, then laughed. "They shall be quite disappointed when you and I do not marry. They probably see you as the answer to their prayers."

He chuckled. "As the plan is for me to be at fault for

the unhappy ending of our engagement, I shall make it a point to avoid them afterward."

"Avoiding my brothers is an excellent idea. As for *your* brother—"

"I do not, in truth, know why Nikolai is here." Alexei sighed in surrender and ignored the fact that he could well guess Nikolai's intentions even if his brother had not yet stated them aloud. "And until I do—"

"You will know today, though, won't you?" she pressed.

"If indeed there is anything to know, and that is yet to be determined." He stared at her. "Why are you so intent upon knowing why my brother is here? Is it that unusual for one brother to visit another?"

"Not at all. I just . . ." She got to her feet and paced the room. "It will sound ridiculous."

"I expect it to."

She ignored him. "From the moment I saw him, I had, well, an odd sort of feeling about him."

He raised a brow. "A feeling?"

"Yes. And you needn't look at me like that."

"Like you were just a bit mad?" he said pleasantly.

"Yes," she snapped, then drew a deep breath. "I assure you I am quite sane."

"I do not know." He shook his head in a solemn manner. "I have always heard that the insane routinely declare themselves to be sane. How do I know that you—"

"Alexei."

"Any moment you could begin batting at invisible flies."

"Alexei!"

"Sorry." He grinned. He did so love it when she was indignant. "Do go on."

"I have a feeling something is going to happen." She paused and stared at him. "Something dreadful."

"Well," he said slowly, "we are engaged. Many might say something dreadful has already—"

"I am quite serious about this." Indignation fairly rang in her voice.

He bit back a grin.

"I would prefer that nothing dreadful, indeed, nothing *fatal*, happen to you."

"That is very kind of you, but if something did indeed happen to me of a fatal nature—"

"Death?" she snapped, as if the idea of his death no longer bothered her but, at the moment at least, was somewhat appealing.

"It would neatly end our engagement, and I would not have to behave in a despicable manner, which I must say I am not looking forward to. Indeed, with my demise you would garner no end of sympathy and, no doubt, many a masculine shoulder to cry on."

"Do be serious." She folded her arms over her chest and glared.

"I am serious. It would be a perfect ending to it all."
She glared at him.

"Very well, I shall try to take this all seriously." He resisted the urge—no—the need to move to her and put his arms around her. "But it will be extremely difficult."

"Nonetheless." She stepped closer to him, concern shining in her eyes. "You will not do anything foolish, will you?"

"Anything foolish?" Blast it all, he was more than ready to do something extremely foolish. With her. Right now. "There are any number of things I should like to do that one might consider foolish."

"Anything dangerous then."

He was certain she had some feelings for him, even if she might still feel a little something for that idiot Penwick. Precisely why being together now would just make it more difficult to be apart when the time came. For both of them. "I shall avoid anything dangerous."

"Dare I believe you?" Her gaze searched his.

On the other hand, being together now would give them both something to look back on in the years to come. "Yes, of course."

"May I have your word then?"

And it was not as if they had not shared his bed before. "You may have whatever you wish."

She stared up at him. "Whatever I wish?"

He nodded.

She rested her hand on his chest, and he tried not to jump. "Anything at all?"

"Anything at all." He grabbed her hand, pulled it to his lips, and kissed her palm. "But you should leave now."

"I don't want to leave."

Nor did he want her to leave. Regardless, it was in her best interest for whatever it was between them to go no farther. Before he broke her heart. Before she broke his.

He released her hand and stepped back. "Pamela, do you not understand what will happen if you remain here? In my bed chamber? At this hour of the night? Dressed like . . . like that?"

"I understand completely."

"I am not a saint. Do not forget my reputation. And I am not used to denial."

"Excellent. In that we agree. I, too, am not fond of denial." Her gaze met his. "You did say anything at all."

"That might have been another mistake on my part."

"Do you think so?" She drew a deep breath, unfastened her robe, pulled it off, and dropped it to the floor. "Pity."

"Yes, I think so," he snapped, scooped the robe up and tossed it at her. "If you are trying to seduce me, I warn you, you will not be successful."

She held the robe out by two fingers and let it drift back to the floor. It was perhaps the most seductive thing he had ever seen. "Oh?"

"Do not play games with me, Pamela."

"But I rather like games." She stepped closer.

"I do not." He stepped back until his back was pressed against the post of the bed. "I am trying to . . . to save you."

"Save me?" She slipped her hands through the opening of his dressing gown and ran her fingers lightly over his chest. His stomach clenched. "From you?"

"More likely from yourself." He caught her hands and glared down at her. "I warn you, Pamela, I shall not resist what you offer for much longer."

"Good." She opened his dressing gown, leaned forward, and placed a kiss in the center of his chest. His resistance shattered, and he pulled her into his arms.

"Pamela." *Serenissima.* He groaned and crushed his lips to hers.

She tasted of fire and passion and memory. Her lips greeted his eagerly, her hunger matched his own. Her mouth opened beneath his, and his tongue plundered hers.

She yanked his dressing gown open and pushed it over his shoulders. He pulled her harder against him, the soft fabric of her nightdress nothing more than a whisper between the heat of his body and hers. Her breasts molded against his chest, and he knew he was lost. And did not care.

He ran his hands over her back and down the curve of her buttocks, cupping them in his hands and pressing her closer against him. His hips ground against hers, his arousal hard and hot and aching. He gathered the fabric of her gown and pulled it up until he could slide his hands over the smooth flesh of the backs of her thighs. He shifted quickly, drew his lips from hers, and in one well-practiced move, pulled her gown over her head and tossed it aside.

"Oh my." She sighed.

He pulled her hard against him, and his lips once more claimed hers. Her naked breasts crushed against his bare chest, the hard tips of her nipples pressing against him. His hands roamed over the planes of her back and the curves of her derriere. Her hands trailed down his side, her touch light and fluttering, as if she wanted to explore every inch of him but was hesitant and unsure. He rather liked that. Innocence and eagerness. Her hands reached the silk of his trousers and skimmed over the fabric to caress his buttocks.

Abruptly, he stepped away.

She drew a deep shuddering breath. "Alexei—"

"Do be quiet, for once, Pamela, I wish to look at you."
As I have not done before. As I have always wished to do.

"I have no wish to be inspected."

He laughed and took her hands. "Nor have I any desire
to inspect." His gaze moved from her eyes to the long
column of her throat and lower. "Only to worship." Her
body caught the light of the lamp and glowed with
warmth like a painting by a renaissance master. Sensual
and golden as if painted by Botticelli himself. A fresco
come to life, an angel to earth. Her breasts were firm and
full, her waist narrow, her hips broad and inviting. She
was exactly as he had pictured her in the quiet hours of
his dreams, the dreams that had filled the years since he
had known her only with his touch.

"Well?" She shifted from foot to foot as if distinctly
uncomfortable. "Have you seen enough then?"

"Never," he murmured, and released her hands.

He stepped closer and cupped her breasts, then lowered his mouth to her nipple. He ran his tongue lightly
over the tip, and she gasped. His tongue trailed around
her nipple, and it tightened and puckered at his touch. He
drew it into his mouth and suckled, and he felt her stomach tighten against him. He turned his attention to the
other breast and feasted on it until her breath came short
and shallow.

Alexei dropped to his knees and clasped her closer to
him and nuzzled his mouth against the soft flesh of her
stomach. Tasting and teasing until her fingers tightened
on his shoulders, and she moaned. He ran his hands along
the backs of her thighs and her calves and caressed her

ankles. And then slowly, so slowly, he felt her hold her breath, drew his hands up between her legs to the soft flesh of her inner thighs and the curls at the juncture of her legs. He nudged her legs apart with one hand and lightly cupped her mound with the other. She sucked in a sharp breath. She was hot and moist against his hand, and his fingers explored the soft, slick folds of flesh. He found the hard sensitive point of her pleasure and caressed it. She gasped and tried to pull away, but he held her tight and stroked her until he felt the tension building within her. And his own arousal throbbed between his legs.

Without warning he rose, scooped her into his arms, and laid her on the bed. Her eyes were glazed with passion, and she could do no more than moan.

He shrugged out of his trousers, then joined her on the bed to kneel between her legs. He spread her legs and lowered his mouth to taste of her. She gasped and arched upward. His tongue caressed her, teased her until she writhed with pleasure. The taste of her, the scent of her aroused him until he knew he could take no more and knew as well she tottered on the brink of release.

He shifted to straddle her, braced himself with one arm and guided his aching member into her.

"Alexei." She sighed and wrapped her arms around him.

He entered her gently and gasped with the intense sensation of her wet heat surrounding him, enveloping him. She was tight and slick with desire, and he resisted the urge to hurry. He pushed with a slow deliberate stroke until he was buried inside her, and she consumed him. He lay still for a long moment, savoring the feel of being one with her. Of her body joined with his. Perfectly and forever.

At last he slid back until he had nearly withdrawn, then pushed forward again, a measured, even stroke designed to heighten her pleasure and his. She wrapped her legs around him and arched her hips up to meet him. He wanted to go on like this forever, but tension built inexorably within him and urged him faster. His pace increased. The feel of her body around his spurred him on. He thrust harder, and she met him with urgency of her own. She whimpered and gripped his shoulders, and he buried his head in her neck. He climbed harder and faster toward release, toward bliss, but would not allow it. Not without her.

Her cries and the labored sound of her breathing mixed and meshed with his, and he no longer knew whose was whose. No longer knew where he ended and she began. No longer cared. Her pleasure was his, his was hers. They were as one, joined in sensation and desire, and they soared toward a pleasure he had but tasted before and never, never like this. And when he thought he could restrain his own urgency no longer, she called out his name and dug her nails hard into his shoulders, and her body exploded beneath his in waves that washed through her and into his very soul. And his own release came hot and intense and convulsed his body as if it would tear him apart, and for a moment he knew without question he could die in her arms without regrets, with a joy he'd never known.

With love.

He wrapped his leg around hers, binding her tightly against him and shifted to the side in a careful manner.

He was not yet ready to withdraw from her. Indeed, the feel of her enveloping him even now in his sated state was a pleasure he did not wish to give up.

She smiled into his eyes. "That was . . ." She heaved a contented sigh. "Very . . ."

"Yes it was." He smiled back. "Very."

She brushed her lips across his. "You are very . . ."

He chuckled. "You are rather very yourself."

"Yes, I am." She smiled with satisfaction. "Do you think I'm wanton, Your Highness?"

"I think you're perfect, Miss Effington."

"I'm not at all certain I wish to be perfect." She tightened around him, and a jolt of pleasure shot through him. "I think I need a lot of practice to become perfect."

He felt himself growing hard again within her. "There is much to be said for practice."

"You, however, do this exceedingly well, Your Highness." She pressed her lips to his in a slow, leisurely manner. "It's all that practice no doubt."

"It doesn't bother you then?"

She swung her leg over his and the next moment was sitting, impaled, grinning down at him. "I am extremely jealous of each and every one, but your past is your past and cannot be changed." She started to rock slowly.

"Oh . . . yes . . . well . . ." Dear God, she felt good. He gripped her waist. "I do not care either, you know, about your past and what, well, however many men . . ."

"Men?" Her eyes closed, and her head dropped back, and he watched the effect of increasing pleasure play across her face. "Certainly not as many . . . oh my . . . as you've had women."

"Ah yes ... half the women ... in Europe." He was not entirely sure what he was saying, his attention was not at all on his words. "Although you surely have not been with ... that many men."

"Of course not ... I ..." She leaned forward, and he caught her breasts in his hands. She moaned. "Does ... does it matter?"

"No ... no." He could barely get out the words. "Not in the least."

"I would think ..."

He rubbed his thumbs over her nipples.

"Dear Lord ... Alexei. ..." She ground her hips harder against his. "Why is it of significance?"

He thrust upward. "What?"

"How many men ... oh yes ..." She bent forward, and he drew her breasts to his mouth. "When the number of women ... you've had ..."

"Because," he murmured against her breasts, "I am a man."

"That's not at all ..." She gasped. "Fair."

"Standards ... are different ..." he raised his hips to meet hers. "For men."

She braced her hands on either side of his shoulders and met his thrusts with hers. "Why?" The word was more a cry than a question.

He gripped her buttocks and pulled her down hard onto him.

"They ... just are."

He pounded himself up into her, and she responded with an eagerness, delightfully wanton, that matched his, and once more he felt himself nearing release. He slipped his hand between them and flicked his fingers over that most sensitive spot of hers, and she screamed and her body jerked and spasmed around his, and his release came with a force he did not expect. It ripped his breath away. And seared his soul.

She collapsed on top of him. Her heart pounded against him, in unison with his. An odd sort of sound came from her, and her body shook on top of his.

"Pamela?" Her head was on his chest and he could not see her face. "Please tell me you are not laughing."

She raised her head and grinned. "I couldn't help it, it was so"—she sighed with utter satisfaction—"delicious."

He chuckled. "It was rather delicious."

"Now then, as we were saying."

"Were we saying something?"

"Indeed we were." She studied him. "Why does it matter how many men there have been in my life—"

He groaned. "Pamela."

"—when it is not supposed to matter how many women there have been in yours?"

"I do not know." He blew a long breath. "A man simply likes to think that the woman that he cares about—"

She arched a brow. "You care about me?"

"Of course, I am your fiancé."

"Ah yes, how silly of me to forget."

"However," he forced himself to go on, "if you can overlook my past, I can certainly overlook yours."

"That's very generous of you." She narrowed her eyes. "What exactly do you wish to know?"

I want to know if Venice was as special to you as it was to me, or was I simply another conquest?

"Nothing." He pulled her lips to his. "Nothing at all."

He held her close for a long moment, his arms wrapped around her. Every inch of her as familiar as his dreams. And just as perfect.

She lifted her head and smiled in a resigned manner. "I should go. It's nearly dawn."

"Yes, you should." He stroked her hair.

"I had not planned on staying this long." She laughed. I had not planned on this at all."

"Nor had I." He heaved a resigned sigh.

She met his gaze. "Was it a mistake then, Alexei?"

He stared into her sable eyes, darker if possible with the sensual glow of a woman well satisfied. "It may well have been, but a rather glorious mistake nonetheless."

"Worth it then, I think." She shifted but seemed as reluctant to leave the warmth of his bed as he was to let her go. "About the other men in my life."

"Good God, Pamela." He grimaced. "I shall not say it again. Your past as well as mine is irrelevant to here and now and the two of us together."

"What about all that I am a man and you are a woman nonsense?"

"I was"—he closed his eyes and prayed for strength—"wrong."

"Were you?" She grinned.

"Yes."

"You don't truly believe that."

He sighed. "Perhaps not."

She laughed softly and slipped out of his arms and out of his bed. She glanced around, found her nightdress, and tossed it on over her head. She considered him thoughtfully, then drew a deep breath. "After George, nearly two years later, I believe, I thought it might be rather interesting to have somewhat more—"

Alexei winced. "I do not know that I wish to hear this."

She ignored him. "Experience. After all, I was already ruined. Chastity at that point seemed rather, well, pointless. Don't you agree?"

"No." He paused. "Possibly."

She picked up her robe and put it on. "Indeed I thought I could become the sort of worldly woman I had met throughout Europe."

He was interested in spite of himself. "And did you?"

"I tried. Once." She paused for a long moment. "In Venice."

He held his breath. "And?"

"And I discovered I was not the type of woman to indiscriminately bed one man after another." She smiled. "And certainly not half the men in Europe."

"Then you did not . . ."

"No, I did not." She smiled slowly. "Until now."

"Until now," he said under his breath. He wanted to ask why. If their night together had indeed meant as much to her, but he could not bring himself to say the words.

"Are you happy now?" She stepped to the bed, leaned over it, and kissed him softly. "Now that you have indeed unraveled all my secrets."

"Blissful." And indeed for this particular moment he was surprised to note he was.

He reached out for her, but she danced out of his way. She paused at the door and looked back at him. "You will tell me what Nikolai says, won't you."

"Of course," he lied.

She narrowed her eyes as if she knew he was lying and shook her head. "Do be careful, Alexei."

"Always, Pamela." He forced a casual smile. "Always."

She looked at him a moment longer, opened the door, and slipped into the corridor, closing it softly behind her.

He stared unseeing at the door for a long time. This night with her was as magical as the last one. More so, really, because she was no mysterious stranger but the woman that he loved.

It would be best if he ended this farce of an engagement as soon as possible. The longer he was with her, the more likely something like this would happen again. Not that he would dislike that; indeed, he would be happy to keep her in his bed forever. And as long as they could simply stay in his bed, as long as the rest of the world paid them no heed they could be happy.

But this was a respite, nothing more. Pamela in his bed, this stay in her house, even their betrothal was nothing more than a holiday of sorts stolen from the reality of his life. Pamela and the farce they were caught up in allowed him to forget, at least for a while, the past and his failures. Allowed him to dwell on something other than the regrets that haunted him.

Dear God he wanted her. In his bed and in his life forever. But how could he do that to her?

He slid out of bed and padded across the room to a chest of drawers. He jerked open the top drawer and pulled out the earbob he had kept for four long years. He stared at it as if it held secrets or answers or just his heart.

She had not been with another man after him. It was at

once gratifying and sobering. He wanted to believe it was because Venice meant as much to her as it had to him. It certainly explained why she had taken such pains not to let him know she was Serenissima. Indeed, if it had been insignificant to her, she could have revealed her masquerade when they first met and no doubt they would have laughed about it. No, it was important to her.

Perhaps he was just being selfish? Perhaps it was wrong for him not to be willing to share his burdens as well as his triumphs with the woman he loved. Not that he anticipated any triumphs in the years to come. Nonetheless, he had never felt about a woman, never in truth believed he could, the way he felt about her. He would not let her share his fate.

They were very much like Romeo and Juliet. Bound together by destiny. Ill-fated and star-crossed.

And their story, too, would not end well.

Fifteen

 I will cherish what little time we have had, but I will have no regrets about not inflicting my life on her. If I love her, I can do nothing less. I shall never see her again.

His Royal Highness,
Prince Alexei Pruzinsky

"*It* is an interesting proposition," Alexei said in a measured manner.

Alexei sat at the desk in the library, Roman stood to his right behind him, just as he had always done. Valentina, who had been allowed to join in the meeting as long as she kept her opinions to herself, was seated off to the side, Dimitri stood nearby. Roman had convinced Lady Overton to invent an errand that would take Pamela out of the house and no one had seen Lady Smythe-Windom all morning. Still, they would not be disturbed.

Alexei surveyed the two men seated before the desk.

Nikolai could barely remain in his seat, and Westerfield appeared distinctly nervous. As well he should.

"You are willing to fund this?" Alexei said to Lord Westerfield. "It will be extraordinarily expensive. Well-equipped armies do not come cheaply."

"We are not talking about an entire army, Alexei." Nikolai leaned forward eagerly. "We are proposing to take a small squad of expert, highly trained troops into Avalonia to take key, strategic positions. They will provide the framework for rebellion." Determination glittered in Nikolai's eyes. "There is a vast network of loyalists in Avalonia who are ready to take up arms against the Russians. They are only waiting for a leader." Nikolai met his brother's gaze directly. "They are waiting for you."

"My funding is dependent upon your participation, Your Highness," Westerfield said slowly. "I will not lend my assistance otherwise."

"For that I am most grateful, my lord." Alexei nodded at the older man. "You have more than likely saved my brother's life."

"Alexei!" Nikolai jumped to his feet.

"Sit down." Alexei's order rang in the room. It was rather gratifying to know he could still summon the proper tone of royal command when necessary.

Nikolai sat.

"Let me ask you this, Lord Westerfield." Alexei chose his words with care. "As the man willing to invest both his money and his council, what do you think of the plan my brother has proposed?"

Westerfield hesitated. "It is clever, Your Highness."

Alexei raised a brow. "And?"

"And"—Westerfield paused to consider his words—"you must understand, Your Highness, my mother's family came to England from Avalonia, and I have relations there still. Indeed, the visits I made there as a boy, and as a man, linger fondly in my memory to this day. As we discussed last night, I have long considered what possible diplomatic remedies might be available even if it is perhaps too late for diplomacy.

"Indeed, I regret that all I can do to aid Avalonia, and her king, is financial in nature. However, I think the proposal as presented to me"—Westerfield blew a long breath—"is ill-advised."

"Ill-advised?" Again Nikolai jumped to his feet, glanced at his brother, and promptly sat back down. "You did not say it was ill-advised when I came to you last night."

"Your Highness." Genuine regret showed on Westerfield's face. "When we spoke after the ball last night, I agreed to give your proposal due consideration. While I think its success is questionable, I continue to stand ready to lend whatever assistance I can." He turned and met Alexei's gaze. "In whatever way His Highness desires."

"Thank you, my lord." Relief coursed through Alexei. Whatever far-fetched plans Nikolai might come up with, he could do little without funds. Alexei stood and reached his hand out to Westerfield. "You are most generous."

His lordship got to his feet at once, Nikolai a mere beat behind, and clasped Alexei's hand. "Do feel free to call on me, Your Highness, for whatever assistance you might need."

Westerfield bid his farewells and took his leave.

Silence hung heavy in the room for an endless moment. Nikolai glared at his brother. "We can triumph in this, Alexei, I am certain of it."

Alexei stared at the younger man and struggled against the desire to shake him or, better yet, beat him soundly for being so headstrong and so very much like himself in his youth. He understood his brother's desire to reclaim their homeland and understood as well his frustration. Still, to give Nikolai due credit, his plan was indeed clever as far as it went. Pity he had not taken into account the vast resources Russia would bring to bear.

"Your Highness." Roman addressed his words to Nikolai. "Perhaps you do not understand the sheer might of the Russian Empire."

Nikolai scoffed in the manner of a man who has not yet tasted his own mortality. Or the mortality of others. "I daresay—"

"Do you realize there are units of the Russian army with more soldiers than the entire population of Avalonia?" Alexei said quietly.

"Certainly, but—"

"Do you understand as well that Russia seized Avalonia not only because we were vulnerable but as a buffer against invasion?"

"Yes, I do but—"

"And do you know that no one in all of Europe, no one"—Alexei braced his hands on his desk and leaned forward—"will come to our aid? Because we are small and insignificant and no one, *no one* will challenge Russia on our behalf."

"I do know that! I know it all!" Nikolai ran his hand through his hair in frustration. "What am I supposed to do, Alexei? Sit back and watch the country of our father and his father's father and all who came before them fade into nothing more than a memory? I cannot be like you. I cannot do nothing!"

"Your Highness!" Roman stepped forward.

Dimitri moved closer. Even Valentina got to her feet.

"Nothing?" Alexei's voice was cold, but rage surged within him. "You think I have done nothing?"

Nikolai's eyes widened with the realization of what he had said. Still, he stood his ground. "You should have fought them. You should have given your own life—"

"And would that have made a difference? Would the deaths of every man in Avalonia, and every woman and child as well, because they would have been the target of Russian reprisal, have made any difference whatsoever?" Bitterness rang in his voice. "Do nothing, Nikolai? From the moment of my birth I have been trained to lead my people. To put their best interests above everything, including my own life. In this case doing nothing, as you put it, was the hardest thing I have ever had to do."

"Alexei, I did not mean—"

"It was the right choice, the only choice, to save my people, my country from certain annihilation, and yet I regret it. I regret it with every breath I take, with every beat of my heart. Dying for my country would have been easy. Living with my regrets, indeed my failure, is the burden I bear, and bear it I shall for the rest of my days."

Nikolai drew a deep breath.

"As for your plan, Nikolai." Alexei's voice was cool.

"Westerfield said, and I agree with him, that it is indeed clever. Unfortunately, it does not take into account reprisal. Nor does it consider what happens in the weeks, months, years to follow. Avalonia will become a battleground. Fields will be laid waste. Entire villages will be slaughtered or populations left to starve. Do not forget—Russia was willing to devastate its own lands to keep Napoleon's troops from finding sustenance. They will do no less to us." Alexei's voice was intense with emotion. "It was made very clear to me that Avalonia would be held up to all the world as an example of the consequences of those who defy her."

Nikolai's face paled. "I had not—"

"You had not considered that, had you, little brother?" Alexei's voice softened. "Nor was it your responsibility to do so. It was mine."

For a long moment the room was quiet. At last Alexei drew a deep breath. "We are all Avalonians in this room. Each and every one of us has given up a great deal to preserve the lives of our people." He sank back into his chair. "The world has changed, but I have always relied on the council of my advisors and indeed my friends. Count Stefanovich." He glanced behind him. "What is your opinion of Nikolai's plan?"

"I too have regrets, Your Highness," Roman said quietly. "I regret that I may never see the friends I have left behind. I regret that the country of my birth will never again be as it once was but"—he paused to choose his words—"I derive some small measure of satisfaction in knowing the people and the land that I love will not be destroyed. And as it remains, so, too, does the heart of

Avalonia." Roman's gaze met Alexei's. "I stand behind your decision, Your Highness, now as I did before."

The oddest lump lodged in Alexei's throat. He ignored it and nodded. "Thank you, Roman." His gaze turned to Dimitri. "Captain Petrov?"

"I am a soldier, Your Highness," Dimitri said slowly. "A warrior. My answer is always to fight, to the death if necessary. I would gladly give up my life in the service of my country and my king. However"—he drew a deep breath—"every battle must be considered in terms of gain and loss. If I thought for so much as a moment there was a possibility of a once-again-independent Avalonia, I would support this proposal or indeed any plan, with my whole heart and soul. But there is no glory in a fight that cannot be won. No honor in death in a cause that is futile." Dimitri's gaze met Alexei's. "I follow Your Highness now as I always have. Without regret and without doubt."

"Captain." Alexei nodded his thanks. Dimitri's first impulse had always been to fight. That he understood why he could not do so now was significant and caught at Alexei's heart.

"Your Highness, Valentina, what do you say?"

"Surely her opinion has no validity here." Nikolai stared in indignation. "She is a vile, treacherous creature who should have been imprisoned years ago."

"It is good to see you, too, cousin," Valentina said wryly.

"She is a princess of the House of Pruzinsky," Alexei said quietly. "Her grandfather is our grandfather. Her blood runs in our veins. Avalonia is her country as it is ours. She has the right to have a say in its fate."

She stared at him. "Thank you, Your Highness."

"Princess." Alexei nodded.

Valentina thought for a moment. "In many ways, God help me, I felt as Petrov did. I, too, thought we should have taken up arms at the outset and fought to the death. I see, now, that perhaps I was"—she rolled her gaze toward the ceiling—"wrong."

She paused to gather her words. "I was brought up to believe my father and I were better suited to rule Avalonia than your branch of the family. But what was apparently lacking in my upbringing was the overriding understanding that the people come first and foremost. Their welfare and their survival. It was a lesson I failed to learn, although I seem to understand it now." She directed her gaze at Alexei. "You have shown me that no matter how great the personal price, the people are all-important. I would have made a good queen but you . . . you would have been a great king."

Alexei stared at her for a long moment, then smiled wryly. "Thank you, cousin. You have changed."

She grimaced. "Nonetheless, I would prefer that you forget I said that, and I shall publicly deny it if necessary. I am not at all sure that this newfound sense of familial loyalty suits me."

Nikolai glared. "I cannot believe—"

"Nikolai." Valentina turned toward him with a long-suffering sigh. "You are extraordinarily young, and even the fact that you are extremely handsome does not make up for the fact that youth carries with it extraordinary stupidity as well. Your brother is endowed with a wisdom well beyond his years, and we should all thank God for that, as he is apparently the only one in the family who is."

Nikolai cast her a disgusted glance, then turned back to his brother. "What are we to do now then?"

"Your Highness," Roman said, "might I ask how vast is this network of loyalists in Avalonia you referred to?"

Nikolai looked distinctly uncomfortable at the question.

Alexei narrowed his gaze. "Well?"

"It sounds worse than it—"

"Well?" Alexei barked.

"No more than a handful really, I suppose, friends mostly." Nikolai sat down in defeat. "And they are here in London, not Avalonia."

"And they are all your age and every bit as passionate." Alexei studied his brother. "Am I right?"

"Yes," Nikolai muttered.

"And you would have had me lead them to their deaths?"

Nikolai's chin shot up. "A glorious death."

"A pointless death," Alexei snapped. He ignored a new surge of anger that his brother's plan was not at all as well considered as he had led them to believe. Alexei's voice hardened. "You will tell them of my decision at once, Nikolai, and, furthermore, you will not continue to pursue this plan of yours. Do you understand?"

"Yes." Nikolai slumped in his chair.

"As to what we do now." Alexei drew a deep breath. "We go on. I intend to buy an estate here in England. You are welcome to join us although I suspect we will all soon choose different paths." He got to his feet. "The past is at an end, Nikolai; we must turn toward the future and build our lives as best we can."

Nikolai stood and met his brother's gaze. "Is it possible to do so then?"

"Where there is life, all things are possible, little brother." Alexei fell silent then shrugged. "By choosing not to fight for her, we may well have given Avalonia the chance at life. And even there, all things are possible."

"Do you think he will do anything foolish?" Alexei asked quietly.

He and Roman were the only two still in the library. The others had taken their leave. Valentina had murmured something about a ride in the park, and Dimitri had dutifully accompanied her, with far less reluctance than usual. Obviously, he too had been moved by her words. Nikolai had promised to consider joining his brother but had mentioned as well resuming his travels. Perhaps the pleasures of Paris were not completely exhausted after all.

Roman chuckled. "I suspect he will do a great many foolish things in the future. But is he off to lead a revolution?" Roman shook his head. "I do not think so, Your Highness."

"Good." Alexei breathed a sigh of relief.

It was a huge weight off his shoulders to know that, at least for now, his brother would not be risking death in a hopeless cause. Still, it was hard not to envy Nikolai his passion and, more, his ability to believe blindly and without question that wrongs can be righted. When had Alexei lost that ability? Or in the realities of being taught to rule, of putting the people above all else, had he ever had it at all? It scarcely mattered he supposed.

Now, he had to do precisely what he had just told Nikolai. Build a new life and go on. Pity he did not believe it was possible. Nikolai was one problem resolved. It was time to resolve the next.

"Roman," Alexei said slowly, "I need to leave London. At once."

"Why?"

"I suspect Miss Effington—Pamela—has significant feelings for me."

"I see," Roman said in a noncommittal manner.

"Worse yet. I am in love with her as well." He met his friend's gaze. "She is indeed the woman I met in Venice."

Roman nodded. "I suspected as much."

"Why?"

"Something Lady Overton said." Roman shrugged. "It is not important." He studied Alexei carefully. "But I am afraid, Your Highness, that I do not see the problem."

"The problem, old friend, is that I cannot allow her any further into my life. God knows I cannot marry her." He pushed away from the desk, stood, and strode across the room to the decanter of brandy the ever-efficient Graham kept well filled. He poured a glass and drank it without pause.

"It is still rather early in the day for brandy, Your Highness."

"I do not need a conscience at the moment, Roman, as much as I do always appreciate your concern." Alexei poured another glass. "And it is far later than you may think. I meant everything I said to you the other day. I did not mean to say it, I did not realize the truth myself until the words came out of my mouth."

Alexei returned to the desk and settled back into his chair. He sipped his brandy, noted in the back of his mind that it was indeed far too early, then stared at his friend over the rim of the glass. "I cannot marry her because I have nothing to offer her save myself, and I am bitter and full of regrets." He raised his glass in a wry toast. "I would not wish to live with me if I had a choice. I am no longer the man she chose to spend a night with in Venice. I have changed, and not for the best."

"Yes, but if she cares for you—"

"If she cares for me, if she loves me, it will be that much worse." He swirled the brandy in his glass and watched it silently. "If she loves me, she will insist on sharing my exile. My demons. If I love her, I cannot permit that."

"That is a problem."

"Indeed it is. The only answer I can see is never to let her know how I feel and, furthermore, to depart from her life as quickly and thoroughly as possible. Pamela would never throw herself at a man who does not want her. Now"—he took a bracing swallow of brandy—"I should like to leave as soon as possible, within the next few days if we can arrange it. We could go to Tatiana's home in the country."

"Excellent idea under other circumstances. However, did your brother not use the word *explode* in reference to your sister?"

"I had forgotten that."

"In addition, unless you are going to leave Valentina behind, I would not expose a woman in an explosive condition to a woman who once held her at gunpoint. As much as we have seen a startling change in the princess, others might well be reluctant to accept her reformation."

"Good point." Alexei thought for a moment. "We shall

go to my cousin's then, Beaumont Abbey. Lord Beaumont and his wife will be more than pleased to see us."

"I beg your pardon, Your Highness, and admittedly I was not there at the time so this could be nothing more than hearsay, but I thought I understood that you had once forced Lady Beaumont to accompany you to Avalonia in an effort to coerce Lord Beaumont's assistance."

"Yes, well." Alexei waved away Roman's comment. "They have long ago forgiven me for that."

"And furthermore was it not your former chief of staff, a cohort of Valentina's, who actually abducted Lady Beaumont and, correct me if I am wrong, eventually shot her?"

"A minor wound." Alexei shrugged. "Nothing of significance. Still, you are right, it might be best . . ." He grinned. "I have it. We shall go to Worthington Castle. Lord Worthington has always been rather fond of me. That is it then. She will never find me there."

"Are you hiding from Miss Effington then?"

"Not at all. I simply do not want our paths to cross accidentally. The idea struck me last night when she and I discussed how much easier it would be to dissolve our engagement if I were dead."

"Dead? That's rather extreme, is it not?"

"Oh, I do not intend to die."

"Your Highness"—Roman's brows drew together—"surely you do not propose to let her think you are dead?"

"No, of course not. Better than dead really." Alexei blew a long breath. "I am going to let her think I'm going to Avalonia to lead the rebellion."

"What?" Roman stared at him with disbelief. "May I speak freely, Your Highness?"

"I expect nothing less."

"You realize this plan smacks of insanity."

"Apparently insane plans run in the family." Alexei paused to gather his thoughts. "In truth, this is the perfect way to end it, publicly at least. I go off to save my country, gallantly freeing her from any obligation to me. I shall be a hero, and she a heroine. No doubt there will be any number of prospective husbands willing to comfort her in my absence."

"Your Highness—"

"If I go, and there is no possibility of my return, she will have no choice but to go on with her life. The life she returned to England to have. Precisely as it should be."

"And what of the future? Will you hide from her for the rest of your days?"

"If I must," Alexei said quietly.

Roman studied him for a long moment. "I shall make arrangements to travel to Worthington Castle as soon as possible."

"Roman." Alexei met his friend's gaze. "As much as I will miss you, I cannot allow you to accompany us. You have Lady Overton to consider."

"Nonsense. My place is now and has always been by your side."

"No, Roman. Your loyalty is appreciated but"—Alexei shook his head—"you will stay here, old friend."

Roman started to protest, then sighed. "As you wish, Your Highness."

Alexei fell silent for a long moment. "Do you think I am a fool, Roman?"

"It is not my place to say."

"Nonetheless, I am—"

"Yes, Your Highness, the worst kind of fool." Roman's tone was blunt. "Doing what is best for your people as a whole is a far cry from doing what you think is best for one woman."

"Nonsense, I—"

"She deserves a choice in her future, Your Highness. She might well like spending the rest of her days with an embittered exiled prince and all of his regrets."

Alexei winced. "Do try not to make it sound so appealing."

Roman shrugged. "Would you care to know what else I think, Your Highness?"

"No," Alexei snapped then sighed. "Go on."

"Of all the regrets you have, of all the sacrifices you have made"—Roman's gaze met his—"this may prove to be the greatest."

"That, my friend"—Alexei raised his glass—"I already know."

"Good day, Graham." Pamela walked briskly into the house and pulled off her gloves.

The very last thing she had wished to do this morning was ride in the park. All she truly wanted was to spend every waking moment, and every night as well, with Alexei. She was certain he loved her. Oh, he hadn't said it, but it was in his touch and more in his eyes. He was well practiced in the art of love, but there was something between them that went beyond mere passion. She knew it in her heart. Now she simply had to get him to admit it.

But Clarissa had been insistent about this morning's

outing, which in itself was exceedingly odd. Clarissa was rarely insistent. "Where is everyone?"

"Lady Smythe-Windom is in the parlor. She requests that you join her as soon as you return," Graham said.

Pamela stopped. Even the glory of last night had not dispelled her qualms about Nikolai. "And His Highness?"

"He is in a meeting in the library, miss."

"Is he indeed?" Pamela turned on her heel and started toward the library.

"Oh, no." Clarissa caught Pamela's arm and steered her toward the parlor. "You are not going to interfere."

"I have no intention of interfering," Pamela lied. "I simply want to know what is being discussed in that room. I know it's important, and as it involves His Highness"—she glanced at Graham—"*my fiancé*, I think I have every right, indeed, it is my responsibility, to find out."

"You may ask when they are finished," Clarissa said firmly, and fairly pushed her toward the parlor. "Aunt Millicent wishes to see us, and that is what we shall do."

"Very well." Pamela sighed, and accompanied her cousin into the parlor.

"My dear darling girls, how are you this fine morning?" Aunt Millicent jumped up from the sofa to embrace each of them in turn. "I have the most wonderful news."

Pamela and Clarissa exchanged wary glances.

"I am going to marry Winchester." Aunt Millicent beamed.

"Winchester?" Clarissa glanced at Pamela.

"The man she almost married," Pamela said.

"I thought you had an aversion to permanence?" Clarissa raised a brow. "I should think marriage is extremely permanent."

"I have apparently gotten over that aversion." Aunt Millicent waved the comment away. "Indeed, permanence with Winchester sounds very much like heaven."

"You do not intend to leave him at the church again, do you?" Pamela asked in a wry manner.

"I didn't intend to do so the first time, my dear," Aunt Millicent said firmly. "It was one of those things that simply happened."

Clarissa studied her. "Will it happen again?"

"Winchester will not allow it to happen again." Aunt Millicent heaved a blissful sigh and sank down on the sofa. "We talked a great deal last night. It seems he still loves me and still wants me, and I shall allow him to have me for the rest of his days."

Pamela stared. "Are you sitting on a pillow?"

"Yes, well, during the course of our conversation, he put me over his knee and spanked me." Aunt Millicent giggled. "It was really quite exciting."

"Good Lord." Pamela groaned.

"Oh my." Clarissa's eyes widened. "How exciting?"

"Clarissa!" Shock rang in Pamela's voice.

"I was just curious," Clarissa murmured.

"Surprisingly exciting." Aunt Millicent leaned forward in a confidential manner. "It was all surprisingly exciting. We had never, well, before last night that is." She sighed at the memory. "It was quite, quite wonderful."

"Are you certain about this?" Pamela sat down beside her aunt.

Aunt Millicent nodded. "Oh my yes, it was perhaps the most wonderful—"

"Not that," Pamela said quickly. She would much prefer not to know any more details of her aunt's night. "You have always said you would not marry without love. That marriage without love was not worth the effort."

"Oh, but he does love me, and I love him as well. Did I fail to mention that?" Aunt Millicent shook her head. "I loved him twelve years ago, but I was too foolish to realize it. And he was too proud to follow me, which makes him a fool as well. Nonetheless, we are both older and definitely wiser, and I do not wish to waste another moment without him. Which, frankly, brings me to the two of you." She patted the seat next to her and Clarissa obediently sat down. "Winchester wishes to marry at once, a special license, probably right here in the house. While I have no intention of changing my mind, I can see why he might be a bit apprehensive about wedding in churches."

"He is wiser," Clarissa said under her breath.

"He has a lovely house here in town and a charming estate in the country." Aunt Millicent glanced from Pamela to Clarissa. "We shall be using those as our primary residences."

"Which means you will not live here," Pamela said slowly.

"Eventually." Aunt Millicent took her nieces' hands. "Winchester completely understands why I cannot allow the two of you to live here alone without a chaperone; therefore, he has agreed to join me here for a while."

Pamela glanced at Clarissa and drew a deep breath. "I'm not entirely sure we can allow that."

Clarissa nodded. "Marriage is rather difficult to become accustomed to, and I would think it might be best if the poor man didn't have a full household of your relations—"

"Your female relations," Pamela said pointedly.

"—To contend with as well as . . . well . . ." Clarissa paused.

"You." Pamela's tone was blunt. "You can be rather overwhelming on occasion."

Aunt Millicent's laughter rang in the room. "Of course I can. I daresay that's what he loves best about me."

A discreet knock sounded at the open door. "Miss Effington," Graham stepped into the room. "You have a caller." He paused, a slight note of disapproval in his voice. "A gentleman caller."

"Excellent," Aunt Millicent said, and rose to her feet. Pamela and Clarissa followed suit. "Show him in at once, Graham."

"As you wish, my lady." Graham nodded and retreated.

"I daresay I hadn't expected anything to happen so quickly." Aunt Millicent grinned with satisfaction. "Why, your engagement was only announced last night, and already you have attracted the interest of an eligible gentleman."

"We have no idea if he is eligible," Pamela said firmly. "Indeed, it could be anyone, one of my brothers perhaps or someone sent by Mr. Corby's office on a matter of business."

"Besides," Clarissa said, "it seems to me a gentleman who would call on a newly engaged woman is not at all the kind of man Pamela would be interested in."

"Yes." Aunt Millicent frowned. "It is rather bad taste,

isn't it? And I really hadn't thought this would happen until you called off your engagement. Well, we shall see."

Graham cleared his throat, and the women turned toward the door.

Pamela winced. "George."

"Lord Penwick." Aunt Millicent said the name as if it left a nasty taste in her mouth. "What are *you* doing here?"

"That does explain the question of bad taste," Clarissa said coolly.

"Lady Smythe-Windom, Lady Overton." George's gaze met Pamela's. She did not like the look in his eye. "Miss Effington. Good day to you all."

"It was a good day," Aunt Millicent said sharply. "What do you want?"

"I should like to have a few words with Miss Effington," George said smoothly.

Pamela sighed. "We have nothing to say to one another."

"I should think His Highness made that perfectly clear to you last night," Clarissa said.

Aunt Millicent leaned toward Clarissa and lowered her voice. "What happened last night?"

"I shall tell you later," Clarissa said under her breath.

"Nonetheless, there is a matter of some importance I wish to discuss with Miss Effington." He paused. "Alone."

"Absolutely not." Aunt Millicent shook her head. "I would be the worst kind of chaperone if I were to leave you alone with her. No, I will not permit it."

"I am not leaving until I speak to her alone." George's mouth pressed into a stubborn line.

Pamela surrendered. Obviously George was not going to leave until he had had his say. It was probably best to get it over with. "It's quite all right, Aunt Millicent. I'm sure that whatever Lord Penwick wishes to discuss, he will be brief"—she leveled him a warning glance—"and to the point. I shall be fine."

"Very well, if you insist." Aunt Millicent nodded at Clarissa and started toward the door. "But we shall be nearby if you need us." Aunt Millicent marched out of the room, Clarissa a step behind. She cast Pamela an encouraging glance and pointedly left the door open behind her.

George chuckled. "Your aunt is quite imposing."

"She can be." Pamela studied him. "Why are you here, George? I thought I made my position perfectly clear last night."

"I have come to ask for your hand."

"What?" She stared in disbelief.

"I wish to marry you."

"Why?"

"Because I love you. I always have, and I always will." He stepped toward her.

She stepped back and thrust out her hand. "Do not take another step toward me, George, or I swear I shall rip your heart out of your chest with my bare hands."

He smiled. "Come now, Pamela, you would never harm me."

"I would, and I would take great pleasure in it," she snapped. "Did you listen to nothing I said last night?"

"Every word." He shrugged. "However, I did not believe you last night, and I do not believe you now."

"Why on earth not?"

He heaved a long-suffering sigh. "Because we are meant to be together. I have missed you every moment of every day. In truth, I prayed for your return, and my prayers were answered. Nothing whatsoever stands between us now. You are back in London, and I am free to wed. Think of the life we shall have together. Why, aside from the passion that we share, my fortune coupled with the fortune you have inherited—"

"How do you know about my inheritance?" For the first time she wondered if George might be substantially more dangerous than she'd suspected.

"The moment I heard you were back I made it my business to find out."

"You wish to marry me for my money?" Her voice rose. "That's what this newfound passion for me is about?"

"Not at all, and my passion is eternal not newfound." Indignation sounded in his voice. "Your money is simply an unexpected, although exceedingly pleasant, benefit."

She clenched her fists by her sides. "Get out, George."

"I think not."

"George." She closed her eyes for a moment and prayed for control. "Aside from the fact that I do not wish to marry you, I am engaged to wed someone else."

He chuckled. "No, you're not."

Her breath caught. "What did you say?"

"Come now, Pamela, I know your engagement to His Highness is nothing but an act. I am not certain of the purpose of it, but I do know it is not legitimate."

She forced a cool note to her voice. "Whatever would make you think such a thing?"

"I overheard you and Lady Overton last night." He shook his head in a chiding manner. "You really should be more cautious of private conversations when in a public gathering."

"Regardless of what you think you might have heard—"

"This is my proposal, Pamela." He clasped his hands behind his back and studied her thoughtfully almost as if she were a broodmare he was considering purchasing. "I shall keep your secret if you end this farce with the prince immediately and marry me."

"First of all, there is no farce. And secondly, even if there was, there is still no force on earth that would induce me to marry you." She forced a smile to her face and an overly pleasant note to her voice. "Now, then, it's long past time for you to leave my house and my life as well."

"Perhaps you did not fully understand." His voice hardened. "You fled England six years ago because you could not face the scandal surrounding us. That will be as nothing compared to the scandal you'll be embroiled in when it is learned you have deceived all of London."

"Do you know how absurd this sounds? How absurd you sound?" A touch of panic rose within her. She crossed her arms over her chest. Disdain sounded in her voice. "No one will ever believe you."

"Perhaps not at first." He shrugged. "But when your engagement does not end in marriage, there will be talk. Speculation. Gossip. This is quite a juicy story. You will be ruined." He paused. "Again."

"Regardless." She jerked her chin up. "I would rather

live with scandal, indeed I would choose to dwell in the fires of hell itself before I would marry you."

"Well said, Miss Effington." Alexei's voice sounded from the doorway. "Well said indeed."

Relief washed through her, and it was all she could do to keep from throwing herself in Alexei's arms.

"Do you make it a habit of listening in on other people's conversations?" George snapped then paused. "Your Highness."

"I suppose I do." Alexei sauntered into the room, his voice was light but a murderous gleam showed in his eye. "One learns so much of interest that way."

"Your Highness." Pamela moved toward Alexei. He ignored her, his attention focused only on George. Good Lord, he was going to kill him. "Alexei—"

"Indeed one does." George stared at Alexei in an assessing manner. "As I have learned the truth about your engagement to Miss Effington."

"Have you?" Alexei's voice was cool. "And are you confident enough in what you think you heard to back it with your life?"

Indecision flashed across George's face but he didn't waver. "I will do whatever is necessary to ensure Pamela marries me."

Pamela snorted. "Never."

Alexei narrowed his eyes. "Pamela is to marry me."

"I had her first," George said staunchly.

Pamela groaned. "Dear Lord."

"I have her now." Alexei's voice was low and carried a tone that ran a chill up her spine.

"No one has me." Pamela scoffed. "I am not a poss—"

"You have questioned Miss Effington's honor." Alexei's gaze bored into George's. George seemed to visibly shrink under his stare. "As well as my own."

George squared his shoulders. "I have said nothing but the truth."

"The truth, Lord Penwick, as are so many things, is a matter of perception. I shall not allow you to threaten Miss Effington in any way, nor shall I allow you to cast aspersions on the good name of the woman I love. Or mine." Alexei shook his head in a regretful manner. "I see you did not believe me last night either."

"I'm afraid I don't know what you mean." George's voice was cautious.

"Simply put, Lord Penwick, while I was inclined to be understanding last night, today that inclination has fled." Alexei smiled pleasantly as if he was discussing nothing more important than an outing in the park, but Pamela caught her breath at the look in his eye. "Do you have a second?"

George's eyes widened. "No."

"You should find someone to serve as your second at once then, as I will have my second contact him later today. Dawn is the usual time I believe." He glanced at Pamela. "Is that customary in your country as well?"

"Alexei, I—"

"I thought it was." Alexei nodded and directed his attention back to George. "Dawn tomorrow then. My second will contact yours as to the place and oh"—he drew his brows together—"since you expressed a preference for swords last night, I assume swords are still your weapon of choice? Or would you now prefer pistols?"

George swallowed hard. "Swords, if I must."

"You must. You do realize, Lord Penwick, you brought this entirely on yourself." Alexei sighed in a regretful manner. "I cannot overlook another *misunderstanding*." His voice hardened. "Nor do I wish to. Indeed, I am quite looking forward to skewering you like a pig on a spit."

George turned an interesting shade of green. In spite of his evident fear, he drew a deep breath and met Alexei's gaze. "I am not unskilled with a sword, Your Highness."

"Excellent." Alexei smiled coldly. "I do so love a challenge."

"Tomorrow then," George said without so much as a quiver in his voice. It obviously took a great deal of effort and would have been admirable in anyone else. "Your Highness. Miss Effington." George nodded and left the parlor, his step measured. That, too, must have taken a great deal of effort.

Alexei grinned. "I must say, this is going to be most enjoyable."

Pamela stared. "You're going to kill him."

He shrugged. "Probably."

"Why?"

"Because he is a vile, nasty man who sees you, and your inheritance, as little more than acquisitions. He lost you once, and he is determined to have you now, in truth, to possess you. And if he cannot have you, because you are far wiser today than you once were—"

"Thank God."

"—then he will make certain no one else does by revealing our charade. Unless, of course," Alexei smiled pleasantly, "I kill him."

She huffed. "You can't kill him."

"I most certainly can unless he is a far better swordsman than I, and I cannot believe that. Or." His gaze met hers, his brown eyes intense. "He is right and you do indeed have feelings for him."

"I have many feelings for him, none of which are the least bit affectionate."

"Excellent." Alexei nodded with a slight but distinct air of relief. "It is decided then. It will not even be much of a challenge, which is something of a pity."

"As much as I would like to see him skewered like a pig on a spit"—she heaved a resigned sigh—"I cannot allow you to do so."

"You, my dear Pamela, have no choice in the matter. Besides, it is the least I can do for you before I leave." His voice was matter-of-fact, as if he were discussing something of no importance whatsoever.

Her heart caught. "What do you mean leave?"

"I intend to depart for Avalonia immediately after slaying Lord Penwick."

She stared at him in disbelief. "What?"

"Oh, I fully intend to slay him," he said casually.

"Not that." She moved closer to him. "The other part."

"Leaving for Avalonia, you mean?"

"Yes."

"It seems my brother has an extremely clever plan for retaking Avalonia involving expert troops and insurgents and, well, they cannot succeed unless they are properly led." He shrugged. "As heir to the throne, it is my duty to do so."

"I knew it. I knew he was dangerous the moment I saw

him." Panic rose within her. "You cannot do this, Alexei. I will not allow it. You'll be killed."

"I am sorry, my dear, but in this, too, you have no say in the matter. As for my death, there is that possibility I suppose although I shall do all in my power to avoid that." He paused for a moment. "Still, there is a certain amount of glory in dying for one's country."

"There is a certain amount of stupidity in dying for a cause one cannot win," she snapped.

"Perhaps."

"Then . . . then . . ." She jerked her chin up in defiance. "Then I shall go with you."

"Do not be absurd. This is not your fight. And as much as I appreciate the offer, I must refuse." He shook his head. "Frankly, you would be nothing but a hindrance."

"My place is with you," she said staunchly.

"Your place?" He chuckled. "Do you forget our engagement is a hoax? Your place is here. It always has been, it always will be."

"But what about"—she held her breath—"us."

"My dear Pamela, we were an act. A very good one I might add."

"Last night—"

"Last night was wonderful, and I shall cherish the memory of it always." He raised her hand to his lips, his gaze boring into hers. "We were but an interlude, Pamela. We were never meant to be anything else."

Her heart lodged in her throat. "I thought you had feelings for me."

"Oh, but I do. I am extremely fond of you, which is precisely why I intend to kill Penwick before I leave. As for anything more, love as it were." He smiled in a wry manner. "I fear I lost my heart sometime ago to a land and a people, and it remains with them still."

"You told George you loved me," she said slowly. "Was that an act as well?"

"And well done, too, if I may say so."

"Alexei." She struggled to hold back tears.

"Pamela." He gently pulled her into his arms. "In another time or another place, indeed in another life altogether, there might well have been a future for us. But here and now we have nothing save a few stolen moments."

"I don't want a few moments. I want forever. With you."

"That is very flattering but I . . ." He shook his head. "I would be very bad for you."

Her voice caught. "I don't care."

"I do." He lowered his lips to hers and kissed her softly, gently, a kiss of farewell. She squeezed her eyes closed tight to hold back tears. She clung to him, and for a long moment he held her. If not for his words she would have sworn he felt far more for her than he admitted. At last he released her and stepped away.

"We shall say circumstances require I release you from our engagement. It will be quite noble of me, to give you up, that is." He smiled in a reluctant manner. "Many will think I am a fool to leave you; indeed, I think so myself at the moment."

"Then don't go!"

"Pamela." He reached out to cup her chin in his hand. "I cannot do anything else. I must return to my country. One makes sacrifices for . . . for love."

She brushed his hand away and forced a calm note to her voice. "Will you be going alone then?"

"No. Captain Petrov and Valentina will join me. It is their country as well." He hesitated. "I am leaving Count Stefanovich behind, and I have released him from all obligation to me."

"Because of Clarissa?"

"Yes, but he is not pleased with me. He, too, thinks my actions are questionable." Alexei shrugged. "Nonetheless, sacrifices—"

"Yes, yes, I know," she said sharply. "For love."

He stared at her for a long moment as if there were any number of things he wished to say but would not.

"Yes?" She couldn't hide the note of hope in her voice.

He ignored it if indeed he noticed it at all. "I have business at the bank to attend to this morning, then meetings, arrangements, that sort of thing that I anticipate will take me well into the night." He drew a deep breath. "It is entirely possible that we will not see one another again."

"So then this is"—she swallowed hard—"good-bye?"

He nodded. "I am afraid so."

"I wish you all the best." Her voice had an odd hollow ring to it. "Please do not let me read of your death."

He chuckled. "I shall do what I can, Pamela." He paused, and his gaze met hers. In spite of his words, regret and something else, something that tore at her heart, shone in his eyes. "I shall treasure these days spent with you for the rest of my life."

"Make certain it is a very long life, Alexei." She could barely get out the words.

He nodded, then turned and took his leave.

For an endless moment shock held her still. It was as if the world itself had crumbled about her. She wanted to scream with frustration or weep with despair.

She turned, stepped to the window, and stared unseeing at the street below. Even if he didn't love her, how could she allow him to risk his life in a hopeless cause? She loved him too much for that, and probably had from the first moment she'd seen him all those years ago in Venice.

Alexei and Stefanovich appeared on the street below her. Would this really be the last time she saw him? She watched Petrov and the princess arrive. The group obviously was discussing their plans, given the serious expressions on those faces she could make out.

She had told Clarissa she was willing to sacrifice everything she'd thought she'd ever wanted, but she could not make him love her. And she would not have him without love. She'd been so certain he'd loved her.

Was she as foolish as George then? He refused to believe she did not love him just as she refused to believe Alexei did not love her. No, her resolve hardened. She wasn't wrong about that. She knew it as she knew the beat of her own heart. Knew it in the very depths of her soul.

And she would not give him up without a fight. Even if that fight was with him.

She had nearly a full day to think of something. He wasn't leaving until tomorrow after he killed George. She would have to stop that as well.

Below her Valentina and Petrov disappeared into the house, Alexei and the count drove off.

Pamela lifted her chin. This would not be the last time

she saw him. Still, she could fight almost anything but his love for his country. It was as much a part of him as his arms or legs or heart.

Her only hope lay in her belief that he loved her as well.

And until that belief was dead and buried, until she was dead and buried, she would never give up.

Sixteen

I will see him again.

Pamela Effington

"*P*amela?" Clarissa's voice sounded from behind her.

"Yes?" Pamela drew a steadying breath and turned away from the window.

"Are you all right?" Clarissa stepped toward her, concern on her face.

"No." Pamela smiled weakly.

"I have something to tell you. While you were in here with George and His Highness, Roman and I spoke." Clarissa drew a deep breath. "He has asked me to marry him."

"Clarissa!" Pamela flew across the room and embraced her cousin. "How wonderful for you."

"Yes it is." Clarissa fairly glowed with happiness. "I accepted, of course, on one condition."

Pamela raised a brow. "A condition?"

"It's really quite simple." Clarissa took her hand, led

her to the sofa, and sat down. Pamela settled beside her. "The condition was honesty."

"That does seem simple."

"Not really." Clarissa's gaze searched her cousin's. "It required the truth about a number of issues."

"Oh?" Pamela's heart thudded.

"First of all," Clarissa paused. "His Highness is not returning to Avalonia."

"What?" Pamela stared. "But his brother has some sort of plan and—"

"Nikolai did indeed have a plan, but everyone agreed it was the height of stupidity."

"Then . . ." Relief swept through her with a vengeance, stole her breath, and doubled her over. Tears flooded her eyes. "Thank God." He was not going off to a certain death. He was not going to throw his life away in a futile cause. He was—she jerked upright. "Then why in the name of all that's holy did he tell me he was? How could he do that to me? Where is he going?"

"He's going off to rusticate in the country somewhere. A castle owned by a distant relative, I believe, although that part seems a little vague. At any rate that is not the point. The point is why."

"I just asked you that," Pamela said, trying to keep impatience from showing in her voice.

"He thinks it's best for you if he is not a part of your life."

"Best for me? How could it possibly be best for me?" She jumped to her feet and paced the room desperately, trying to recall every word of every conversation they'd ever had. "He certainly wasn't reluctant for me to be a part of his life four years ago."

"Four years ago he had not lost his country," Clarissa said quietly.

Pamela pulled up short and met her cousin's gaze. "Do you think that's it then?"

"There's more, Pamela. According to Roman, His Highness knows"—Clarissa winced—"everything."

"What do you mean everything?" Pamela said slowly.

"He knows you were the lady in Venice." Clarissa studied her thoughtfully. "Furthermore, that night has lingered in his mind just as it has in yours."

Pamela stared at her cousin, the most absurd sense of delight swelling within her. "Has it really? All these years?"

"Indeed it has."

"A man with his reputation?"

Clarissa grinned.

"Then this makes no sense at all." Pamela pulled her brows together and tried to comprehend the male mind. "If I am the woman of his dreams—" She glanced at Clarissa. "He has dreamed about me, hasn't he? I have certainly dreamed about him."

"If you recall, I was not instructed to ask about dreams."

"Yes, of course. I should have included that."

Clarissa snorted.

"As I was saying, this makes no sense."

"Roman says he feels he has nothing to offer a wife. Nothing to offer *you*."

"Nothing?" Pamela shook her head. "I don't—"

One makes sacrifices for love.

Pamela stared at Clarissa. "He's willing to give me up to save me then? From a life with him because he's lost everything? Is that it?"

Clarissa shrugged helplessly, as if she, too, had her doubts about the workings of the male mind.

"How absurd. He has absolutely no idea that I would rather spend my life with him and have nothing than have all the treasures of the world without him." Pamela shook her head. "So he decides to decide my fate for me? Rather arrogant of him I think. A bit sweet as well."

"I believe he loves you," Clarissa said slowly.

"Of course he loves me, I knew it all along." Pamela grinned with sheer delight. "What a dear, wonderful, arrogant fool he is."

"Now that you know all this, what are you going to do—"

Without warning Valentina swept into the room, Petrov at her heels. "I am about to do, God help me," she shuddered, "a good deed."

"You are not," Petrov said firmly.

Pamela and Clarissa traded glances.

"You are such an annoying creature." Valentina grabbed the lapels of his coat with both hands and stared into his eyes. "Is it not your duty to serve His Highness?"

"Yes," he said cautiously.

"And does that not mean doing whatever is necessary to ensure his well-being and happiness?"

"I suppose."

"Then do be quiet and let me talk." Valentina smiled suggestively and released him. "I shall see you are well rewarded for it later."

Petrov cast her a suspicious glare but held his tongue.

"Pamela." Valentina turned toward her. "You should know my cousin has not broken off your engagement because he is off to fight the Russians but rather is going to hide in the country and make all of us accompany him, by the way, to some dreadful place at the very edge of nowhere, and he has done all this because"—she paused dramatically—"he loves you."

Pamela bit back a grin. "Yes, I know."

"You do?" Valentina's brows drew together. "Then my good deed was for nothing?"

"Not at all," Pamela said quickly. "It is most appreciated."

"Well, that is something, I suppose." Valentina huffed and collapsed into the nearest chair. "So much for good deeds."

Petrov leaned toward her. "It was an exceptionally good deed, though."

"Your opinion is of no consequence." Valentina sighed then muttered. "You have my thanks nonetheless."

"You may yet help however," Pamela said. "We are trying to determine what I do now. How I convince His Highness of the error of his high-handed and arrogant ways."

Valentine scoffed. "I shall give it my complete attention, but I should warn you—we, the House of Pruzinsky, that is—are a stubborn lot when we have a made a decision. Even if it is completely wrong."

"Pamela." George burst into the room.

"Good Lord, George." Pamela crossed her arms over her chest. "I have neither the time nor the desire to deal with you now. What ever possessed you to return? If His Highness sees you—"

"I waited until I was sure he was gone." For the first time George noticed they were not alone. He nodded at the gathering. "Good day."

"Who is this?" Valentina studied him curiously.

Clarissa sniffed. "He's a vile, despicable creature who should be put out of his misery."

"Pity I've given up vile, despicable creatures. I have always had a fondness for fair-haired men." Valentina glanced at the dark-haired Petrov and sighed. "Apparently I've given that up as well."

Petrov bit back a grin.

George stared at her for a moment, then shook his head as if to clear it and turned back to Pamela. "Do you really want him to kill me?"

Pamela considered him for a moment then sighed. "I suppose not."

George smiled smugly. "Because you love m—"

"Because I love him," Pamela said firmly.

George studied her with obvious disbelief. "Are you certain?"

"I have never been more certain of anything in my life."

"I see." He narrowed his eyes suspiciously. "And do you really intend to marry him?"

"I do." Pamela had never spoken truer words.

"Then, well"—George nodded firmly—"you have my abject apologies."

"That's it, George?" She raised a brow. "You threaten to ruin my life and you think an apology is enough?"

"He threatened to ruin her life?" Valentina said in an aside to Clarissa. "How?"

"I have no idea." Clarissa glared. "But I'm sure it was quite wicked."

"Really?" Valentina cast George an appraising glance.

"You're right, a mere apology is probably not enough. Does it matter at all that my threat was that of a man desperate to win the hand of the woman he loved?" A hopeful note sounded in George's voice.

"No!" Pamela stared in disbelief. How could she ever have been fool enough to believe she had loved this man? Indeed, if he hadn't been such a cad, she would probably be married to him today and . . . abruptly relief and a fair amount of gratitude rushed through her. George had been a dreadful mistake, but her mistake could have been so much worse.

George heaved a sigh of sheer misery. "You are going to let him kill me then, aren't you?"

"No," she snapped. "Not tomorrow at any rate, but I shall keep it as a possibility for the future." She waved him toward the door. "I strongly suggest you leave right now and for God's sake do not show up tomorrow. Indeed, it would be best if you do not so much as show your face anywhere near His Highness for quite some time. Ever would be best. I would strongly advise you not to leave your house at all for a while. Hide, George, it's your only hope. I shall take care of the matter."

He started toward the door, then hesitated. "But what of my honor.

"He'll kill you," Pamela said sharply. "And given your behavior, he shall probably take a fair amount of pleasure in it. The loss of your honor pales in comparison to the loss of your life."

"Yes, I suppose." George nodded and again headed toward the door.

"Furthermore, I would suggest, to stay out of his path, it might be wise for you to leave London altogether."

George brightened. "I could go to the country I suppose."

"That is the wisest thing I have ever heard you say. And George." She leveled him her most threatening look. "At the moment, this is a private affair. I intend to keep it that way in which case your honor"—she snorted—"shall not be questioned. However, do keep in mind that that can change at any moment. An offhand comment to a friend one trusts, who then passes it on to another friend and before you know what has happened the entire world knows. Do you understand?"

George swallowed. "Indeed I do." He paused. "It's not at all nice of you."

"I told you I have changed. Nice is no longer a possibility." Pamela practically shoved him toward the door. "Not where you are concerned."

"Pamela." He cast her a longing look. "Should you ever decide—"

"Thank you, George." She steered him toward the door. "Get out."

"So that is the man Alexei wants dead," Valentina said thoughtfully.

"Oh, I don't think he really wants him—" Pamela sighed. "That's the one."

"And you are certain he will not appear tomorrow?"

Pamela nodded. "I would wager a great deal on it."

"Then I have a brilliant idea." Valentina jumped to her feet and spread her arms in a dramatic gesture. "It shall be my next good deed."

"Forgive me for saying so, Your Highness," Clarissa said slowly, "but for one as unaccustomed to good deeds as you, perhaps it would be best if you started with one on a smaller scale. Something like, I don't know, spreading bread crumbs for birds?"

"Birds?" Valentina stared at Clarissa as if she had sprouted wings and would fly off. "Why on earth would I wish to feed birds?"

"It was just a thought," Clarissa murmured.

"This is much better than feeding birds." The princess rejected Clarissa's suggestion with a dismissive wave, then turned to Pamela. "Do you by any chance know anything about fencing?"

Pamela stared at her, then abruptly realized what Valentina's idea was. Far-fetched, of course, and completely improper, but inspired nonetheless. She grinned slowly. "Your Highness, that is indeed brilliant."

Valentina beamed. "I thought it was." She leaned toward Pamela in a confidential manner. "But just a bit wicked as well, do you not think so? In a good sort of way, I mean."

"Oh very good. Very good indeed, Princess."

"I thought so. In truth, Pamela dear, its brilliance was never in question," Valentina said smugly, then paused. "The question is whether or not it will work."

"Where is the blasted man?" Alexei paced to and fro in the clearing where his duel with Penwick was to take place if the man had the courage to show up. Alexei had no idea precisely where they were, somewhere on the outskirts of London he thought, nor did he particularly care. He simply wanted to get it over and done with.

"I have no idea, Your Highness," Roman said mildly.

Graham stood nearby, stiffly erect, holding up a sword in each hand.

"Good God, Graham, you can put those down until he gets here." Alexei sighed. The man was an excellent butler, but it was obvious he had had no experience acting in this capacity save what he might have seen in a play. Still, he had managed to find a physician to accompany them, at a rather exorbitant cost, who even now waited in the carriage.

"Thank you, Your Highness," Graham said, and gratefully lowered the swords to the ground.

"If Penwick does not appear soon, I shall have to flush him out wherever he may be hiding. I have things to attend to, and I cannot wait here all day." Alexei glanced at Roman. "Are our travel arrangements taken care of?"

"You have asked me that several times, Your Highness, and the answer, once again, is yes."

"Good," Alexei snapped.

"May I say, Your Highness, you are in an exceptionally foul mood this morning." Roman smiled pleasantly.

"Of course I am in a foul mood. I am about to kill a man."

"Yes, I thought that was it."

Alexei glared at his friend and resumed pacing. Roman knew full well it was not the thought of this absurd duel that had knotted Alexei's stomach. Why, he probably wouldn't even kill Penwick at all, just make him suffer a bit. Possibly a strategic wound would suffice. Perhaps the loss of his nose would be appropriate. Yes, Alexei liked that.

No, it was not Penwick behind Alexei's ill temper this morning. It was Pamela.

Alexei had made it a point to stay away from the house, away from her, all day yesterday and well into the night. When at last he had fallen into bed, he was unable to sleep and spent most of the night jumping at any unexpected sound in the corridor. Hoping she would once again appear at his door. Praying she would not. It was hard enough to say good-bye to her once. He was not sure if he could do it again.

"This is damned inconsiderate of the man." Alexei grit his teeth. "He should have been here by now."

"It is extremely bad form to be late for one's own killing," Roman said mildly. "I assume you still intend to kill him?"

"I have not decided yet. Killing him might well cause no end of problems for Miss Effington once we are gone." Alexei smiled grimly. "But I will make certain he does not threaten her again."

A carriage pulled up a short distance away. Graham once again jerked the swords upright. Alexei rolled his gaze toward the sky.

The carriage door opened, and a footman helped three cloaked, hooded figures descend.

"That is a bit overly dramatic," Roman said.

Alexei shrugged. "Penwick is an idiot. The man has probably never dueled before."

The figures came toward them briskly, one a few steps in front of the others. Odd, Alexei had thought Penwick was about his height and not as slight as he appeared now.

Obviously, it was a trick of the early-morning light coupled with the cloak that made him appear otherwise.

The closest figure stopped and brushed back the hood. Long, golden hair tumbled forward.

Alexei clenched his jaw. "Pamela."

"Good morning, Your Highness," Pamela said brightly. "Excellent day for a duel, don't you think?"

"What are you doing here?" he snapped. "And where is that coward, Penwick."

"I told him not to come." She smiled pleasantly. "I am taking his place."

"You what?" He stared. "You cannot do that!"

"Oh, but I can. According to the British Code of Duels, rules and conduct, current edition, fourth page, third paragraph, the challenged may choose a champion to substitute for him." A smug note sounded in her voice. "I am the champion."

He glared at her. "I have never heard of such a thing."

"Of course not." She shrugged "It's an English rule."

"Nor have I ever heard of the British code of whatever." He narrowed his eyes. "You are making it up."

"Regardless," she said loftily. "I am here, and Penwick is not."

"But you are a woman. Even in England, I doubt women are allowed to duel."

"I am indeed a woman and thank you for noticing." She shook her head. "It's an odd thing about that. I read the entire code—"

"The code you made up," he snapped.

"—and it doesn't say anything about women not being allowed to duel. Perhaps it's understood or a simple mistake; regardless, there is nothing specifically forbidding women participating in duels, and, therefore, I am here." She cast him a brilliant smile. "And I am prepared."

Alexei looked at Roman, who shrugged helplessly.

Pamela stepped to Graham, studied the swords he offered, then wrinkled her nose in distaste. "These won't do at all. Neither is to my liking." She glanced at Alexei. "Do you mind if I use my own?"

He scoffed. "You have your own sword?"

"Indeed I do." She stepped to the closest hooded figure, her second apparently and, no doubt, Lady Overton.

"Did you know about this?" Alexei said under his breath to Roman.

"No." Roman stared forbiddingly at the as-yet-unrevealed second. "I certainly would not have permitted it."

"That is something at any rate," Alexei muttered. "Although even with the well-behaved Lady Overton I doubt you would have had much to say about it."

Pamela pulled off her cloak and Alexei gasped.

"You have on breeches!" He stared in disbelief. "Breeches!"

"I've never worn them before, and they are extremely comfortable. I quite like them." She smoothed the fabric over her hip. "Besides, you don't expect me to duel in a dress, do you?"

"I do not expect you to duel at all!"

Pamela ignored him. "That would be most unfair, dueling in a dress, unless, of course, you would be willing to wear a dress as well?"

"Don't be absurd." He snorted in disdain. "I have no intention of ever wearing women's clothing again."

"Again?" She raised a brow.

"It was an unavoidable disguise," he muttered.

She chuckled. "I imagine you were quite fetching."

"Quite," he snapped.

Pamela choked back a laugh and turned toward the other woman, who pulled a sword from beneath her cloak, then shook her hood free.

Alexei groaned.

"Good day to you, cousin." Valentina grinned.

"Thank God," Roman said, and stared at the third figure, who still lingered a few feet behind the others.

"This is your idea no doubt," Alexei said sharply.

"Not entirely, but I did have a certain hand in it and consider it a good deed as well. And"—a note of pride rang in Valentina's voice—"they are my breeches. Do you like them?"

"No!" Although in truth he found them quite fetching. They molded to Pamela's skin in a most becoming, completely improper, and altogether erotic manner. It would indeed be fairer if he donned a dress. Pamela in those breeches was extraordinarily distracting.

He blew a frustrated breath. "Where is Dimitri?"

"We tied him to a chair and left him at the house." Valentina shrugged in a blithe manner.

"I am here, Your Highness." The third figure pushed the hood from his head and stepped forward. Dimitri cast a disgusted look at the women. "They made me wear this."

"Made you?" Alexei's voice rose. "Made you?"

Dimitri nodded at Valentina. "I told you she was a witch."

Valentina laughed.

"And you are a man. A soldier. A warrior." Alexei glared at his friend.

"Indeed I am, Your Highness." Dimitri coolly met Alexei's gaze. "And I owe my allegiance first and fore-most to you. You commanded me to watch the princess day and night—"

Pamela made an odd sort of choking sound.

"—and I have done so. You did not, however, command me to prevent her from taking actions that"—he squared his shoulders—"may well be in your best interest."

"How is this"—Alexei gestured wildly at the women— "in my best interest?"

"Oh, I do think I shall keep him," Valentina murmured.

"Do give it up, Alexei," Pamela said, with a resigned sigh. "You've lost this argument, and we have better things to do."

She took her sword from Valentina, a rather delicate-looking thing. Italian, he thought, and possibly quite effec-tive.

"You call that a sword?" Alexei scoffed, and accepted his own somewhat more substantial blade.

Pamela flexed it and assumed the en garde position. Properly, he noted. "Are you quite ready?"

"I am not going to fight you," he said firmly.

She thrust her sword toward him. He parried it easily. "Why are you doing this for Penwick?"

"I am not doing it for Penwick." She thrust again, and

again he parried. Not quite as easily this time. "I'm doing it for myself."

"What do you mean for yourself?" Again he batted away her blade. "He threatened you. He questioned your honor. Dammit all, Pamela, he stole your virtue!"

"You stole my heart!" She lunged, and he countered. "Why did you want me to believe you were going off to your certain death?"

"It was the best way to set you free." He parried her thrust once again, and the battle began in earnest.

The sounds of swords clashing rang in the morning air. He had no intention of hurting her but, by God, if she insisted on continuing this absurd behavior, he would certainly teach her a lesson she would not soon forget. Still, she was far more skilled than he had imagined.

"She's been practicing all night," Valentina called.

"Not enough," he muttered, and expertly slashed the loose fabric of her sleeve.

Her gaze narrowed, but her efforts did not falter. "The difference between you and George, Your Highness, is that he was an idiot who was not intelligent enough to know what he was losing."

"I know what I am losing." He lunged toward her.

She jumped back expertly. "You are a fool then."

"Perhaps. But I did it for you." The advantage was his. He thrust forward, and she retreated. "I have regrets, Pamela, you have no idea of my regrets. They eat at me. Every day, every night."

"You need me, and I love you." She met his sword with hers. "Don't allow me to be yet another regret."

"You cannot imagine what demons haunt me." He

forced himself to remain calm, to focus on the work at hand. He did not want to harm her in any way. "I will not inflict that on you."

"I want to spend my life with you, Alexei." She punctuated her words with the thrust of her sword.

"Are you not listening to me? I have failed my country and my family and my people!" He slashed his sword across hers.

"Do not fail me then as well!" She was weakening, he could tell. Still, she would not give up.

"I warn you, life with me would not be pleasant." They circled one another.

"I do not want pleasant. I could have had pleasant. I want you!"

She was quicker than he had thought, and the memory of just how agile she could be flashed through his mind, and he faltered. She took the advantage offered and slashed at his midsection, just enough to tear the linen of his shirt.

"Oh, that was not at all nice."

"It was not intended to be." She lunged toward him, and he trapped her sword with his. For a moment they stared at one another.

"It is time to end this." He ducked under her sword, stepped around her with blinding speed until he was at her back. She turned at once. He thrust his sword with great precision to catch the grip just above her hand and flick the sword from her grasp. It was a move he had long ago perfected.

Her eyes widened, she stepped back, stumbled, and fell to the ground. He stood over her, aiming his sword at her midsection.

"Have you had enough then?" He smiled smugly down at her.

"No." She rolled quickly, caught his ankle with her foot, and he tumbled to the ground. Before he could recover she scrambled to her knees, grabbed his sword, and held it against his chest. "You're right, it is time to end this."

He looked at the sword and winced. "Do be careful with that. You could inflict a great deal of harm."

"Exactly." She stared at him and pressed the sword a fraction closer. "Do you love me?"

He glanced pointedly at the blade, then back at her. "Do I have a choice?"

She raised a brow. "Do you?"

He gazed into her sable eyes and knew he was lost. God help him. God help them both. He sighed in surrender. "Yes."

She caught her breath. "Really?"

He carefully took the sword from her hand, tossed it aside and got to his knees, his gaze never leaving hers. "Roman, my waistcoat please." A moment later Roman handed him the garment. He pulled her earbob from the waistcoat pocket and held it out to her. "I believe this belongs to you."

She picked it up and looked at it, her brow furrowed in confusion. "Good Lord, that's mine. I thought I lost it years ago."

"You did," he said softly. "In my bed. In Venice."

She sucked in a sharp breath. "And you kept it?"

He nodded. "As a talisman really. A memory caught in glass." He paused to gather his thoughts. "It should have been no different than any other enjoyable evening spent with a beautiful woman, but something remarkable happened that night in Venice. A night of magic. I do not know what or why, indeed I did not realize it at the time, but I met the woman who was half of my soul. Who captured my heart then and has held it ever since. Serenissima."

"It was one night. I am not . . ." She shook her head. "I am scarcely serene."

"And then I met another woman, when my life as I had always known it had ended." He brushed her hair away from her face and gazed into her eyes. "She is outspoken and annoying and obstinate and not the least bit serene. And she, too, is half of my soul."

"Alexei—" She bit back a sob. "I never forgot Venice either. I never forgot you. Not for a day, not for a moment."

"I never hoped to find you again. Never dared to dream . . ."

Emotion glittered in her eyes. "From the first moment you possessed my heart."

"It is a mutual possession." He drew a steadying breath. "There remains Penwick to be dealt with, you know. And I see only one way to keep him quiet."

She groaned. "You are not still going to kill him?"

"No."

"We can leave England."

"No. This is your home. It is where you belong, and you have been gone far too long." He shrugged. "I shall simply have to marry you after all."

She stared in suspicion. "To keep Penwick quiet?"

"Of course." He smiled slowly. "And because I love you. I always have."

"I knew you did." She threw her arms around his neck and clung to him for a moment, then drew back. A serious light showed in her dark eyes. "You should know, I want to marry you, but as long as I have your love, I don't care about anything else. If you do not wish marriage, I will still spend the rest of my days with you as whatever you wish."

"That is an interesting offer." He pulled her closer. "I have nothing left to give you save the respectability and propriety you once wanted, and I will give you that."

"And your heart." Her voice was firm.

"And my heart although it has always been yours." He shook his head. "Marriage to me will not be easy."

"Nor shall it be dull." She smiled in a wicked manner. "And I daresay I shall give as good as I get."

"I should warn you as well, Pamela, Serenissima"—his gaze searched hers—"I said good-bye to you four years ago when I did not know what I was losing and again yesterday when I did. I shall not say good-bye to you again."

She laughed, a sound of pure joy that echoed in his heart. In his soul. "Nor shall I let you until the moment you draw your last breath. You shall never be rid of me."

"I can ask for nothing more although I should very much like to kiss you now." His voice was low and intense with the emotion that swelled within him. "But we are not alone."

"Ah well, so much for propriety." She sighed and drew his lips to her.

For a long moment he lost himself in the feel of her mouth on his, his body pressed to hers, her life now and always entwined with his. Halves of a whole at last reunited. A soul rejoined.

They were star-crossed no more.

And their ending would be very, very good.